Barbara has written a beautiful story that touched a deep place of love and connection for me. Reading Angelic Wavelength reminded me that we all have angels guiding us: if only I am willing to be quiet and listen, I, too, will be aware of what they are telling me. Now, I'm paying attention in a different way. I'm grateful to Barbara for painting this beautiful picture to nourish all of our hearts."

—*SUSAN COLLINS, Ph.D.*
Professional Certified Coach
Later Stage Leadership, LLC

Barbara Quijano has written a wise and wonderful book. *Angelic Wavelength* shimmers with life-affirming lessons about love, forgiveness, redemption, and ultimately hope.

—*CINDY ATLEE, partner*
The Story Branding Group

ANGELIC

WAVELENGTH

BARBARA QUIJANO

This book is dedicated to my special angel, my father Reuben.

Always the teacher and the artist, he modeled the simple joy of losing oneself in the creative flow.

PART ONE

PROLOGUE

The heavens rarely shine brighter, nor the angelic choirs sing as joyously as the day a baby is born.

True, this is not an unusual circumstance. In fact, the heavenly corridors echo ceaselessly in angelic hymns as each new life is ushered forth. However, never is the miracle of birth lost nor the glory of life dimmed. Each new child is serenaded as a king. A timeless symphony of hope and love emanate from the heights of heaven and filter to the earth below.

Such is the miracle of birth both in heaven and on earth that it is also noted by the heavenly record keepers who precisely log the arrival of each human soul.

An angelic guide is dispatched to shepherd the babe along his new journey. It is an awesome task and one never taken lightly. Angels are sent out with lightning speed to attend to their new charges and guide them along the path of life. They become that child's constant companion and closest external link to all that is good, right, holy and Divine.

This angel has been chosen at the time of conception and has spent nine months, give or take a few weeks, preparing for the adventure. It is a time of devotion to the Source of all Life. It is not a simple assignment but rather one filled with reverence and love. The angels are the Universe's gift to each child. It is part of the great plan created from Source, the interconnection of the Universe and all that coexists within.

And so began the life of Jordan Michael Collingsworth on February 10th. He came into the world, eight pounds and nine ounces of screaming and hollering fury. His proud parents, Charlene and Daniel, awed by the miracle of birth, were filled with unspeakable love for their new son.

The heavens filled with song as well, and Anioch—a novice guardian angel—was dispatched to Jordan's side.

CHAPTER I

Anioch arrived in the delivery room as Jordan was grabbed by Dr. Janus. With smart and efficient motions the babe was handed off to the attending nurses. Anioch anticipated each of these actions thanks to nine months of meticulous studies. The more experienced angels had bestowed heaps of advice upon the novices. Anioch could only hope he had captured that wisdom as well as Dr. Janus had caught Jordan.

For months he had practiced the fine art of intervention without notice, of diligence and patience, corporeal embodiment, and other necessary duties. Anioch vowed to become a perfect messenger of angelic love and devotion. But he had never faced full guardianship duties before. He felt excited and humbled. *Wow, this is real. I'm on the earthly plane with my beautiful human being. Welcome to earth, little one. This is going to be amazing!*

His angelic thoughts were interrupted by the high-pitched wail of his charge.

Anioch had paid close attention to courses on human anger and the barbaric practices of corporal punishment. He watched as the nurse poked, prodded, injected, and appeared to be altogether too rough with the screaming newborn.

His initial reaction was to somehow soften the rough handling by these gloved and masked humans. *I don't remember this being part of the birth ritual.* A sinking feeling began to rise within. *Oh my God, what am I supposed to do?* Anioch looked to Mr. and Mrs. Collingsworth who did not seem overly concerned. He decided to wait and see what would happen next.

Anioch looked at the small helpless child, wrinkled and red and covered in a pasty white film. Still crying and clearly not pleased with the brusque treatment of hospital staff, he was now cradled in his mother's loving arms.

Charlene's eyes held infinite love. Anioch's anxiety diminished as he recognized the mother as a true ally. Lessons on maternal love had revealed its resemblance to the love of the Divine, perhaps as close as earthly souls could get to heavenly Love. He figured he would do well to pay close attention to her and her reactions to her infant son since her duty was not unlike his own.

The fledgling angel stayed near the new family. He was relieved to see Charlene's and Daniel's angelic guides as they passed him inside the hospital corridors, looking perfectly pleased and happy, as if they too were proud new parents. Both angels nodded to Anioch and offered a slight bow of acknowledgment and respect.

He desperately wanted to ask for their sage advice, but they merely smiled, bowed and turned. Their silence held acceptance, reverence and an unspoken communication of celestial beings. Anioch was one of them—the select guardian of the Universe's preferred.

His heart leapt and he sang a prayer to the Divine Source.

Jordan's eyelids fluttered and Charlene smiled. She gently bent over and whispered, "An angel has just arrived," as she kissed her newborn son.

The first days and months of Jordan's life and Anioch's tenure were remarkably uneventful. Jordan settled into a routine of sleeping and nursing, punctuated by brief periods of alertness.

Anioch began to relax in his new role and explore his earthly surroundings. He had not visited the material plane shared with man and beast for any protracted time. Being young—as far as angels are concerned—he was fascinated by humans and their reactions to life. They seemed at times a contradiction. Signs of near godliness were followed by unexpected flights of fear, rage, anger, doubt and all forms of unholy attributes.

Daniel's nightly ritual watching the evening news brought strange and disturbing images into the Collingsworth living room. As far as Anioch could tell, humans were a wholly confused lot. He was glad that Charlene often dozed during most of the broadcast.

Human nature amused and bemused the angel. He enjoyed studying their moves, their words and their motives from his unperceived perch. He was intrigued when a few days after Charlene and baby Jordan came home, a large bouquet of beautiful roses arrived. It seemed as if there were a saintly holiday of which Anioch had been unaware.

"Oh Daniel, thank you. The flowers are so beautiful. I totally forgot it was Valentine's Day. I have a card somewhere that I bought before the baby was born." Charlene gently caressed her husband's arm as they sat close to each other while Jordan slept.

"Well, you are my special lady. I love you."

"And I love you. Thank you. You always make me feel special."

Anioch was curious why there was a day set aside for cards and flowers to express love. He looked out the large window that opened to a magnificent garden just waiting to bloom into full life. Flowers were there for their pleasure every day. Humans were funny that way. They didn't seem to notice the beauty and blessings that surrounded them.

On Daniel's runs he plugged a contraption into his ears to block out the sound of birds and the hum of nature. Anioch noticed a human tendency to look at things from a small perspective—like the complaints when the skies would open and shower the earth with loving and nourishing rain. *Oh great, I just got the car washed.* Anioch wondered why rain was bad for cars. Yes, humans were an interesting species.

The angel figured the All Knowing had definitely spiced up the universe when he created these creatures, though in his heart he knew Source had a Divine Purpose and plan. But his initial conclusion was it would take all the love of the heavenly hosts to protect man from man.

These humans seemed to fear so many things he knew nothing about, such as "loss" and "death." Yet to the novice angel it seemed that fear would be better reserved for the strange perception of their human condition. Fear was a human construct and not an outflowing from Divine Creation. *Strange creatures.* He continued to love and praise the Source of all Life for the divine wisdom and infinite love that was the essence of the one *I AM.*

Anioch's duties were limited in those early days—prayer and devotion, along with his angelic observations of these rather perplexing human beings. He knew he had not been assigned to tend to anybody other than Jordan and so was wise to avoid intervention with other humans. In fact, except for the brief moment at Jordan's delivery, Anioch had not felt any need to intervene. Jordan was well cared for and loved by his mother and father.

Anioch spent his time dutifully near Jordan, never tiring of watching over the sleeping babe. They bonded in a most angelic way. He would hover near as Charlene cuddled and sang to her young son. Anioch would harmonize with her beautiful human voice and shower Jordan with heavenly love and prayers of hope.

The angel felt that Jordan knew he was there along with his mother. Sometimes those baby eyes would stare at him, a fleeting smile lighting his face.

This inevitably would fill Charlene with great joy and pride. She would look around to see what had captured Jordan's attention, then giggle, "Whatcha looking at, my precious one? There's no one here but your mamma." She would lose herself in thought and casually answer her own question. "You must be following the light and shadows." But the angel knew Jordan could see him in all of his glory and light.

Indeed Jordan was mesmerized by the radiance and intensity. When his face burst with that brief baby smile, Anioch's heart also swelled. Life was balanced and beautiful for everyone. A near inaudible hum of energy emerged as the material plane vibrated a bit higher with the love and connection of human and angel.

Anioch praised the Creator for allowing him the honor of being guardian and messenger of Perfect Divine Love. He began to realize it was all part of The Universal Plan; his love would increase as would his duty. Flawed though the human spirit may be, humans needed angels, and angels needed them. So perfect was the Cosmic Plan. It was in giving that the angel received. In becoming the blessing, he was blessed. Anioch was humbled and awed.

CHAPTER 2

At three months of age, Jordan began learning the basic law of physics: *an object once set in motion remains in motion until acted upon by an outside force.* Anioch's duties adapted necessarily to protect Jordan from the harsher effects of gravity.

People had begun to comment that Jordan was a very alert and bright child. Anioch took pride in these comments, not unlike Charlene and Daniel who also believed their child was special.

Jordan was awake now for longer periods of time and enjoyed watching the world from his infant seat.

In the late afternoons, Charlene would ceremoniously place his carrier in the middle of the counter while preparing supper. Jordan would follow his mother's every move and respond to her chatter with baby babblings of his own. Jordan sometimes would spy Anioch as well, and coo his regards to the angel. This made Anioch dance about for the baby and draw rainbows of light and colors. Jordan marveled at the spectacle and quivered in sheer delight.

Charlene would sometimes stop cold as if she sensed their play. Delighted at Jordan's attention and spontaneous bursts of laughter, she also seemed to sense another presence, like a barely perceptible charge of electricity.

This afternoon Charlene hummed to herself and hefted Jordan's infant carrier onto the kitchen counter once more. She pushed it back against the wall as far as it would go, and angled it slightly toward where she would be cooking. With a smile, she attached an assortment of dangling toys to the carrier's handle. Jordan batted the red one with his foot.

Anioch stifled a yawn during this sweet mother-son bonding moment. Being a guardian angel was far easier than he'd imagined. *I guess I really have the gift!* The Masters had said his angelic nature would guide him. Of course it helped that Jordan was infinitely loveable.

Charlene was busy in the kitchen, music playing softly in the background. She gently rocked to the beat as she took out an assortment of bowls, measuring cups and a mixer. Cooking filled a void she only half acknowledged, some small part of the excitement from her life before Jordan. She missed the connection with other people.

She glided effortlessly across the room while Jordan followed her every move, mother and child both in rhythm with the music. Charlene hummed. Jordan cooed.

The phone rang. Charlene grabbed her cell phone. "Hello?" Her voice was bright.

It was Kate. Charlene smiled at the sound of her friend's voice. Turning her back to the utensils and baby on the counter, she looked dreamily out the bay window that framed the kitchen. The garden was now in full bloom with a radiant burst of color and prisms of light dancing among the trees. She gazed out into the world just beyond and was immediately lost in conversation.

An electric cord hung loosely from the standing mixer. It bounced and danced just out of Jordan's pudgy reach. Ever curious, he discovered that those hands sometimes responded to what his little baby mind willed. Early lessons on cause and effect had been practiced, batting and beating on soft toys and rattles that his parents placed within reach. But the cord looked more challenging. It swayed and twisted.

Jordan tried to grab it. He swung at it. He grunted at it. It hung there just beyond him.

Anioch was amused. Jordan was tenacious. The angel watched only half engaged, knowing the baby would soon lose interest.

Jordan reached and grabbed with feet and hands in a singular motion as if they were invisibly connected. Settling back, it looked like the baby had given up. Jordan unenthusiastically tapped his familiar toys with his bare feet.

Anioch smiled. "The little guy is done," he chuckled.

But indeed the active three month old's mind was already planning its next move. Jordan tapped the well-worn toys as he willed hands, feet and body to move. In one swift push, the baby lunged for the fascinating tangle and swirl of plastic. He didn't meet the usual resistance like when he had tried this move before. In her rush to start dinner, Charlene had forgotten to secure the baby strap. Jordan thrust forward with full force now, happily reaching the beckoning cord.

Anioch immediately recognized his call to service. In a split second that only angelic beings can distinguish, he coolly assessed the situation. Boy and chair would tumble over the counter. Charlene was distracted and too far away to catch him. Recalling his lessons, Anioch flew to Jordan's side, opened the cupboard door just enough to catch the falling chair, and tightened the loosely looped strap.

It stopped Jordan's fall. Both chair and baby wedged into the cabinet door. Jordan squealed with delight.

Charlene heard the clamor. "Oh my God, Kate. I've got to go!"

She tossed the phone on the counter and lunged across the kitchen to pull Jordan out of the precariously dangling seat. Once he was unfastened, the carrier crashed to the floor. Charlene held her son close to her pounding chest.

She kissed his head and whispered, "Oh my God, oh my God."

Jordan grabbed the object of his fascination still dangling, now near Charlene's shoulder. He was delighted to finally feel and taste this new toy.

Charlene batted it from his hand. Jordan hollered. Anioch retreated. He let out a deep sigh and smiled to himself. *Close call, but I passed my first test.* He'd protected the small child without any trace of angelic intervention. The fallen carrier wedged in the cabinet would be a fine storyline. The cupboard door somehow broke Jordan's fall. So strange, but so lucky.

Charlene held the baby and comforted him, adrenaline pumping. Her legs became weak. She chastised herself for being so careless, and spoke softly to her son. She would never let him get hurt, she would always watch over him. She promised him. She promised herself.

Anioch watched. Somewhere deep inside his being, he knew Charlene was making a promise she wouldn't be able to keep. For the first time Anioch had felt the full measure of his assignment as guardian angel. A flash of insight struck him. Source, in infinite wisdom, knew the limits of human love. The need to protect and guide was the complement and gift of the angelic realm.

Anioch sang softly to the creator, "Thank you for the gift to serve. In giving, I receive. In blessing, I am blessed. In serving, I am fulfilling my purpose. And so it is, as it always has been and always will be." The angel passed a soft protective wing over Charlene and her child. In that moment, he knew they sensed his presence. In that same moment of connection, he also sensed Charlene shift from fear to love.

The mother stopped and peered in Anioch's direction, momentarily transfixed by an invisible force. Her breathing slowed. The mundane prayer, "Thank you, God," now felt hollow and insignificant. Charlene felt moved to whisper a new prayer. "Thank you, Lord for watching over my baby. Bless this child in your love and keep him safe."

It was as it should be. *All praise unto the Creator*, thought Anioch. Merely the facilitator, the messenger, the instrument, he joined Charlene in a prayer of thanks to the Divine.

Jordan reached for the brilliant aura while Charlene gathered her child nearer, filled with an unspeakable warmth. Charlene felt a charge pass through her as if drawn into a radiant circle of light.

Anioch spread his magnificent wings and bent deeply with them stretched toward the heavens. Outside the bay window the birds gathered and joined in the song of praise.

CHAPTER 3

Jordan continued to grow as babies do. With each passing day, he became a little more active and a little more mischievous. Jordan loved his swing, the stroller, his Johnny Jumper. All were unspoken challenges as to how to climb up, squeeze out, or wiggle in. Crawling was followed by stair climbing, furniture scaling, and lessons on the measurement and size of his head in proportion to gates and grates.

One warm fall afternoon Charlene was out in the garden prepping the soil for the change in seasons. The baby monitor was nearby on a glass patio table. Lost in the sun's warmth, Charlene hummed to herself. The smell of earth, leaves, dew and her own sweat mixed, and she let the textures of soil and small stones caress her.

She patted down the earth and plucked away random patches of weeds. Looking at her watch, she was startled to see she had been outside for almost two hours. Two hours without a single sound of Jordan stirring. Her mind snapped into alert mode.

Charlene rushed to the monitor and discovered the volume was turned off. Panic grabbed her and tied a knot in her stomach. She ran upstairs to find the nursery door wide open. Her mind raced, trying to recall if she had forgotten to close the door. Hoping to see Jordan cuddled into his favorite patch-quilt blanket, her heart sank when she took a full quick view of the room. No blanket. No baby.

"Jordan, honey. Where are you?" she called out to the empty room. All she heard was her own voice echoing in the monitor, still sitting out on the patio, now at full volume. "Oh my God, where are you?" Her terrified voice echoed again.

She checked the closet to see if he might have crawled in. Charlene began a frantic rush through the house opening closet doors, checking behind furniture. As she passed each room her level of panic steadily rose.

Anioch was nearby and dutifully watching over Jordan. He couldn't fully understand Charlene's agitation. He wouldn't let harm come to their baby. Anioch watched as she checked under tables and opened drawers that would never fit a small child.

Though Charlene's angelic guide, Murial, was also close by the distraught young mother, Anioch noticed something different in her angelic presence. Murial held his gaze, calling him into action. "Fix this." Charlene's sobs filled the empty home.

Anioch was briefly confused, not a comfortable place for a Divine Guardian. A strange sensation of unease spread through him. He rose and opened his wings. As he stirred, his thoughts were interrupted again with a short, *"NOW!"*

A flash of awareness struck. He felt Murial's steady stare. He immediately understood that while his mission was to guard Jordan, he would be wise to be aware of the web of love surrounding this child. All things and Beings are connected.

Charlene got up and went to the phone while Anioch flew toward the still sleeping infant, comfortably nestled in the laundry basket piled high with towels and blankets. He gently brushed his wing against Jordan's cheek. Jordan stirred and opened his eyes, smiling then giggling.

At the sound, Charlene dropped the phone. "Jordan, sweetie, where are you?"

"Mama," replied the laughing boy as he wiggled out of the basket.

Charlene rushed into the laundry room and swooped up her warm son who smelled of laundry detergent. His tousled hair mixed with her tears.

Anioch gave a slight nod to Murial and thanked her for the lesson. She answered with a barely perceptible smile, still fully focused on her special child, Charlene.

That evening Charlene told Daniel what happened, leaving out the sheer terror and guilt that had rushed through her. "You know, Daniel. I am convinced you can't turn your back on him for a second. He is just a bundle of wild energy. What will he be like when he gets older? Maybe we need to put a chip in him."

Daniel looked up and saw a slight smile on his wife's face. But her eyes didn't match the lightness in her voice.

"Or a leash," he responded hoping to change the mood. "He's fine, honey. Just a curious, smart and healthy little boy. We will laugh about this when he is older." Daniel reached over and patted his wife's hand.

Charlene didn't speak of the dull new feeling that still weighed on her, a feeling Murial and Anioch both sensed. A dark raw energy slowly seeped in and hung between the pauses.

Daniel renamed his son, *Houdini*, like the great escape artist. While Anioch did not like the name it seemed to be a source of great amusement to Daniels's friends and family.

Anioch's involvement increased exponentially with Jordan's unquenchable curiosity. Things needed to be tested, tasted, handled, dismembered, crashed, smashed, mashed, sucked on, chewed on, inhaled and sometimes expelled. Small objects went into every orifice.

Anioch knew now to be more aware of how Jordan impacted his parents and tried to stay closer to them as well. Anioch and Charlene played an unending game of hide and seek. Jordan would hide while Anioch and Charlene were forced to seek: seek Jordan, seek his blankey, seek his sucky, seek the keys, seek the rattle, seek the bead, the raisin, any small object left in his path that would disappear in his hands, mouth, ear, nose, under chairs, in toilets, under rugs.

Jordan's zest for conquest was exhilarating and exhausting. But Anioch continued to thank Source for this wonderful challenge. He was filled with vitality and energy, for an angel never tires, his love and patience are endless. His purpose is to impart and thereby receive the essence of unconditional love.

With each passing day, Anioch realized why the Creator had assigned guardians to humans; they were a terribly inquisitive lot that often lacked judgment.

But Anioch loved this child and would work overtime—a concept foreign to angels but which he'd overheard Daniel discuss. He understood it to be a call of duty. Jordan had an uncanny knack for being at the wrong place at precisely the right time, requiring quick and creative thinking by his guardian.

Anioch noticed that Jordan's perpetual motion was taking a toll on Charlene. Since the day of Jordan's first disappearance in the laundry room, something had changed. Their daily walks to the park were slowly turning into every other or every third day. She spent less time in the garden and weeds began to flourish while the falling leaves piled up. Things that once brought joy, like cooking, were reduced to the simplest task, now measured in five ingredients or less.

Overheard conversations made Anioch wonder if that dark energy was taking root.

"Honey, how about we make a date night this weekend? I could ask my parents to come watch Jordan?" Daniel watched his wife's reaction, hoping to see her eyes light up.

Charlene looked up as she expertly changed Jordan's diaper, grabbing his squirming feet when he tried to roll away. "Oh that sounds really nice, but I am so tired. I don't even know what we would do."

Jordan grunted.

"Dinner and a movie would be nice." Daniel pushed the conversation forward.

"But I am so out of it. I don't even think I could stay awake through a whole show."

They both fell silent. Daniel stopped prodding. "How about I take Jordan to the park for a bit? You can have a nice long bath."

"That sounds lovely, but we just went to the park yesterday. We can go together later if you want."

It didn't matter what Daniel offered. Charlene clung tighter to the role of motherhood.

An insidious presence sent a current of electricity through the house. Anioch wasn't sure what it was but he noticed that this new vibration sucked up the light and joy. Jordan would stop his babbling and pull away. A new tone painted a heavy patina over words that had once been wrapped in love.

"Jordan, stop it!" Charlene would snap, wrestling the wriggling child into his car seat.

As Jordan's back straightened to avoid confinement, the once caressing hands grabbed harder and pushed. Charlene caught herself though and took a step back. "Come on, Jordie, does everything have to be a battle?"

Over dinner, the couple spoke of their day. Charlene kept the conversation light, but wove in simple statements with carefully chosen words. "You know this is sometimes harder than I expected. I wonder if other new moms feel like this."

Daniel glanced at the paper while eating supper and let her statements pass by, hoping the feeling of exhaustion would pass as well.

Charlene continued, "It's like he's constantly testing his strength and endurance."

And your resolve, Daniel thought.

That pure love Anioch had so easily recognized before was still there—in the quiet moments—but at other times there was frustration, impatience and twinges of hostility. Tension did not translate into love.

Impatience and exasperation were new to Anioch. That wasn't part of an angel's nature. He had only felt complete and total love, without reproach. As a messenger of that Pure Love, he knew it was humanly possible to experience it because he had seen and felt it during those quiet moments. But something had changed. He loved Jordan and did not tire of the endless interventions and creative responses to the child's ceaseless assault on the world. Charlene however, seemed worn, with no more love or patience to give. Anioch wondered at those times what her guardian was doing.

A radiant Being of Light, Murial hovered ever so slightly above the denser material plane. Anioch turned in reverent observation to Charlene's angelic guide. The young angel shifted his gaze and stepped into her magnificent aura. There was Divine Order in the Angelic realm with an energy field for Divine Communion. As a novice guardian, Anioch knew that wisdom was always present and his to freely tap. He quietly shifted his attention to open himself to observe and learn from Murial.

"Dear sister," he began the almost-telepathic conversation.

Murial shifted her gaze and slightly opened her wings. She was a blaze of beautiful lights. Her purpose in all things was to serve. "Yes, brother? What is it?"

"This earthly space is a strange and mystifying place. There is so much that is beautiful and I feel great joy. But I am feeling something else lately. It seems that the mother..."

"Charlene," Murial quietly added.

"Yes, Charlene. Well she has a new aura of darkness surrounding her. I am not sure what that means or what I am to do about that. I know my duty is to love and protect my child. Am I also to protect him from her?" Anioch regretted the words the moment he spoke them.

Murial smiled. Nearly regal in her presence, an aura of radiant light emanated and bathed Charlene. "Well, my dear one. She is human and as such, she has to fight with what she believes are her two natures. She is very tired and now worried. It would serve us all well if the child..."

Now it was Anioch's turn to interrupt, "Jordan."

"Yes, Jordan. As I was saying, it would help bring back peace and balance if the babe, Jordan, was a little less curious and active. Charlene is now fighting fear and love." As Murial spoke, Anioch noticed that she showered tenderness around the young mother. "Dear One, I know you had your training and I am confident you learned of our code. We in the angelic realm must wait to be called upon. We stay alert as the call can come in many ways." She explained in her calm manner that she was vigilant to any calls for help or intercession.

During Novice Training, Anioch had learned the relationship between human and angel changes over what humans refer to as *time*.

"We are called to not just know this," communicated Muriel, "but rather to live according to the Divine Code of Intervention: Ask and you shall receive. Human free will must be respected at all times."

The lesson ended. Anioch stayed silent, sensing it was a good time for reflection. Divine Order was at play on the angelic realm. On this day, Muriel had not only served her human charge, but him as well. He sang praise to Source and the infinite wisdom that surrounded all of life.

Anioch began to understand. His beloved child did not need to make a request for help now, but in time, their relationship would evolve; a human plea, however slight, would need to be made for the angel to intervene.

"Murial, why can't they just be at peace and happy? Don't they know that all things are always working for their greater good?"

"Like I said before, they fight with all their mind to make sense out of things. Because they do not surrender to the simple Truth—that they are Beloved and in fact Beings of Love—and in this not knowing they are unhappy. They believe they are separate from Source, and that separation brings imbalance."

Anioch pondered. The human spirit was complex and demanding. He still could not fully understand why these humans couldn't just open their eyes and see the truth, instead of sinking into lower vibrations that drained and blocked the energy of love that was always present. "I suppose that is why we are here. If they were fully awake, they would be in communion with us. Right, sister?"

"Indeed. What purpose would we serve? What would we guard? Just shine your light, Anioch, and love with your whole being. That is what is ours to do."

Anioch vowed he would do that, always. But still he contemplated these strange creatures who were so loved by the Creator, yet spent their energy avoiding the Truth, oblivious to the higher vibrations where peace and joy resided. "Yes, and I will do it with my whole being. I will love and protect my child. I will also expand my awareness to include the wellness of all who love him."

CHAPTER 4

Life continued with the human hurricane known as Jordan. Anioch remained vigilant. A gifted athlete, Jordan was blessed with a kind soul and a matching mischievous heart. He yearned to be outside, always in motion.

As a toddler, he savored riding on the back of his father's bike. People would remark at the little boy with outstretched arms, "It looks like he's flying." On these days, Jordan's eyes focused on the sky, an expression of pure bliss covering his face. He squealed while racing his beloved angel.

The first day of swimming lessons, Jordan ran past a small group of youngsters and jumped straight into the deep end. Terrified parents screamed when the young boy sank. An instructor jumped in while the other children stood and stared.

At the sound of screams, Charlene looked up from her cell phone. "Oh God! It's Jordie." She raced to the other side of the pool.

The instructor emerged carrying her son who was laughing and delighted. "Again! Again!" he cried.

"Jordan, you need to pay attention and listen to the teacher," Charlene said as she took her son from the swim instructor. "You hear me? You can't jump in. That's dangerous."

Jordan looked at his mom and nodded. He saw Anioch nearby and smiled. The angel had pushed him up to the water's surface moments earlier. "Yes, Mommy. But it was fun."

Charlene held him close and tucked the fear deep inside her heart.

The "near misses" always ended with Jordan saved at the last minute. Daniel was left wondering. Charlene was left worried. Both left thanking God for Jordan's good fortune.

With each new incident, Jordan expanded his own awe, joy and love for life.

Charlene waited for her son to come home from school, quickly surveying his arms, legs, elbows, knees and scraped face for possible damage. "Jordan, you tore your pants again."

"Sorry, Mom. I had the best run from first base to third. I slid right in. It was amazing."

Charlene smiled. Torn jeans were the least of her worry. She made dinner.

As time passed, the incidents grew more serious and increasingly perilous.

"Did you know they have a skateboard club at school?" Jordan asked. "Can I join? I tried Mitch's skateboard and it's amazing. We made a ramp after school behind Jack and Payton's house and I got up the highest and almost made a full body spin."

"Maybe the chess club would be fun, son. Something different?"

Jordan held his fork mid-air. "You're kidding, Mom. Chess? That sounds boring."

⋘∙⋙

After dinner, Daniel and Charlene remained in the kitchen. Daniel sipped his wine while Charlene cleared the dishes.

"Daniel, I think we need to talk to Jordie. This skate club really worries me. I don't know if he has the judgment to not do something stupid."

"Club or no club, it's pretty clear he's going to do these things anyway. Didn't you hear him talk about the ramp? Hopefully the club will teach safety and maybe he will listen to someone else. He thinks we are too smothering."

Charlene flinched. She wanted to argue that she wasn't smothering anyone, just being the grown-up. But she stayed silent.

"Chess club, honey? Really?"

Charlene continued drying the dishes. Jordan was in the backyard swinging higher and higher, pulling the legs of the swing set momentarily out of the dirt. She knew he would launch himself in the next few passes. She rapped on the window, her sign to slow down. Jordan ignored her completely. *Smothering,* she thought. She told herself to not get angry. *It's not about me. It's about Jordan.*

"Daniel, one day we are going to get a call from school or a friend's parent that he has really hurt himself."

"Yup, that goes with having a healthy, curious, happy kid. We can't protect him from everything." Daniel picked up his paper and started reading.

Charlene stared into the deep green of their fenced-in yard. *What's wrong with protecting him?* But she stayed silent, keeping a mental inventory of all the near-misses.

Charlene felt alone. She needed an ally. On the phone later, her mother also chastised, "Getting yourself into this state of near panic doesn't help. I'm more worried about you." Charlene listened to her mother, silently arguing, *You don't understand! He's not like my brothers. Jordan's different. He scares me.*

Jordan's grandmother had raised Charlene, her one daughter and five boys and wasn't even affected by the report of his second-story fall that ended with Jordan crashing through the screen only to catch his coat on the awning below. "Boys will be boys," was her pat response.

Anioch listened and remembered. Jordan had smiled at his guardian while swinging midair, oblivious to the danger that lay below.

Murial was nearby also listening to the conversation and telegraphed a look, no doubt remembering Charlene's bone chilling screams. *Be mindful of those who share in the web of love.*

Anioch felt the telepathic words and knew they held a lesson.

Daniel reflected in silence as well. Normally the voice of calm reason, he too looked as if he were beginning to wonder if theirs was a wildly lucky child. He phoned a childhood friend who coached youth soccer and had been a bit of a thrill seeker. Needing an ally, his heart raced when his friend answered. The conversation flowed, and Anioch could hear pieces of it. "I think we might have a bit of an Evil Knievel on our hands. Not sure if I should be more worried."

Bob recalled a few of his own crazy stunts with safe landings and happy memories and encouraged Daniel to grab a beer.

Daniel carried the phone into the next room where Jordan was playing and continued. "I never told Charlene about the time Jordan fell into a rushing creek on one of our walks. I was teaching him to maneuver on slippery rocks, just holding his hand. Out of nowhere the wind gusted past and that little guy looked up into the sky and leapt, tumbling head first into the swollen creek. Had me calling out to God, that one did." Daniel took a long drag from his beer. "Luckily there was a branch jutting out ahead and Jordan grabbed on until I could reach him. Scared the hell out of me."

Jordan looked up at his dad's use of the "h" word and interrupted, "I was fine, Daddy. My friend Ani was with me. I saw him fly in the wind and I was chasing him."

Daniel patted his son with his free hand. "Jordan honey, please. You have to be more careful. And you have to stop daydreaming about your friend."

Daniel carried the phone into the office but left the door open behind him. Anioch continued to listen.

"Now he wants to join this skateboarding club. Charlene is dead set against it. He is young for this but I just want to make sure he'll keep telling me what he's doing. I don't want to say no so many times that he shuts down. I ask him when we're alone what's going on. So he tells me about this big hill and it sounds pretty fun until I figured out it's Kite Hill and he's all excited to tell me how he's roaring down... with no helmet." Daniel drained his beer in one last long pull. "And I'm thinking, holy crap that kid has a death wish. But he tells me how he hit a crack or a drain and got tossed up into the air before the intersection. Landed on some old mattress that was set out for trash. Another near miraculous last-minute twist of fate. This kid is starting to scare me."

Bob listened, letting Daniel take the time to work through his emotions. He understood and offered support and reassurance. "They outgrow it, Dan. Remember the crazy stuff we did? And we survived. Gotta respect our dads for letting us figure it out."

Anioch listened as well. He praised his Creator for the chance to serve and guide. He sang a prayer of love for the little boy who would look up with eyes full of wonder, once more saved from harm. *If only they knew what was really going on. I bet they would build a shrine to me if they knew how many times I've saved Jordan.*

Murial shot a look his way, as if reading his angelic mind. "Hubris, my dear brother, is not of the angelic realm."

CHAPTER 5

Word began to spread among the guardians. This peculiar child required near incessant intervention. Other angels clustered round to witness and applaud Anioch's creative rescues. But Anioch remembered Murial's words on hubris and tried to keep his thoughts within the higher vibration.

"Ani, let's go and fly together," Jordan said.

Charlene looked up to see her son run into the backyard wearing his superhero cape. What she and her husband had earlier dismissed as childish prater was now a source of concern.

"Honey, do we need to talk to someone about his imagination?" she asked Daniel. "I know you keep telling me he'll outgrow this, but..." her voice was thick with worry.

Daniel looked at his wife and stayed silent. The silence hung and filled the room. Daniel finally looked up and responded, "I want what is best for Jordan and for you." His voice was deep and heavy. His words were slow as if speaking to himself. "But I don't want the doctors to medicate that joy out of him." Daniel leaned forward with his head in his hands. "He's just a little boy. Before we know it, he'll be grown and never get to play like this."

"Play?" Charlene stopped herself. She hadn't meant to react so strongly. She paused and then continued, her voice less sharp. "I guess I wouldn't worry so much if it was just play. Can we at least talk to the school counselor? I feel like we have to do something."

Daniel agreed, but only because he saw his wife becoming paralyzed with fear every time the phone rang. *Is it the school nurse, the hospital, or the police calling to say Jordan's been severely injured?* He looked at his wife who was beginning to show now. *Another one on the way,* he sighed and lost himself in thought.

Anioch noticed Daniel grow remote and disconnected.

༺༻

It was the opening night of the annual spring church festival, Jordan talked excitedly about the rides and games. "Dad, am I tall enough to ride the big rollercoaster by myself?"

Daniel smiled and showed him the line on the sign. "There you go, buddy. Forty-eight inches. But you know I'd be happy to tag along."

"Thanks, Dad, but I think Ani will love it. We'll really be flying together this time."

Charlene shot Daniel a look he knew all too well as she snuggled the new baby slung close to her chest.

Daniel handed Jordan five tickets for the "grown-up" rollercoaster and they waited in line together until it was his turn. Jordan ran along the track to the very last car, smiling ear to ear, still carrying the superhero knock-off he'd won earlier at the ring toss.

The rollercoaster took off and headed into a swirl of curves and turns.

Daniel watched his son as he dipped and flew by. Daniel saw something fly out of the last car. For a moment he thought it was Jordan but then realized it was the Batman prize. He let out his breath.

But then, as if in slow motion, Daniel realized Jordan was now wiggling and climbing on his knees trying to reach for the toy. "Get your belt back on, Jordan!" Daniel screamed.

The boy stretched out of the car trying to reach his lost prize that had landed on the distant rail below. Daniel ran toward the distracted carnival worker who was looking at his phone. No one seemed to notice Jordan in a near stand in the back car.

As Daniel reached the worker, he heard a gasp from the crowd. In one clean sweep the coaster jerked to the left, heading into a turn... while Jordan flew to the right.

Daniel caught sight of his son mid-flight but just as quickly the child disappeared from view. The entire carnival site lost power. Lights switched off dramatically. All music ceased, and a strange hush enveloped the crowd.

The rollercoaster operator applied the manual break, bringing the ride to a screeching halt several excruciating seconds later. Daniel's heart skipped a beat.

The crowd, now bathed in darkness, let out an audible gasp. Parents ran to various rides to find their children stuck in different stages of lifts and drops. The carnival lights flickered and with a loud hum came back on.

Charlene screamed when she saw where her son was perched.

Mere feet in front of the rollercoaster's nose, on the rail where it had been stopped from its rocketing descent, sat Jordan holding his blue Batman and waving enthusiastically down at them.

"My God, Daniel! Enough," Charlene hissed. "We have to do something."

They watched with breath held tightly as the coaster operator painstakingly climbed the metal track to the precariously seated boy, then carried Jordan back to the platform.

Daniel ran to get his son, still pondering the event and knowing in his heart his wife was right.

"Jordan honey, what were you thinking?" Charlene pulled the child into her arms and smothered him alongside the baby at her chest.

Jordan could hear his mother's racing heart. His parents were scared. *He* had scared them. "I just wanted to rescue my toy. I didn't mean to shut off the lights. I think that must have been Ani."

"Stop it, Jordan! No more talk about this 'Ani'," Daniel scoffed. "You could have been killed."

Jordan looked at his father earnestly. "Ani wouldn't let me get hurt." He glanced to his guardian angel, who shivered visibly in the summer-like heat.

Anioch saw Murial extend her beautiful wings in a protective arch around Charlene. The angelic calming presence did not extend to Anioch, into whose eyes her displeasure bore. *This needs to change, dear brother. Too many people are being hurt.*

Anioch floated backward and moved upward to a higher perch. From this new vantage point, more angels came into view. They hovered near their charges, offering light and love to frightened children and anxious parents caught in the power outage. Some glanced at Anioch with awe, but more mirrored Murial's reprimand. *You let it go too far, dear one. The child needs better control.*

The novice angel wondered if perhaps he had been too flamboyant. Maybe he should have intervened sooner. Anioch turned to Source for guidance. At that moment he felt a brief delay in the connection. The novice turned as if trying to find the energy current he knew was always present. Something was different. His angelic mind filled with a fast flow of questions. Had his love for playing with Jordan separated him from his true angelic duty? Had his pride separated him from the Eternal Source? Was it even possible to disconnect from Source?

Anioch felt heavy as if he were sinking into the material plane, pulled into the denser vibration. He struggled to stay in his higher place. In a moment of clarity, the questions pierced him and the answer formed. His purpose was to be in Loving Service. It was simple. His joy was derived from fully being in Service.

The question hung in the ether: was he more focused on the thrill of the intercession than the act of Service?

Murial looked up and caught Anioch's eye. She nodded slightly and silently communicated, "Source is ever-present. It is you who are disconnected. Be an act of Love always and you will never be disconnected from Source."

Within that moment of questioning and the clarity which followed, Anioch knew he must extend his presence outward. He was connected to more than just Jordan. When he glanced at the magnificence that was Murial, he suddenly understood that he was only one of several angels assigned to this earthly family. For the first time, he had a meaningful connection with another angelic Being.

He looked with an open and humbled heart and took in Daniel's angelic guide, Roshan. Roshan stepped forward and bowed. Anioch bowed in return, curious why this older angel had remained on the outer margins. Roshan held Anioch's glance but did not communicate. Despite the silence, Anioch sensed that together they were entering a new phase of their parallel and conjoined journeys.

While Murial was strong and ablaze in her brilliance, Roshan was more distant as if caught in a slight ebb outside of the immediate space of this special family's angelic orbit. His aura was beautiful but did not radiate like Murial's.

Anioch held his questions at bay. He knew this was a time to be still and learn.

Murial's voice came to him, "You have much to learn, brother. It is best to go into reflection and not fill yourself with a thousand questions."

Anioch heard her words but couldn't stop the swirl. Was he too steeped in the earthly plane? Was his angelic mind losing its softness and becoming more human, lost in an endless cacophony of idle thoughts? For the first time he felt a tinge of emotion. It was unknown and strange. He couldn't name the tug that pulled him down.

Murial's gaze reminded him to fill his angelic mind with pure thoughts of grace and mercy. *Be still now. Be strong. Be alert. Awaken and know love conquers fear.*

Fear? Was that what he felt pulling on him? Anioch looked at her and screamed out, "Fear?" The very word made him feel even worse. How could that emotion enter the angelic realm?

Murial kept a calm gaze. "Look at our brother. He is here to teach you. Be wise and learn from him."

Anioch shifted his mind from the racing thoughts and noticed a counter-flow of energy pushing Roshan slightly out and away. Roshan was not in the same space as Anioch and Murial. Anioch could see the actual vibration emanating from the humans. He also saw that Daniel's fear was vibrating dark and dense within the material plane.

"Sister, I can see the fear. It has power. It is shutting out the pure energy of Love."

"Yes. And it is pushing out our dear brother, Roshan. For love is his true essence."

Anioch looked at Roshan. Understanding dawned. Roshan was there, always there. Just like Source. He waited, always waiting. He wouldn't leave, but rather it was Daniel's choice, always a choice. Anioch sent a surge of energy to his brother and Roshan smiled.

In that moment, Anioch knew Murial's powerful and wise affirmation was not meant just for him but for Roshan as well. Stay in love. The circle of Love is where I am strong for Jordan, for myself, and my brother and sister and the whole family.

Murial looked at Anioch and smiled. *You are learning, little brother.*

A new chapter began. Jordan was sent to numerous doctors and psychologists who tried to understand his nature. Kind but serious professionals would talk and listen, probe and poke. "So tell me, Jordan, about your friend."

Jordan would fumble with the action figures or crayons they gave, trying to coax him into role playing or drawing. His dad secretly told him not to share too much about Ani. This time Jordan obeyed.

The visits continued but the questions were pretty much the same. Jordan attended and behaved. The child glanced at Anioch who was always nearby. At first, Jordan sat quietly, but that seemed to force more frequent visits. So Jordan began to answer in short sentences: "He is nice," "He is very strong," "He makes me feel safe," "He sings the most beautiful songs."

Whenever they asked if his friend was here now, Jordan would steal a sideways glance to Anioch who would gently shake his head.

"No, not now."

Anioch loved his child with his whole Being. He didn't like these sessions. He didn't understand what was going on but sensed the grown-ups' worry. Maybe Jordan was too brave. After the carnival incident and the hushed reproach from the other angels, Anioch had decided to be less active. Murial supported this.

One summer day, Jordan was taken to a new doctor. The office was set up like a school with lots of activity tables. This young doctor was not like the others. She didn't wear a suit, but instead jeans and sandals and her hair was pulled back in a ponytail. There was a small but cheerful garden filled with bright sunflowers and other meadow flowers in the back where a yellow Labrador lay curled up in the sun.

Jordan liked it here, and he liked the doctor. She spoke easily with the child. As Jordan gently petted, the friendly dog wagged his tail. Sometimes it would peer in Anioch's direction and bark in joyous bursts. Jordan liked that Zee Boy, the dog, could see Ani. Anioch heard Jordan's thoughts, silently telling the dog that the angel had to be their secret. Anioch smiled and the dog answered with a new burst of barking.

But Jordan also told Dr. Jamie about his friend. As he painted with bright colors, he spoke of the magnificent rainbows. "Oh, you would love the colors Ani paints. They aren't like these," he said as he slapped yellows and oranges in a swirl. "The rainbows he draws are huge, and they sparkle."

Dr. Jamie smiled as she drew small flowers on her white paper. "Does Ani talk to you?"

"Yes, that's how I know his name. It's really longer than 'Ani', but I was a baby when we met. 'Ani' was easier to say. And I think he likes it."

"You saw Ani when you were a baby?" the doctor asked.

"I've always seen Ani. I mean I don't ever remember not having him with me. He's like Mommy and Dad."

"Can you see him now?"

Jordan paused. He remembered his dad's cautionary words. But he liked Dr. Jamie. He didn't think she would hurt Ani. "I don't know," he answered. "Well, maybe. But if I say he is here, will you try to take him away?"

"Jordan, why would you think I would do that?"

"Because I don't think grown-ups understand. Mommy doesn't like it when I talk to Ani and my dad told me not to tell people about him. My friends think I'm weird. So now I just try to ignore him. But I think that makes him sad."

Jordan dipped his brush in water. He grew quiet.

Dr. Jamie waited. She and Jordan talked about other things like bikes and flying. "Do you ever get afraid when you are trying something new? Do you think maybe you might get hurt? Or... hurt someone else?"

Jordan looked up from his play. "No. I can't get hurt. Ani told me that. He said he's here to protect me. And I would never hurt anyone. Mom and Dad taught me that and Ani always tells me to be kind."

Anioch beamed. He enjoyed the sessions when Jordan would describe him as a "secret friend." Anioch sensed the love as his young charge described blinding lights and dancing rainbows.

Dr. Jamie asked other questions about school, his parents, his new baby brother and of course his "special friend." Jordan had many visits with her, and sometimes she would leave him with Zee while she went into her office to speak to his parents.

"He is healthy and very smart. He tests high on creativity and verbal skills, and doesn't show any inclinations to harm himself or others. But he does seem to be a bit disconnected with reality and on the spectrum for hyperactivity. He'll probably grow out of this, but we could help calm him and provide focus with some mild medications."

Charlene nodded her head eagerly. Daniel remained silent.

The doctor recommended joint therapy sessions and handed a prescription to Daniel. He folded it and sighed.

"You seem concerned," the kind physician prompted.

"Just worried," Daniel responded. "I don't think the answer is to medicate him. He's just a happy creative kid. This will change his brain chemistry."

Dr. Jamie smiled. Her voice was calm and reassuring. "It is mild and short term, with no severe side effects. I have to be frank. I can see what his behavior is doing to you as a family. While he may not be self-destructive in nature, I don't want you to think that his impulsive behavior isn't dangerous. From what you've told me, you all have been incredibly lucky."

Charlene continued to nod in agreement.

Roshan leaned in to send light to his child. Daniel sat up. "Okay, I know you are right. It just seems wrong on some level."

Murial stayed near, knowing that husband and wife needed to be in agreement. She reached out to Roshan to join in light and love.

So, with the calming effect of the medication, Jordan began to change. Over time, he heeded the gentle warnings of his parents, teachers, grandparents, counselors and concerned relatives.

A weight lifted from Charlene. She gave thanks that the human whirlwind known as Jordan began to unwind and the bizarre accidents stopped.

Daniel withdrew a bit more. He watched his son settle into the couch to watch television. "Hey buddy, wanna go play on the swing set?"

"Nah, Dad. Maybe later."

The bike stayed in the garage. The superhero cape stayed hung on its hook. Jordan settled into the routine of a "normal" young boy.

Anioch stayed near, as always, but the rainbows, laughter, and fun became a distant memory.

Sometimes at night as the boy slept and dreamed, his angel would whisper to him, "Don't forget me, Jordan. Please don't forget me."

And sometimes Jordan would wake up remembering his dream and the amazing adventures, riding into the wind and chasing some magical being. But even those dreams began to fade.

At last there was order, and Anioch's heart ached.

CHAPTER 6

The years passed and Jordan grew, as children tend to do. Anioch, the ever-present guardian, was always near as the boy matured in strength and beauty. With time and medication, the colors in Jordan's world faded and the memory of his secret friend and the brilliant lights which once awed him, now dimmed.

Charlene appreciated the new calm and let go of the anxiety and fear which had taken root in her heart. Murial appeared pleased as well. Daniel watched his son, feeling at once relieved and saddened. Yes, Jordan was less rambunctious... but also less effervescent. Mystery had been replaced with mundane, grace with the practical, and joy with conformity.

"Hey Jordan, we got the new camping catalog. I'm thinking maybe this year we can plan a longer trip and add in a few days of river rafting. What do you think?" Daniel eyed his son who was once again lost in the flashing screen of a video game. "Jordie, hey. I'm talking to you." Daniel leaned forward and tapped his son on the shoulder.

"Wait a sec, Dad. Let me finish this level."

Daniel set down the catalog. He was learning to wait. He missed how they'd once played together and the crazy stories his little boy had spun. Now their only conversations came in short declaratives: "Yes," "No," "Later."

Anioch watched as Roshan sent love to his charge, knowing the unspoken sense of loss that Daniel kept hidden in his heart.

Daniel approached his wife, who was busy preparing school lunches. She was humming softly when he said, "Jordie's school paper looked good. He really seems to have settled down."

"Yeah," Charlene replied. "I made some corrections but he did most of the work. I have to tell you, Dan, I used to worry that he would never be able to sit for long enough to read a book or write a paper."

"I know, right?" Daniel chuckled, hoping to keep his wife's mood light for the conversation he had planned. "Hey honey, do you ever wonder if somehow Jordan just isn't quite the same kid, sort of a little flat?"

Charlene looked up quizzically. "Come on, Dan, he was a wild child. Are you forgetting all that?"

Daniel glanced at Jordan in the family room resting on the floor, earphones plugged in and phone in hand. "No, I haven't forgotten. But look at him. He never goes out to play. I don't see him smiling or hear that excitement that used to just light him up."

"I think this is normal adolescent stuff. I mean he's doing well in school. And finally he isn't getting hurt or in trouble. I don't know about you, honey, but I used to live in fear each day afraid of what might happen."

Anioch listened with a tinge of guilt. He too found himself feeling relief that life had become much easier. He no longer needed to intervene quickly or think up new and creative ways to save his charge. But he also understood Daniel. Something was missing—the once etheric connection between angel and child.

"Yeah, I know," Daniel said, "and there is a lot I don't miss. But there was something magical in how he would describe those rainbows he saw. I just hope we didn't make the wrong choice..." Daniel's voice trailed off.

Anioch noticed Roshan lower his head.

❧

Daniel walked into the family room and laid down next to his son. "Hey kiddo, let's go take a bike ride. It's beautiful out tonight. We haven't caught a sunset for a long time."

Jordan took out his earphones. "I have homework."

"You can do it a little later. Maybe just a short ride. I need some fresh air." Daniel was stretching.

"But the game is going to start," Jordan said, pointing to the TV.

"We'll be back for the second half. Come on, son. Make your old man happy."

Jordan stole a glance at his mother in the kitchen. She nodded.

Anioch felt a wave of excitement. *Yes! I will paint him the most beautiful evening sky.*

As father and son rode past the well-manicured lawns and out onto the old railroad path into open fields, Anioch flew nearby and added to the brilliance of the setting sun with deep reds and oranges.

"Look, Jordan. Look at the beauty that is all around you. Can't you see it? Can't you see me?"

Jordan's head tilted back, letting the wind race across his face and dance through his hair. His lips curved in a smile.

"Oh, my beautiful boy, how I love you. I miss you, my sweet child."

Jordan looked up at the disappearing sun as it faded into a sliver of golden light. He stopped his bike.

Daniel slid up beside him.

Anioch and Roshan stayed near, both grateful for this time together. The wind stirred again, and the first stars began to sparkle in the darkening sky. Jordan stared into the fading lights and momentarily felt a flicker of a memory. Then it was gone.

Jordan shivered even though the night still held late summer's warmth. Slowly his smile faded. "Let's go, Dad. It's getting late. I gotta finish my homework and I bet the Lakers are up by twenty points."

As the years passed, Anioch's love remained constant and strong, though the distance between angel and his child deepened. No longer a boy, Jordan's curiosity, spontaneity and awe were replaced by complacency and boredom.

The angel tried to leave small signs of the miraculous: whispers in dreams, a passing of his wing, a random feather. Jordan seemed to sense something, but a nameless void took root and grew in the young man's heart.

At fifteen, Jordan's family—along with his sister and brother— moved to a small seaside town. He had read about the ocean but never visited. He loved the color, depth, power and strength of the ocean. His sophomore year began at Mar Vista High School, just a few blocks from the vast expanse of the Pacific Ocean.

Through the Surf Club, Jordan hoped to make new friends. The first meeting was held near a long wooden pier that stood as sentry, luring fishermen, surfers, and young couples. The tanned and trim teenagers stood near the water's edge holding boards and casually talking. Several more seasoned surfers were out past the sandbar dotting the hazy horizon, patiently waiting for the next good set of waves.

A new friend, Zach, called to several of the teens, "So this is Jordan's first time on the board. I told him we'd help him out. You know those east-coasters don't know much about surfing."

Jordan smiled.

"We all remember our first time out," Zach continued. "It was probably on a boogey board when were like two or something."

A boy named Sean joked, "No way, I was on a long board when I was still wearing pampers."

One of the girls in the group responded without pause, "Yeah right, Sean, you're still in pampers."

Anioch sensed that his child was stepping into the warmth of new friends and hopefully reigniting a connection with the energy of the earth. The angel blazed in a way he hadn't in quite some time.

Despite the long summer days, the ocean water felt cool and invigorating. Jordan stretched out on his board and began to paddle against the rolling tides. Spray hit him in the face as he moved in a rhythmic motion. Anioch flew beside the teenager, loving the mixture of sea and salt air.

Jordan's new friends coached him on how to wait for the right set and to time his entry into the forming swell. Jordan's heart raced as he let himself sink into the rolling waves. A surge of energy he had long forgotten connected him to something outside his own body. He felt a pulse beyond his own, closing his eyes and reveling in the freedom and excitement.

Anioch's heart sang.

The rest of the surf club watched in amazement as the graceful young man became lost in the mist and currents. Jordan rode the wave to the end of its crest.

"Well, bro, I'd say you're a natural," Zach shouted over the sound of the crashing water, and tossed Jordan a towel.

"I don't know about that," Jordan responded, "but that was even better than a rollercoaster."

Anioch paused. His memories of rollercoasters weren't happy ones.

CHAPTER 7

Jordan's life became the ocean, waves and the thrill he found in conquering the challenge of the pounding surf. The years passed and Anioch's boy grew into a strong and beautiful man. He gained fame and spoke boldly of living life on the edge. He professed a philosophy of "no fear." But silently something inside of him pulled like an invisible current, drawing him further and further away from his True Center.

Despite Jordan's outward bravado, something inside him stirred. It was nothing more than a mere flutter. The prayers from Anioch and messages of love did not reach him but rather ever so slightly whispered and called at some deeper sealed off level. Somewhere buried within Jordan was a void-like space that silently cried out, *"Feel me."*

The young man boldly professed that he conquered fear. With each new triumph he faced down great walls of water and power, yet inside he slowly was turning numb. As his fame grew, he further disconnected from his family, his friends and his passion. The empty space grew.

In truth, the fearless champion was silently consumed with one thing: he feared to fully live. And from that place of illusion, he denied his True Self. He lived from that void and saw the world from that empty spot and in that disconnection he created his own private hell.

Jordan arrived early in Australia for one of the biggest competition events of the season. He wanted to adjust to the time zone and re-familiarize himself with the unique currents of the beach. The weather was setting up to create near perfect surf conditions. A large storm was brewing off the coast but close enough to create huge regular sets. "This could be one for the record books," he causally remarked to Kyle, his agent. "The storm track is just perfect. I don't think it's going to slide close enough to chop up the water or sheer the winds. This could be some pretty amazing rides."

"For sure. You should be pretty damn awesome. Looks like conditions are setting up for you. There's no one out there who can beat you on the monster waves." Kyle paused and looked at Jordan who was staring at the ocean. "You okay, bro?" Kyle asked.

"Me? Yeah, I'm good," Jordan answered looking up. "Why you asking?"

"I don't know. You just seem a little distracted lately. Just checking. We need you in the zone. But I can see the surf report has you pumped." Kyle put down his coffee and gazed out to the wide expanse of beach. He'd been watching Jordan surf since high school days, and had signed him on the pro circuit. Jordan was an agent's dream, winning competitions and raking in new commercial endorsements. *It doesn't hurt that you're so damn photogenic*, the agent mused.

Jordan turned toward Kyle. "Yeah, well you know we've been on the road for a long time this season. A few days here will help me focus. I've been thinking maybe I should take a little bit of time off after this one. My mom keeps asking when I will come home for a visit. Grandma and Grandpa are having this anniversary dinner. Thinking maybe I should go."

Kyle nodded in agreement. "A break could do us all good. We have some photo and promo shoots scheduled for you afterwards but let me know and we can move them around."

Jordan stretched. He hadn't really thought of going home but somehow the idea popped in and felt right. "Nah, it's all good. I love it here. No worries, man."

Anioch buzzed with excitement. *Home! Oh yes, that would be perfect, my child. Back to where you are loved.* Anioch thought of Murial and Roshan and his angelic heart sang. He gave thanks to Source for lighting Jordan's mind with the idea.

Jordan spent several days surfing the majestic and churning Aussie sea. Crowds formed to watch him fly in and over the waves. Jordan felt the current pull, and effortlessly shifted into the energy of the wave. He lost himself in the moment and became one with the ocean. It was in these moments that he would feel the faint pull calling him back to a place of joy.

Anioch could feel the energy shift and would move in even closer. He would sail along the mist and sing with complete abandon, hoping that somewhere the slumbering child could still hear him. But the moment would pass. The ride would end. The crowd would roar and Jordan would forget the moment.

34

So the surfing legend and his angel surfed. As always, together. Anioch took his place alongside his child, adding the sublime touch of the Divine and raising the dance of man, angel and sea to near glorious perfection. He sang songs of praise to Source knowing this was a gift of pleasure and connection. In those moments, Jordan would awaken and feel the energy return. It was his secret lifeline.

But then the darkness would creep in as the sun set. Anioch watched and worried as Jordan lost himself in a life of endless parties. Anioch's angelic heart ached when he saw his beautiful child end his nights in a haze of confusion, mixing drugs and drinks with nameless friends all looking for a piece of the action. Countless sunrises were missed as Jordan woke up not remembering what town he was in, or who the woman was sleeping next to him.

The angel watched and worried. "Clear your head, my beautiful son. Clear your eyes. There is a beautiful world waiting for you to wake up. Clear your heart and return to that place of joy." Anioch prayed for strength, not knowing how to intervene in this destructive behavior. Stopping rollercoasters was easier than this.

The day of the final competition arrived. Jordan was well ahead in the scores and the spectator stands were buzzing with excitement about how the champ had surfed near flawless sets. There was little doubt who would win and the real race was for second and third. But folks streamed into the stands anticipating a thrilling show.

The predicted conditions were as near perfect as possible with massive sets coming in steady intervals on strong currents with minimal wind to flatten the waves. Jordan felt calm and assured. He readied himself and swam out rhythmically past the white foam and spray line. He began his ritual of emptying his mind, slipping into that special place where he surrendered himself into the current and the power of the wave. In that moment, man and wave became one.

Jordan felt the ocean swell before it could be seen on the surface. He readied every muscle and instinctively shifted his breath. For a brief second he closed his eyes and released his outer breath as he leaned into the wave.

Anioch could feel it. He too had learned to become a part of the dance. It was the perfect wave, rising up and carrying man and angel into the swirl of sea and air. The different shades of blue blended into a crescent that slowly wrapped the moving ocean. A magnificent curl stretched out from the powerful wave and slowly enveloped the lone surfer. Jordan caught the current and began his solitary flight within the magical space formed by air and water. It was perfect stillness in that magical tube. It was the point where Jordan felt peace merging into the space, free from the outside world.

Anioch knew they were flying together in the eye of a singular storm. The angel sang and laughed, fully alive in the throbbing energy. Jordan remained silent and at one with his board, his body, the current, wind and sea. It was in these brief seconds that he felt alive. It was pure magic. *I've got this,* both man and angel thought.

The crowd stood and watched as the wave and curl grew bigger. They momentarily lost sight of the surfer, now dwarfed by the looming wall of water. The energy in the crowd shifted. Perhaps the sea was too angry today. Some had voiced concerns over the storm predictions. The wave continued its march toward shore and the curl tightened. Within a small space shaped like the opening to a magical vortex, the steady surfer could be seen gliding on the smallest edge of the line. The crowd roared. Jordan flew through the end of the curl and emerged like a god on a golden chariot ablaze in light.

This was his most perfect and glorious set. Jordan was greeted by cheers. The video footage made him an instant legend in the surfing community. Anioch was breathless with excitement. He had been there orchestrating every small move, feeling the danger of the unchained ocean and its pulsing currents, but he too had perfected the art of surfing. He knew how to gently coax his child and calm the pull of the tide.

Anioch was certain that Jordan had to have felt his angelic presence, sharing the silent canopy of the wave. But Jordan felt nothing. Hubris obscured the holy. He heard the crowd. He watched the news clip and marveled, yet nothing inside him moved. The passion was gone. He smiled and went through the motions of celebration. He raised his cup in cheer but his heart was empty. Jordan felt strangely numb even in his moment of triumph.

The long flight home gave the hero time to think. Jordan sat in silence staring out the window to the shapeless clouds that covered his view. *I thought I could fly when I was a kid. I remember that feeling.* Jordan closed his eyes. Fame and success was his, yet something was missing. He was living his dream. He rode the power of the waves but lately couldn't feel that burning excitement which had been his life force. *What the hell is wrong with me?*

Anioch also thought of flying. It was his natural state. But being locked in this giant metal tube was not flying. Yet he sensed his child and the inner torment. This was an emotion that did not belong in the angelic realm. He worried that he had failed his charge. His whole purpose was to guide and protect, to journey with this human on this path of life toward the ultimate goal of an eternal life fully connected with Source. Yet Jordan appeared to be retreating further, on a path of self-destruction.

The angel's worry rose and formed dark questions. *Did I bring this on with my incessant interventions? Maybe I was too good?* Had he so deftly hidden the miraculous, the wonderous, and connection to the spiritual that Jordan no longer respected life or cared for his soul? Had Jordan come to believe that the power rested within his own humanity? The angel was filled with his first taste of despair. And in that moment he remembered Murial's affirmation from what now seemed like another lifetime: *"Be still now. Be strong. Be alert. Awaken and know that Love conquers fear."*

Anioch shuddered with this thought that perhaps he had overstepped his role and duties as a Guardian and thus played a part in the unfolding descent of man. Anioch prayed with unbridled energy for Divine enlightenment. He beseeched the Universe to restore him to his angelic vibration and resisted the slide into the dense material energy field. Unknowingly angel and man were descending below their blessed and balanced state. In a moment of horrific clarity, Anioch wondered if somehow both he and his child's connected souls were at stake. Anioch shuddered again as the plane entered into turbulence.

The small seaside town celebrated the return of their hometown celebrity. Charlene welcomed her child with open arms and tears in her eyes. Years of worry and pain melted away when she saw her grown son, golden and bronzed. He was beautiful.

Jordan could not respond from the heart but rather continued in the role of triumphant hero. As he hugged his mother, he didn't look into her eyes to see the depth of her love—or the extent of her pain. He ached. But he couldn't acknowledge the pain. Below the dull numb non-feeling, the abandoned young boy ached for something long forgotten and so deeply buried it seemed lost.

Daniel was there as well to greet his son. But he was remote. He hugged Jordan and then turned away, distancing himself through silence and disengagement. He saw the flamboyance, recognized the arrogance, and felt the soulless charade and impenetrable cold façade his son had devised. There was no pain in Daniel's eyes—indeed there was not even love—instead a look of blank withdrawal, Daniel's own protective facade.

Soon the celebration, fanfare and novelty wore off. Jordan began to question the wisdom of coming home.

Anioch watched and prayed. He hurt for the rejected mother. He hurt to see her love turned away. He hurt for the father who seemed to have given up. He hurt for the emptiness that consumed Jordan's soul. Anioch sang a prayer to the Most High, a prayer of love and a request for renewal. When would this tormented soul see the light? What was his angelic purpose if he could not impart love, grace and hope?

With Jordan's return home, Anioch rejoined his angelic circle and sphere of love with Murial and Roshan. But something was different. He felt it. The vibrations of both humans and angels had changed. The luminous aura that had surrounded and radiated from Murial was dimmer, as if covered in opaque gauze. Roshan was even further outside of the angelic vibrational reach. *Do I look and feel different, too?*

Murial looked up and smiled. "Welcome back, dear brother. We've missed you so. There is emptiness here without you and your child." Her eyes were warm and her smile brilliant.

Anioch understood. Their circle had temporarily been broken. The three angels bowed in grateful acknowledgment that they were rejoined.

Murial gently stroked Anioch with her wing. A deep flow of warmth entered Anioch's energy field. He had forgotten the pure bliss that came with a simple touch. "Oh sister, I missed you. It is like something was taken from me. I am so grateful to be with you."

Roshan looked on. Anioch reached out to him and returned the act of kindness he'd received from Murial. His beautiful white wing gently brushed Roshan. The three angels joined in a flow of giving and receiving. Collectively they blazed and their joy emitted a deep hum.

At that moment, the three humans who shared the space each sensed an energy shift. In that same moment of renewal, Anioch came to understand he had unwittingly joined in Jordan's descent into darkness. He had shut himself off to both giving and receiving. He had stepped out of the flow.

Murial's smile was warm and wise. For a brief time it broke through the haze and she shined with luminous brilliance.

Charlene was out in her garden. Pausing, she saw the clouds break and rays of light dance among the swaying trees. She sensed a lightening around her. For the first time in a long time, her heart felt a surge of hope. Her son was home and that was good. She looked at the bounty before her. *I'm going to make him a fresh salad.* She began collecting an assortment of vegetables and placed them in her basket.

Roshan watched and bowed. "Brother, we missed you. We are now complete." Despite whatever distance Daniel had created with his Angelic Guide, Roshan had been supported by the constant Love that emanated from Murial. With the power of that love, there was order and balance even within the darkened environment.

In that moment of reconnection, Anioch understood he had been severed not just from Jordan but also from this sacred circle. It wasn't because of the human illusion of space. Rather it was because Anioch had chosen to focus on the impermanence offered by the material plane such as fame, glory, adventure and conquest. In that separation from Divine Love and Source, he had come to connect instead with fear and despair, mirroring the lost soul of his beautiful and beloved child.

Anioch ached as he recognized this truth and in that instance of awareness, the Angelic Beings joined in a prayer to the One: *"We are instruments of Divine Love. Let us serve that sacred Purpose. Renew us as we join and rejoin our prayer of healing and transformative Love."*

Enlightenment came as the vibration lifted. Anioch's ease returned. There were no more questions. He too had come home, and for that glorious gift he gave thanks.

CHAPTER 8

Jordan suffered in silence for the next few days. Charlene tried to make small talk to draw him out, and Daniel offered to go on outings, but Jordan responded without enthusiasm. Though he spent time with his brother and sister, he realized he barely knew them. He watched as Jenna and Jake talked with an easy grace borne of years of deep connection. *I don't belong here anymore.*

"We're going down to the pier for a burger. Wanna join us?" Jenna shouted to Jordan as she ran upstairs to get her purse.

Jordan wasn't hungry but he was anxious sitting at home, sleeping in his old room, eating at the family table. "Sure. I haven't been there in forever. Is JoJo's still at the end of the pier?"

"Yup, best greasy burgers in town," Jake replied.

"Or you can get a veggie burger if you aren't into that," Jenna yelled from upstairs.

"Why would I want a veggie burger? But a poke bowl would be amazing," he shouted back.

Jenna popped her head out of her bedroom door. "I dunno. I'm not sure what you like or don't like. Maybe you're gross like Jake and dip your fries in your shake."

Jake's voice carried from behind the bathroom door. "Nothing gross about that. Maybe the champ doesn't eat junk food. You know his body is a temple. I mean he's plastered all over surf shops downtown. Can't get away from his winsome gaze." Jake started laughing. As he came out he laughingly continued, "Oh yeah, JoJo's has awesome poke bowls. I mean it is really quite the foodie hot spot, bro. Get real." He continued to laugh to himself.

Jordan smiled but felt a slight sting.

Jenna came out of her room with her purse. "Just ignore him. He's jealous. He tried surfing but wasn't very good at it. Baseball is his thing. You should ask him about it."

Baseball, Jordan thought. *Man, I remember little league days. He kind of sucked.* "Oh, thanks for the intel. And how about you, what's your thing?"

Jenna shot her brother a smile. "My thing? I don't know. For now trying not to be a jock like my brothers."

Jordan didn't respond.

The three siblings walked on the well-worn pier. Jordan marveled at how little had changed. He breathed in the salt air. Funny, how the ocean smelled the same all over the world, but here there was something just a bit different. It smelled like home.

He watched the local surfers bob like phantom figures in the rolling tide. As he and his siblings walked to the pier's end, some people recognized him and shouted welcomes. Jordan smiled but inside felt pangs of regret and loss.

The familiar aroma of frying oil, greasy fries, and grilled burgers helped, but he ate mostly in silence while his brother and sister joked and laughed. They tried to bring him into the conversation. They knew little about him and nothing of his life, and he realized he knew even less about them.

Again his thoughts drifted. *I don't belong here.*

That night Charlene asked Jordan if he would help her move some boxes in the garage. "Oh my gosh, look! These are your old paintings from back when you were a little kid. You loved to paint." She stopped, remembering the most elaborate ones had been created with his secret friend. She held out the multi-colored rainbow outlined in stars and bright rays of light.

Jordan stared at it and felt a surge of sadness. "Wow, Mom. I can't believe you still have that. I was a regular Picasso." Jordan's words fell flat. Jordan pulled at the boxes. "I can go through these in my room. Guessing they are in your way. I didn't know you had kept all this old stuff." He grabbed several and went inside.

Charlene sighed. She had hoped to spark a conversation or stir a warm memory. She wanted her little boy back for a moment. She was left alone surrounded by dusty mementos and an aching heart.

Upstairs in his room, Jordan mused over old forgotten and discarded childhood junk that his mother had painstakingly wrapped and stored. Memories came back in flashes. He vaguely recalled times of great happiness, chasing rainbows and singing long forgotten songs. He remembered a time when he felt calm and secure. Anger boiled up within him because he knew these were moments he would never recapture. *"You don't belong here!"* his mind shouted again.

He dismissed his inner voice and the yearnings for that long lost time. He rationalized that feelings of awe, excitement, joy and love of life were for kids. He cursed at his stupidity. There really was no way to go back to the fantasy of home.

Anioch sat with Jordan as he picked through his past, comforting the man with a touch of his wing. But Jordan couldn't feel it. Jordan pushed all his old paintings and long forgotten childhood artifacts back into the boxes. *I'm not that kid anymore. He's been gone a long time.* He hauled the boxes out to the side yard near the garbage cans.

Daniel watched from behind the blinds in the den. His heart hurt. Roshan's heart hurt.

Jordan decided he had stayed long enough. *I gotta get out of here. What was I thinking?* He called his agent to make arrangements to meet up with the team. "Sure, I can be there in a few days. Family is good, but time to get back to my real life. You know, this straight edge existence is killing me. Make sure you score me some of the good stuff." Jordan hung up as Charlene passed by.

Murial shot one of her looks at Anioch.

"I know. But what can I do? You were the one who told me to give him space."

Murial returned a look of disbelief. "Oh dear brother, be mindful of your words. Even for angels they have power."

Anioch returned to his duties, more mindful of his words and thoughts.

Jordan had a flight scheduled for the weekend. He spent large portions of his day on the beach. Anioch stayed near. They walked along the beach and Anioch blazed across the western sky, illuminating the canvas with radiant bursts of color and light. But Jordan couldn't see. Anioch sang childhood hymns of love and hope. But Jordan couldn't hear. *Really, Divine Source, what am I to do?*

Anioch brushed his child with pure power and energy. But Jordan was numb. Jordan was nothing more than a beautiful empty shell— incapable of perceiving, much less recognizing, the Divine that protected him and dwelled deep within his aching soul.

On the last afternoon of his trip, Jordan went to the garage and took out his old surfboard. Larger than the ones he now used, it had been badly dinged by his reckless youth.

He grabbed the board and headed to the empty beach. The surf was high and choppy because of a tropical storm brewing in the south. Red flags dotted the beach with small craft warnings posted along the coast.

Anioch followed, feeling darkness hanging over his child. He had seen Jordan in every state of human emotion but there was something sinister in the air. A chill consumed the space between angel and man—evil, black and tormenting. Anioch called upon the Almighty, the Power of Love and Creation. He stayed near, completely energized, protective and alert while the winds blew and the sky grew darker.

Jordan sat alone on the shore, staring out at the vast sea. His eyes filled with tears as he traced circles in the sand with his bare toes.

Anioch smiled as he saw how those toes had grown, as if only yesterday Jordan had been batting his toys and rattles. Anioch's angelic heart swelled with love.

Jordan began to mutter to himself. The surf was high and powerful. Waves leapt like giant citadels of foam and mist that crashed upon the shore with fury and unbridled power. Jordan jumped up. His mind was a churning vortex of jumbled thoughts. He would tempt the fates one last time. He screamed into the howling wind, "Okay, I'm here. Bring it on. Who's gonna save me now?"

The words echoed in the angel's heart and filled him with dread. Anioch prayed as he had never prayed before. He was suddenly faced with the unthinkable question that angels should never ask... *"What should I do?"*

In that instant Anioch was filled with a dark and powerful image of a tectonic struggle. He felt and fully understood what his child was thinking. Anioch would have to protect Jordan from his own dark and destructive side. But he knew the law of intervention, and he froze, alert to any semblance of a call for help.

He sang out to the Power of Heaven and rose in grace and glory and shone with the light of Love that is the essence of the Angelic Being. In dazzling light and majesty he manifested himself in front of the young man he had loved and cared for since before his birth.

Jordan stopped and stared in amazement. He could see the angel.

"Don't be afraid. It is I, your secret friend, your angelic guide," Anioch intoned with power and might.

Jordan stood frozen in disbelief. He had convinced himself over the years that it had been the imaginings of a young child. That anguish and despair which had lived so long in his heart reached into his lungs and caused him to struggle to breathe. What could this angel offer him now? He had turned away every person who had simply and completely loved him, including Anioch. He had been forced to turn away from his secret friend Ani. Sadness and anger blended as Jordan leaned into and surrendered to the sense of total loss and despair.

Jordan started to walk. It wasn't awe that pushed him but rather unbound rage. "You abandoned me and left me totally alone. Now you show up. Now? I don't need you. I don't want you. I... I don't even... I don't even believe in you..." Jordan's voice was strangled, caught in a hoarse and raw growl of utter hopelessness.

Anioch stood startled before his child, ablaze on the empty beach amidst the crash of the raging sea. He recognized the look as hatred. It pierced him.

"Even you can't save me this time," Jordan taunted. "You abandoned me. Everyone told me you didn't exist, and you left me. I don't want to feel anymore because all I feel is empty. If this is all there is, then I am tired and done. Where were you when I cried out all alone still believing in something?"

Anioch dug deep into his angelic core and blazed brighter, demanding attention. "I have always been here. I never left your side. It was you who turned away and stopped believing in me. But I never stopped loving you."

"Bullshit!" Jordan hissed into the whipping wind. "They told me I was crazy. You're not real. If you were real, how come I feel so hopeless and alone?"

Anioch surrendered to his Higher Self. How could he answer these questions that tore at his very essence? He was but a novice angel. In the darkening world, Anioch lost faith in his Divine Purpose, feeling as lost and abandoned as his child. All he had ever done was love and serve. But that didn't seem to be enough.

Anioch cried out, his voice booming over the crashing waves, "Jordan, it's always been your choice. You chose this life. You chose every moment to live, either in fear or love. You chose your thoughts. You chose what to see and what to feel. The Truth remains constant and unchanged: Love is. But it is a choice. Hope is. But it is a choice. Happiness and Joy are. But they are a choice. Grace is always present whether you know or accept it. It is a free gift that we never really

44

deserve. That was and is the Universe's Divine choice. Right now, this very moment everything boils down to this: It is your choice."

"A choice? Are you kidding me? I believed in you. That was my choice and they told me I was crazy. I'm crazy right now. Stone cold insane standing here talking to an empty beach. I didn't choose the pills. I didn't choose to slowly shut down and die inside. When I needed you most, I looked for you and you were gone. Joy, happiness, love? What good is all of that when your whole world, your reality opens up and crushes you? I'm done—it's all a big lie and illusion."

A dark wave of energy struck at the angel. Anioch had never felt anger before, but he had seen the destruction it wrought on the earthly plane. He did not believe angels could feel this emotion but the swirl of negativity clawed at him and it scared him. With a flash of insight, he wondered if he had descended to such a low vibration where anger and despair existed. He bellowed into the gathering storm, "This is your choice. You see me. You feel me. You know this to be true." And without thinking, Anioch exhaled into the raging wind and filled the air with Murial's command: *"Jordan, be still now. Be strong. Be alert. Awaken and know love conquers fear."* Then he added, "Love conquers death."

Jordan paused. The words sent a shiver down his entire spine and throughout his body. His mind raced. His heart froze. With one deep breath, he stood, surfboard under his arm and walked into the churning surf. He did not look back.

Anioch was crushed. Jordan had turned his back on him. *I failed.*

The angel stayed on the shore and watched his child paddle against the raging waves. The beach was deserted as the storm manifested itself in all its fury in the crashing tide. This was the first time since Jordan's birth that Anioch was not by his side. He did not stay near him. He couldn't. He didn't sing a prayer. He couldn't. He didn't bedazzle the sky. He silently stood on the shore and watched. He did not fly. He did not hover. He stood.

He wondered if Jordan's final hour had arrived. He knew, as an angel must, that he would be near at that time. The final passage would be their crowning moment together—the end of their earthly journey.

But Anioch stayed on the beach, confused and hurt by Jordan's rejection. His sorrow paralyzed him as he became a mere spectator. The angel sank deeper into the heavy vibration of the earthly plane as Jordan paddled out into the raging storm.

Jordan began to ride the waves with complete fearlessness. He cut across the tops and was thrown crashing from the crests. Suddenly one massive wave rose above the dark outer reaches of the black ocean and began its forceful and methodical ride toward land. Anioch could see Jordan off in the distance, a small bobbing figure. He was positioning himself for the ride. As the wave began to rise and gain speed and force, the heavens opened. A loud rumble and roar filled the air as a host of angels appeared.

Anioch was shaken and Jordan looked up. He lost sight of the wave that came crashing upon him.

"It is not your place to decide the time of passage," boomed the commanding angel. The statement rattled the shore like a clap of thunder and filled the air with an electric current of unchained power and might.

Anioch shuttered. He had been consumed by anger, sadness and despair, with thoughts of failure and loss. These were human emotions foreign to the angelic realm. This Divine pronouncement shook him out of his stupor and called him into action.

The heavens remained open as Seraphim and Cherubim circled the beach. Thunder and lightning roiled the seaside town.

Jordan tumbled and crashed among the pounding waves. He had sought this end and was suddenly filled with fear. He was not being saved as he always had. He had tempted fate once too often. He had seen the angel and turned his back on him. In his heart he knew this was the moment of his death and he cried out in fear and sorrow. He had wasted so much. He had been given so much, but right now had so little. He cried to the heavens to save his soul. He feared not death but the emptiness he knew that would consume his soul if he let himself go into the darkness of the oceanic abyss.

As Jordan was thrown between the waves and the air, he glimpsed a sight of the heavens filled with radiant Beings. He heard the angels singing and was reminded of the songs he had heard as a child. He desperately wanted to be folded into those loving wings one last time. He thought of his mother and yearned for the comfort of her loving embrace. *"Help me,"* his soul cried out.

Anoich heard the silent request... the plea he had prayed for. He was being asked to intercede, to intervene. He felt a surge of energy race through his being, lifting him up. At that moment angel and man connected.

Boy and angel together in unison, matching each other, riding on an angelic wavelength where singular phrases began and ended in one thought.

"I'm so sorry, my beautiful child..."

—"Please forgive me, my secret friend and guardian angel. Be with me now..."

"I am here."

—"I love you..."

"All I've ever done is love you."

The scattered words formed a prayer, a plea, a statement, a truth. Jordan let go, knowing in his heart that he had truly failed in everything that really mattered. He prayed for forgiveness for his arrogance and selfishness. At that moment a fierce wave dragged him down and sucked him into the turbulent currents below.

Anioch followed, diving into the thrashing surf as he was thrown amidst the pounding waves. He reached Jordan's side, and with a mixture of grace and strength wrapped himself around the limp body of his child, pulling the boy to shore.

The Angels from on high spoke once more: "It is our duty to guide, protect and impart Love. We do not decide nor hasten the course of events. Man was made with a free will which makes him blessed in the Creator's eyes. Anioch, you are young and have been given a difficult task. Remember to remain true to your purpose—Love is the message. Be Love. That is your task."

With that the heavens closed and Anioch was left alone with Jordan's limp body. Anioch knew that Jordan had been given a second chance; in truth, he humbly recognized that he had as well.

CHAPTER 9

The young angel took human form. He became an Angel Unawares and descended into the dense material plane. The cold crash of the waves and the stinging wind whipped against his skin. Momentarily disoriented, Anioch's wings morphed into arms—arms that now needed to plow through the water to save his drowning child. He felt his lungs fill with cold air and tasted the salt from the waves. Movement took effort and he felt fatigue for the first time as he lumbered toward the shore feeling the weight of gravity pull at him.

The young stranger stood in the damp sand. "Act like a human," Anioch whispered to himself. This was not a time for him to intervene too dramatically. He reached into the soaked clothes and found a phone. "Thank you," he softly whispered, glancing up to the now clearing sky. Other forces were clearly protecting them on this heavy earth plane.

He stared at the device and tried to recall what Jordan had done so many times. As the angelic-man stared at the phone, lights flashed and the numbers 911 appeared on the screen. Anioch put the phone to his ear and heard a calm human voice say, "911, what is your emergency?"

Anioch cleared his throat and spoke. His human voice sounded strange. It was deep and strong and felt so different, along with the new sensation of human lungs inhaling and exhaling. "There is a drowning victim here near Tower 33. He is non-responsive." As he spoke, he began to shiver in the strong wind. He had never known what it felt like to be cold. Everything on this earthly plane was so foreign. Every part of his human body seemed to be alive and screaming at him for attention. He wondered if acting like a human was really the right response. He pushed the rambling thoughts aside. *Stay centered*, he willed himself.

"Okay, we are dispatching emergency personnel now," the operator responded. "I will need you to help me until the paramedics arrive. Can you do that?"

Anioch smiled. Oh yes, I can do so much more... but I won't.

"Sir, are you still with me?"

"Yes, yes, I am here and will do whatever I am asked." Anioch set the phone down and followed instructions. He rolled his child over. A wall of emotion crashed over him and tears welled in his human eyes. *What is happening to my vision?* Momentary panic gripped him as he wrestled with the strange interplay of emotions in his human body. Anioch was stunned at the strength of the human feelings and began to realize his transformation onto the human plane was not merely physical. He felt a moment of deep empathy for the human condition. It was so much more complicated than he had ever thought. He pushed these insights aside. *Concentrate!*

Focusing on the operator's directives, Anioch cleared Jordan's airways, and started compression. A small crowd began to form and Anioch heard sirens in the distance. As he pushed and breathed into his beloved child, finally the young man violently lunged forward. "He appears to be breathing." Anioch kept his voice calm, suppressing the urge to sing an angelic song of praise.

"Great, be gentle, keep him calm," the voice on the phone urged. "We don't know the extent of his injuries. Don't let him move."

Jordan's eyes briefly fluttered open. The angel held his gaze and softly spoke, "I am with you, Jordan. Be still."

Jordan blinked. At that moment, Anioch knew that his child could see him and knew who he was. Jordan briefly squeezed his angel's now human hand. A wave of energy passed through both men. Anioch's heart soared. Jordan's breathing was shallow. His pulse weak.

Anioch stroked Jordan's wet hair as the ambulance and firetrucks arrived. Uniformed men ran toward the shoreline, and the crowd scattered. Anioch stepped aside to make room for the first responders.

In the blink of an eye, the surf-soaked stranger who moments before had been calmly whispering to the injured man disappeared, shedding his human form and taking his angelic position once again just above his child.

Anioch took a deep breath and realigned with his angelic form. He spread his wings and surrounded the small crowd with an arc of light. At that moment, some on the shore saw the sun peek out from the dark and ominous clouds that still held the power of the passing storm. Some felt a pulse of energy pass through them. Some felt moved to pray while others wept. There was a brief moment of deep spiritual connection on that shoreline. These connected souls pondered what they saw and felt, and held these thoughts in their hearts for many hours, days and months. Such was the power of Divine interaction.

As the paramedics tended to the near lifeless man, one member of the team moved among the crowd trying to identify the 911 caller. People whispered and wondered. No one could explain how the man had left unnoticed. He had simply disappeared.

Anioch stayed near, his only call to action was to hold a space of grace for his child and the people gathered to assist. He prayed for healing. He prayed for forgiveness. He prayed affirming Divine Order. His mind swirled with competing thoughts. Still straddling two worlds, he felt the pull of confusion from the human level of consciousness. He willed his mind to be still and to focus. He was here to simply embody Love.

The small gathering of on-lookers wondered who the hero was. No one had gotten his name or recognized him. Later the newspaper accounts wrote about the world class surfer and merely described the stranger as a passerby who had heroically jumped into the pounding surf to pull the champion to shore. The 911 call traced the stranger's phone to an unknown number. The rescue was shrouded in mystery. *All is as it should be*, the young guardian thought.

Jordan was carefully placed on a backboard, his neck braced. As he was loaded onto the ambulance, Anioch slid into the cramped space and stationed himself near the motionless man. Sirens blared and traffic parted. The air was heavy and the atmosphere tense. Anioch looked at the maze of wires, glimmering steel surfaces, clipped words, static interrupting and exploding, accompanied by the calm precision-like movements of the paramedics.

The angel could still feel the heavy pull of the material plane. He wondered how long it would take to shed the lower vibration and come back to his full angelic realm of light.

He prayed for Jordan, trying to lift himself to the higher energetic realm, but raw emotions of sadness and regret swirled in his heart. His mind raced, what had he done? How had he strayed so far from his simple assignment? *Love, serve and protect... that is it. I failed, and here you are, my beautiful child... alone, broken and in despair. What have I done?* Anioch's heart shattered.

While praying for forgiveness, Anioch's wing touched Jordan's hand and again he felt a tiny surge of energy. In that moment, Anioch realized he had become a mirror to Jordan's soul. They were connected by an invisible luminous ray of light. Angel and man shared the same Divine energy and drew life from the same wellspring.

In this same flash of illumination, Anioch knew he must be the one to shift. He must be the instrument of love. If he could mirror Jordan's soul, then Jordan could become the mirror of Anioch's angelic soul. Healing and redemption rested in that space of shared grace. Anioch envisioned himself carrying his child on an angelic wave of Divine and Healing Grace.

I am light. I am love. I am whole and complete as a creation of Source.

Jordan squirmed and the paramedic assessed the vital signs displayed on the monitors. Anioch listened to the short bursts of conversation.

"He's one lucky guy," the younger man spoke to his colleague. "Not out of the woods, but at least he's alive. Wonder who the unsung hero was? Pretty strange."

The two paramedics continued laboring. Anioch noticed how the older one stopped for a brief moment and glanced up in the angel's direction. Anioch wondered if perhaps the man had felt a shift and sensed his presence. Anioch focused on the man and sent him love.

The paramedic lightly touched Jordan and smiled. "Feeling a bit of energy in here," he casually said to his colleagues.

The uniformed crew nodded and smiled, each knowing what the other meant. They all had stories of how they felt energy shifts during certain rescues. It was as if the air was suddenly purified or some stream of light was able to enter the sealed off space of the life-supporting vehicle.

The monitors pulsed, reducing Jordan's vital signs to electronic dots and waves. Anioch saw the paramedic lean over his child and whisper, "You're gonna be fine, buddy. Someone is watching out for you."

He knows. In that moment of recognition, Anioch saw the man gently bow toward him. Anioch spread his wings and deeply bowed back, humbled by the mystery of it all.

The rescue crew, with angel in tow, finally arrived at South Bay Medical Center. The transfer was performed with the speed and efficiency of a well-choreographed dance. Jordan remained motionless while Anioch struggled to keep his focus off the organized chaos surrounding his child. He let go of unholy feelings such as sadness, guilt and despair and returned again and again to love.

Through endless tests and assessments, Anioch hovered nearby, holding a vision of healing and wholeness. *You are a child of God and wholeness is your birthright.* These words became the angel's mantra, as much for his child as for himself.

Jordan was admitted to the I.C.U. It was a small well-equipped area where every square inch served a lifesaving purpose. An almost solemn-like hush filled the unit with a holy vibration of healing that felt sacred as Anioch continued his vigil sending unceasing vibrations of hope and love.

He meditated on the significance of the past few hours. This was a turning point for Anioch and he fully suspected it would be for Jordan as well. In reflection, Anioch recognized his heart was filled with gratitude that his Teachers had come forward and saved both man and angel. He knew his descent into the material plane had been a master lesson and thanked his soul Guides for their love.

And so, the journey continued. Neither Jordan nor Anioch knew the path they were beginning. For now, Anioch focused on the moment, reminded by the mechanically measured metronome of the monitors. Each heartbeat spoke of continued life and hope.

As Jordan was situated into the healing cocoon of the I.C.U., Anioch watched the admitting nurse. She approached the still patient with near-reverence. Tending to Jordan, she paused and glanced over her shoulder, as if looking upon Anioch. Though the angel knew he had returned to being invisible on the human plane, he was startled by her smile and what seemed her knowing nod.

The angel bowed back, confused but feeling a surge of joy. Twice in a span of hours, he had found another human ally, a friend. *Thank you.*

The woman in green scrubs checked medical records, recorded important information, worked in a methodical manner. Anioch noticed her slight smile as she went about her tasks. She had a kind face with warm eyes that had a luminous quality radiating outward. She filled the room with positive energy.

Anioch could feel the shift in the atmosphere. *Pay attention to her,* he quietly willed himself. Anioch liked her. He was happy that she would spend the first night with his child.

As the nurse finalized her assessment, she placed a small hand on the bandaged, plugged in, motionless patient, then closed her eyes and bowed her head.

Anioch watched with intent focus. Her lips moved as she recited a silent prayer. He could see healing energy emanate from her heart to the bandaged forehead of his child. The two become encircled in an aura of light. Anioch had never seen a human being as radiant and beautiful as this woman. *Who is she?*

The nurse opened her eyes, gently patted the foot of the bed, and turned to leave. Just before closing the door, she took a final peek toward Anioch.

She knows I am here. Who is she?

"Protect, guide and love your child," she whispered. "God's will be done." With that, she left.

The room was bathed in light, and Anioch was greatly moved. He—the angelic messenger for Source—had been given a simple command from a human counterpart. In his heart he realized the Universe's creations blended in perfect harmony when allowed to freely connect. Or as Jordan would say, *"They were on the same wavelength."* Anioch wondered if the blessed wavelength was human or angelic. Either way he received it with humility and gratitude.

Anioch pondered the deep significance of the past few hours. There was so much to learn. Out of his failure, he was being offered great lessons and great gifts. His heart was full. In the holy sepulcher of the South Bay Medical Center's I.C.U., Anioch began to untangle the mysteries and let the healing light bathe over him as well as his beloved child.

Time stood still. There was little to do. Anioch only needed to be present while Jordan rested. The healing would take its own time. Anioch knew that it was all an illusion constructed for humans and, as he now understood, angels as well to learn on the earthly plane.

As Anioch's vigil continued, Charlene and Daniel entered the I.C.U. and opened the curtain that separated Jordan from the other patients. Anioch watched as they cautiously approached their son. He could see deep fear in their red-rimmed eyes.

Charlene leaned into her husband and buried her head into his shoulders. "Oh Jordie, my poor Jordan. What happened?" As she looked at her motionless son, her mind raced to grapple with the reality of her worst nightmare slowly being realized. Charlene began to sob.

Anioch sent her light, and he watched as Murial wrapped her dear child in a large protective wing. Guilt swept through Anioch when he caught the silent reproach in Murial's eyes. He fought to not slide back into the still lapping emotional riptides that threatened to drag him into the dark energy of fear.

Daniel stood quietly holding his wife, gently caressing her. The small space they shared shrank as the silence was punctured by low sobs and the background hiss of life-support machines. Daniel's face remained blank. His eyes didn't focus. He didn't look at his son. He stared off into the distance. A darkness swirled around him. Roshan hovered in the shadows. His eyes were downcast but his wings extended out, reaching into the small space where the grieving couple stood watch.

Anioch sensed Daniel's despair, but also something else—anger. Tiny ripples of regret washed over the angel. He watched the tableau play out in front of him; parents and accompanying angels knotted together in a circle of love, ripples of worry churning into pounding waves of sorrow and regret. *I am so sorry for what I did. I hurt my earthly family and angelic family. Please forgive me. I will make this right. I can make this right.* He suddenly knew this tragic trajectory had been set years before today.

Murial looked at Anioch and softly responded, "You cannot and will not make this right. The lesson, my dear brother, is to let go and know that it is not our will which must be done."

Anioch nodded. Of course she was right. That was the message he received at the height of the storm on the surf-pounded beach. He moved back.

Daniel shifted and slowly whispered to Charlene, "They said we only have a few minutes at a time in here. We can come back later."

Charlene lifted her head from her husband's shoulder. She stepped closer to the bed, softly touching her son's hand. She noticed all the tubes that were attached and bandages that covered his head.

She turned to the monitor that gave her some comfort, seeing the steady beat of her son's strong heart. "Let me just be with him for another minute, please. He's alive. Let me just touch him and feel his warmth," she softly implored.

Daniel didn't answer but stepped back, giving mother and child space. Charlene drew closer and softly rested her hand on her son's arm. She whispered into his ear, "Rest, Jordie. We are here with you. You're going to be okay. You just need to rest right now. We love you." Her voice broke as she felt her heart break. "Oh Jordie, what happened?" Charlene began to sob.

Daniel stood and waited. In his heart he knew that was all they could do. Wait. Daniel drew near and pulled his wife into his arms. "Let's let him be. He's sleeping and that is good. Let's let him sleep."

The couple left the room and Roshan turned to Anioch and bowed. Anioch did not feel the same reproach as from Murial but instead felt compassion and empathy.

Mother and father began their own vigil in the waiting area where doctors would eventually meet with them. All they knew was that Jordan had been in a serious surfing accident. They didn't know the extent of the injury, which had been classified as "critical."

They spoke in short sentences. Long pauses filled the space between their words. "What was he thinking? He knew this was a bad storm. There were surf warnings all along the coast." Daniel seemed to be speaking to himself.

Charlene looked at him. She didn't answer right away. When she finally did speak, she stared at her hands. "What does that matter, Daniel? That doesn't fix anything. We need to be here for him. What he did or why he did it just doesn't matter at all." Charlene stood and walked to the waiting room door, then said, "I need to get some air."

Daniel stayed seated. "I'll wait for the doctor. I will text you if he comes by."

Roshan sat with his ward. He had learned over the years that the best he could do was to simply be present. So father and angel sat and waited.

Daniel let his mind wander, recalling the carefree child who spoke of a secret friend who danced and sang for him. Daniel's heart ached.

Where was that little boy now? Who was singing to him now? *What have I done?* Tears rose and a cry of anguish pierced the empty room.

Roshan heard and felt his child's pain and softly whispered, "You are not alone, my child. I am here. I always have been. Please feel my presence and know that all is as it should be."

Daniel lowered his head into his hands and continued to weep.

Doctors and nurses came and went from the large electronic door that separated the waiting area from the I.C.U. Families huddled in small groups, each lost in their own private worlds, accented by worry, fear, loss and hope. This became the new living space for Charlene and Daniel.

Family and friends cycled in to offer words of support. Jordan's brother and sister would come to visit but would leave after a short stay, unable to fully comprehend the seriousness of the situation.

Jake sat quietly slumped in one of the overstuffed chairs. He stared out the small window wishing to be anywhere but there. He got up and hugged his mom. "I'm going to get a soda. Can I get you anything?"

Charlene patted her son's back and shook her head. "I'll text you if anything changes." She could feel Jake's unease.

Jenna watched and felt the pool of despair wrapping itself around her family. "Jordan is going to be fine, Mom. He's brave and fierce."

Days blended into night and back into day, everything melting in a swirl reduced in time and space to a small, bland non-descript, sterile waiting room.

Jordan slumbered, lost in a deep sleep. He was medicated so his body could rest. But his spirit soared. Free from his body and the crush of his self-created hell, in the sacred space free of time with no constraints from the past or fear of the future, he reconnected to his deepest hopes and dreams. His soul reawakened as he felt the flow of grace fill him and carry him back to the safety of the shore. He saw lights and rainbows. He heard ancient songs he had long forgotten. He felt the presence of his childhood friend, Ani. He was free and whole.

While Jordan slumbered, his parents worried. His angel rejoiced.

Doctors spoke in hushed and clipped tones to the worried family members. They measured his progress in outward manifestations—pulse rates, oxygen levels, brain function. The physical healing was slow. In fact, the doctors were not even sure of the full extent of Jordan's injuries.

Murial and Roshan stayed near and listened.

The lead doctor began his latest assessment, "There are concerns with infection in his airways and lungs. We are monitoring that and administering antibiotics. His vital signs look strong and his brainwaves don't show any type of abnormality to cause us concern with brain function. We will know more about the possibility of paralysis from the spinal cord damage when the swelling reduces and as we bring him out of the coma. He is strong and in good shape and that is a big plus."

Charlene and Daniel listened. Words like "coma," "oxygen deprivation," "spinal cord damage," and "paralysis" slipped in and out of the flow of conversation. Words they had never imagined contemplating or speaking now entered their world.

Charlene was too afraid to ask, *"Will my son be able to walk?"* For now he was alive and that was good enough. Instead she moved into her new mantra. It became her immediate and ready response no matter what facts or information were conveyed: "He's a fighter. He has the heart of a champion."

For Daniel the questions gnawed at a deeper level. He worried who might emerge from the induced coma. How would the world-class surfer react to legs that couldn't walk, or arms that couldn't swim? He worried in silence, always returning to the question steeped in deep regret: *"What more can we take away from him before we crush his soul?"* In his mind's eye he always saw the enthusiastic young boy chasing his secret friend. *Where is that beautiful child?*

Daniel refused to go any deeper into the questions. The possible answers frightened him. So both parents sat stoically and listened. Both spoke words of hope but silently faced their own fears, stepping only so close before they shut down and went no further. And each day they waited as the vigil continued.

PART TWO

CHAPTER 10

Jordan lay motionless—his signs of life displayed in undulating hypnotic lights, flashes and accompanying beeps. Anioch was deeply aware of the comings and goings of friends and family. He felt the energy of each person and would extend his wings to accept the positive and shield his child from the negative forces.

In the small space of the I.C.U., as people were ushered in, they saw Jordan hooked up to shiny and impersonal instruments. Tubes protruded, whizzing and whining. The champion's act of desperation and unacknowledged self-destruction rippled out into Jordan's circle of family and friends. It took on an undercurrent of power like a slow cresting wave that ebbed and flowed, moving each person in intimate and sometimes painful ways. The waves pulled with the hidden power of a riptide. They lapped or crashed in a mix of sorrow, loss, fear, anger and guilt. *What happened? Were there signs I missed? How could you have done this, Jordan? What's going to happen now?* With somber and intimate processing of the event, each person entered the space and offered his or her silent homage. Anioch held his vigil and spread his wings wider.

News spread quickly of the surfing accident that had almost taken the life of the world's premier competitor. Endless calls and texts from fans, friends, agents and well-wishers streamed across social media and passed through the hospital. Words of support were spoken. Silent questions lingered.

Anioch ignored the human tidal wave of emotions. He knew the Heavens had allowed both man and angel a chance to make amends and grow in their own understanding of the Universe's mysteries of suffering and loss—of letting go, surrendering and ultimately forgiveness always moving toward awakening. He knew what no human could know and so he did not share in their worry and anguish. Instead the angelic being meditated on the causes and effects of his own angelic actions and inactions. *Forgive me, please.*

The angel rested in the simple moment. In this blessed Now, he was grateful for both the certainty as well as the uncertainty. He knew his child needed to sleep in order to fully awaken. Anioch felt the restorative flow of grace wash over him and through it strengthen his charge. In that outpouring of Divine Love, the angelic guardian was humbled and renewed. His lesson again was made clear: Do not question the will of Source. Instead stand in service. Be the Source. And so Anioch stood and offered endless thanksgiving and praise. *Thy will be done.*

Charlene kept her own private bedside vigil. Once again mother and angel watched over their special child. Anioch recalled those early days and noticed that the mother's love had remained true and strong despite repeated heartbreaks, rebukes and rejections. Charlene prayed for divine intervention for the healing of her son. She wept as she thought about her brave and daring child who had always wanted to push out to... and perhaps beyond the edge to tempt the fates. She longed to look into the eyes of the young boy who loved life and saw beauty in all things. She was now forced to face the fear directly that she had so often tried to bury: her son was facing death. Yet he was still here and she held tightly to her belief in miracles and second chances—both for her and her child.

In the long and seemingly endless wait, she pondered the slow descent of her beloved son. She wrestled with her inner thoughts that perhaps this had not been an accident, and allowed the flickering doubt to enter her mind and bring form to the nearly unthinkable. With each breath, she dared to believe there was a plan. She imagined and held as a sacred intention that in that plan her son would be whole and happy again, filled with light and joy like he had been so many years before.

Knowing that Charlene had stepped into a powerful level of prayer, Anioch matched his angelic intention, creating a blessed union. *"Thy will be done,"* mother and angel silently intoned.

The afternoon sun dipped behind the trees that framed the windows, creating shadows on the waiting room floor. Charlene sat quietly in the corner of the room in an overstuffed chair that had become hers during the days-long vigil.

A woman with a kind face came in and sat down next to her. Sensing the new presence, Charlene looked up from her reading. Her eyes brightened as she leaned forward. "Jen," she whispered her friend's name. A smile softened Charlene's brow. She put down her book and stood, leaning in to a deep embrace.

"Charlie, I am so sorry. I am so so sorry." Jen's voice was low but the other visitors shifted in their seats as the ritual of waiting welcomed a new member.

Charlene let another smile escape. It felt good to hear the nickname. It felt good to smile. It felt good to hold a steady hand. It felt good to have a connection to happier times.

The women hugged. Charlene could feel a slow rhythm as her more shallow breathing gave way to low gentle sobs.

"It's okay, sweetie," Jen said. "You just need to let it out." Both women slowly sank into the waiting chairs, hands still grasped.

Charlene looked into her friend's face and saw compassion and love.

"Oh Charlie, I came as soon as I could."

As Charlene studied her friend's face, she wondered how long it had been since they had been together.

Jen patted her hand as if reading Charlene's mind. "It's been way too long. I was trying to remember the last time we saw each other. I'm thinking it might have been when the boys went off to surf camp."

Charlene flashed on an image of two lanky teenage boys running off to the passenger van, filled with happy carefree youths all waving goodbye to their mothers. In that moment, she could once more feel the warmth of the early summer sun and hear the cacophony of excited teenagers shouting.

"Oh, that was a good time. Those two boys off together for their summer adventure."

Jen let out a soft chuckle. People holding private vigils in the waiting room shifted again at the strange yet welcome sound.

"Oh my gosh, those two wild-eyed boys ready to conquer the waves of the southern beaches—" Jen's eyes raised to meet Charlene. Breath caught in her throat.

Charlene nodded. "It's okay. That's who he is. That's what he does. He loves the ocean, and those are great memories."

Jen squeezed her hand.

Charlene paused to steady her voice. "I don't think that was when we were last together. The boys were only in high school. So many good times." Charlene dabbed her eyes and continued. "I love remembering them like that. All full of life and energy."

"Yup. Your bronzed and newly converted beach bum son dragging along my already preppy east-coast nerd. Pretty funny to think about it."

Charlene felt a loosening of the strangling grip that had held her in a clutch for days. She let the good memories enter and wash over her. "You have no idea how happy I am to see you."

"Me too. I mean, not the reason I wanted to come here. Jim and I were in London visiting Stephen, just making sure he's adjusting to the changes. I think I might worry a bit too much. You know graduate school in a foreign country... but he's going totally native and acting just like a Brit. So we were with him and he saw it on Facebook first. Then we caught it on the sports news. I don't know how much they got right, but I left as soon as I could."

There was a pause. Charlene stared off into the large window. The early evening sky was painted in deep reds. She dreaded giving the update, again. As friends and family stopped in, she and Daniel had to go back over the details. Each time she spoke the words, the reality of the situation burrowed deeper into the core of her being.

"You know, it is really hard to talk about this. Every day it seems I have to tell someone about Jordan and how he is laying there just beyond those doors and we don't know how he is going to be tomorrow. There is some little voice inside of me that is afraid every time I say certain words, they take on more power and become more real."

Jen's gaze met Charlene's unmasked sadness and fear. "Well then, I say we just affirm right here, right now, that Jordan is surrounded in light. He is whole and the healing that is taking place is complete. That's what I say."

Charlene smiled and hugged her dear friend. "That is absolutely perfect."

Murial, always nearby, sang a song of praise.

"Okay, so I am thinking it's just about tea time. At least I think it is in London. How about we take a step outside and get you a change of scenery, my dear Charlie?"

"I feel like I need to stay close by. You know, maybe they will call me." Charlene's voice was hesitant.

"Well they might, but how long have you been sitting here waiting?"

"I'm not even sure what day it is. I do go home and sleep for a few hours when Dan comes over to relieve me. Sometimes I shower. Look at me. But I feel like I need to be here." Charlene was pulling at her zipper and biting her lip.

"I get it. I do. But I think it would be fine for us to go out for just a little bit. Jordie is in good hands. Plus they have your number and we won't wander too far. I think you deserve a piece of pie or ice cream." Jen tugged at her arm. "Come on, Char. We are the Fierce Moms, remember?"

Charlene remembered. Fierce Moms. They had coined the phrase after one too many episodes of tracking down their sons following some Jordan-led adventure. She loved Jen. They had met in a Mommy & Me class when the boys were toddlers and became fast friends. Over the years, the families spent holidays and vacations together. Charlene felt closer to Jen than her own sister.

"You don't need permission to give yourself a little bit of gentle kindness. It's not like we're going to get a mani-pedi."

Charlene smiled. Jen always had a bright sunny side. "Did I tell you how happy I am that you're here?"

"Yes, you did." She gently pushed Charlene's hair back. "So, let's go somewhere we can talk and not whisper."

"Okay, let's check in with the nurse. They let me visit for a few minutes every hour. I don't want to miss that. They will let you in, too. I mean, you are my sister after all." Charlene's voice was stronger and had a brighter tone.

"Oh you bet. My sista from another mista, like we always said."

Charlene felt the laugh rush to every part of her body and it felt good. She felt strangely alive for the first time since the call. *Whoever brought her to me, thank you.*

The two women passed through the electronic doors. Charlene felt the shift as the air pressure closed the doors behind them. The stillness weighed heavily. Muffled sounds of life wove into the backdrop of hissing machinery. She felt Jen pull her near.

"He's over here," Charlene said. "He doesn't look like himself. He is pretty swollen and bruised. But I whisper to him. I know he can hear me. He will be really happy to hear your voice. I know he will."

Jen slid behind the curtain and looked at the still man covered in sheets and bandages. She gasped. Then she took a deep breath, squared her shoulders and moved toward the bed.

"Hey Jordie, it's me, Aunt Jenni. Steve sends you his love. So does Uncle Jim. There are so many people who love you and are holding you in prayers. You just need to rest right now and let your body heal. I know what a scrappy kid you are. I mean, who can forget our little wild child. Right? My goodness, I remember how you would scare your poor mom. Always finding something that could make you go faster or fly higher."

Anioch listened. He felt her energy. She was one of the good ones. "I remember when you got your new bike. You were maybe seven years old. When you rode that thing, it was like you became a different person. You talked to your imaginary friend and sped along the sidewalks chasing every made-up bad guy you could think of. You got so caught up in your game, you ditched poor Stevie. He came home crying, saying you were ignoring him and only talking to your pretend cop radio friend."

Anioch smiled. He remembered playing cops and robbers with Jordan. He knew the imaginary voice that Jordan spoke to had been him.

"Well, then it got dark and you didn't come home. Your mom came over and was so worried. She was ready to call the real cops when there you were riding down the street, not a care in the world."

Charlene remembered that day. How she wished that it could be that simple right now to see Jordan wake up and flash his big bright smile. *"Sorry, Mom..."*

"And there you were all smiles. 'Hey, Mom and Aunt Jenni,' you said. 'We got the bad guys. They went really far trying to run away, but we got them.' I swear I was sure that this time your mom was going to spank you. I mean she was so worried. But there you were with your big heart so full of love that when you looked at her, you immediately knew she was scared and worried. You jumped off that bike and ran to her. I can still see you in your cowboy boots and blue cape, running with your arms wide open shouting, 'Oh Mommy, don't look so sad. I'm fine. I am always fine. I will always be fine. I'm special and protected'."

Charlene felt hot tears running down her cheek.

"And your mom just hugged you and loved you. That's all she has ever done, sweetheart. Because Jordan, you are special and so very loved. And I know you are protected. You are surrounded by love and that is the strongest power on earth. You, my dear one, are perfect. Know that. You are absolutely perfect..." Jen's voice dropped.

Charlene watched in amazement as her dear friend spoke the simple words of truth that she knew her son needed to hear.

66

"Jordan, honey, you rest and know we are all here waiting to hug you. Whatever you were thinking, or whatever happened, that's all in the past. We love you and want our little wild child with the big heart and m-magical s-smile back..." Jen's voice cracked.

Charlene moved near the edge of the bed. "Jordan, honey. Not one day has passed where I don't thank God for you. I love being your mom. You have brought me such joy and love. Rest, my sweet child. We are all here for you. And we love you."

Anioch hovered and marveled at how perfectly life's moments came together. The blending of the past in a simple story allowed for words of love and forgiveness. He knew his child heard the words and felt the warm glow of the shared energy.

"Thank you," Charlene whispered to her friend. "You are the best."

Both women bent to gently kiss the top of Jordan's head. Each softly whispered into his ear, "You are surrounded by light." And Anioch smiled. They had both spoken Truth and the light expanded.

Charlene returned to the hospital alone. Her time with Jen had been like a magic elixir. Over tea and scones, childhood memories were shared along with laughter and tears. As she returned to the hospital, in the lobby she saw a man who looked vaguely familiar. Dressed casually in khakis and a polo, there was an air of rushed impatience about him. He was speaking on the phone. Charlene picked up a few of the words, her interest piqued.

"I don't know, man. He looks pretty bad. His dad was there and was able to get me into the I.C.U. for a few minutes. I gotta say, it doesn't look good. They wouldn't tell me much. I'm not even sure they know anything."

Charlene paused and moved closer, digging in her purse as if distracted. *Who is this guy? Is he talking about Jordan?*

"Well, I don't think we can do anything yet. I'll look at the contracts when I get back to the office. He's got tournaments coming up that we'll have to cancel, but we need to look at the sponsorships, too. That's where the financial risks are for us."

Charlene felt a knot of anger tighten in her stomach. Her son was in a hospital bed hooked to machines to breathe while this stranger was worried about contracts and sponsors.

"I'll call you once I check out the legal stuff. We can spin this. We need to keep the drugs and shit out of the press."

Charlene had heard enough. Her pulse quickened. Moving close to the man, she remembered the agent's name. "Hello, Kyle. We met once during one of the competitions. I couldn't help but overhear your conversation. It's best that you are leaving. Just know that Jordan is a fighter. He will heal and come back. And he will be better." Charlene's voice was strong and clear. "But he doesn't need people like you who see him as a commodity to trade and sell. So please, I am asking you to stay away. The I.C.U. is for family. For people who love the ones who are in there fighting for their lives. Just tell your crew to stay the hell away."

She pushed past the doors not bothering to look back. She felt strong and focused. This was her son and she was going to fight for him.

CHAPTER II

Jordan remained in a deep sleep for several weeks in an induced coma to aid the healing. Doctors were optimistic that no permanent damage had been sustained. They spoke hopefully of recovery but still in guarded terms.

Anioch watched as family and friends sat by Jordan's side and spoke openly and lovingly. He also noticed that the new friends who had partied with Jordan and were happy to share in the flash of fame had now disappeared. Anioch believed this was part of the blessing that had come from the accident. Those who stayed close were from Jordan's past and had known the free spirited joy-filled child.

He knew Jordan could hear the beautiful words of love and support. Anioch held as his constant prayer that Jordan would recognize his own goodness and worth and begin to fill that emptiness that had gripped and shattered him.

Anioch did not leave Jordan's side. He did not venture into the long endless corridors. He remained ever-near. Finally one day, amidst his ceaseless prayers, Anioch noticed movement in the bed below. Jordan began to stir under the tightly spread covers. Jordan's eyes fluttered; hesitantly he opened them and moved his head toward the direction of the undetectable light that emanated from the looming guardian.

Anioch's angelic heart raced, could it be that his child could see him? Anioch stayed perfectly still.

Jordan allowed a small smile to cross his parched lips. His eyes twinkled ever so slightly as they adjusted to the light. The heavy gauze of the deep slumber lifted and Jordan slowly reentered the living world. As he peered around the unfamiliar surroundings, a flicker of hope entered his aching chest and recognition registered. He was in the presence of his secret friend. He looked at the radiant light that filled the space and knew this was the same being that had tried to stop his fateful ride on that deserted beach. *Am I dead?*

He wondered for a second if perhaps he was in some holding place. But his thought was interrupted by the low wheezing sounds of machines hooked up to his body. He blinked, trying to clear his eyes.

69

He noticed monitors measuring his vital signs and felt tubes in his throat and arms. He slowly felt sensation return to his body. *I'm alive. But where am I?*

He looked at his angel and bent his head ever so slightly. The light refracted and reflected in a burst of brilliance that drew prisms on the plain walls. His heart stirred. The monitor raised an alert. He remembered that glorious light from his childhood. *Am I dreaming or delirious? Where am I?*

His mind raced. He had convinced himself that his memories of a light being were those of a delusional child. But here he was enveloped in that light in the cool darkness of this unfamiliar space. And he felt at peace. *I'm alone.* His mind filled with a thousand questions and thoughts. *But I'm not alone. You are here with me. Have you always been here with me?*

Anioch bowed and answered softly, "Since before your birth, my beloved. I've been with you since before time and will be with you long after time passes."

The room filled with light as the monitors sent off a cacophony of sounds.

As the angel radiated love toward his child, the curtain parted and the nurse who had commanded Anioch to his call of duty on that first day entered. She'd heard the alarms and came in with a sense of urgency.

As she drew near, she stood completely still in the shadow draped by the pale blue curtain. She sensed the heightened energy in the room and saw the slight smile on the once slumbering man. But there was more. Anioch stopped speaking and Jordan smiled. It was a moment of grace. She was witnessing a miracle—the instantaneous shift of reconciliation, return, and awakening to truth.

The kind nurse looked as the lights subtly shifted and the air moved. She waited. The alarms quieted. As she watched from her place of shadows, she saw the beautiful young man who had lain in this bed for the past weeks in a motionless coma smiling at an invisible force. She felt a surge of electricity and power. This was a place of healing. She was in the presence of a holy being and she stayed discreetly at a distance.

Anioch saw the middle-aged nurse and knew that she sensed his presence. Jordan turned toward the door, saw the nurse and smiled again.

She was filled with joy and awe. That presence she had felt since the first day of admission had not been an angel of death that stood watch, waiting for the right moment to guide the human soul to heaven. Rather his was a guardian and keeper who would heal and hold the vigil of love. She bowed in Anioch's direction. "I too am here to serve."

Anioch gasped and Jordan watched in amazement. *Who is she? Where am I?*

The nurse walked toward the pale young man, his bronze tan long since faded. "Hello, Jordan," she spoke softly. Her voice was soft and calming.

Anioch was touched by the serenity and love that voice conveyed. He sensed this was a special human, one consciously connected to the Divine. The young angel felt somewhat exposed. She was a human who was somehow aligned with angels, believed deeply and knew Truth. Her words echoed. *"I too am here to serve."* *Indeed,* and for that he was grateful.

She looked toward Anioch, as if acknowledging his presence. She then turned to Jordan while she moved efficiently, resetting the monitors. As she gently touched his forehead she softly spoke, "You suffered a very serious accident but you're going to be all right. Your mind and body have been through a lot, but you have been well looked after." She smiled and again slightly bowed in Anioch's direction.

He bowed in response. *Can she see me?*

Jordan followed the kind stranger with his eyes. He noticed that she had a slight glow to her, not as brilliant as his secret friend's, but he instinctively trusted her and felt peaceful in her presence.

The nurse checked his vital signs and summoned a doctor. She gently patted her patient and reassured him. She was efficient yet loving. "I'm going to send for your mother," the nurse said. "She has been by your side for a long time."

More than you could ever know, Anioch thought.

Jordan watched her leave and wondered how long he had been in the hospital. The last thing he could remember was being dragged under a massive wave and seeing the sky fill with angels and all sorts of otherworldly beings. As he tried to remember what happened, he recalled seeing Ani looking at him from behind near-human eyes. *My*

God, none of this makes any sense. He sank lower in his bed. *Man, everything hurts.* He closed his eyes as his body began to scream back to life.

Anioch watched and sang praise for the miracle of life—renewed life—and all the hope it held.

Charlene ran through the double doors and pushed back the curtain. She fell to her knees in front of the tall metal bed. She wept with joy as she gently cradled her son's face in her outstretched hands. Her prayers had been answered. Her son was awake, he was alive. He had escaped death and risen from his deep slumber. Jordan opened his eyes. They shone brightly, different and new. She gently kissed his hands and caressed each finger.

Jordan watched as his mother rocked and cried. She did not speak, but he understood. The weight of worry and fear had been released from her heart. Jordan felt genuine love for this woman and a deep pang of regret for the years he had denied that love.

Jordan reached out and tentatively touched his mother's face. With a weak trembling hand he brushed away her tears. He softly whispered in a voice frail and raspy, "I'm sorry, Mom." He looked into her dark eyes and saw love. Connecting for a brief instant, a moment of fleeting eternity, he had to look away; the mix of love and sorrow were too real and raw. Tears pooled in his eyes. "I'm so sorry."

He had not looked into his mother's eyes for many years. He could not look at that unmasked love or the buried hurt. He had known then, as he knew now, that he had been a source of pain and worry. As he lay strapped in the confining bed, he reflected on his mother's face— drained and exhausted. He felt regret and shame. He knew he had caused her great pain. The refrain echoed in his mind: *What have I done?*

He glanced up to his secret friend who hovered and watched, motionless and serene. Jordan felt a second stronger pang of guilt and failure. All of the pain and emptiness and despair of the past came forward and gripped at his tormented soul. He buried his face in his mother's arms and let the tears come.

She softly spoke to her son, "It's all over, Jordie. The past is in the past. We are all sorry for what was. I let you down. But we have today and tomorrow. We are so very lucky that we have you back, and that is all that matters."

Again, mother and son cradled together, sharing unspoken love in a hospital room with an angel nearby singing songs of gratitude for that love, and new life.

Jordan listened to his mother's word. She spoke of new beginnings. She spoke of forgiveness. She spoke of luck. Yet in his heart, Jordan knew it had not been luck. He remembered the heavens opening and the heavenly hosts descending and orchestrating his rescue. He felt humbled, awed. Silently he wondered what divine plan awaited him, the lost and repentant son.

Questions swirled in his head as he tried to reconcile the past with this moment. He didn't know what had happened or how badly hurt he was. But he was being offered a second chance. He could see his secret friend. That was no coincidence but he knew he had caused everyone pain. He felt exhausted.

The kind nurse came by and told Charlene that Jordan needed to rest.

Jordan smiled briefly. It hurt to speak. "We are good, Mom."

That was enough for Charlene. She needed to make calls and share the good news.

As Jordan sank back, a question rose from a deep hidden place within his soul. He assumed he had been close to death, or at least it felt that way. But he was here. *Why am I still alive? What do I need to know?*

With those thoughts he drifted off to sleep. And his angel stayed near, measuring his breath without the need of wheezing machines. *All is well and as it should be,* the angel rejoiced.

CHAPTER 12

Jordan continued his journey of healing. He stepped onto the new and curved path of recovery, both physically and figuratively. He found strange comfort in the pain of weakened muscles forced to stretch through physical therapy. The pain meant he was alive and healing.

"Okay Jordan, I need you to do one more rep," the therapist coached. "Slow it down and lift the weight from your core. Remember... balance."

Jordan took a deep breath. He was covered in a fine film of sweat. He looked at Sam, his physical therapist. Built like a wrestler, the man had an easy way and a quick smile. But he also knew when and how far to push. "Hey man, my back is screaming at me right now. Can we take a break for just a sec?" Jordan moved the pulley, fully focused, feet planted on the ground. Every part of his body shook under the pressure of movement. He closed his eyes.

"Sure, we can rest when you finish. Earn that rest, brother. We're happy to get you out of that bed, remember? We have to get you strong again. The ocean's calling for you, Mr. Pro." Sam chuckled, gently realigning Jordan's back and feet.

Mr. Pro, Jordan thought. If only you knew. "You're right on that. I gotta get these legs back, but man, my back is just so sore. I can't believe there is that much space in my body to hurt."

"You know you're lucky, right? Most people don't come back this fast from that kind of accident. When I saw your chart, I was surprised I wasn't taking you out of a chair to begin PT. You are one lucky dude."

Luck, Jordan pondered. His mom had used that word. He heard it a lot. But he knew it wasn't luck. He knew he had to push himself because he wasn't lucky. He kept the memories of that day to himself. But in the memory, he was more certain with each day that there was something for him to do. And he needed to be strong.

"Well, I guess someone was watching over me. I can't imagine life like that."

Jordan leaned into the move and regulated his breathing. He mentally counted the reps. The pain was real and intense and he fought the urge to tighten.

"Good job. Slow it down. Slow it down. Make it count. This is good, Jordan. You're going to be out there winning those competitions in no time."

Jordan closed his eyes and surrendered to the movement. Anioch was there measuring every count. He marveled at Jordan's strength and determination. He saw the pain etched deeply on the young man's face. He felt the push and pull and release of energy as Jordan willed himself to pick up one more weight. He knew his child's heart and it was pure.

"Okay, Jordan. Let go. We're good for today. You're gonna feel this tomorrow. Maybe tonight. But that's good. Right?" Sam fist-bumped the slouched young man who draped a towel over his head.

"Oh, you know it. It's all good." Jordan took a long drink from the water bottle and eased himself into position, steadying himself on the shiny walker. *Traded in my board for this,* he thought with a sense of irony. "It's all good," he repeated and shifted the thought to a prayer. "It really is all good. Thank you for your help."

Sam smiled and patted his shoulders. "You bet. I'll be right there on shore when you come sailing on that wave."

Jordan looked up and smiled.

As Jordan worked his body, he awakened to the understanding that there was more he needed to develop and strengthen. In silence and solitude he tended to the healing of his soul. Jordan felt the angelic presence and was comforted in its warmth. He wanted to speak to his secret friend but did not know how. But he thought about him and remembered him.

That was enough for Anioch. *He doesn't deny me.* And for that Anioch was grateful.

Jordan spoke instead with his mother who continued her daily visits. He rediscovered a dear friend in her. Somehow he had vilified her all those years for no other reason than to support his own rebellion and descent into despair.

The hours spent together in the dimly lit hospital room were nourishment for the souls of both mother and son. A long forgotten and immeasurable love nearly lost slowly restored itself. In the seclusion of the hospital and rigor of recovery, Charlene rejoiced in her son's return to the grounding love that had never stopped being available. Like a hidden stream it had always been there waiting for him to dip into and refresh himself.

Sun streamed into the big window covered by plastic peach-colored drapes. "Good morning!" Charlene's voice was light. She came into the room carrying a cup of tea and a few bags.

"Hey, Mom." Jordan shifted in his seat, where he'd moved to stay out of the bed as much as possible.

"I brought you a few books. You seem to be devouring them."

Jordan had become fascinated by the interconnectedness of the mind and body. He was learning how positive thoughts supported the healing process and he had begun to dabble in creating intentions and visualizing. It was curious how he had instinctively done that while surfing, envisioning the perfect place to sink into the perfect ride.

"It might help me heal," he said, visualizing strong legs and a straight back. "I get really tired with the PT but my mind seems to ask a lot of questions. Reading helps focus me. I'm learning how our thoughts and moods affect our body chemistry. Makes me wonder what happened when I was a kid and my mood just sort of changed."

Charlene sat quietly. She heard the question and felt her stomach turn. She knew there were deep conversations in their future. But she looked at her son and saw how weak his body was. His mind was clear and his will as strong as ever, and she didn't want to open up old wounds. This was a time for healing.

"Oh honey, you were a beautiful and curious boy. You were love and joy all wrapped up in a bundle of constant motion. You saw the world from a place of innocence. It was amazing to watch as you played. You had this gift to see beauty all around you. I remember how you would look at the night sky and just marvel at the stars and ask a million questions about the universe. You would stop and stare at the sunsets and say they were more beautiful than any painting. In fact when you drew you would say how perfect nature was, and how no crayon could match it." Charlene stopped and sighed. *And then you changed.* But she let that thought stay silent.

"I think I remember that. There was this rush of feeling alive. But then I didn't feel that rush anymore. Maybe that's part of growing up. But everything kind of went gray."

Charlene listened and her heart hurt.

Jordan continued, "But I felt it after we moved and I took up surfing. I think that's why I love it so much. Some part of me connected again with nature and how raw and wild it was. I felt alive when I surfed. Or at least I did in the beginning. But there was always something dark pulling at me. That scares me, you know. Because I don't want that to come back and draw me in." Jordan dropped his eyes.

Charlene listened and stilled the small voice of worry. "We can talk about that, honey. Or find someone to talk to. You've been through a lot. Things could seem scary."

Jordan shifted and moved in his chair.

Charlene stood up. "You want to walk a bit?"

"Yeah, get the blood flowing."

Charlene shifted the walker closer. As mother and son slowly moved down the hall, Charlene leaned close to him. "Jordan, you are my hero. I am so proud of you. Not just because of this and how brave you are facing these challenges. I haven't heard you complain once. There's something in you that is really special. I hope you know that. Maybe it's the heart of the champion... you're just born with it. But as I look at you and watch you handling this nightmare with such surrender and grace, it makes me proud to call you my son." Charlene's heart raced.

Jordan took a step forward, leaning on his walker for support. He slowly bent over and kissed his mother's cheek. "I love you, Mom. You have been my constant support. Thank you for that... and for loving me even when I was a total jerk. I promise I will do something good with my life. I think I have to now."

Mother and son slowly moved along the long corridor, together.

Anioch marveled anew at the deep capacity for human love. From his vantage point it seemed that true love was rarely felt nor freely shared on the material plane. Here, mother and son served as a conduit of pure love. The angel reconfirmed his initial belief that the connection between mother and child was truly a beautiful and divine gift which closely mirrored the love of Source—complete, affirming, restorative, transformative and pure creative love. *All is well*, he silently affirmed.

One late afternoon, Jordan was resting in the chair, pulled close to the window. He enjoyed watching the world unfold just outside this space that was now the extent of his world. He found comfort and peace in the marvels of nature. He began to awaken and appreciate the small movements that he somehow had ignored in the busyness of life. He saw the trees sway and bend in the wind. Birds took flight and landed with remarkable grace on lilting branches that appeared too fragile to support their weight. Passing clouds reconnected him with the simple joy he had felt as a young boy.

Lost in the serenity of the moment, Jordan didn't hear the door creak open. Out of nowhere a bright rainbow mylar balloon floated in. Jordan leaned forward trying to reach his walker. *A visitor,* he thought.

The balloon floated in and up, followed by a sudden burst of foam arrows flying into the small room, scattering on the floor and bed.

Jordan smiled. "Hey, who is it?" His voice was bright. Finally a wave of wrapped goodies flew across the room sliding at Jordan's feet. "Tastykakes!" Jordan shouted. "Chocolate ones. Is that you, Steve?" Jordan laughed as he leaned down to pick up the snack.

A tall young man with long brown hair and bookish glasses jumped into the room. His face was radiant. "Is it Steve, he asks? Really? Who else would shower you with Tastykakes?"

Jordan broke into a louder laugh. "Come on dude, you know we only eat Hostess on the Left Coast."

"Ding Dongs, bro!" Stephen responded between laughs. "No man, it's Ho Hos."

Both men filled the room with their laughter. Anioch was brimming with excitement. *"Stevie!"* he sang.

Jordan stood and steadied himself, reaching for his walker as he moved toward his friend. Stephen put down the bag and wrapped Jordan in a hug. They held each other for a long time. Joy filled the room.

"Look at you." Stephen stepped back from Jordan. "I mean I expected you to be all like The Return of the Mummy wrapped in bandages." Stephen's voice was filled with good humor.

Jordan felt his energy lift. "Yeah, I bet you did. Well I gotta say you still look like the intellectual nerd we all knew. You've got the whole Harry Potter thing going on. Man, it is great to see you. When did you get in?"

"Last night. You messed up my first break. I was ready to head to Rome and check out the Italian ladies. But no, as always Jordan has to change everything up." Stephen paused and looked at his friend. His smile faded. "You know, I was seriously worried about you. Mom told me about her visit and it sounded really bad. I couldn't imagine not coming here and seeing you. You stupid jerk." The young man paused and slowly whispered, "You big dumbass, I love you like a brother..." Stephen's voice trailed off and he looked away.

Jordan took a step forward. "I know. I love you too, and thank you. This whole thing has really messed with my head but in a good way. I am so happy to see you. Look at you bringing me rainbows, nerf arrows and cakes. I mean who else would do that? Childhood madness all accounted for."

"Who else? Well no one. 'Cuz they all think you're some kind of wonder jock. But I know the deep inner nerd. I remember you and your crazy stories about flying and seeing lights and rainbows and talking to secret friends or weird cosmic alien beings. All that shit that somehow always managed to get me into trouble."

Jordan laughed. "You were the dumbass to follow me."

Stephen laughed. "That is true, my friend." He moved the small table near the guest chairs and picked up his bag, bringing out a chess set.

Jordan clapped. "You are the *GOAT*."

"The goat?" Stephen stared at his friend.

Jordan let out a loud chuckle. "Oh sorry, I guess in Cambridge they don't speak our surfer slang. *Greatest Of All Time*. Chess! Man, I haven't played that in forever."

"I guessed as much. I mean you've been living the life with those surfer slackers. I wouldn't imagine they are the chess-playing type. You can tell me all about your derelict life while we play."

Stephen set up the board as Jordan settled into his comfortable chair. "My derelict life. I guess it was. It really was."

"I followed you. I couldn't believe it. There you were, the world champion. You were unbelievable. I watched those clips and they scared the shit out of me. You are one fearless human being."

Jordan lowered his eyes. "Yeah, I was fearless, or stupid. Or both."

Stephen waited while Jordan stared at the board, pondering his next move. Anioch waited as well. He knew healing came in different forms.

"I'm really kinda in this weird space right now. I think you hit it right on the head. I was fearless. I mean, some part of me really believed that I could do anything and I'd always be okay. That isn't very normal, right?"

"Normal? Come on, Jordan. There's never been anything normal about you. I was afraid of almost everything, but you pushed me to do stuff and we had fun. Your not being normal helped me be normal."

79

"Stevie, it somehow always comes back to you. I think I must have failed on the making you normal front. But we did have fun. Yeah, we did. Until something happened." Jordan's voice cracked and his eyes began to well with tears. "Then it wasn't fun anymore. I mean then it became dark for me. I think some part of me wanted to see how far I could push. And I pushed. I just kept pushing. Now look at me."

Stephen moved closer and leaned in. "Yeah, look at you. You are here, alive. Pushing yourself to walk and heal. Maybe this whole thing is giving you a dose of respect for life... and knowing you aren't superman is okay. Sorry to tell you this, but you are a mere mortal. Bones break, man." Stephen sat back in his chair, a slight grin on his face.

"I know that. And I guess there's a part of me that is actually grateful to feel this pain and know I am human. But the part that is messing with me is that I wanted to be normal before, so I tried to shut off what made me different. Now that I feel more normal, I think I'm supposed to embrace what makes me different. It doesn't make sense."

Stephen stood. "Sometimes we just need to be patient. I don't have answers for you. These questions are yours to figure out. It's okay to be afraid. That's part of the human condition. Some fear is probably a good thing... especially for you..." Stephen's voice hung in the air.

Jordan nodded. "You're right. Mom thinks I should talk to someone."

Stephen nodded as well. "Yeah, I think our moms have been right a lot." He sat back down. "So, I say we put aside this heavy shit. I'm only in my first year of graduate school so I haven't had too much experience in the therapy realm yet, bro, so give me a break. I do thank you for all the years of observing your delusions but I can't even charge you yet."

CHAPTER 13

Jordan looked forward to the admitting nurse's visits. He knew the rotation schedules and anticipated days when she would be doing the rounds. He felt safe in Anne Marie's presence. It was as if they shared some type of mystical bond. She had been there when he first arrived near death. She had been there to witness his rebirth. And she felt his secret friend's presence. Jordan did not speak of his angel, though. He hadn't forgotten how the honesty of the little boy had led to the dark psychiatric exile of his angelic guide. Yet he believed deep in his heart that she knew.

During one of her visits, Jordan nervously began, "Anne Marie, I have a question for you." His voice was halting. Anne Marie stopped jotting down her notes and looked at the young man. Jordan continued his eyes darting, "It might sound kind of crazy, but I get the feeling you won't think I'm totally nuts."

"Ask me anything. I promise to tell you the truth, Jordan." Her voice was soft.

"Okay, I have had these ideas for a long time. Well, not really ideas, I guess... more like experiences. I've had them since I was very little. But then I stopped having them and I think that's when life got sort of sad for me. But I had an experience during my accident that is making me question everything. I get the feeling you might understand me. Or at least I hope you will." Jordan paused.

The kind nurse leaned in. "Go on. I'm listening."

"Well, I don't know what I saw, but I guess I am wondering, I'm asking you... do you believe in things like angels?"

Anne Marie paused. She breathed deeply and looked at him, directly in his eyes.

Jordan's heart jumped. Only his mother had ever looked at him that way. He tried not to look away from the truth he saw reflected there. Without realizing, he held his breath.

In a near whisper, Anne Marie spoke deliberately. "I believe in a Divine Source that is One, ever present and all good. I believe in heaven and I believe that through our thoughts and choices we design our own reality which can be some degree of heaven or even hell. I believe we are called and chosen, and that we each have a Divine purpose. I believe we are each bestowed with a guide, our own angelic guardian who is a messenger from the Divine Source. We are loved and protected; our angel is the Universe's gift to us."

She paused and held Jordan's gaze. Jordan's heart raced. *She doesn't think I'm crazy!*

Anioch held his angelic breath and felt the power of the words fill the room. He sensed the energy flow from nurse to patient. The Truth of her conviction washed over the young man like gentle lapping waves. Anioch was delighted.

Jordan felt the impact as if his center of balance changed. In that simple statement, she'd validated the one true thing he had been forced to reject. In a voice choked with emotion he said, "You don't think I'm crazy?"

"No… I think you are blessed."

The gentle cadence of her words did not belie their powerful impact. Jordan's whole tortured reality was being ripped open and laid bare. Years of denial and the hard protective shell he had wrapped around his heart were being crushed by this kind and unassuming woman.

"You believe in angels, for real?" He had to repeat the question, not wanting to risk mistaking her response.

"Yes, I do. I believe it is all part of the Divine plan and Divine order. I believe we each have our own free will and can turn away from that Love—that we can wrap ourselves in fear, hatred, anxiety and untimely death of the soul and the body. It's our choice. We must choose every day between the gifts of Love or the slow march toward emptiness that is separation from that Love."

Jordan closed his eyes, trying to absorb the depth of her words. "Yeah, emptiness. That's a good word. I know that feeling. But I didn't choose that—it chose me. I was forced to stop believing. They thought I was delusional."

"I know, I know," Anne Marie nodded. "And sometimes it is at that point of total loss, when we stop believing and lose all hope that we just surrender. At that moment we can find our True Self. Maybe it's only a glimmer of our True Self. The last real thing that remains."

She paused and the room was silent.

"Death isn't the end, though. The end and the void is the not knowing—not knowing that we are Love. Not sharing Love. That is death to the soul. I believe in miracles, and the redemptive and restorative power of Love. That is who we are, and ultimately what we return to."

Jordan's mind was swirling. She made it sound so easy. "Love? That's it? How can it be so simple? I'm not sure I even know what love is. Is it the angel I saw? Or the pain I feel when I look into my mom's eyes?" Jordan struggled to piece together the words. Silence filled the space. Jordan closed his eyes and continued, his voice dropped. "Or is it the power I sense when I look at the ocean and see the sky bend into the horizon... when I think I can almost touch eternity?"

Anne Marie nodded slightly and smiled. "I believe that Divine Love is within each of us and we either choose to connect with it and step into our heaven, or we choose to live a life that is disconnected, incomplete and empty."

Anioch was intrigued and in awe. It was strange and exciting to hear human words explain all the beauty and mystery of what he knew to be Universal Truths. He shifted his vision slightly to expand and see Anne Marie's angelic guide. Anioch had seen him before and knew he was magnificent—an ancient and wise guide. Radiant and imbued in a rich blue light, Valyrin bowed to Anioch. *"Be silent and listen. Listen deeply with your Divine Flame and learn. We are all on a path of learning."* Anioch felt a surge of energy pass through him and in that brief moment on the earthly plane both Angel and Jordan paused, knowing this was a time of grace.

Jordan's heart leapt. There was a shift. Something changed, expanded.

Anne Marie paused as well, caught her breath, then continued, "We are all children of Divine Source. We are Divine Beings. Believing and really knowing that simple truth changes everything. Once you know that and come to believe it, deep down in the farthest reaches of your soul, you are transformed. You simply can't look at life the same. You can't look at another human being the same. We are Divine Love. Just sit with that thought, Jordan, and contemplate what it means. We are here as extensions of the Divine, doing and being a part of that mysterious and creative energy flow, eternal and timeless."

Jordan felt weightless, as if carried away on some invisible current that pulled him deeper into an ancient stream. His soul drifted into a tidal rhythm that felt strangely comforting and relaxing. His inner voice told him to let go of limiting thoughts and to just sit in the silence.

Anne Marie lowered her gaze. Her words took on the slow rhythmic cadence of an ancient tidal current. "So yes, Jordan. I believe in angels. I have not seen my angel but I know he is with me and I can feel the presence of others. I have sensed your angel here with you... since the first day you were brought in."

Jordan felt the air leave his body. She knew and believed. She didn't think he was crazy. She'd answered him truthfully, openly. Stated her creed without hesitation. Jordan's eyes filled with tears.

Anne Marie reached out and touched him, warm yet firm.

Jordan knew his life had just changed. He knew he could either believe and step into the reality of angelic guidance, or deny the presence of indwelling Divine Love. He could embrace heaven on earth and create a new reality... or return to the emptiness that had nearly destroyed him. The choice was his.

"I believe you when you say you wanted to die, Jordan. But Source has a plan for you. It was not your time. You have a lot of people who love you. You have a purpose. Find it. Cherish the gift of life and get to know your angelic guide. Don't turn your back on those who love you. Death is not to be feared, but rather the loss of love and the emptiness we cause when we turn away and deny our True Nature."

Jordan shook. He hadn't discussed his attempted suicide with anybody. He hadn't told anyone about the angels he had seen and heard as he was thrashed in those massive waves. Yet she knew. She understood. She offered hope.

He allowed the tears to flow, and Anne Marie held him as he released years of pent up torment and anguish. He wept for the little boy who had been forced to let go of his angel and in it the connection to everything pure and real. He wept for the pain of separation and the destruction it had wrought on so many lives. He wept in humbling recognition of the new life that awaited him.

Anioch watched, bewildered and in awe. His angelic mind raced with a jumble of questions. *I know Jordan has seen me. Why can't my beloved child believe his own eyes?* He was curious, as he had been since he first descended to the earthly plane, why the concept of angelic guides was so foreign and difficult for the frail human mind to comprehend. He watched as his child cried with wild abandon. He knew there was surrender, cleansing the soul of all its doubts, disbeliefs, hurts and pains of alienation. *Why do so few acknowledge the truth?* Anioch pondered. *Why do they not see the truth and remain separated in their delusion and doubt and in that haze of ignorance, that they call truth, choose a life of want and fear?* These were great mysteries that the young angel could not understand. *Human beings are very strange creatures.*

The nurse's magnificent guide drew near and bowed to the novice angel. He began, in a deep and rich tone, to sing a song of praise. Anioch opened his wings. Together, Anioch and Valyrin joined in an angelic hymn of gratitude. Through that connection of the human and spirit world there was healing and the opening of a Divine space for both the entry and release of light and grace. Anioch was filled with immense love for the Creator and saw in that moment the beautiful mirror of restorative energy reflected in his young charge as he surrendered to the Truth.

Much like a human angel, Anne Marie was called and she answered. Through her presence and faith, she served as an instrument of Divine Grace. In this place and at this time, healing began through her act of intervention because Jordan needed her. Her words were what Jordan needed to hear and what he could understand. Anioch's songs and energy had been felt but some part of the practical human mind could not comprehend or fully accept it. The human touch was the channel for this healing grace.

Jordan stopped crying and looked directly at Anne Marie. He wanted to ask her a million questions, but hesitated. "I need help." That was all he could say and the simple plea spoke volumes.

She nodded at him and smiled knowingly. Perhaps she had heard the plea before.

"Yes, dear one. You need help, and it's here. Just be patient because the Universe's time is not our time. There is an old saying, 'God's will has no whys.' When we accept that truth, we can begin to balance our lives. When we let go of our need to orchestrate everything, the unfolding symphony of our life song is truly magnificent. Be the instrument, Jordan... and let Source work through you."

Jordan smiled and breathed deeply. A warm sense of peace and love flowed through his whole body. For the first time in a long time, he felt safe.

Anne Marie stood then gently patted his hands. She left the room, quietly, reverently bowing slightly in Anioch's direction. Jordan noticed. *I know he is there and she does too. I can't see him anymore but I can feel him. And I'm not crazy. I am blessed.* He felt a healing vibration envelop his whole body. He laid down and fell into a deep, restful sleep.

CHAPTER 14

As Jordan continued to heal, he spent the long hours of late night and early mornings alone. It was the first time in his life he wasn't active and fully absorbed in something: school, sports or partying. In the slowness demanded by recovery, he found the stillness to be strangely peaceful. He read and allowed himself the space to think and contemplate the events of his young life. He felt slightly disoriented but tried to piece things together as he pondered what new meaning his life was taking on. He thought about the choices he had made and what choices had been made for him. He lived the consequences every day in brief moments of excruciating pain or more often the numb throb of constant discomfort.

Jordan took stock of his life and tried to make sense of things. He acknowledged there was a new presence of hope but also a creeping competing pull of fear. He sat with them both and tried to reconcile the push and pull of past and future.

In the darkness and embracing quiet of his hospital room, he thought of the simple words spoken by Anne Marie. While few, they grabbed him in a deep almost visceral way. *"You are a child of the Divine." What does that mean?* His mind struggled with the profound implications. He knew he could never go back to his old way of life. *If I am a child of the Divine, who am I?* His heart called out for answers to the rush of questions that filled him during these hours of solitude.

His body was healing. "Miraculous" was the word used to describe it. *But if it was a miracle, then why?* This question was always followed by thoughts of his angel. *If he's real, and I know now that he is, then what does that say about me and my life?*

Jordan began to take long walks at night. The hospital staff knew him and left him alone as he pushed himself on his own training circuit through the solitary hallways. For Jordan the steady pace became a type of medication. He moved his body, purposefully noting each step. He worked on his balance and felt each muscle move in concert to support him without the aid of his walker.

As he moved, he wondered what secrets lay behind those closed doors. He thought about the patients who shared this place with him.

Were they awake as well, contemplating life, healing, illness or death? He was curious what they thought of life and deeper thoughts about purpose and the meaning of it all. *Where are their angels?*

In the hours, after the flow of visitors left and patients slept, a heavy quiet hung in the building. *It feels like a tomb.* He changed his focus and thoughts. *Or perhaps a womb.* Jordan walked and became almost invisible to the night staff who now nodded at him reflexively. No one saw the angel who kept pace with the young man.

Anioch stayed near and measured his child's energy. The angel pondered things as well. *He is getting stronger and his mind is alert.* The guardian continued to sing praise and shine light on his ward. Anioch knew his child's heart and understood this was a time of awakening. "Be patient, my dear child. The answers will come," he whispered into the empty halls.

Sometimes Jordan wandered back to the I.C.U., feeling drawn to the most critical of the patients. It was as if some invisible energy called to him. He walked and he thought. He thought and he prayed. Patients slept, some aided by medication, others maintained by technology; some clinging to life, many in their slumbered state secretly holding on to their vision of life, be it heaven or hell. Jordan walked and remembered. He passed distraught families clinging to their own hope, praying for the miracle. He bowed in silence as he sent them love and asked for forgiveness, knowing now the pain he had caused.

Jordan walked and took it all in. *What are they hanging on to? What do they believe in? What are they afraid of? What really matters right here and right now?* These thoughts and many others raced through Jordan's mind as he exercised his healing muscles. And his angel followed his every step and his every thought.

In the daylight, Jordan continued his routine. Today Sam patted Jordan on the back. "You are one big bold badass, my brother. I can't believe how far you've come. Look at you."

Jordan looked up and saw the joy in Sam's eyes. "Well, I have you to thank for riding me like some kind of insane drill sergeant. I'd say it's been fun. But I'd be lying." Jordan stood and the two men embraced. "Thank you, Sam. I'm not sure I can express to you how grateful I am. You made me dig deep and it hurt. It really hurt. I know I'm standing here today because you pushed me. But I think it's more than that. You believed in me. And knowing that was huge. Thank you for that."

Sam smiled and began to chuckle. "Well Mr. Pro, you just get out there and be the champ I know you are. Man, you have heart and it has been a pleasure and honor to push you."

Jordan smiled. *I'm going to miss him.*

Jordan's medical team was pleased with his progress. Bones had fused. Brainwaves were good. Lungs were strong. A new doctor was added to his list of caretakers—a quiet yet self-assured psychologist. Dr. Blair had met with his mom. They'd discussed Jordan's childhood. "He was so wild. I mean my husband and I were at our wits end. I just had this terrible feeling that he would hurt himself or someone else." Charlene told him of the medications and Jordan's slow march into what he now called his grey world.

Dr. Blair listened. He understood that the once exuberant thrill seeker, the life of the party and serial charmer was now replaced by a quiet, gentle, contemplative man who preferred to listen and observe. "It is not uncommon for people who have suffered this type of trauma to retreat for a while. He is processing a lot right now." The psychologist was concerned about addiction since toxicology reports after Jordan's accident indicated a mix of drugs and alcohol and the possibility that it was not an accident. Those were areas he hoped to explore with the young man.

Jordan met with the doctor in preparation for his discharge. Dr. Blair came to Jordan's room. "Hello, I'm Dr. Blair." He extended his hand. Jordan shook it. "Man, do people tell you that you look a lot like—"

The doctor cut him off. "Yes, all the time. But my ears are smaller and my hair isn't grey. More like a young Barack, I'd say." There was a slight chuckle in the doctor's voice.

Jordan studied his face. He looked to be maybe forty and had an easy way about him. Jordan sat quietly while the doctor talked about out-patient care. Jordan's mind wandered. He was careful, trying to get a sense of the man. *Wonder what he does for fun. Man, what is he going to know or understand about me?* Jordan wasn't listening. His mind was racing and he felt a swell of fear rising in his chest. He instinctively knew he could not discuss what his mind and soul were pondering. The truths his heart was discovering were far too beautiful, far too real and true to share. The last time he had been truthful with a psychiatrist, they'd medicated his honesty. He would not risk that emptiness and loss again.

The man had stopped talking. Jordan looked up. "It's okay, Jordan. We can talk later when you are home." Jordan looked up. He felt himself blushing. *Shit, he's been talking to me.*

A slight smile lit the doctor's face and fine lines framed his warm eyes. Jordan smiled back. "Sorry Dr. Blair, I am not really paying good attention right now. I am kind of distracted with the thought of going home. But I heard you about the out-patient stuff and I know my parents think that would be good. I will try, but I have to be honest... I'm not a big fan of the mental health profession."

Dr. Blair nodded. "I hear you, Jordan, and that's fine. I just want to make sure you are adjusting okay. You've been through a lot. We will take it slow and can just talk. No pressure."

Jordan shrugged. "Okay, that sounds cool." He felt he owed his parents that much.

"If you feel like you want to talk sooner than that, please call me." Dr. Blair handed Jordan a business card. With that the doctor got up to leave, but turned and smiled at Jordan before he closed the door. "It's going to be okay. You'll see."

Jordan's mind shouted, *If you only knew!* "See ya around," he called instead.

The doctor met briefly with Charlene to provide an initial assessment. "He's holding back," he reported. "There won't be any breakthroughs at this point. We'll continue sessions once he's left the hospital. These things take time but he seems to be in a good place."

Charlene thanked him. Yet she sensed something was already changing in her son. Stillness and near prayerfulness filled Jordan's room when she entered unannounced. It was like a ripple on the ocean, an energy that was fleeting, barely perceivable, nothing more than a shiver that would run down her spine. Those once wild eyes—fearless and daring, rebellious and angry—were replaced by soulful, meditative, gentle and calm ones.

He was changing but Charlene couldn't define it or put the feeling into words. The anger and hostility had vanished. Though withdrawn, Jordan seemed to have embarked on that long journey of self-discovery. Charlene felt hopeful that her son's return would be a true homecoming for her son, her real son.

On his final night in the hospital, Jordan walked the darkened and stilled corridors for the last time. His mind raced, filled with endless thoughts and a crashing swirl of mixed emotions. He was excited, yet frightened. "It sucks here in the hospital, but I'm safe. I'm cared for," he'd confessed earlier that evening in a call to Stephen.

"You'll be fine," his friend consoled. "You've got people who will care for you. And way better food."

As he walked, Jordan thought of his life. Here the temptations had been limited. "Man, I can't go back to that," he softly whispered to himself.

Anioch sent him love. Jordan kept walking and forced himself to focus on something beyond himself and his doubts and fears. He recognized the negative thoughts that tried to seep in and knew all too well the pain they inevitably brought.

Jordan slowed his pace. Anne Marie taught him to turn to his heart to focus instead on gratitude. She told him to learn to train his mind to see beyond his own needs. With each step he thought of her wise words, *"Step outside of your self-pity. Think of three things you are grateful for. It can be as simple as 'I am grateful for my breath. I am grateful for the air I breathe. I am grateful for my lungs that breathe without my thinking.' Then turn and pray for someone else. Send someone love. Go beyond yourself. You will be tapping into a power bigger than you."*

Okay, he thought. *I can do that.* As he silently walked, he stated his gratitude for his legs, for his feet, for the healing bones and muscles. He then visualized the people behind the doors. He prayed for those patients lying alone and frightened right there separated from him by one closed door. He repeated a prayer, almost a mantra that had come to him: "I am grateful. I am at peace. Be still now."

Jordan turned a corner. He saw a woman leaving one of the nondescript rooms. She looked harried and confused. He noticed that she held an unlit cigarette. Her red hair was pulled back into a loosely held bun. She wore dark glasses even though it was nighttime. She rushed down the hallway fumbling with her purse, pulling out a cell phone. Jordan continued down the long corridor, his slow footsteps echoing on the well-polished linoleum. He continued his internal dialogue focusing on gratitude and sending love.

As he drew closer to the small waiting room, he heard a woman's voice speaking in a low tone. Her voice was raspy, rushed and raw with emotion. "They are moving her again. They say there's nothing more they can do. It's a nightmare, just a nightmare. I can't believe I am saying these god awful things about my baby girl. They are telling me her organs are shutting down."

The woman broke into deep sobs, then an almost guttural howl filled the space. Jordan stopped. *My God, she is alone. There is no one there to comfort her.* Jordan wondered if he should turn into the small area and offer something to the woman. As his mind raced, he saw a nurse heading toward him. She nodded at Jordan and turned into the waiting room.

He heard the nurse softly speak, "I know this is hard. Is there someone we can call for you? Maybe the chaplain?"

The frantic woman slowly calmed her breathing and in a near whisper answered, "I will be okay. I didn't think she was that sick. That's my only child and I just told them to unplug her. Oh my God, I gave up on her." The sobbing filled the entire space.

Jordan felt as if he was intruding. He silently offered the woman and her daughter a prayer for strength and love. He looked at his image in the well-placed mirror up in the intersection of the halls and realized he indeed had much to be grateful for. He continued on his walk lost in deep thought.

His circuit half complete, Jordan looped back toward his room. He passed by the door where the distraught woman had rushed out. He paused. The door was slightly ajar. He took a step closer. He expected it to be empty. Instead, he could see a small figure motionless in the large metal bed, bathed in the dim yellow light of the nurse's call monitor. The young woman barely seemed to breathe. She looked lost in the bed, tiny, sunken, nearly consumed. Her face was white, drawn and almost lifeless. Tubes were inserted into her veins, nourishing her emaciated body, oxygen feeding her cells. The ventilator pumped in a dull rhythmic motion. Jordan shivered. He had heard the conversation and now it was real. *I guess they haven't taken her off life support yet.*

Anioch sensed that the young woman's body lay near death. There was a deep stillness and the air hung heavy. *Left alone,* the angel thought. *Just like my beautiful child.*

Both man and angel felt a strange pull in the dark space. Jordan wanted to get out, feeling like an unwelcomed stranger. Anioch sensed that this young woman's Guide was weak as well. "You poor child. Here you are alone, tiny, and frail. Where is your angelic guide?" he whispered into the darkness.

Anioch adjusted his vision and saw the tiny frame of the angelic being, like a dimming candle. Her eyes were large and pleading. Anioch shuddered with recognition. He bowed and softly said, "I send you love. I know the dark pull of the material plane. But I also know the power of our purpose. Be strong, my beloved." Then he spread his wings and sent light into the upper reaches of the room.

Jordan wanted to leave but felt called to offer another prayer for the stranger. He prayed for her body to heal, for her spirit to soar, for her heart to mend and for her soul to be saved. He tried to remember words that Anne Marie offered him but he couldn't think of any. So he simply stated, "I wish you peace and healing. May your heart be strong and your soul at peace." He ended his petition as he had learned to end all petitions, "Thy will be done." It was proper and right to release the outcome to Divine Grace and Wisdom.

Jordan turned. He felt he had already invaded the space and was sure the mother or doctors would return. His heart felt heavy as he looked one more time at the young stranger. *What happened to you? I wish I could do something for you. I would, if I knew what you needed.*

As Jordan grabbed for the door, Anioch noticed the frail body move, ever so slightly. He saw a small spark rise above her head. He stopped. Then he felt it, a small burst of energy that flashed and fluttered. A mere whisper of Spirit renewed. Anioch smiled and sent angelic love to fill and lift the vibration of the room.

CHAPTER 15

The next day Jordan was released from South Bay Medical Center. The near lifeless surfer who weeks before had been brought into the emergency room was now transformed into a young man filled with renewed hope, a calm presence, inner strength and a new perspective and respect for life.

Jordan readied himself for his discharge. His mind and heart were filled with a swirl of competing emotions—a bittersweet mix of joy, anticipation, anxiety and sadness.

Many of the nurses, physical therapists and others who were part of his caregiving team came to wish him well. He took the time to say goodbye to each of them. His final hug was saved for Anne Marie, the kind nurse who now stood off to the side.

Jordan walked toward her, a slight limp slowing his pace. She smiled and opened her arms. Jordan embraced her and whispered into her ear, "This is not goodbye."

Anne Marie wiped away a tear and looked at Jordan. Her heart swelled with deep love. She then bowed ever so slightly toward Anioch.

The angel bowed in return. "Blessings," he quietly wished her. The nurse smiled. The angel smiled back. He recognized her as a special gift—a wise human, deeply blessed, full of grace and grounded in love. He watched as she slipped Jordan a small package neatly wrapped.

"Someday you will connect with this and its purpose will be clear to you," she whispered.

Jordan held the tiny package and felt his heart leap. *She is always filled with wonderful surprises.* Jordan held her gaze and answered with a final heartfelt, "Thank you." He paused. His voice was deep and filled with emotion. "I am here today because of you. I love you."

Anne Marie closed her eyes and let the warm sun and the powerful words wash over her. "And I love you, Jordan. You've blessed me more than you will ever know."

Jordan returned to his parents' house. This was a different homecoming, a blend of profound happiness mixed with an unspoken worry about the future. Emotions flooded Jordan's heart as the car pulled into the tree-lined street. Friends and neighbors stood outside on their lawns, smiling and waving to him. Yet this time he was not returning as the town hero. He wasn't being welcomed home as a celebrity. Instead there was joy but also a hint of reverence. People held their thoughts close to their hearts, contemplating instead the living proof of the miraculous, along with the unspoken undercurrent of suspicion in a darker secret that lay brooding below.

The old feelings of despair, emptiness and loneliness that had nearly consumed his soul started to beckon and call. It was muted but present. Jordan feared that he could fall prey to that call, getting caught in the riptide and eventual fury of a massive emotional tidal wave.

The neighborhood, his home, the faces, meticulously drawn in refined details of familiarity and timelessness stirred old haunting feelings. Jordan closed his eyes and intentionally silenced the past with a centering prayer. Quick in-breath—restorative and healing—then an out-breath with release and surrender. *It's time for a new story and a new reality.* He squared his shoulders, closed his eyes and stepped out of the car.

Anioch felt everything. He remained vigilant and aware. He touched his child with angelic warmth, whispering, "Be strong. Face the past. Bless it. Then let it go." The guardian knew the past only had the power that Jordan afforded it. The guilt his child felt right now for all his past sins had no place in the present. "Let it go," he intoned.

Jordan opened his eyes and faced his family, embracing each member. Daniel was the last one. Jordan hesitated; he had not yet made amends with his father. *There's work here,* his still small inner voice spoke.

He stepped forward and reached out to hug Daniel. The warmth, acceptance and love he felt from everyone else was not there. Instead Jordan felt a cold space between them. It was a tangible and real divide. His father felt distant and reserved. He looked at his father and saw it, fresh and raw. There was hurt—deep and ancient—in those eyes.

His mother had frequently visited in the hospital. "My rock," he had called her. Yet his father stayed away. Jordan tried to make sense of it and thought his father was probably afraid to be hurt again. *Maybe he's had it with me. I've caused him a lot of grief.* Jordan tried to put himself in his father's place and contemplated the sense of loss he must have felt watching his son slowly implode. *I can't blame him if he's afraid to believe that I've changed.* Jordan opened his heart and understood.

Anioch whispered, "All things in their right season."

The days that followed were a time of healing and reconnecting with the people, place and rhythm of a past Jordan had long forgotten. He kept the lapping waves of negative emotions at bay. It felt good to be home. He knew this was a gift and that it was up to him to mine it for the treasures it held. He searched for balance, knowing he needed to focus on his body as well as his heart and spirit.

Anioch whispered, "Let the blessings unfold in their own time."

Charlene knew that Jordan needed time and space and she generously offered both.

"Don't push him," Dr. Blair had offered. "Be present but don't press."

Charlene kept those words as her silent command. "Hey kiddo, you want to give me a hand, please?" Charlene grabbed her large-brimmed sunhat and gardening gloves from the workbench in the garage.

"Sure Mom, what do you need?"

Charlene pointed to a large bag of mulch in the corner near the back door. "If you could carry that over to the garden for me, I'd really appreciate it." Charlene went through the door and stepped into her own private oasis. *I hope he decides to stay with me,* she silently wished. She remembered their last encounter in the garage.

Jordan picked up the big bag and followed his mother. He felt the cool grass between his toes and the warm sun on his skin. His mother's garden was always a special place, although he couldn't recall the last time he had spent any time in it. He heard the chirping of the birds and noticed that his heart felt lighter. "Where do you want this?"

Charlene pointed to a wheelbarrow leaning against the wooden fence.

Jordan smiled. *She could have used that instead.* "The garden's looking good, Mom."

"Thanks. I've planted some new flowers this year. I'm hoping they will take. I started them from seedlings so we'll see how they do. I've also started the vegetable garden over there. We had a really good crop of tomatoes last year." Charlene was already busying herself, squatting low to the ground pushing aside leaves and pulling up the small weeds.

"I remember doing the seed packets with you when I was little. That was so cool, Mom. I remember being excited when those tiny shoots started to pop up." Jordan sat down on the small stool.

Charlene kept digging. She was happy that he had stayed. "Oh, you loved to garden when you were a kid. You talked all the time about the magical seeds and how they grew while we slept. You were such a storyteller."

Magic. "Yeah, it did seem like magic. You know we would put those hard seeds that looked like nothing into dirt and then we would wait. And I thought if we just trusted time we would then get flowers or peppers or whatever. Now I think I would use the word 'miracle'." He paused and tilted his face toward the sun. It felt good. With eyes closed he continued. "Miracle... You know, every seed holds in it its own future, its imprint. It will become what it is meant to become. A sunflower is a sunflower. An apple is an apple."

The mother heard the wisdom in her son's words and felt humbled. The angel heard the truth in his child's words and felt hope.

Charlene stood and reached for a small spade. She handed some gloves to Jordan. The moment was a gift she held close to her heart. She didn't want it to end. "It's that simple really, isn't it? We just complicate it. Here, get into the dirt, kiddo. It feels good."

Jordan slid off the stool and began to move the soil, staying near his mother. They worked together under the morning sun, talking about seeds, miracles, Jordan's imagination, vegetables and the simple things in life.

Charlene's heart was filled with joy.

Jordan's heart was filled with gratitude. "This is nice, Mom. Really nice. Thank you."

Charlene got up on one knee and looked at her son. "Yes, it is. It's so good to have you back."

Charlene treasured the hours in the garden with her son, and thanked the Universe he had been allowed a second chance. Their conversations meandered like a slow running creek. Charlene gave her son the gift of time and space. The garden became a haven.

"You know, I've been thinking that I probably need to figure out what I am going to do next. I've been avoiding the calls from my sponsors. But I will have to answer them. I don't think I want to go back into the competition scene."

Charlene slowly watered the vegetable beds. "Well, you don't need to make any big decisions right now. Give yourself some time. Your dad and I support you."

"Yeah, I know that. I think I need to figure something else out. I just don't know what that is. The whole accident thing has made me look at life differently."

There was silence. Charlene stayed present. She knew her words wouldn't add to the strength of the silence. So she let the silence sit.

Jordan slowly scraped with the hoe, digging up small weeds. Finally he stopped and stretched. "I think I'm supposed to take this time to figure out what I am here to do. And for now, I am preparing the soil."

Charlene laughed. "I like that, Jordan. I really do."

"Yeah?" Jordan was smiling.

"Oh, it's perfect, kiddo. I mean, it's the prep work that pays off. No one sees you when you are clearing the land and preparing the soil. It's hard work. You have to clear out the stones and stuff that will impede the growth. You have to do that work alone. Then you have to add the nutrient and find the right balance. You can't just plant seeds in any old soil. Well, you can, but you won't get much to grow. People look at the garden and are amazed at the beauty. I look at the garden and see the miracle. Those tiny seeds are planted with love and faith. Like you said, they are pure potential. And with time, and proper care, they blossom. So, my dear son, you take your time and prepare that soil."

Charlene moved toward her son and gathered him in her arms. Jordan sank deeply into the hug. It felt good.

Jordan watched his brother and sister as they went about their lives. He felt strangely disconnected from them. He was amazed how little he knew about these people who shared his childhood and his blood. He recognized how absent he had been as a big brother. *They probably think I'm a total jerk.*

"Hey Jake, you know my car is sitting in the garage collecting dust. You can use it if you want."

His brother was moving clothes and water bottles into his backpack, getting ready for baseball practice. "Thanks bro, I'm cool with my bike. It gets me warmed up. Besides, your car is kind of your baby. I wouldn't want to wreck it."

"I'm serious. It really needs to be driven and I'm not interested in that right now."

"Okay, well maybe later." Jake grabbed his cap off the hook in the mudroom.

"So, when is your next game? I'd like to come. I haven't seen you play since you were in the peewees and we'd yell, 'Batter, batter, batter,' to distract those poor kids."

"Too funny. I remember that. It embarrassed me." Jake didn't look up.

Jordan stopped. He didn't want to push. *Seeds,* he thought. *All I can do is plant them and nurture them.* He ached for the lost time and was sorry for whatever pain he had caused. But he was grateful for this chance to discover the beauty of his family.

His sister, Jenna, was more receptive.

Jordan felt a connection to his little sister. They would sit together and watch TV or spend time in the yard. Sometimes she joined him on his walks. She was curious about her big brother.

"You know," she said, "I have these memories of playing with you when I was little. I think Mom would make you watch me sometimes when she needed to get stuff done. You would do the weirdest things... like try and make things move, telling me you had secret super powers."

"I did that?" Jordan laughed. "Yeah, I was kind of weird."

"Well, I thought it was cool because, you know, sometimes things would move and I thought you were a magician. I mean, I still wonder what you did to make lights turn on and swings move."

Jordan smiled.

Anioch recalled their games and chuckled, remembering the little girl in pigtails squealing with delight.

"Then when I'd watch you surf, it did seem like you had secret powers. It scared me but it also was so awesome."

"Nope, sorry to burst your bubble, but here I am made of flesh and bones. And I am here to tell you that these bones hurt when they break."

Jenna grabbed her brother's arm and squeezed it. "I'm glad you're home. I was really afraid when you got hurt. I couldn't imagine not having you in my life." She paused and blinked, holding back tears. "I missed you. And Mom and Dad always seemed so worried. I think they're happy too. At least Mom is way more chill now." Jenna let out a giggle.

"Yeah, I'm glad to be home, too. I think I missed out on a lot."

"No worries, we have time to catch up." Brother and sister stopped and hugged, feeling a deep sense of gratitude and hope.

During one of their walks together Jenna stopped her brother. A few surfers were clustered together past the pier. "So do you think you're going to surf again?" Jordan didn't answer. Jenna must have sensed the shift in him and backpedaled, "I'm sorry, I shouldn't have asked that. I didn't mean to pry."

Jordan remained in the pause. There was power in the question. It was one he asked himself every day. He turned to Jenna and said, "No worries. It's a fair question. Truth is, I don't know."

"Really? You are so good at it. You don't seem like a quitter to me."

"Is that what they are saying, that I'm a quitter?" Jordan turned to look at his sister.

She looked down, kicking at the wet sand. "No, no one is saying that. I'm just guessing some people are thinking it. I mean, you are a champion."

"Yeah, but I don't really even think that matters. I don't know what I'm going to do. But I feel like I need to do something that has a little more value than just chasing waves."

"I guess. But you could do it for fun, you know?"

"Yup. I can do lots of things for fun. Right now it doesn't sound fun."

"Are you afraid, Jordan?"

The question cut deep. The wind shifted. Jordan felt the power of both deep in his gut. Three small words summed up his world. *Are you afraid?* "I don't know what I am right now. Maybe I am afraid. But I don't know if I'm afraid of the ocean. Or maybe I'm afraid of who I am when I surf. But for now, I'm cool just being near the water."

Jenna grabbed her brother and hugged him. "Well, at least now I know I can beat you in a race. So... race ya to lifeguard stand #23." Jenna began to laugh as she broke into a trot.

Jordan followed her. He felt the wind in his face. His back ached and his legs screamed but the movement and burst of energy felt good. "Just wait, you little brat. I'll catch up. Just watch."

Brother and sister laughed while Anioch sang an ancient song of praise. *"All is as it should be."*

Yet Daniel still remained... there but always one step beyond.

Jordan tried to reach out to his father but the distance and resistance remained. He knew the time for healing would come. He prayed for discernment and patience. He thought of the garden and knew that a seed had been planted. He would wait. He would nurture that seed. He knew it was a path for two yet a journey of one. The path would be made clear in time.

Jordan spent much of his days reading, reflecting, working out and walking on the beach. His soul was rejuvenated on those shores. He found peace and strength as he watched the power of the waves. The long lost wonder and awe of life, of nature, of Source and Spirit was being restored and expanded one step at a time, each day greater than ever before. Jordan reflected on his life as he walked along the white sands. He talked to the Universe and his Angel.

Anioch listened and was filled with immeasurable joy to once again be part of his child's life. He watched as his child traveled his path of discovery, tending to the deep roots, doing the important interior work.

Jordan knew there was a reason he had been spared death. He asked for guidance. He prayed as the sun set amidst a burst of color. The sea gave him comfort and strength, a grounding of past, present and future. He could sense and catch a glimpse at eternity as the ocean continued its ancient dance and the sun disappeared into the horizon.

As he looked out at the endless horizon he could still feel the pull from the past. *I can't keep ignoring it.* But he was afraid to acknowledge it, fearing that would give it power.

"What am I afraid of?" he spoke into the evening wind. "What's out there beyond the safety of this shore?"

Something inside of him stirred.

"Be still," it whispered. *"All is well."*

But he knew there was unfinished business. He slowly walked into the lapping waves. He stopped. The water felt cold. He saw the small swirl of salt water circle around his bare feet. *One step at a time*, the voice reminded. The breeze passed over him and he shivered. "Be still. All is well," this time Jordan repeated it before turning and walking back to the shore.

CHAPTER 16

As the days turned into weeks, Jordan sensed a change in his father. He felt a slow thaw in the ice wall that had formed over many years. Jordan would linger in the room when his father entered, catch his gaze and smile with true love. Jordan had learned patience and that healing takes time... and sometimes requires pain.

Also, Divine time is not our time.

Jordan waited. He invited his father on one of his daily walks.

Daniel hesitated. Jordan saw his mother turn away, afraid of again witnessing a rejection. But this time Daniel accepted. He grabbed his sweatshirt and hat and followed Jordan.

Father and son set out on a trek of physical and spiritual exercise. No words passed for a long time. Jordan sensed the hesitation. He stopped along the sand at a turn in the shore. He looked back at the beautiful cove, empty and quiet, deserted like the day he had tempted fate.

His father stopped and looked beyond him.

Jordan felt the nudge of his Angel. Unexpectedly his mouth opened and the words flowed, "Dad, I haven't told anyone this. But I was in a really bad place the day of the accident. I felt empty. Something inside of me was done with everything." He paused.

Daniel waited.

Anioch prayed.

"I went straight into that storm and I knew it was dumb and dangerous. I didn't care. I wanted to tempt whatever crazy power or protector I believed I had. But really, I just wanted to escape the emptiness that was crushing me." He paused again, choking this time on his words.

Daniel held back tears.

Anioch continued to pray.

Finally Jordan broke the silence. "You know, I wanted to die that day."

There, I said it. For the first time Jordan had allowed the words to be spoken. Face to face in front of his father.

He hadn't planned to have this dialogue, but it was what needed to be said. It was what his father needed to know.

Daniel turned toward his son. Tears glistened in those dark brown eyes. He looked at this man—his son, the child he had saved so many times. He turned, trying to hide his pain. There was nowhere to go, only stretches of open, empty sand. It felt as desolate and empty as his soul.

"Son, I knew that. I felt it in my heart. I felt your despair. I worried about you when you came back home. Heck, I've worried about you for years. But this last time, you seemed like an empty shell; you had shut out everybody from your life. I knew something awful was going to happen. I heard a voice that kept saying over and over again, 'Talk to him, reach out to him.' But I couldn't. I didn't know how to reach you. I was afraid of your anger and rejection. I had tried so many times before, so I let you go."

Tears were swelling in both father's and son's eyes.

Daniel continued, cleansing his soul with the confession of guilt that had racked him since that fateful day on this lonely stretch of sand. "I blame myself. I let it happen. Everybody thought it was an accident. I knew in my heart what you set out to do. But I had stepped aside and let you go. I was a coward and gave into my own sense of worthlessness. A part of me died that day. I prayed for you, but was afraid to have you back. You were driven by anger... anger against the world, anger against everyone who loved you. A part of me was willing to let you die to allow us some peace... to offer you final peace. I hate myself for that. I couldn't watch you torment yourself or your mother. I wanted my son to live, but not a life of hatred, emptiness or blind rebellion. I felt that by my inaction I had willed you to try to take your life."

Jordan struggled to breathe. He had never wished this guilt and despair on his father. He thought he alone had felt the emptiness, the loneliness, the void. How could that have passed to his father? *What have I done?*

He stared at Daniel, speechless. He had broken his father's spirit through his selfish and destructive anger. His father now blamed himself for Jordan's behavior and choices. Gripped by a sense of disbelief recognizing that the path of destruction he had blazed was so vast and complete it had virtually consumed everything in its path that was true and good, Jordan had thought of no one but himself in his hour of despair. Now he could see that he had nearly broken the spirit of his entire family.

Jordan stepped forward and hesitated. He saw his father bent in sorrow. What could he say? What could ever make this right? His mind raced and his heart ached as his inner voice cried out, *Dear God, what have I done?*

"It wasn't you, Dad." Jordan felt all the emotions he had buried come crashing forward with the power and fury of a violent and deadly storm. He was dizzy as if once again thrashing helplessly in the pounding surf. "It was me, all me. I couldn't handle your love. I couldn't accept it. I thought I didn't deserve it. You never let me down. I shut you out and everything and everybody that made me believe in myself or that validated me. I stopped believing in the miracle of life because I got caught up in a bunch of empty and useless stuff. You were always there for me, you did everything you could. There is so much you don't know. But you have to believe that you didn't push me away. I couldn't accept your love because I didn't love myself. I wanted something, anything, a rush. I needed that to feel alive. But the rushes didn't come anymore. I didn't feel that joy when I surfed. I was high all the time trying to numb the pain of my emptiness. Dad, I lost my spirit and was dead when I got in that water. It wasn't you or Mom. It was me." Jordan's voice broke as emotion consumed him.

Daniel took a deep breath and knew that he had to let go of the knot that had tightly wrapped itself around his heart. He wasn't sure how to begin or even what exactly he felt. He had avoided even putting the thoughts into silent words because he had buried and silenced that inner voice for so many years. Yet Daniel knew this was a moment he had to step into.

"I sense that you have changed, and so I am asking you to listen to me from your heart. I don't really know how to say what I feel, but I hope maybe someday you'll forgive me." Daniel's voice was low but strong and steady. He looked out at the horizon as if searching for some far off sign.

Jordan stood still. His heart was racing. He couldn't quite understand why he felt such apprehension or why the beach suddenly felt charged with an added pulse of energy. "Sure, Dad. I'm listening."

The wind picked up and the waves echoed as they crashed on the shore.

Anioch was listening, too. The angel felt the altered environment and was wondering what shift had just taken place on the human plane. Anioch looked to Roshan. He was blazing, fully embracing Daniel, a strong and grounded presence. Anioch once again sensed the shift that signaled a miracle in the making.

With eyes still focused on the distant horizon, Daniel spoke with a rhythmic calm. "I always felt that you were a special child. All you kids are special and I love each of you with my whole heart. But you were different. I knew that about you from a very young age. I watched you and recognized something in you that I think I had when I was very young. You had this incredible energy and joy. I guess you were a daredevil, but there was something else. You weren't crazy wild, just filled with excitement and curiosity. You had an openness that was a beautiful gift. You were never sad or angry and just seemed to love everything and everybody. You connected with people and animals. The best word I can think of is Radiance. You radiated pure love, pure joy."

Jordan listened, wondering where this conversation was headed. He pushed his own thoughts away so he could stay focused on his dad's words. He noticed that as his father spoke he leaned deeper into the horizon as if reaching out for something.

"You talked about your secret friend. At first it was kind of cute. That isn't so unusual for kids. But then you seemed to be getting lost in your secret world and you were becoming more and more daring. Your mother and grandparents were concerned. I was worried too but not for the same reasons. I haven't told anyone what I am about to tell you. And actually, if my instinct is wrong here, you might think I'm totally nuts." Daniel took a deep breath and closed his eyes.

For a moment, Jordan got the distinct impression that his father was somehow steadying himself almost as if preparing to jump. He turned toward Jordan, his gaze more intense than ever before.

Daniel cleared his throat and shifted, widening his stance.

He's grounding himself, Jordan mused.

Daniel's voice was deep and strong, rising above the wind and surf. "We did everything we could to keep you safe and to protect you. We took you to get better and to help you put aside your childhood fantasies. But I saw how you changed once that secret friend of yours was gone. That beautiful radiance in you disappeared. Your specialness died out. I always wondered if somehow we killed that spark of joy. I worried that your destructive streak, and all that followed, was because of my pushing you to *be normal*. I'm afraid I forced you to conform, and through that you lost touch with your inner spirit. Jordan, what I was really afraid was that I did to you what I had done to myself a long, long time ago."

Daniel stepped forward, closer to the incoming tide. His focus again shifted to the horizon. He was lost in his thoughts and words. Jordan felt the words hit him and the truth in them slowly started to sink in.

"Dad, what do you mean?" Jordan's heart was pounding so hard he was sure his father could hear it. He noticed that the wind had started to pick up.

Roshan was blazing in the setting sun. He was a Radiant Being of Light. Anioch stood transfixed.

"Son, I have a faint memory of some kind of special friend... or guide, or someone or something that was beside me when I was little. I've never told anyone about this—not your nana or your mom. I really had pretty much forgotten about it and vaguely remembered it like some childhood daydream. But as you grew up and talked about your special friend I had this little voice inside of me who told me to believe. But I couldn't. I would watch you sometimes and I could see you totally lost in your own world. I sort of remembered having been like that and I remembered how safe and protected I had felt as a child. But I turned away, intentionally, from whatever connection I had created with that fantasy world." Daniel's words were no more than a hoarse whisper. "As I watched you grow up, I started to have not only a pang of regret, but a sense of fear."

The strength he had displayed earlier had faded. The wind was getting stronger still and the air shifted.

"Jordan, I resisted for a long time but your mom was consumed with worry. I hoped and prayed you would outgrow your fantasies. But then it started to get really scary. I couldn't just wish it away. I had to do something. I'm sorry I was weak. But I gave in and took you to the doctors. I had to do something."

Again the pause.

"I was afraid that maybe there was some type of genetic inclination toward delusion. Your mother and I didn't agree initially with the medication, but you really were beginning to scare us with all of your crazy antics. Then later I worried that by forcing you to let go and become *normal,* I somehow... killed a divine part of you... your spirit."

Jordan noticed tears forming in his father's eyes. Jordan was struggling to fully connect with what he was hearing. Had his father once seen or felt his own guardian? His mind was filled with a barrage of questions. What had his father seen, heard or felt? Why did he turn away? How did he turn away? How did that disconnection feel for him?

Silence enveloped father and son. Jordan let the words sink in. He looked at his father. The man's face was tired, body slumped as if spent. Jordan's heart ached for the hurt he saw etched there. He was filled with an overwhelming wave of love.

"Dad, I don't really know what to say. You did what you thought was right for me. I'm still really trying to figure out what is going on in my life and what I'm supposed to do. I mean I haven't even told you the whole story about what happened here on the beach that day. But man, Dad, you are kind of blowing me away right now."

Jordan had never intended to tell his parents about the angels or the changes he was going through. But here was his dad telling him of his own deliberate act of turning away from the light.

"Come on," Jordan said. "Really, none of this is your fault. In my heart I know that this had to happen. It is part of my bigger life lesson. There is more to all of this than you know."

The wind began to whip up the waves and push sand against them. Side by side they continued to walk. They didn't speak as each contemplated the enormity of what had been shared.

A sudden gust of wind swept the hat off Daniel's head. He started to run after it and Jordan trotted slowly to catch up with him. It hurt but somehow the pain made the moment that much more real. They chased down that empty beach after a flying hat, followed by two invisible angels, all of them just out of reach. Both men started to laugh at the absurdity. Daniel stopped and waited for his son.

Jordan grabbed his father by the shoulders and took him into his arms. They had not embraced or connected for so many years. In that moment, father and son let go of the hurt and sorrow that had surrounded them. "I love you, son."

"I know that, Dad. I always have."

Anioch watched. The frozen wall was shattered by Jordan's own admission of self-hatred and Daniel's confession of guilt. Father and son now shared something deeper that connected them at a psychic level. The healing could only come with total release, forgiveness and grace. The scars of the past loss ran deeply through their shared spirit.

Daniel and Jordan stayed on the beach. The healing process began while Anioch and Roshan blazed in the setting sun.

CHAPTER 17

Jordan's new life continued to unfold, taking on a routine that included weekly therapy sessions with Dr. Blair. The day of his appointment, Jordan would feel faint stirrings of unease. While the sessions were low-key and conversational, there was an unspoken tension. Jordan couldn't quite put his finger on what he felt. He didn't know if it was his continued apprehension around reconnecting with his "soul-space," as he and his father now called it, or his fear of revealing this awakening to the doctor. His inner voice told him to be careful. His angel agreed.

Jordan honored the promise he'd made to his mother that morning before he left the hospital. He now knew the promise had been as much to her as it was to his own True Self. With each day, his spirit and body grew stronger. The accident had broken some part of him, but in the breaking, a crack had opened and light began to enter. New ideas like surrender and trust entered into his consciousness and he stayed with these thoughts. So he trusted that the weekly sessions with Dr. Blair were part of the journey.

"You've told me a lot about what drove you before. That competitive drive to be the best and to... what did you say... suck the juice from the marrow of life?" Dr. Blair paused and smiled at the young man, clearly enjoying his company.

"Yeah, something like that. I needed to feel alive. Something deep down inside of me was so hungry. To the point of being numb. Does that even make sense? It was like I was always looking for the next big wave. The next high. It was never enough." Jordan played the old story over in his head a million times.

"And the question is, now what?" The doctor paused. It had become a theme. "How do you suck the marrow out of life now? Or is the question instead, 'Is that something you even want to do now'?" The doctor let both questions hang in the air.

Jordan was the first to break the silence. "That's just it, Doc. I don't know what's next. I can kind of define it more by what I don't want. I know I don't ever want to feel so disconnected from my family and friends. I don't ever want to feel so alone thinking no one understands or cares about me. I don't want to be defined by the anger and blind rage that shut me off from everything that made life beautiful before. I don't want to feel so empty and self-absorbed that nothing touches or inspires me. I don't want to feel like I have nothing to lose. I don't want to live life like I'm already dead. I don't ever want that again."

Dr. Blair leaned forward in his big leather chair. He looked at Jordan and with kindness in his eyes said, "It is good to say what you don't want. It is also very powerful to say what you do want. Through affirmations we can reframe our way of thinking, and by changing our thoughts we can change our lives." He leaned back as Jordan leaned in. The two men again sat in silence.

Jordan didn't answer but in his heart he knew there was power and truth in the words he heard. Again, Jordan finally broke the silence. "Okay, so how do I do that? If I don't want fear—because that is what it all boils down to—what do I say? I want courage? Are you telling me it's that simple?"

"Yes, it is simple," the doctor replied. "But it isn't easy. Let's start off simple, Jordan. You say you don't want fear. Okay. So you can deny that fear by reframing it in a way to not put your attention on it. It's okay to acknowledge the fear. Fear can be helpful but it's a question of who's in control. The next step is... what do you affirm? What do you stand for? Another way to ask this is what is your personal statement of how you are going to live and show up?"

"What do I stand for?" Jordan asked. "I don't know. Right now I am just staying open and trusting in the process." His mind filled with half-formed thoughts. The conversation was pushing him into a new place. He slowly repeated, "What do I stand for? I think right now I stand for... *hope*."

Anioch smiled. Hope! Yes, hope.

"That is a great start. 'I stand for hope.' Let that guide you for the week and see how it feels."

Jordan took the cue, time was up. "Thanks, Doc. This was good. It feels good to be moving past my past." Jordan grabbed his jacket and the two men shook hands.

As Jordan drove home he thought about reframing his thoughts. He pondered what his future might look like putting fear in perspective and focusing on hope. *It's not courage, man. I didn't lack courage. I had way stupid courage. Hell, I was fearless and full of courage.*

What I didn't have was hope. I was hopeless. So yeah, I stand for hope.

With hope as his mantra, Jordan focused on his immediate future. He knew soon he would need to move on and begin a new life. The safety of his parents' home had provided the space for physical and emotional healing, but in his heart he knew that deep healing and mending of past ruptures was progressing as it should. The next phase of his journey, like the seed cradled deep within the earth, was slowly unfolding and made manifest at its own pace. "I stand for hope," Jordan spoke out loud.

While Jordan remained puzzled and unclear as to the future, he surrendered to its uncertainty. He remembered Dr. Blair's words and didn't let fear gain control. He added to his affirmation, "I stand for hope, and affirm that all is well."

Jordan continued his daily walks on the beach although each day he pushed himself, adding small bursts of sprints as he built up muscle and lung capacity. He loved the time on the beach and felt connected to the greater power displayed magnificently in nature. His heart and spirit soared as he walked and ran on those familiar shores. But his soul knew there was another type of energy present as well. Wise now to the inner voice, instead of denying it, he paid attention. He recognized the pull of unease and acknowledged it. He named it as uncertainty, anxiousness, even fear. He let the shadow of fear stay in the space but chose not to give it the loudest voice. *Fear cannot abide alongside hope*, he mused.

"Well Jordan, if you had a conversation with that big feeling you call fear, what do you think it would sound like?"

"What would fear sound like? You mean like a growl?" Jordan was half playing with Dr. Blair.

"No, not what would fear sound like. What would it say?"

"What would it say?" Jordan repeated, trying to adjust his mind to the thoughts. "It would tempt me. Like a seductress. I mean, lately fear comes to me in the familiar form of the ocean. She tempts me. I am there every day and she calls to me asking me to return to her. But she turned on me. Or maybe I turned on her. She was angry and wild and I challenged her. And she won." Jordan stopped. He closed his eyes and felt his heart racing.

"Go on, Jordan. You are telling me about the ocean. But what is fear saying to you?"

"I don't know. That's the thing. I never really knew fear. I always thought I could beat it. I always had. So now fear is a giant black ball of energy that is just there. I don't know that it speaks to me. I think it laughs." Jordan sat with his eyes closed. He tried to listen to his inner voice but all he could hear was the pounding of his heart.

"It laughs at me and mocks me. It says, 'You think you are special but you're not special. You were number one but now you are nothing. You thought you were the best and everyone loved you. But they didn't love you. They only loved you for what you did, not for who you were.' So now what am I? Who am I? Fear makes me doubt myself." Jordan opened his eyes and felt the sting of tears. He looked at the man who sat across from him whose eyes were soft and kind.

"And what do you say back to that voice, Jordan?" Silence hung like a heavy mist, drawing the two men into an intimate circle of shadow and light.

"I look across that big endless ocean and I thank her for what she gave me and what she gives me. I am not afraid of her. It isn't the power of the ocean that scares me. I know her and respect her. It's me I'm scared of. I'm scared of the uncontrolled part of me that doesn't believe in me. I have to speak to that dark side."

"Okay, and what do you say to him?"

Jordan took several deep breaths. He cleared his mind and thought of his mother's garden. He saw a young boy standing under the shade of the large blooming fruit tree, arms outstretched. *Hope*, he thought. *Love*, his inner voice replied. He remembered how he planted seeds and trusted life and the cycle of each season. The blossoms spoke of a future rich harvest. The boy spoke of joy. He smiled and the words poured out.

"Fear, you don't speak for me. You don't know me. You are small and uninspired. You are strong only when I am small. You hide in shadow and darkness. You think of me only as a fragmented part of my True Self. But when I step into the light, I silence you. I affirm my wholeness. I stand for hope. I stand for love. I stand waiting as I slowly emerge and step into my full potential and purpose. Fear does not serve me. Patience, faith, love and hope serve me and I serve them." As Jordan finished his voice broke and sobs rose from deep inside.

Dr. Blair remained seated. "Good," he said. "Very good."

Time passed. Jordan sat with the questions and did not push. He began to look forward to his sessions, realizing that he was being gently coaxed to go deeper. "This is the nutrient I need." The quiet inner voice grew stronger, seeking a reason, a passion and a purpose. *I'm developing deep roots.*

Dr. Blair challenged him to look at things in a different way. "You can sit *with* the question or *in* the question."

Jordan would look at him puzzled. "I swear sometimes you sound like freaking Yoda."

Both men laughed.

As mornings faded into evenings and days passed, Jordan shifted to be more in the question. And as he silenced his mind, the answers quietly came drifting in on a hidden current dropping silently at his feet in the lapping tide.

One day Jordan finally admitted, "Well I can confidently say, I am not returning to competitive surfing."

"Then what does that mean for you?"

"It means I don't have a job."

"Is that what it was for you?" Dr. Blair leaned back in his chair.

Jordan knew they were going to begin one of their verbal volley games. "It was what I did. So yeah, I guess it was my job. This is your job, right? I surfed waves for a living and you ask questions."

"Indeed. Well if you define a job by how we earn a living then yes, this is my job. I ask questions." A faint smile was beginning to spread across the doctor's face.

"What are you saying? You don't think of this as your job?"

"So I guess you're asking the questions now? That's good. I don't so much think of this as my job. I do this because it's what I am called to do. This is mine to do."

"How do you know that?" Jordan was genuinely curious. He had been thinking a lot about what he was meant to do.

"How do you or I know anything, Jordan?"

"I guess we just try it, right?"

"Or we don't. You won't swim right now so how do you know surfing isn't your thing?" Dr. Blair was jotting notes down in his black leather binder.

"Because I can feel it in my bones." Jordan could feel a slight wave of excitement stir. He liked the energy during these exchanges.

"That's good. Our bodies can tell us a lot. They don't lie to us. I listen to my body. When I am here with you, I am really present and connected. I feel positive and fully alive. That helps tell me that this is mine to do."

"How can you be so sure, Doc?"

"Again you are asking me the questions. You're not going to get off that easy, Jordan. Ask yourself the big questions."

Jordan laughed. "Hey, I thought you were supposed to ask me the questions. Remember that's your purpose and calling? I don't know what mine is."

Both men smiled. There was radiant warmth in the office.

The big questions came and Jordan stayed with them. *Who am I? What is my purpose? What is mine to do?* The questions stayed and he learned to remain open and explore the answers with curiosity and kindness. Patience was the elixir. With Dr. Blair's help, Jordan rested in silence and welcomed the not knowing.

It was during one session that Jordan stopped and asked the doctor to repeat a question. "What are you asking me?" There they were again together on that empty, stormy and angry shore.

Dr. Blair lowered his voice and slowly repeated, "At that moment what did you have left to lose?"

Jordan looked directly into the wise doctor's eyes. "Nothing. Absolutely nothing."

"And what did that mean for you?"

The wise man had known there was something there still anchoring Jordan to that moment. Some part of the story still held him. Together they had gone over the years, the hours, up to the moment of the accident so many times. But Jordan always held back. They had worked through the anger, the emptiness, the fear, but he had never owned the despair and hopelessness even as he chose to affirm hope.

"It meant I wanted it to stop. I simply wanted it all to stop."

They both sat in the heaviness of the words. It wasn't a revelation for either man. But they needed it to be fully acknowledged to be laid bare.

"What did 'stopping it all' mean for you, Jordan?"

"I had nothing left to live for. I was alone. I felt nothing. No joy. Even the anger was gone. I somehow lost the ability to feel, to dream, to believe. I felt unworthy. I was wholly disconnected from everything. I was totally alone. In a weird way I was going to give it one last shot to see if anything happened. If something saved me or tried to save me. Something always saved me. But this time I was alone..." Jordan's voice trailed off.

Anioch watched, knowing his child was only telling a part of the story.

Jordan sat silently. He couldn't speak about the connections with his angelic guide. He had only shared this with his father and intuitively with Anne Marie. Even his mother didn't know. The little boy didn't trust anyone else and shouted through the illusion of space and time. *Don't say it. They disconnected me from my angel before. They said he wasn't real. They said I was crazy. The color was gone. Remember the shadows. Don't let that happen again.* The voice was loud and desperate. He could feel the little boy clawing inside his chest.

Jordan stood up and stretched. He felt dizzy. "I don't know. I wanted to die. I had no reason to live. I thought that if something didn't save me then really none of this stuff mattered anymore."

Dr. Blair didn't push. "That is a big thing to admit, Jordan. Thank you for your honesty. How do you feel?"

"How do I feel?" Jordan paused. He felt unsteady and tasted bitter metal on his tongue. But he knew that he was responding to the past. "I'm not going to speak from my past. Right here, right now, I'm different. I really am. Things have changed. I'm working through this. And I have to thank you for a lot of the changes. I don't see myself ever going back to that dark place. I won't go there again." Jordan wanted to leave and have some space to quiet the still nagging little boy who was screaming in his head.

"You are doing all the hard work. You are very open to ideas and practices. Like they say, practice makes progress."

"I thought it was *perfect*. Practice makes perfect," Jordan corrected.

"Well, whoever said that was not very wise and put a lot of pressure on people. Be kind to yourself. I am here if you need to talk."

The sessions continued. The physician gently prodded the young man to test his intellectual and psychic curiosity. Jordan sensed Dr. Blair was a vast reservoir of wisdom, but could tell his wise mentor was only willing to reflect back the same energy that Jordan was willing to commit. Intrigued, he often left sessions feeling like Dr. Blair knew more than he said and was sitting back patiently waiting to see what Jordan would discover and eventually reveal.

"You ask a lot of questions about purpose. Well wait, Jordan, let me reframe that because you are a peculiar patient." Dr. Blair was chuckling.

Jordan smiled and leaned in, waiting for the question. There was always the next question.

"Because I like you, I answer those questions. But now I want to ask you, when you sit with the idea of purpose in your life, what answers are you receiving?"

"I don't know really. I am beginning to think maybe purpose is something we try to define just to give us some semblance of order. Maybe I'm making too big of a deal about it."

"Go on. So if purpose can be something smaller, how does that suddenly feel?"

Jordan knew that was a cue to do a quick body check. He closed his eyes and scanned for any tension. He knew his spots and paid attention to his jaw and shoulders. He took a deep breath and loosened his shoulders, rolled his neck. He opened his eyes and looked at Dr. Blair who had a slight smile on his face. *Where is he going with this?* "Well if it is smaller, it is more doable but also more immediate. I guess it becomes an answer to that question you have me ask every morning—'What is mine to do today?' That can be my purpose, for now."

"So if you can right size purpose, how does that affect it?"

"It actually makes me more excited. I can do smaller things and still be purposeful. Maybe I can again take off my hero's cape and not have to save everybody from everything. You know when I try and do the superhero thing, I just freeze myself into inaction. But I can do the small acts of kindness. I can do that." Jordan smiled back at the doctor. "So what's up with your Cheshire cat grin?"

Dr. Blair let out a deep laugh. "Am I that transparent?"

"Man, I'd love to play poker with you because I think you would probably suck."

"Jordan, I am wondering if you would be interested—I'm starting a new group session, and I think you have an amazing perspective to share with these folks. It occurred to me that you can both give and receive in this group dynamic. It's kind of an eclectic group of people... you all are survivors, really we are all survivors. I can't get into backgrounds, but there are powerful stories here, each of you a special piece of what could turn into a beautiful mosaic."

Jordan listened. He knew he needed to expand his circle of friends since so many had dropped away. A small voice inside whispered to him that there was something deeper at play. An unspoken reason for this invitation. He hoped it was part of that elusive purpose he'd been searching for. So he answered simply, "Yes."

CHAPTER 18

Jordan's mother and brother sat at the kitchen table going over the stack of papers in front of them. "When is the deadline for this, Jake?"

Jordan watched his brother input information into the laptop. He noticed the fine lines that framed his mother's eyes. She looked tired.

"The school counselor says we need to get the loan stuff in by the end of the month," Jake answered. "I'm getting all my applications ready for the scholarships. I really hope I don't need any student loans, but they are saying it's smart to get the whole package done."

"It will be fine. I just need to make sure I have all the business stuff current. You know how much I love doing this." Charlene let out a nervous laugh.

Jordan pulled up a chair. He knew things had gotten a bit tight. He'd overheard his parents talking about his dad's job and how the company was consolidating and shipping jobs overseas. "Anything I can do to help?" he offered.

His brother and mother looked up. Charlene gently patted his hand. "I don't recall math being your favorite subject."

Jake rolled his eyes.

"Ouch, Mom. Maybe I can help with Jake's essays or something. Or I can make tea."

"Tea would be lovely," she mumbled, still flipping through files. "We've got this. Right, boys? I don't want to bug your dad. He's working long hours and doesn't need anything more on his plate. Like your nanna used to say, 'Time to put my big girl panties on'."

"So how much are they whacking folks at State these days?" Jordan asked. He had no idea what tuition cost, since he had always envisioned his life as one of tours and travel.

"Depends on whether I live at home or go somewhere else," Jake answered. "I'm hoping for a baseball scholarship." He continued typing numbers into the computer.

"That would be great," Jordan said, now busy at the stove. "When I was at your game last week I heard some guys talking and saying there were scouts in the crowd."

"It doesn't have to be an athletic scholarship," Charlene chimed in. "Your grades and SATs are also really strong. We just need to be patient and hopeful."

"So how much is it?" Jordan asked again. "I mean I always hear how people carry this student loan debt with them forever."

"If I stay in-state it isn't too bad. Maybe twenty grand if I live on campus. But I can stay at home and reduce it by a lot."

"No, Jake. We want you to have the full college experience. We'll figure it out. Who wants to live at home at your age?" Charlene caught herself and immediately regretted her words. She looked up to catch Jordan's eyes. "You know what I mean, Jordan. Right?"

"No worries, Mom. It wasn't my plan, and you guys have been great. But she's right, Jake. You've got a lot of life ahead of you. Who knows? Maybe you'll inspire me."

Jake looked up perplexed. "What, you thinking of college?" he asked dismissively.

"You aren't making the process look too appealing." Jordan poured the boiling water into his mother's favorite mug. "But I have to figure something out because I don't have too many marketable skills. Not much work for a retired surfer. Maybe we could be roommates and save some money?"

Jake smiled. "Sure. I can hang out with the oldest freshman on campus. But that could be a positive… since you can legally buy beer."

Charlene sipped her tea. "I'm not putting the house up for hock for that."

Jordan shot his brother a look. "Don't think so, bro. Those days are over for me. But I can lure in the 'chicks,' as gramps says." Jordan bent over and gave his mom a hug.

"Where are you going?" she asked.

"To meet Anne Marie for lunch." Jordan felt he could talk to his newest friend about anything. He was grateful for her friendship.

"Please say hello from me. Maybe one day I can join you guys." Charlene stood to give Jordan another big hug. "Love you. Be safe."

Jordan enjoyed this new ritual. "Love you too, Mom." He saw Jake roll his eyes again. Jordan knew his brother didn't understand. He yelled out as he left through the garage door, "Good luck, you two. It will all work out."

As Jordan drove toward the hospital, he knew it was time to make some sort of plans for his future. *I can't live at Mom and Dad's forever.*

He knew his mother hadn't meant to be hurtful. It simply was the truth.

He pulled up to the small café where Anne Marie was already sitting on a bench outside. She waved at him and her face lit up. "Well hello there, my Treasure from the Sea." They both hugged and laughed.

"Hello, Florence."

"And the machine?" Anne Marie responded.

"Nope, Nightingale."

"Look at you! Your hair is getting all long again. Going for the beach bum look?"

"Just holding off on my expenses. Saving on haircuts and razorblades." Jordan felt his heart swell with joy. He loved being in this woman's presence. "You look good, too. Got your early summer tan going. What've you been up to?"

"Dr. Summer is going to yell at me. I've been working in the garden. We're getting the house ready."

Jordan followed Anne Marie as she led him to a table. "Dr. Summer? You okay?"

"I'm fine. She's my dermatologist. It goes with living here by the beach. I am assuming you're being smart."

"Your dermatologist's name is Summer?" Jordan chuckled. "Kinda like my math teacher's name was Ms. Trygg."

Anne Marie put down the menu and sipped ice water. "You still seeing Dr. Blair?"

"Yeah, we've been getting into some heavy stuff but I really like it. In fact it's making me think about what my next steps might be. I've decided to quit the surfing world. It's not what I want to do with my life."

"That's a big decision. You okay with that?"

"Yeah, in fact Jake's been doing all the college admissions stuff and it hit a nerve. A part of me wants to find a way to help people reconnect with that part of them that is joy and magic. Maybe school could help." Jordan took a bite of the sandwich he had ordered.

Anne Marie grabbed a fry off his plate. "You want to be a teacher? They get long vacations. Not a bad gig."

"Not really sure. I'm wondering if I could do something like what Dr. Blair does. Not a doctor, but maybe some type of coach or a therapist. I love the back and forth questions. It's actually pretty fun."

"Well, you don't need to choose your major right away. Keep exploring. I mean, look at me. Here I am at this point in my life trying to figure out what my next chapter will be."

"Really? You are like the uber nurse. You are amazing. I would have a hard time thinking of you as anything other than my Florence."

"Well you know there's a season for everything. And I am beginning to feel a little stirring. We will see where it takes me. I'm just staying open to the faint whisper."

The two sat in the sun and let the conversation flow.

"Want to split a dessert?" Anne Marie's eyes danced. "I've been really good and deserve a reward."

"Sure. I've been really bad so what the hell." Jordan pushed away his empty plate and leaned back. "Here's what's really on my mind. It's time to start looking for my own place. I think the school thing is a good idea but I need to find a job. I just never had to think about work or money before... and I don't like it. So far, I've been okay with the royalty checks still coming in from the endorsements and ad campaigns. But that's gonna dry up. I have no idea what I can do as far as a job and it's freaking me out a little."

"Understandable. But just like everything else in this world, there are some basic universal spiritual laws at play. You know how everyone talks about karma?"

"How can there be a spiritual law around money? Pardon my French, but the pursuit of fame—and the money that came with it— kind of f'ed me up." Jordan took a bite of the deep dish pie.

"Money didn't do that. Just like everything else, you let it mess with your head. You're the one who gave it the power."

"Okay, but if I want to live on my own and go to school, I need a way to make money."

"That's a related but separate issue, Jordan. The unspoken statement you made is that you don't have money and that's a problem. That's a statement coming from a place of scarcity."

"It's a statement from a place of truth," Jordan pressed. "I don't have a real income flow. So money is scarce."

"I know this can be uncomfortable. It's taken me a long time to open my heart and know that there is abundance of every type in my life. When I can find that place of openness and ease, it seems the abundance just flows more freely through me. It's the idea of being a pass-through that really changed my view on money. If I don't have to hold on to it so tightly... because I'm afraid I might lose it... then instead it easily flows to and through me. I can positively impact others by being mindful where I send it."

Jordan felt a knot in his stomach. He pushed the pie aside. "Sounds pretty woo-woo." But Jordan had learned to trust this gentle woman. He knew she was in his life for a reason.

"No pressure. Just stay open to the idea. This is a big lesson and many people never get it. Be grateful for all the abundance you have right here and now... and relax. The more you open yourself up as a channel for abundance, the more you'll attract."

Jordan didn't respond. Anne Marie let the silence fill the space. The friends sat together quietly and were comfortable. Anne Marie sipped her drink and leaned forward.

"The time and energy and love we put out there comes back to us, because everything flows to and from us. I struggled with the idea of doing what you love because there were a lot of days I didn't really love nursing. Rude doctors... Mean patients. But over time I learned to reframe it and saw that I was serving a higher purpose. When I put love into what I did, it changed everything. And I am so richly blessed. It's opened me up to think of doing something deeper."

The knot in Jordan's gut began to loosen.

"Don't think of what you lack. That's your small-self speaking. Your True Self is whole and complete and has everything it needs. You can give without a care in the world if you are in that place. You can give, knowing the well never runs dry. Give, knowing you will be taken care of. There is enough to go around. But also give from a place of love. Prepare for school if that's what you're called to do. The money will come. Just watch. Don't hold back and don't be afraid. Do it from a place of grace. The Universe wants to move through open channels. Be that open space." Anne Marie took one last sip of water and looked at her vibrating phone. "Luke's wondering what happened to me. I should probably get home."

Jordan got up and hugged his human angel. "Thank you. You inspire me."

When Jordan returned home, his mother was still sitting at the kitchen table. A look of sadness and worry etched her face. A few stray gray hairs had popped out of her messy bun. *I have to help somehow. Let me be that channel Anne Marie talked about.*

Jordan put down his keys and his mother looked up. Her expression immediately shifted. "Oh hey, I didn't hear you come in.

Looks like your brother and I got this done. Exciting times." Her voice was light but her eyes still held the worry.

"You know, Mom, we are a family and life has been good to me. I'm still getting paid for my endorsements and stuff. Please let me help. It would really mean a lot to me. I'd feel like I'm contributing and in some small way paying it forward." He didn't add that he had no idea when the money would dry up, but for now he felt a warm energy wash over him.

Charlene tilted her head, surprise glinting in her eyes. "Oh, we are fine, honey. I really appreciate the offer, but you have your life."

"Mom, please. You and Dad missed a lot of work while I was in the hospital, and I'm living here without expenses. Shoot, I used to spend money like a drunken sailor—more like a drunken surfer."

Jordan saw Charlene's telltale glisten of tears. "I am sure everything will be fine. Your dad thinks his job is secure for now. And I'm looking to add some hours subbing."

Jordan wasn't exactly sure what emotions he was seeing. Pride in her son? Worry for the future? Shame for something?

"Okay, but I'm serious. This is part of a lesson I'm supposed to learn from Dr. Blair, so you can't say no."

CHAPTER 19

The boxes were stacked up in the corner of the empty room. Jordan opened the window and took in the sound of the crashing waves and breathed in the smell of the salt air. He went into the small kitchen and turned on the overhead light. It hummed while the fluorescent bulb flickered on. He smiled to himself. *Who'd have thought I'd be here living right off Pacific Coast Highway?* He chuckled softly. Life had taken some interesting turns and he felt deep gratitude in his heart.

The apartment was small but comfortable. Decorated in a mismatched array of furniture he'd been gifted by his parents and family friends, "Bohemian" was the word his sister Jenna used. He liked that. He didn't need neat and conforming. Bohemian was a good word to describe his life. He was learning to set intentions in a broad open manner and leave the details to the Universe.

He found humor in the way random events pulled together to place opportunities and blessings in his hands. Each time these little synchronicities happened, he felt both blessed and humbled. Even when something seemed liked an obstacle, he tried to stay open and grateful, trusting that all things would lean toward good. *"Find the blessing,"* Anne Marie told him.

Jordan checked his phone. He still had time before he needed to go downstairs to the surf shop. He called his brother to check in. Jake was in his first semester at State. All the worry and stress his parents silently struggled with ultimately gave way to a combined academic and athletic scholarship.

Jordan had seen the lines of tension lift when the acceptance letter arrived. *"Mom, I'm in. But better yet, listen to this, 'We are pleased to inform you that based on your academic record and information contained in your application, you qualify for a 50% academic scholarship.' Can you believe this? Holy cow, this plus the baseball scholarship covers me, Mom!"*

Jordan smiled as he remembered how they all danced together. He listened to the phone ringing as he stayed with the memory. It was good and made him feel warm and happy.

The phone continued to ring. Jordan let the happy memory play out, remembering how later, his mom came to his room and hugged him. *"Thank you, Jordie. Thank you for being so kind and loving. We won't need your help now with your brother. But I will always remember how you stepped up and offered with such an open heart. I love you so much."*

Jordan beamed. His act of open-heartedness to help finance his brother's college costs had worked just like Anne Marie suggested. Once he began to let go of the need to know and control, things started falling into place. Jordan took each sign as a positive affirmation from the Universe. *All is well.*

The phone stopped ringing and went to voicemail. "Hey, this is Jake. I can't take your call right now. But you know the drill... text me or leave a message."

"Little brother, it's me. Just calling to say hi and see how it's going. Moving into my new apartment right across from the pier and was thinking of you, wondering how you are doing in your new place. Hope all is well. Love you, bro. Talk to you later."

Jordan grabbed his sweatshirt and went downstairs to work. The surf shop was small and crammed with an array of beach ware, tee-shirts, hats, flip flops, bikinis, board shorts, magazines, board wax, sunscreen, and every imaginable piece of hardware for the beginner to seasoned surfer. Surfboards were stacked in the back and boogie boards lined the aisles. Music filled the store and he was greeted by the smells of summer: suntan oil, sweat, sand and sea salt.

"Hey Greg, how's it going, bro?"

The young man behind the counter looked up. "Whatsup?" Greg jumped up from the stool, grabbing his energy drink. "Glad to see ya. I know your commute is a total bitch."

Jordan smiled. "Fifteen steps, man."

"Well, I got class. It's been slow. The inventory sheets are done, so your night should be pretty chill." Greg fist-bumped Jordan then pulled out his skateboard from the small closet. "See ya."

Jordan had been looking for a job but wasn't sure what he wanted to do. He struggled with the idea that he had no real marketable skills yet didn't want to flip burgers or wait tables. Dr. Blair told him to pay attention to his thoughts and "listen to your body." At first Jordan didn't quite understand. But as he scoured online sites for job postings he began to notice how his stomach responded to certain ads or his energy shifted when he read job descriptions. Nothing seemed to really interest or excite him. He fought the urge to become frustrated and instead set an intention that he would find work that would meet his needs and be the right fit for now.

The chime on the door sounded. Jordan looked up from the magazine he had been absentmindedly flipping through. "Well, if it isn't my hero. Man, it's good to see you."

Jordan jumped out from the counter and embraced the customer.

"Oh boy, Jordan. I heard you were back and recovering from the accident. I've been wanting to see you but had to finish up the senior circuit." Both men laughed. The customer's hazel eyes danced. Jordan noticed flecks of gray and fine lines etched on his face. "How's my star pupil? I've missed watching you. I mean it's not the same, will never have another one like you. Raw talent." The man continued to gently pat Jordan's back.

"I think you called it raw, unbridled bat shit crazy talent," Jordan laughed.

"Probably could have gotten in trouble for that. But no one cuts a set like you. How are you, son?"

Jordan looked at his former coach. The years had been kind to him. He sensed a hidden purpose to this meeting and he silenced his racing mind. "I'm doing good. I just started here at the shop. It's a sweet deal. Mr. Tyler needed someone to manage the store at night and I had nothing but time on my hands. The cool thing is, he threw in the upstairs apartment as part of the pay. So here I am. Couldn't say no to living right on the beach."

The coach smiled. "Well, I'm sure you're helping business. I mean, who better to manage a surf shop than the world champ? We all know old surfers never die... we just paddle off into the sunset looking for the big one to ride home."

"Something like that." Jordan knew where the conversation was heading. It was the same question he got every day.

"You going back on the circuit soon?"

Jordan heard the shift in the older man's tone. He sensed care and concern, no judgment. "I don't think so. I haven't even gone back in for a set yet. I'm trying to figure some things out. For now this job is good. It keeps me connected and it gives me time. I'm starting at Coast Community College next week. I'll take a few classes and see what calls to me. Things seem to be falling into place. So... no rush, if you know what I mean." Jordan waited.

"That sounds really smart. Sometimes in life we have to hit the pause button. Sounds like you are doing that."

"Might even be the reset button for me. But it feels good. I just don't know what the next couple of years are supposed to look like. This friend tells me it's good sometimes to not know. She says it's in times of uncertainty when the good stuff starts to come together. So... how's the team this year?"

"Pretty good. We've got some talent. Not raw unbridled bat shit crazy talent. I think that only comes along once in a coach's life. But good solid talent. Maybe you'd like to come by practice one day. I think these guys and gals would be pretty pumped to see you."

Jordan nodded. He could feel something stirring deep down. He stayed open and didn't rush to a quick no. "Yeah, that would be fun. I'd love to watch the next generation of legends."

"Great. Practices are same time, same place. Funny how little things change." The coach began to pull some items from the nearby shelf.

Or how totally some things change, Jordan thought. "Hey, let me help with that, coach." Jordan grabbed a small basket and handed it to the man.

"So college? That sounds exciting. Any idea what you might want to major in?"

"Not sure. My brother's up at State. He got a full scholarship which is what got me thinking about school. I remember how you used to tell us to dream big because we were unlimited and only as big as our biggest dream. It sounded like motivational stuff at the time and I didn't really believe it. But I've learned some lessons lately and some new teachers have come into my life. I'm guessing you might get some of this."

The man stopped, turned and nodded. Jordan felt the inner nudge to share how things had unfolded for him and his family in the last few months. Somewhere in his heart, Jordan knew that none of the interconnected events were mere coincidence. He heard Dr. Blair's calm voice proclaim, *"There are no coincidences in life, Jordan. It's all a matter of perception. I call them miracles."*

Jordan continued as his former coach listened, "Before we found out about the scholarships, I offered to help my parents with my brother's school. It's crazy but for some reason the print ad stuff I did for some of the clothing companies is still paying off. So that money stream just seems to be flowing. Kind of weird, but cool weird. You know what I mean? I'm not counting on it and thought if it could be put to good use, I'd use it to help my family. Well, anyway, I thought I'd stay local and dabble for a bit to see what might catch my interest. So here I am and my rent is covered... so I really don't need that money. Community college makes more sense for me. I'm thinking maybe something in psychology or coaching."

The coach looked up and smiled. "Looks like the Universe is conspiring in your favor. Makes your old coach happy. Gonna follow in my footsteps?"

"Maybe another type of coaching. But who knows? Like I said, I'm just going to explore for a while."

"That is wise, Jordan. Sounds like things are in a good place for you. Think about the offer... we'd love to have you stop by. Who knows? Maybe you can dabble in a bit of coaching on the side."

The man paid for the merchandise and turned back to Jordan.

"Things happen for a reason. Out of our biggest losses or hardest battles we emerge new and better. You are special, Jordan. You always have been. So follow your heart. You've got a big one and it sounds like the Universe has some plans for you."

The two men hugged and Jordan knew that at that moment he was exactly where he was meant to be.

Jordan pulled into the sprawling parking lot and gathered his laptop and backpack. He was excited but slightly apprehensive. The small voice in his head demanded center stage. "*You are going to be the oldest student in class. You were a lousy student before. What makes you think you can do it now? The only thing you know is how to surf and you can't do that because you are too scared.*"

Jordan closed his eyes and took a deep breath. "All is well," he spoke out loud, and let it sink into his bones.

He moved along the footpath past teenagers walking in small groups. Skateboarders veered in and out of the passing students. Jordan noticed a mix of people: young and old, some dressed in shorts and jeans and a few in khakis and polo shirts, sundresses. *You'll be fine,* he silently repeated.

When he was younger, Jordan found most of the classes boring and was often caught daydreaming or doodling, lost in his own world.

He hoped that with the passing years, he would find joy in learning and perhaps had gained some discipline and focus.

He turned left on the asphalt path and headed toward the nondescript two-story building. As he climbed a small set of cement stairs he moved closer into the narrowing stream of people pushing into the double glass doors. He heard bits and pieces of conversations. The long corridor brought back a rush of memories. He found room 201-A. A few students sat at desks unpacking their iPads or texting on their smartphones. He logged into the class syllabus for Psychology 101. Jordan smiled to himself. *A year ago who'd have thought I'd be doing this?* Now that he had quieted the cacophony of doubting voices, he was excited to begin this new chapter.

Jordan settled into his new life as a student. The initial apprehension faded when he dove enthusiastically into classes. As he got busier between school, work, and the new informal coaching with the high school surf team... and his continuing sessions with Dr. Blair... he felt more energetic and excited for his future. Time seemed to expand instead of contract. He didn't know what the future held but he was finally moving in the right direction. *At least I'm moving,* he told himself.

He looked forward to his sessions with Dr. Blair. Jordan never knew where the conversations would go but he trusted the process. Lately they had been focusing more on Jordan's feelings around connection. These were new and unsettling feelings. He struggled to turn them into words.

"I know I'm not alone. In fact, I have more people in my life than ever before—and these are good people who aren't just hooking up with me because they think I have something they want." Jordan tried to express the gnawing unnamed feelings. "I mean, there are kids at school that I see going down that stupid path of partying and trying to fit in. I'm really grateful I waited until now to go back to school. I see that lifestyle for what it is. I learned my lesson. And it's not that I feel that I'm missing out—I love hanging out with the surf club. Those kids are amazing and I really feel I am serving a purpose with them. Coach is awesome and he gets me and the stuff you and I talk about." Jordan paused.

Dr. Blair sat quietly, waiting.

"And things with my family are great. I mean, even Jake's coming along. I don't know why I can't just relax and be grateful. It's like I'm creating some stupid drama where I don't need it. Everything is good.

So what's up with this nagging thing that's holding me back from being content?"

Dr. Blair uncrossed his legs and leaned forward. "If you had to name this feeling, what is it?"

"I don't know, Doc. That's the thing. I'm not sad. I'm not lonely. It's not really a feeling. It's like energy. Like a nagging dull ache. A sort of emptiness." Jordan paused and breathed in. "It's not a something that's there. It's a something that's missing."

"That's good. Just feel the emptiness and acknowledge it. You can honor it for making its presence known."

Jordan didn't fully understand but he trusted the kind doctor.

Dr. Blair asked him to try and just observe his thoughts around relationships and not judge the thoughts or feelings.

It still didn't make sense. But slowly Jordan got more comfortable sitting with the dull pit. He would wonder, *How do I fill it? What's missing?* But he didn't do anything with it but accepted it. He observed it.

Anioch stayed present. The angel sensed that in observing these new questions, his child was digging deeper. He knew these questions weren't forcing Jordan to look outside for the answers... but rather his charge began searching inward. "That is good, my child," the angel whispered. "All the true questions have their answers deep inside your Being."

Jordan sensed his angel's presence and was grateful for it. He recognized that when he was in the right space he would feel the angelic energy and it gave him comfort. He sat with the empty space and didn't try to fill it. He knew he wasn't alone. He also didn't feel that the empty place spoke to hopelessness like that aching hurt of loss from his past. In the quiet space, Jordan felt an inner voice enter into the silence. It was as if he—or some part of him—was filling the empty space.

Who are you? he would silently ask.

I am you. The real you. I am here with you observing. What do you want?

He would continue his questions. I am asking nothing of you. I am complete. I am whole. I am the space that you look to fill. But in me there is no space between us.

For a fleeting second the puzzling words made sense to Jordan, but then their meaning slipped away. But he found that as he stayed in silence, the empty pit became still and less demanding.

He struggled to explain this to Dr. Blair. "So I think you might be pushing me to the edge of crazy. I sit, like you asked me to. And there is silence. But it's the silence that speaks. I'm hearing voices and it sounds kinda nuts."

"Perhaps it is crazy or brilliant. Hard to say where those lines might intersect."

"Oh well, that makes me feel so much better." Jordan's shoulders tightened, a sure sign he was shutting off. He fought the urge to retreat.

Dr. Blair continued, ignoring the tinge of sarcasm. "So, what does the silence say?"

"Here's the weird part. It tells me that the silence is me. That I am part of the silence. That somehow the aching emptiness is only empty because I choose that. It says it waits and by waiting it ultimately is and in that, it will be filled by me. When I start thinking like that, the emptiness seems much less empty or nagging. It just is. And at that moment it's okay." Jordan heard his words and felt embarrassed. "I say this stuff and when I hear it come out of my mouth I really feel dumb."

"Why would you feel dumb? What part of this is making you feel uncomfortable?"

"All of it. None of it makes sense. I feel empty. But I am not empty because I can fill that emptiness. I mean... I feel kind of like I am having some weird conversation with myself and I am afraid it might be bordering on madness." Jordan felt a heaviness creeping in.

Anioch stayed alert. *Embrace the light, my child. What you are saying is Truth. Stay open and listen with your heart.*

"So if for a moment we accept that you having a conversation with yourself isn't any type of mental illness, what part of your inner-self inviting you to fill the space is scary?"

In that moment, Jordan felt the darkness recede. *Okay man, why is this scary? Am I scared?* He took a deep breath and answered, "I don't know that I would say this is scary. It's different. Maybe more unsettling. I guess it's trying to balance the idea that I really am in a good place right now. I know I have people in my life who I love, and they love me. It's so different than before. Back then I felt cut off from everything. I don't feel that now. In fact, I feel grounded and connected. So it's that ache and recognizing that silent place that is unsettling. I don't know what I am supposed to do with it. And when I acknowledge it, it answers me with a riddle."

"Where's the riddle, Jordan? I hear it saying something simple to you."

"Really? Well, you have more experience with this Zen-master double speak stuff."

"Okay, so is it real?"

"Is what real? The ache? The emptiness? The stillness? The voice? The space between me and that pit?"

Dr. Blair sat perfectly still and waited. "Any of it."

Jordan leaned back and closed his eyes. His mind dashed in a million different directions, all broken and diffused like the sparkled swirl of changing patterns in a kaleidoscope.

"Man, I don't know. You are kind of blowing my mind." Jordan didn't want to continue. "Is our time up?" Jordan leaned forward and looked into the doctor's eyes.

"No, Jordan. We have time." Silence hung between them.

Jordan kept his eyes closed and gently rocked back and forth on the back legs of his chair. "It's as real as I am willing to make it. But when I step into that space, I am there. It's not me, right? That's the point—it is me, but a different part of me. That's it. I am more than this. I am that as well. I am that deep space inside of me. It calls like an ache, but it's not an ache. It's calling me in. And when I pay attention, it's not empty. I am there." Tears began to stream down Jordan's face. He didn't know where the words came from but as he spoke he felt his heart open.

Anioch blazed.

"I am that silence," Jordan continued. "I am that space. I am that hunger. It's not scary because it's just me. The response to fear is always love. It's a call to love. That's it, isn't it? I am looking for something, a deeper love. That's the ache. But it isn't out there. It's in here." Jordan tapped softly on his chest. His face broke into a smile.

"Yes, Jordan. That's it. And love answers love. Be patient. Be kind to yourself." Dr. Blair stood.

"So, now our time is up?" Jordan laughed.

"Time? Is time real?" Dr. Blair joked. "For now, yes, our time is up."

CHAPTER 20

Finally, after several months and false starts, the group session Dr. Blair invited Jordan to join was ready for its launch. Jordan's studies had been interrupted by fleeting thoughts of what these people would be like. He had come to recognize that most events in his life were not mere coincidence or fancy, but rather purposeful. Courses in psychology and philosophy revealed that universal truths were stated over and over, just with different dictum. *Synchronicity* was a new word that tickled him. Divine intervention. Divine coincidence. He knew it was his Angel's presence. Jordan knew he was connected to some larger energy field. He began and ended every day with words of thanksgiving. Nothing was taken for granted anymore.

Each day was a gift, as was he. He embraced the notion that the blessed became the blessing and in that knowledge, Jordan waited. The aching pit that had threatened to drag him down into the abyss was now transformed into a secluded grotto where he came to rest. The silence became his companion as the fear turned to peace. He knew he was Love and he tried to approach each encounter and each moment with his heart, mind and body tuned and turned to love. He learned to recognize each moment as a call to love. To connect with that pure essence and energy of Life. *I am the manifestation of Divine Love.*

Jordan drove to Dr. Blair's small office. The group session would be held in the conference room. Jordan felt strangely nervous. He was amused at this reaction. He had not been nervous for some time. He strived to be in service and to focus his energy on positive flow for himself and those he encountered. There were no coincidences but rather opportunities to co-create.

Anne Marie had long ago said, *"God's will has no whys,"* so he ended each day with "Amen. And so it is." He knew that things would unfold as they should and in their proper time as long as he remained open and humble. He heard someone once say that worry was a waste of creative energy. He agreed. He learned to stay with the awe and wonder available in the magnificent moment of now and not get too far ahead of things.

Yet, here he was sitting in the conference room with several strangers, each looking in some way mildly uncomfortable. He smiled at those who had already taken their seats in the circle. He closed his eyes and prayed silently to his angel.

Anioch was there. The angel noticed how weak the spirits of some of these strangers appeared. Before him a group of slightly broken and spent people were quietly assembled. Anioch's Divine power blazed brightly over Jordan's head. Anioch also wondered what Source's purpose was. He too was filled with the sense that there was something more to this meeting. Energy of anticipation filled the room.

Jordan believed he was where he was supposed to be, and somehow he was meant to be more than just a participant. Dr. Blair all but admitted that to him. Jordan and Anioch both silently questioned if Dr. Blair was even fully cognizant of his reasons for wanting Jordan to participate.

So Jordan reflected and steadied himself and his energies for whatever Greater Purpose, grand or small, there was to be at this session. Silently he recited the words of St. Francis, *"Lord make me an instrument of your peace,"* a long forgotten childhood prayer that now spoke directly to his soul.

A thin young woman entered. Anioch, who had been eyeing each group member and assessing their spiritual flame and energy, felt an immediate pang of recognition. This woman, dressed in blue jeans, an oversized red sweater and sandals, touched him. She looked uncomfortable, shy and somewhat withdrawn. She did not greet any of the furtive glances from the others who shifted in their seats. Her blue-grey eyes remained downcast, unwilling to make contact.

When Dr. Blair entered, Jordan stirred. The doctor was dressed casually yet with an understated fashion sense—designer jeans, pressed tailored shirt, polished leather boots and a matching belt. His cool composure, assured posture and visible success stood in unspoken contrast to those who sat in steel-backed chairs, filled with nervous hesitation, withdrawn, insecure.

Anioch sensed that Dr. Blair was a wise old soul who had a Divine Purpose that he was joyfully fulfilling. The doctor's Angelic Being was a study in serene presence.

Dr. Blair welcomed the members. He then set down ground rules regarding confidentiality, interrupting, and setting aside judgment. Each member agreed and committed to showing up, being present, respectful and honest. Dr. Blair then offered for each member to introduce themselves.

As each gave their name, Jordan noticed for the first time the quiet young woman who had sparked Anioch's interest. She sat almost directly across from Jordan. Perfectly still, her hands folded in her lap, slowly and methodically her right foot swung. Her face was impassive, yet her eyes were downcast. She wore her blonde hair pulled close to her head in a tight ponytail. Her neck was long and thin. Indeed she was quite thin, giving her face a pinched look. Not pretty but attractive. *Like the too-thin super models*, Jordan thought.

A sense of familiarity struck him. He began to try to place a name to go with the face, but forced himself to be present and honor each person. As they went around the circle, they each offered a tiny statement of who they were, adding a brief glimpse into the story that had brought them into this closed circle.

The slight woman seemed to sense him and briefly locked his gaze. Jordan's heart leaped, and he could not understand why. There was a burst of energy, a momentary spark. He had never felt a surge like that before. It was strange. It lasted a millisecond. He couldn't explain it and as quickly as it came, it went. Jordan sat wondering what this strange circle held for him. He watched and observed his thoughts. There she was, an almost painfully shy girl, nondescript in appearance, who for the briefest moment had held his gaze and lit a spark. Something in those eyes reached out to him, beckoned and drew him in.

He waited until it was her turn to speak. He guessed that her voice would be a whisper, thin as her build. Indeed it was.

"My name is Amanda Martin," she said almost apologetically. "I moved here several years ago. I'm from up north near Holyfield. I have been working with Dr. Blair for almost two years." She offered no more.

Jordan watched her, hoping to lock eyes one more time. But she looked down. Hands folded. Foot swinging. No spark. No energy burst.

Anioch also watched. Undefined and loose energy slowly rolled up and coiled inward, but he was at a loss as to what was going on. As he looked at the young woman, he shifted his focus and noticed her spirit was very weak. Whatever Divine Being had been sent to surround and guide her was present but incapable of infusing the woman with much more than a mere glimmer of inner light. *A near lost soul,* the young angel mused.

Jordan felt his own spirit move as Anioch reached toward the heavens to pray for spiritual healing. He sensed a shift in the air. His pulse quickened. He looked at the woman, drawn again to her. He noticed Amanda's eyes flutter. She breathed deeply, as if reaching into the depths of her being. At that moment he felt something. There was something there. It was some unnamed connection. It wasn't the same energy burst but more of a pulling in as if he were caught in an invisible current. It was real. He was part of it. He shut his eyes too and allowed the energy to flow. Angels, man and woman for the briefest moment of time connected, sharing in a passage of Divine Healing.

Jordan was puzzled; he had never felt like this. It was beyond him, bigger than him. He felt disoriented as if he had stepped into another place. When he opened his eyes, Dr. Blair was looking directly at him with a puzzled look. Jordan blinked. Everyone was staring at him. *My God,* he thought, *how long have I been spaced out?*

"It's your turn, Jordan."

Jordan cleared his throat, "Sorry, my name is Jordan Collingsworth. I'm a student at State, majoring in Psychology and Philosophy. I used to be a pro surfer until I suffered a near fatal accident. I still love the ocean although from the shore for now. I also love to read, love music and good food. Sorry, I know that sounds cheesy, and in case you are wondering... no, I am not on Match." The small group chuckled. Jordan noticed a few folks smiled and nodded to him.

The young woman, Amanda Martin he recalled, was still looking into her hands.

And so the first session continued. Jordan did not participate much, but rather listened and tried to connect with the strange feelings he was experiencing. He didn't understand what was going on. He knew that now wasn't the time to make sense of any of this. He was learning to let things be and to go back in stillness and reflect. But something in him told him that he and this woman had something that was theirs to do. *Who is she? Where do I know her from? I can feel her sadness. She seems lost and alone.* He acknowledged the feelings and sent her love. The session was ending. "All is well," he whispered softly and got his things together.

Anioch stretched his wings and agreed, repeating the mantra, *"All is well."* And as angel and man rose, the small angelic being that hovered near the woman bowed and reached into the blazing color radiating from Jordan and Anioch.

"And as it should be, dear brother. As it must be."

CHAPTER 21

The meeting broke up, and a few people gathered near Dr. Blair. He was the link that connected all of them. Jordan grabbed his jacket and headed toward the exit. As he moved down the dimly lit corridor to the elevator, he noticed Amanda standing alone by the stairwell. Jordan turned and decided to take the stairs.

Jordan caught up with Amanda who was a few stairs down. She turned and smiled at him. She had a beautiful smile which gave life to her eyes and lit up her face. *Wow, she's beautiful.*

"Umm, it was nice to meet you, Amanda." Jordan offered his hand.

The woman hesitantly offered hers, a tentative shake. Jordan didn't feel any rush of energy. He wondered now if perhaps he had only imagined it. Amanda continued down the stairs. He noticed that she moved with a lightness and grace like a dancer.

"So, you were a professional surfer? That's very exciting. I'm sure you have been to some beautiful places."

Her voice was a little fuller, the syntax less chopped. Amanda felt better. Surprisingly, the session had lifted her spirits. It felt good talking to someone new. She had shied away for so long, choosing intentionally to avoid groups and awkward small talk. Instead she'd wrapped herself in her small safe world.

The session had touched her in a strange way. She didn't understand it, especially given her resistance to attend. Dr. Blair had been very persistent. But she now felt like a breath of fresh air had swept in and in some strange way invigorated her spirit. She looked at the young man before her and felt something stir inside. She listened to his voice. It was calm and warm.

"Yeah, I've probably surfed on every shore this planet has to offer. I'd love to go back now and enjoy them with a clear head."

Amanda shyly smiled. She knew what he meant... they probably all did. She figured that was why they had been brought together. They were survivors, people who had reached the end of their proverbial ropes, let go, taken the fall and still lived to tell about it. At least that is what she understood when Dr. Blair told her about the group. While he didn't explicitly state it, she took his words and created a story based on her own experience. As she had watched and listened to each group member she tried to imagine their life. What had they lived through? How had they responded? What painful story had they immersed themselves in? She imagined that each person responded in some self-destructive harmful way and in that isolation, they were now brought together to share their stories and perhaps build something new and better. *We each have a part in this play,* she mused.

Amanda didn't want to open herself up and share but she honored the doctor's request because she trusted him. She'd begun her private sessions with Dr. Blair after years of dark struggles borne over many years of neglect and self-loathing.

She wondered what demons haunted this handsome and gregarious man. Perhaps the lifestyle as champion surfer had offered a lot of different means for self-destruction. "I think we would all like to go back sometimes and walk those shores again," she said softly.

Her words hit Jordan. There was a deep sadness in them. He saw the smoldering pain in her eyes that now echoed in her voice. The stirring began again. He looked at her and wondered aloud, "You know, it's funny but the first time I saw you tonight I thought you looked familiar. I swear I have met you before. But I can't place your name or face."

Amanda looked at him, puzzled. "How funny. I got the same feeling, but I know I've never met you. I think I would remember. I mean... you're the type of person I would remember, umm... because you sound interesting... and like, you've done a lot of exciting things. But it's weird because there is something about you that seems familiar. Comfortable." She regretted the words the moment they came out. She picked up the pace as she went down the stairs. *Way to go, Amanda. Already saying dumb things. Just shut up.* She bounded down the last few steps, her feet barely touching the concrete.

Jordan followed, matching her stride. When they reached the bottom of the stairs he said, "I hope we can talk again." Jordan heard the words and realized they sounded forced.

Amanda smiled. "Well, I am sure we will next week."

Jordan winced. He tried to recover. "Yeah, for sure. I'm already looking forward to it. I'm glad Dr. Blair asked me to come. I think it will be good to meet new people." Jordan felt slightly flustered. He held the door as Amanda exited.

The night air rushed at them and Amanda shivered. The parking lot was pitch dark. She hated the dark.

Jordan noticed her hesitation. "Can I walk you to your car? It's pretty dark out here."

Amanda gratefully accepted but her inner voice made her nervous. *Go slowly. You don't know him. You are fine in the world you've created. Don't complicate things.* They walked in silence in the near-deserted parking lot. She quieted the swirling thoughts, noticing instead that she felt safe walking with the former surfer by her side. Amanda pointed out her blue Honda Civic. They headed in that direction. She fumbled for her keys and unlocked the door.

Jordan then asked, "Would you mind if I called you?" He didn't quite know why he asked but felt a tapping feeling, and he had come to acknowledge and respect it. He was learning to not fight the subtle shifts and knowings that Spirit manifested in myriad ways.

Amanda hesitated. She had turned nearly every person out of her life. She was a master at isolation. And she liked it that way. No one to warn her of her weight loss, or later to remind her of the diabetes. No one to see her binges and purging, dangerous highs and lows that threw her body into turmoil. Isolation allowed her to be in control. In the solitude, she believed she found freedom.

But she was trying desperately to put that response to life behind her. Something inside her told her to lower the barriers a bit. For a brief moment the thought came that perhaps this man was a gift. He was here to walk her to her car. Feeling safe for this small moment of time felt good. She felt comfortable with this stranger and decided for once to just trust her heart. "Yeah, okay, that would be nice." She took out her phone and they exchanged numbers.

Jordan smiled and put his phone away. He gently shut the driver's side door. He stood back as the Civic's engine rumbled.

Amanda backed out and began to drive away. She turned briefly and waved goodbye.

Jordan walked to his Audi. He still loved speed and the accompanying thrill, but now felt safer when secured in seatbelts than on the crest of a wave. He knew it was a fear he would have to overcome, but he wasn't quite ready. He pushed the thought away. As he turned the key and the engine roared to life, he sat back and thought about the evening.

He was filled with thoughts and half-asked questions. Who were all these new people who suddenly were introduced into his life? What was Dr. Blair doing bringing them all together? What was his to do? What was his to learn? He thought of Amanda. Why had he responded to her in that way? He sensed their paths were intentionally crossed but couldn't understand why. Was she a piece of his life's puzzle? In his gut he knew their meeting was more than coincidence. He had felt it, and guessed that she had, too... and maybe even Dr. Blair.

As the engine purred, Jordan decided these were questions he could not answer. Instead he decided to trust that all was as it should be and unfolding in its own way. He decided not to add to the story and just let it be. *All is well,* he silently prayed. *Just enjoy the ride,* he told himself as he moved his car into gear. His heart felt light. He hit the button and the roof pulled back. He let the night air wrap itself around him.

Anioch stayed near and wondered as well. The angel sang songs of praise as he danced in the dark space above the racing car. He saw the mystery and it gave him great joy. He knew the connection between Jordan and Amanda had been deeper. The Angel's heart soared. His voice boomed. The Heavens vibrated with an added intensity.

Jordan drove along the highway with the waves rolling in on the shore, filling the night air with the sound of unleashed power. The stars glimmered, cutting a path of flickering light in the ink black night sky. His angel blazed with the radiance of the rising sun, and Jordan felt strangely alive and awake. Jordan laughed out loud. *Just enjoy the ride!* The car punched into high speed and disappeared into the night.

CHAPTER 22

Amanda slowly drove through the back canyons. She opened the windows. Maneuvering the tight curves, she breathed in the night air. Sage mixed with the heavy dew that gently settled on the dry brush, joining the breeze as a subtle sweet perfume. She replayed the evening. She hadn't wanted to join the group. But now she felt a strange energy pulling at her. She hummed as she leaned into the twists and turns and felt the cool air caress her face. Something felt different. The dull numbness of her well organized life seemed slightly churned. She smiled. It felt good.

As she pulled into the hidden alley and parked her car, a small wave of gratitude washed over her. She walked the pebbled beach-stone path to her tiny cottage and stopped. *I feel happy right now.* "I just feel happy," she repeated, this time aloud. She opened the door and walked into her home. Everything was the way she had left it only a few hours earlier but somehow it was different, brighter. She continued to hum.

The days passed and Amanda quietly noticed the new sense of energy remained with her. She couldn't quite put her finger on what had changed. She just noticed that something inside her felt more alive, awakened. She went about her normal routines. At the boutique she ordered new merchandise, managed accounts and helped customers. She went to the gym and yoga. In the evening she immersed herself in a new novel, sitting near the bay window that framed the common patio. Things were much the same but somehow different. It was like the light had shifted, slightly, but just enough that the old looked new, fresh, layered in a film of gauzy promise.

Amanda liked this new feeling. She allowed her mind to daydream, something she had almost forgotten how to do. She bought bright yellow sunflowers for her small studio apartment, and giggled when she placed them in the painted ceramic vase from her childhood. She studied the vase and let the wash of memories bathe her. *There were some happy times.* The flowers lit up the entire room. *I am happy.* She let the thought again frame her.

Diffused morning sun filtered into the small room. Another day and the nearly imperceptible pulse of joy was still present. Amanda woke and looked at the clock near her bed. "My God, it's nine o'clock!" She couldn't remember the last time she had slept in. She checked her phone and looked outside at the blanket of grey mist hugging the ground pierced by the sun's rays fighting to break through.

She had a midweek day off with no plans or commitments. As she relaxed over a cup of tea, she decided to take a drive to the beach. Throwing on her comfortable sweats, she grabbed a book. She felt a slight vibration of energy like a tiny developing wave, barely perceivable but present just below the surface. It was like a faint feeling of anticipation, as if something new was emerging.

Dr. Blair had told her she needed to pay attention to these types of things such as small inner callings. Amanda was an expert at controlling her feelings, ordering all of her longings, sorting and stacking every detail of her life. But rather than turning off these new stirrings she willed herself to stay present and just notice them. She refused to wish them away or quiet them. Instead she acknowledged them and waited. In a strange way, the not quite knowing and slight disorder made her feel more alive. She smiled as she looked at the sunlight filtering through the mist. *My life feels like that right now: sunlight filtering through the grey fog.*

Amanda switched the satellite channel to the '70's station, listening to old songs her mother once sang to her, as she drove south along the Coast Highway. She loosened her hair out of the ponytail and let the wind carry it.

Jordan began his day as he did most days. He ran down the small flight of stairs and started off on his morning jog. He didn't have classes until later so he decided to extend his usual run and head toward the cove.

Mornings on the beach had become a vital part of his day. It was a time of reflection and prayer. It was here that Jordan was able to reconnect with nature, his angel, and energy source. He felt deep gratitude as he passed along the shore. He felt the morning sun on his skin and slight spray of the waves on his face. He noticed the fog lifting off the shore and watched as the mist sailed to the south.

Keenly alive this morning, his body pulsated with energy. A cooling breeze blew over him, and the salt air entered his lungs. He concentrated on the in-breath and released it with thoughts of love and gratitude. *I am blessed,* he thought and smiled.

Amanda drove along the flat and nearly empty two-lane road. She'd set out without a plan. She didn't have a sense of where to stop. She simply enjoyed the ride, the soft music, and the sunlight that danced behind the billowing clouds. She noticed a turn-off leading to the jutting beach that sloped below the red clay-coated rocks. She turned and parked along the near deserted highway, then took off her shoes and headed toward the cove. The beach was almost empty except for a few people jogging or walking. Despite the newly emerging sense of joy, Amanda walked as she normally did, eyes cast down.

Jordan was lost in his own world. Anioch, his steadfast companion, joined him as always, grateful to his Creator that he had been assigned to this untiring man. He wondered how other angels dealt with what he considered the mundane lifestyles of their charges. Anioch noticed other humans who seemed to *exist* rather than live.

As the angel followed his running man-child, he felt empathy for other angelic beings assigned to those men and women, who chose to not reach out and grab life, to live it to the fullest. Anioch vicariously lived the runs, the vigor, the fatigue and rush of endorphins. But as always, Anioch would end his thoughts with the firm belief that the Creator, source of Infinite Wisdom, knew the nature of all universal beings and matched them accordingly. Anioch believed that his spirit was fed by Jordan and was confident that Jordan was blessed by him.

Approaching the curve in the damp sand, Jordan paced himself, breathing deeply, steadily. He did not notice the woman who gazed out over the dark purple ocean.

Anioch sensed her presence and knew immediately that this was one of life's purposeful coincidences. He gently guided Jordan closer to the jagged rocks that jutted out from the cove where the young woman stood lost in contemplation.

Jordan did not think. He instinctively moved as his divine friend directed.

Amanda caught the jogging figure out of the corner of her eye. She initially paid him no attention, rather continued her contemplative gaze across the vast horizon. But a sudden shift in light drew her attention to the young man. As she refocused, recognition registered, and she smiled to herself. *What a pleasant surprise.*

Almost skipping in the sand, Amanda stood and approached him. "Jordan, Jordan, hi." Her voice was light, cheerful and carried easily on the sea breeze.

Roused from a place of deep concentration, Jordan slowed his pace and followed the voice. He was confused. He saw the young woman, but only slowly recognized Amanda. His heart leapt... it was that strange feeling again. He took a deep breath and smiled.

"Well, hello there. I was thinking about you this morning. In fact, I was going to call you tonight." Jordan immediately regretted the words as soon as he spoke them. They rang hollow.

But Amanda didn't seem to notice.

"What are you doing down here?" he asked, bent over catching his breath. His brow was glazed in sweat, his chest heaving.

"Well I had the day off, and it just seemed like a nice morning to take in the beach. I've been feeling like I needed to find some open spaces lately." Amanda's voice had lost the earlier lightness and almost seemed as if she was trying to explain things to herself.

"I must say this is a real nice surprise. I always take these surprises as little gifts." Jordan headed up the gently sloping shoreline.

"Why? Do you get a lot of them in your life?" Amanda asked.

"Yeah, I guess I do. They are what I call happy coincidences, or as my professor might say, 'synchronicity.' Like little pats on the back, they remind me that I am where I should be and doing what I am supposed to be doing. It's like my angel smiling down on me, saying, *'All is right with the world today'.*"

Anioch beamed.

Amanda looked at Jordan with a strange expression. She wanted to ask him something but couldn't find the right words. These were odd thoughts, especially from a man and a virtual stranger. A breeze rose behind her and a chill ran down her back. She clutched her sweater closer to her waist. But the breeze and energy felt pleasant. She sensed an aliveness in the moment. Her eyes, ears and entire body was awake, seeing, hearing, feeling. She could even taste the slight saltiness in the air. She was fully present in the moment. She slowed her thoughts and noticed that some part of her was waiting. She liked the feeling of being grounded in the moment and the sense of deeper energy flowing through her.

She smiled and Jordan again noticed how her eyes lit up. The breeze caught her hair and framed her face. *She is beautiful*, he thought. "You have the day off? I'm free until later this afternoon. Would you like to join me for a cup of coffee? There's a great coffee house up the beach. It has outside tables that overlook the ocean." Jordan noticed she'd fallen in step next to him.

"Sure, that would be nice. It's getting a little cold here. Well, at least for me. I'm parked just up there." Amanda pointed toward the highway and her car off in the distance.

"We can walk, if you don't mind. It will give me time to cool down. You caught me mid-run."

She shivered, and Jordan offered her his sweatshirt that he had wrapped around his waist.

Anioch watched as the two walked along this familiar stretch of beach. He mused how connected Jordan's life seemed to the ocean. Important events always seemed to find this shore. He followed along, feeling the exchange of energy.

The angel tried to tune into Amanda's Guiding Spirit. He knew it was there; he could sense her presence. But it remained guarded and tentative. Anioch did not connect often with Angelic Beings other than Charlene's, Daniel's or Anne Marie's. He remained true to his divine task: focused and centered on Jordan. He remember how he had interacted briefly with the Higher Beings on that momentous day that now seemed an eternity past. In that moment he relearned how petition and requests worked both in the material and angelic realms. He was sure that his own requests and faith in Divine Response had given him strength during difficult times with his Divine Mission.

As Anioch contemplated and prayed for Amanda and her angel, he noticed briefly the opaque appearance of Amanda's angelic guide. He bowed and focused his attention, noticing that she was a magnificent creature, beautiful in outline, fairly glowing. But while still a Being of Divine Light, Anioch sensed a heaviness about her that was foreign. It was as if her vibration had been lowered, pulsing just above the denser earthly plane.

The angel connected with Anioch; she bowed in acknowledgment to his Higher Spirit. It both awed and startled him. While she was clearly made of Angelic beauty and grace, she reached out her wing in a gesture of request. She needed to be touched by a Being connected to Source. In that moment, Anioch understood that the woman's disconnection from Spirit had drained her and her angel and further isolated her from Source Energy. *You and your child have been isolated. Come join us. Blessings to you, my beloved sister.*

In a brief instance of awareness, Anioch wondered how he had looked and if he had vibrated at an even lower level on that fateful day here on these shores. He shuddered with the thought. Anioch blazed brightly for this angel, and bowed as her wing extended to touch his aura. In the fleeting passing of earth time, they touched and illuminated the space with sparks. There was an audible crack like electricity passing. The two angels swirled in a blaze of light.

Jordan noticed that Amanda had grown quiet. She almost stood still, hesitating in the sand. Another visible shiver passed through her. The breeze picked up. There was a strange rise of wind, sea, and spray, as if matter was set in motion in a choreographed dance. Something had changed. He felt it in his body and he knew it in his soul. *Maybe a storm is coming.*

Amanda shifted and smiled shyly. "It's something. There's a raw power here. Somehow the pure expansiveness of the ocean wakes me up. It makes me feel small but also like I'm part of this big open world. I forgot how much I love spending time on the beach. I used to come here all the time when I was in high school. I haven't come since I got sick. It is so big and powerful. It moves me." Amanda was surprised by her openness. Her inner voice raged at her to step back from the shore, to not get pulled in.

She stayed still. It seemed she could not leave the spot. Jordan watched. He felt something pass in the air, and again wondered if a thunderstorm was approaching. His senses felt heightened and he was alert, awake and fully present. "Yeah, me too. I don't think I could ever live far from here. I need the space. I need the power, the majesty. I get centered here. I find myself, my soul here." Jordan spoke his truths without hesitation.

Amanda listened and was touched. This was a different language. She felt her heart open. She let the words wash over her. This type of honesty was not something she was used to hearing. This young man, former surfer, student, maybe friend was very different than anyone she had ever met. She smiled. The sense of pause and waiting stayed with her and it felt right. The childhood notion of waiting for a gift from

Santa or a secret friend flashed in her mind. She looked at Jordan and slightly bowed. She felt a warmth surround her and a pull of energy drawing her in. She moved closer to Jordan who offered his arm. They walked along the shore with the waves pounding the sand, the sun dancing behind the clouds and two angels connected in an arc of brilliant dazzling light.

CHAPTER 23

Jordan and Amanda continued their walk to the beachfront café. A few people stood in line waiting for steaming mugs of milk and coffee. The smell was rich and enticing. Amanda felt content and silently gave herself permission to be happy. She eyed the pastry counter and ordered a nonfat latte and a Greek yogurt. Jordan ordered a double espresso with a breakfast sandwich on sourdough.

They took their food to an outside table under a heater. From the raised patio, they had a view of the expansive coast with the cresting waves and dotted surfers bouncing out beyond the wave line. Gulls squawked in the distance. Amanda let her heart open.

Their conversation flowed easily and Amanda felt her defenses falling. She found herself slowly opening up and laughing at Jordan's stories. She pushed aside the small voice that tried to distract her, willing herself instead to relish the moment.

Time passed quickly. With food and drink finished, Jordan checked his phone. "Sorry, I think I've lost track of time. I've got a little bit of homework left."

Amanda took the cue, smiled and set her napkin on the table. "I should be going, too. I've got some errands to run." Even though she had no real plans she didn't want to overstay. The small inner voice moved to judgment. *He's being kind. Just stop being silly. He's travelled the world and you've barely been out of state. Get real.*

Jordan grabbed the check and went to the counter to pay.

"Hey, I've got this," she said, following behind him.

"Next time." He winked as he handed the server his card.

Next time, a less familiar voice repeated. This one was softer and gentler. Amanda sighed and smiled at him.

Jordan walked Amanda to her car. As Amanda fumbled for her keys, he casually asked, "Hey, I'm going to a concert here in town Friday night with a few friends." Stunned, Amanda stopped and looked up as he continued, "It's pretty casual, just a local band, but it should be fun. I'd love for you to come."

Amanda didn't answer right away. Her mind raced as a choir of half-formed words rushed at her. Her hand instinctively found the keys she'd been searching for and unlocked the car.

Jordan reached over and opened the door for her.

She stood awkwardly halfway into the opened car door. *Oh God, is he asking me out on a date?* Her stomach tightened. She'd avoided dating, going out, or whatever the word was. She had set herself up for too many hurts in the past and chose instead to avoid the eventual heartbreak by creating her now comfortable yet insular world. That was how she kept the pain away.

You like this life, Amanda. The voice that spoke the loudest grabbed her attention. Amanda turned toward Jordan and silently demanded it to be quiet. She was drawn to this man. When they were together she felt safe and somehow warm and alive. She heard a faint echo of Dr. Blair's voice reassuring her, *"There's a whole life out there waiting for you, Amanda. It's up to you to open yourself to it. It might be messy but it's real."*

Jordan watched and noticed her hesitation. Something told him to be patient. He knew in his heart that this chance encounter was meant to be. He sensed that she carried a lot of pain and hurt. *No pressure here,* he silently encouraged.

Jordan let go of the door, not wanting to make Amanda uncomfortable. He simply wanted to offer his authentic self and to just be present. As he grew deeper and let go of the past distractions and false narratives, he was more comfortable just being himself.

Conversations with this woman were easy. He felt as if the words flowed from him without filtering. He noticed a lightness when they spoke as if he were in a different space. In some way it was similar to his connection to Anne Marie, suspended, tapping into her energy and listening with deep attention. But here the roles seemed reversed. He recalled the old adage: when the student is ready, the teacher will come. Right behind that thought, a new refrain popped up. *"We teach what we are meant to learn."* Jordan held on to the thought knowing there was a truth for him.

He began to turn and was ready to say his goodbyes. *No need to push.*

"Yeah sure, that would be great," Amanda finally chimed in. "I work Friday until closing but I should be out of the store by 9:30. Is that too late?"

"No, that's perfect. Do you want me to pick you up?"

Amanda's mind immediately jumped back into a race of wild thoughts. *Don't let him in!* She invited only a few people over to her apartment. Something cold gripped her and hissed, *Guard your space, Amanda. You've fought too hard for this freedom.* The voice was shrill and angry. Amanda froze. Again, the softer voice whispered to her, *Loneliness isn't freedom.*

Amanda swallowed hard. She held Jordan's gaze. His eyes were calm and kind.

She tried to speak nonchalantly. "No, it'll be late. I'll meet you there, is that okay?"

Jordan sensed a darkness as if something was pushing him away, and didn't press the issue. A quick thought, almost a prayer, came to mind. *Make me an instrument.* He let the energy go. Jordan was learning that if he stayed open as a channel of Divine Love, then all would be in balance.

"Sure. It's on Fifth and Waterfront—The Golden Bear. It looks like an old dive bar. Well... it is an old dive bar, but it's great. I'll wait for you outside." With that he backed away when Amanda grabbed for the door.

She looked at him and forced a smile.

Jordan waved as she pulled away.

Heading back toward the pier, Jordan realized something had happened. He had touched a nerve. In a moment, the light sense of positive energy disappeared. The clouds hid the sun and the wind blew colder. He put on his sweatshirt. *Curious,* he thought.

Anioch stayed beside his child. *Curious, indeed.* The angel felt a surge of protective energy release. He prayed for his child. *This is a troubled woman.* As he flew above the damp shoreline, he wondered if maybe Jordan should just move on. But he knew his child wouldn't let go. He too felt a connection, something bigger at play.

He thought of his own interaction within the angelic realm. This woman had a loving Guide reaching out for help. Anioch knew deep down that indeed both he and Jordan were being called.

As the angel flew along the familiar shore, he found humor in the situation. *It is I who must learn here.* In that moment, Anioch understood and he let go. It was not his place to judge or interfere. He didn't need another lesson.

So be it, he thought. He would stay close and guard. "God's will has no why," he sang and the heavens echoed in response.

As Jordan walked home, he wondered what, if any, plan was at play. He quietly prayed for wisdom and discernment to know how far ... or when to let go. Perhaps he was but a vessel there to serve some small purpose in Amanda's life, to be a friend, to listen or offer a piece of wisdom or a hug. Jordan figured there was little more he could do.

He thought again of St. Francis' prayer, "O Divine Master, grant that I may not so much seek to be consoled as to console; to be understood as to understand; to be loved as to love." Jordan turned the curve onto the open beach and raced toward the pier.

Amanda decided to close the shop early. Few people ventured in from the storm and she let the sales clerk go home early. She sorted and straightened everything, leaving the accounting for last.

She looked at the time. It was still early. She was excited but nervous about the concert. She liked Jordan yet a knot of anxiety gripped her chest. She wondered what his friends might be like. Mingling and making small talk weren't her favorite things. Since that morning at the café, Amanda heard the slow rising voices in her head. Desperately she tried to tune them out. She knew these voices. They gave form to her unnamed fears.

Sometimes they sounded like her mother, sugar-coated but at the core cold and stern, judging. *"Oh my, look at that... give it to me... I guess I will have to do that one myself. You can't seem to get it right."* Amanda felt the pain of the little girl as the words cut into her adult body.

From those ancient voices she wore the labels and scars of her childhood—"forgetful," "selfish," "slow," "careless." As the words cut, she shrank, wishing to make herself invisible. She hid in the shadows.

Yet even now the voices still found her. She heard her grandfather's voice, detached and void of feeling, telling her every detail of what was wrong or bad and never good enough.. *"You'll never amount to anything if you don't get your head out of the clouds. Pay attention, child!"* She felt the shame still raw. The pain of humiliation presented like an open wound.

Her aunt's voice joined the choir, shrill and demanding, always needing something from her. *"Oh Mandy, come sit with your auntie. We've got another mess on our hands."*

Amanda tried to push the voices away. As the storm pounded against the windows, she turned the music up. *There's no "we" here,* she answered to that memory. Alone in the store she fought the phantom voices.

The ancient and relentless choir was a mixture of nameless and faceless people from her past: teachers, her mother's many boyfriends, her own boyfriends, would-be friends... all somehow hurt her deeply with their words, actions, inactions, and rejections. The competing voices vied for her attention. They had been her constant companion for years.

Now in the silence of the small shop, she remembered the old story Dr. Blair had told her about the wolves... *"The one you feed is the one you give the power."* She pushed aside the old voices of shame and unworthiness and stood firm. *I'm not going to retreat. I deserve to be happy. I'm not feeding this pack of wolves.* She trusted Jordan and for now that was enough.

Amanda turned to her task. She emptied the register and began to add up the day's receipts. Music filtered throughout the store. Music was always an entry point for her to move to higher ground. Jordan was different. He listened. He met her gaze and held it with honesty and compassion. He didn't say hurtful words. She felt safe with him. But the old voices rattled on, *"You silly child, you can't do that. Get your head out of the clouds."*

By the time Amanda turned off the lights and closed the metal gates, she was near emotional exhaustion. *Those voices don't serve me.* Amanda stayed with the dialogue feeling the strength flow in. *I am no longer defined by my past.* She affirmed, *I have control of my life.* Leaning into the feelings the words created, she felt free. She felt strong. She felt calm. From that place of emerging balance, she added a new thought... *Control does not mean isolation.*

Slowly she sucked in air, methodically letting it out. Release, release. Relax, relax. It's a concert. I can sit back and listen to the music. It's okay. No one knows me. They don't expect anything. I am free to be myself. And that's good enough. I am good enough.

As Amanda turned on her car, she called Jordan to say that she was on her way. She could hear the cacophony of voices and music in the background. *This will be fun.* She felt herself loosening up. *Fun.* A new word she wanted to embrace.

Amanda drove in the pounding rain to Fifth Street and Waterfront. The marquis announced the show. She'd never heard of the group. Running to the door, she found Jordan standing off in a corner. He grabbed her with calm assurance and brought her in from the rain. He felt warm and welcoming. His smile made her heart race. She was immediately relieved. She was glad she hadn't given in to her fears.

The choir of voices faded as the clamor from the club, sounds of life, laughter and happiness filtered in and wrapped Amanda in an energy of joy. She breathed in deeply and felt relief. *I am enough,* she silently repeated. She took Jordan's hand and moved through the tables filled with smiling, laughing people. And in that moment her Guide blazed with a new light. Amanda smiled and let herself be happy.

CHAPTER 24

As the concert drew to a close, Jordan noticed that Amanda had relaxed and seemed to be having fun. During one of the sets, she'd moved over to an open space and danced with a small group. She moved with the ease and grace of a dancer. Jordan went to the end of the table where she was smiling and chatting with his friends. He heard her laugh and it made him feel happy. He smiled at her and again was struck by her simple beauty. *I think she is having fun.* He was grateful that his friends had been sensitive to her initial reserve and gently brought her into the conversation. He felt blessed to have found true friends.

The music had been good, the food delicious as always, and the atmosphere warm. Jordan noticed that Amanda ate very little, mostly nibbling on raw vegetables and sipping mineral water. She was very thin but didn't seem to want to eat the wonderful assortment of pastas, breads and salads the rest of the group shared. *I wonder what her story is. She said she was sick.* He let the thought go. Right now it didn't matter.

"So, Amanda, what do you think of our little dive bar?" Jordan was holding the umbrella and her raincoat.

"I think your dive bar is quite lovely. Thank you for inviting me. It was wonderful." Her face was dazzling and her voice light. Her cheeks were pink and her hair flowing. She stepped into her coat. She hugged a few of her new friends goodbye. She turned to Jordan and hugged him, too. He chuckled.

"That's for being patient with me." Jordan held her and breathed in the smells of perfume and sweat. It was nice. He let go and smiled. Amanda followed the group toward the door. Jordan gently took her arm and led her through the exiting cars. It had stopped raining but it was still drizzling and there was a cold biting breeze. She pressed herself close to him to stay under his umbrella.

He wished he could drive her home, but knew he shouldn't push.

Amanda looked up to him, ready to say goodnight. Instead her blue-grey eyes filled with tears, and she looked away. She physically moved away and in a small hushed voice whispered, "There I go, making a fool of myself. I'm sorry, Jordan."

He set the umbrella down and gently took her hands and answered in a calm assuring voice, "Please Amanda, don't ever apologize for being real."

His words were kind. She heard them and they touched her. There was no reproach, no laughter, no turning away. She had lived her whole life apologizing for every personality trait. She had never been bright enough, fast enough, good enough, pretty enough, loud enough; and she always apologized. She even apologized for apologizing.

"Thank you. Thank you for that, for being so kind. I don't know why I am feeling like this. I guess this whole evening has been really different for me. Your friends were sweet and made me feel so welcome. I really struggled with the idea of coming out. But I am so glad that I did." She paused. Jordan stayed in the silence gently stroking her hands. She looked down. He waited. "I don't want this to sound weird but, Jordan, I haven't met anyone like you before." Amanda spoke quietly, almost in a whisper. "I don't want to scare you or make this too heavy or more than it is, but I feel like you are somehow letting me take back some part of my life. Even just tonight, made me realize I can have fun. It's like I am giving myself permission to have fun. I really can't thank you enough for that."

The rain began again. It beat down on them. Jordan left the umbrella on the car. He didn't care. It felt good. He felt alive. He took her head in his hands and looked into her eyes brimming with tears. There was pain there, he had seen it before, but now he saw something else—a flicker—and he wondered if it was a spark of hope. She let a faint smile cross her lips. They stood in the pouring rain neither wanting to move. He felt her close by, slowly relaxing into him.

In slow motion, his lips moved toward hers. She didn't pull away. Her eyes fluttered closed. Then he kissed her, softly and gently.

She didn't recoil, but flowed with the kiss. They became part of the moment, feeling the wind, the rain and the race of electricity that passed between them.

Anioch watched. He had been there during countless kisses. He wasn't impressed by this form of physical communication. The Creator, in infinite wisdom had designed human beings with the physical need to express love. But what Anioch had seen about human physical love up to now seemed shallow and wholly devoid of the essence of Love.

Anioch tried not to be judgmental and remain faithful to the Angelic code to serve and guide but decided long ago that this was one of the Divine mysteries he simply would leave as a mystery.

Yet the young angel sensed something different. He turned and watched. In this kiss, the touch and energy were different. There was tenderness, and something beyond mere physical communication, a connection of heart and soul. He felt the power. He noticed the Angelic Being beside Amanda rise and glow.

In that moment the angel knew Jordan had touched Amanda's spirit. Anioch marveled. Was this a glimpse of the real power of love? Love: Restorative, transformative, life-giving and healing. He pondered. Could it be that there were levels of love and here he glimpsed an energy not unlike Pure Divine Love? He wondered at the mystery and was humbled and awed.

PART THREE

CHAPTER 25

And so began the newest chapter in the lives of Jordan Collingsworth and Amanda Martin. Two souls who had cried out in desperation as they lay broken and spent were somehow brought together. A relationship based upon honesty, openness, hope and grace blossomed.

Jordan sensed that he could speak openly to her, and she listened. She really listened, with her whole mind and body, open and present. Maybe only someone who had lost all hope—who had faced stepping into that great void—could understand what his heart was expressing. She listened with her heart.

Amanda continued her sessions with Dr. Blair, which mirrored the deepening of her relationship with Jordan. They discovered a thread which had been woven within each part of her story: Fear. It was the one constant that continued to show up in all of its masked and unmasked power.

Slowly she came to recognize that at every turn her response to recoil was rooted in some deep and raw form of fear. It would appear, boldly grabbing her whole being. Subtly shifting her breath or posture. A constant presence. It held her.

"I don't know, Dr. Blair. I just can't face it."

"You can't, or you won't?" he challenged.

"Does it really matter?" The words were hard and cold and Amanda knew what would come next.

"I don't know, Amanda. *Does* it matter?"

So she would sit in the silence. The invisible thread of fear tying it back, always back, to inaction. But a small voice would whisper to her, *"Yes, yes. It really does matter."* In that deep place, Amanda was beginning to discover that she did care. Running was no longer an option.

In truth she had run for so long, but had never really gotten away. It was only when she began to identify what she was running from that she realized it would always follow her... because it was inside of her. The fear was always there and would resurface. Each time, somehow more powerful. The thread pulled the weave tighter. It wove a destructive tapestry. It gripped and froze her, leaving her mind in a swirling pool of bottomless anguish.

"Yeah, it matters. I don't want to define my life anymore by what I can't or won't do." Amanda felt a shift in her body as she spoke the words. Something stirred and she noticed the tug.

"Okay, so what is it you want to do?"

There it was: the big question. Caught between the inhale and exhale, it rose and hung in that breathless space. The simple yet deep question grabbed her soul.

"I want to live a full life," Amanda breathed out the words in a gasp.

"A full life," Dr. Blair repeated as if rolling an errant pebble in a swirling tide. "I wonder, Amanda, what a full life looks like."

There it was again, a question laying bare the response. Dig deeper, it implored. Reach into the swirling tide and grab that pebble before the water recedes and takes it back.

"Oh, wow. I guess it would look rich. Full of emotions and color. Exciting but somehow calm. There would be magic, but something very real at the same time. Deep yet also light, free. A messy but joyful blur. I know I'm not making sense."

"Really? Listen to the complexity of what you are saying."

Amanda paused. The words had just flowed out of her as if some deep hidden spring had been tapped. She thought about her structured and organized life. She had purposefully brought control into every aspect, yet when she described a full life it came out as one open to infinite possibilities. It sounded like near chaos... but a joyous vibrant chaos! Amanda felt her pulse quicken.

"What do you feel when you describe this full life?" Dr. Blair asked.

Amanda closed her eyes. She was an expert at controlling her body but she wanted to give herself permission to let her body speak. "I feel a different energy. A good energy. I feel sort of excited. Curious. I guess maybe you could call it passion."

"Passion," Dr. Blair repeated.

It sounded foreign. Amanda had never associated with that word. Her inner voice affirmed, *Yes, passion. Passion.* But some part of her began to fill in the space arguing, *You can't control passion. Passion will control you.* Amanda breathed. It was all foreign. But it felt good.

Dr. Blair watched Amanda and quietly repeated, "Passion. That's good. How does that sound? So a full life has passion?" It was more a statement than a question.

"Yeah, it does sound good. It would, right? I mean a life without passion is just kind of grey. My life is grey. It's covered in a fog and the lines are blurred. I want blue. I want to turn my life into bright blue." Amanda was gazing past the room.

"That's interesting. How can you do that now? How do you shift a little of that grey to blue?" The doctor's tone was soft and disarming in its offhanded manner.

"Hmm, maybe I can begin to let go of the control. Relax a little. I wonder if I'm actually squeezing the color out."

"What happens if you don't control or you don't squeeze so hard?"

There it was: the simple statement digging below the flesh to extract the hidden gem.

"I'm afraid to let go because I can hear those old voices. The words are there, playing over and over. I have to control them. I have to shut them off. I have to shut them out. They are always there." Amanda began to fidget.

"They're just thoughts, Amanda. Just words. What power are you giving them?"

"Power?" Amanda stopped, lost in the question. Was she giving the voices power? She tried to bury them but she reacted the same anyway. Freeze and recoil.

"Yes, what power are you giving them? What are they telling you to do? And what are you doing?"

Amanda's eyes closed. "I give them power over my action. Power over my feelings. Power over my own thoughts. I am not squeezing. I am giving up and letting the voices suck me into that world of grey. I've given them the power to color my world. My full life is reduced by them. I am listening to voices that aren't even there." She opened her eyes and finished, "They scream inside my head and tell me I can't."

"Who is saying you can't?" Dr. Blair asked.

Amanda inhaled slowly. She knew these voices. They had been her constant companions. She fought them by never facing them. That was how she gave them power. But now an energy filled the room. She closed her eyes once more and heard a new voice: *"Step into the question. There is a healing stream. Rest in the waters. You can listen without surrendering. Face the voices. Face the fear."*

"Who is saying you can't?" Dr. Blair repeated.

"I am. I say I can't." She opened her eyes. Dr. Blair's expression flickered. He bowed slightly. She held his gaze. "I say I can't." She repeated the phrase. "But I want to say, 'I can'. I want to stop living in grey. I want to dance. I want to sing. I have a song—I know I do. I can hear it when I quiet the voices and give myself a little space. But I'm afraid to sing it." Amanda began to softly weep.

The singular moment of speaking her truth, of facing the voices and the fear washed away. She had been brave. She was brave.

At her most vulnerable she was ultimately her strongest.

"So if you are the one saying 'I can't,' but you also have a small inner voice begging you to reach for color, passion and life... to dance, sing and be joyful.... which voice will you follow? Which voice is real?"

"They are both real. They are both very real."

"Yes, they are. But you get to choose which one you listen to. Our thoughts and what we put our attention on is always a choice. Which one do you feed? Which one do you take and move beyond a whisper or a howl to turn into something real?"

"I guess I usually pay attention to the one that is screaming the loudest."

"You alone are choosing to give it that power. Is it really about the volume, Amanda? Which voice will you listen to, the small faint whisper that is new or the old blaring one that you know by heart?"

"I want to listen to my voice. I want my life to be narrated by my own voice. I want to sing my song with my own voice." Amanda smiled. It was barely a smile but she felt her heart leap.

"Okay, and what does that voice say? Who does that voice speak for?" Dr. Blair was leading her in a stream of consciousness, unblocked and unfiltered.

"I speak for myself. But you know the other voices speak for me, too. They are giving voice to the frightened version of me."

"Who is the frightened you? Who is she?"

Once again two simple questions plunged Amanda deeper. There wasn't a simple answer.

"She's me. She's the little girl. She's the one who learned not to speak out. She's the one who couldn't say the truth, her truth. She's the one who ran away and hid even if she had to stay put. She's the one who would close her eyes and pray to just disappear. She's the one who learned that to stop the hurt you had to stop feeling, so she hid her heart. She hid it so no one could hurt her anymore. She buried it so deep she isn't even sure now where it really is. She's the one who believed that if she slid behind the curtain no one would see her. If she turned to grey, she could be like a shadow. It was safe in the shadow, unnoticed. But she could still hear the voices even when she hid. She could still hear them. They screamed at her. They said hurtful things in the silence: *No one ever wanted you. No one ever loved you. You don't matter because no one will ever love you.*" Amanda broke down into soft sobs that overtook her small body. The floodgates were open and she was awash in a sea of deep emotion.

Dr. Blair paused and let the silence sit.

"Yes, I know," he eventually said. "I know. Those other voices speak. But I'm not sure they're speaking for you, Amanda. They are shouting at the little girl to scare her, to keep her in the shadows, hidden and grey. They are afraid because they know that if that little girl ever faced them, they would lose their power. So they don't want a conversation. They just want to shout."

Silence again filled the room. Amanda looked up and wiped her eyes.

Dr. Blair asked one final question. "If you could speak to that little girl, Amanda, what would you say?"

The dark and heavy fear she had carried with her now shifted. Amanda sat up tall in her seat and announced, "I would tell her not to listen to them."

CHAPTER 26

Amanda clutched a soft leather-bound journal. As she settled into the comfortable chair, she opened the notebook, ready to share. Dr. Blair leaned forward in a welcoming pose. "I sense some excitement here. Is there a little less grey in your world?"

Amanda smiled and gave him a slight nod. "Jordan has been helping me with these meditations and something just changed. I can feel it. I started listening to the voices and thought of myself not as the little girl but as the grown-up who needed to speak for her. The writing just flowed."

"What do you think shifted?"

"Funny, but after I peeled back all of the sadness and trappings of her as a victim, I could see her instead as the bright beautiful girl. I found myself opening up to her. I didn't feel afraid for her anymore. I began to feel love. There was a kind of magic and she started to come out of the shadow. I can't really explain it, but we were connected."

Dr. Blair listened to the tale of transformation, an almost rebirth. "As you see this young girl come into light and life, are there any voices?"

"Yes, but funny thing is... the more understanding I offer her, the more love I wrap her in, the less dream-like she becomes. It seems that as I open my heart to her, she becomes more real. It feels like as she takes on this stronger personality, a part of me is integrating with her. Does that even make sense?" Amanda paused as if waiting for some sort of validation.

"I think the question is... does this make sense to you?" Dr. Blair sat perfectly still while his eyes danced.

"Yes, it does. As I listen to the little girl, her voice is stronger. And when that gets stronger, I can hear my own voice louder. It's like, as I give her the freedom to come forward, to express, and I see her as a lovely child, I am finding some part of myself and finding my more authentic voice. I am speaking for her."

"And as you speak for her, what are you saying?"

Amanda sat in silence and closed her eyes. "She is saying, 'Love me.' And I am saying to her, 'I love you and always have. Come into the light and be with me'."

Dr. Blair leaned forward, elbows on his knees. "And how do you feel?"

"How do I feel?" Amanda repeated the question. "Well, I guess I feel a sense of confidence. Maybe I'm less timid. Something in me feels more solid, like I am a little more rooted or grounded." Amanda stopped as if searching for the words. "Does that make sense?"

Dr. Blair smiled. "Again, does that make sense to you? That's what matters. You make the meaning here."

Amanda shifted in her seat. "Yeah, I know. I guess my new phrase should be 'does that make sense?' instead of 'I'm sorry'." She let out a small nervous laugh.

"So what does that mean for you to feel more grounded?"

"Well that small child, she is there. She is here. She isn't hiding behind the curtain or trying to disappear. She is coming forward and being present. She is demanding her place. She is asking for love. She is more grounded." Amanda's voice grew stronger. "As she comes forward, some part of me feels more real and honest. It's weird.'

"Who is she?"

Amanda's eyes grew brighter. "She's that part of me that hid from life. Sometimes she still wants to hide, but the real me—the grown-up me—wants to embrace her and make her whole." Amanda's voice caught. "I want to make *me* whole."

"Do you know how to do that, to make yourself whole?"

"Like I said, as I hold her in love—just love her and honor her and forgive her—she gets brighter. And as she gets brighter, she delights me." Amanda's face was drawn in a radiant smile as tears welled in her eyes.

Dr. Blair softly whispered, "Go on..."

"You know, I think I have to really love her before anyone else can."

"That's wise, Amanda."

"You know what, I actually speak to her. I hope that's not crazy."

Soft lines framed Dr. Blair's face as a smile emerged. "No, there's nothing crazy about that. Integrating all the pieces of you into a happy, healthy whole is quite sane and wonderful."

Amanda let out a small chuckle. "Okay good, just checking. So hopefully it's okay, or wonderful that I named her."

"Really?" asked Dr. Blair. "What's her name?"

"Baby Blue," Amanda answered.

"Ah... a lighter shade of grey," he observed.

Amanda smiled. "Yes. Like I said, when I speak for her I feel myself getting lighter but somehow stronger. I like the voice. When I'm with her the old cruel voices seem to fade."

"That's powerful. Do you mind sharing what your voice is saying not for her but when you are together?"

"You asked me to journal. And I did. But I took the words and wrote a poem, then turned it into a song. I heard it before in very quiet moments, but now it's there and it's real. It says that my words—my song—is good and that I should share it. It tells me that I have worth." Amanda paused.

"So tell me how this poem or song makes you feel."

"There is something pure about the place when we are together. There is stillness but something deep inside calls to me and I feel like I should honor it. It's both from me but not. Does that make sense?"

"Yes, it does, Amanda. You feel like you should honor it. I am curious how you would do that."

"I've been asking myself the same question. My answer is nudging me. I've stayed very private and wrapped in my own space. Baby Blue demands me to step out from behind the curtain and shadow."

"Do you want to share it with me now?"

Amanda looked directly into his eyes. "My heart is telling me to do this even bigger. Does that even make sense?"

"If your heart is speaking to you, then stay open."

"So I was wondering if maybe I could share it with the group on Wednesday."

Dr. Blair smiled. "I think that is perfect."

Amanda studied the gentle man's face. His eyes were warm and generous and his lips always held a hint of a smile. She nodded in agreement and waited. She watched as he gracefully leaned back and folded his arms behind his head. *Here it comes,* she thought. *He's moving into his space.*

"Yes, I think that is perfect. When we allow ourselves to tap into that creative space, like you are doing when you are journaling, writing poems or songs, we clear away the clutter and allow a crack to open. In that tiny opening, the light can enter and shine. When we go into stillness, we can listen to that small but powerful inner voice that dwells in the silence. It is there that we find inspiration." Dr. Blair paused. Amanda listened.

"To be inspired. That's where the magic happens. The words comes from the Greek word *inspiritus*... to let Spirit in."

The kind doctor leaned forward. The brief lesson done, Amanda felt a flutter in her chest. *There's always a wise spirit guiding us when I'm here.*

Wednesday arrived and Amanda readied herself for the session. She felt a wave of excitement surround her. While there was a nervousness that fluttered below the surface, she reminded herself that Dr. Blair always created a safe space. The small group had built a community where each member knew they could speak openly of their struggles. They understood each other and from that place of recognition, they were able to offer empathy and insights.

As the evening had drawn closer, Amanda was surprised that she remained calm. *I have to face this fear.* She knew in her heart that this moment of sharing and vulnerability was important. She recognized that by standing alone in front of this beloved group she would take the first step to silence the older and deeper voices of her past that fed her fear. She promised herself this would be her first stand to reclaim her true voice.

Amanda arrived by herself. She'd chosen to drive alone, wanting the time to center herself. When she entered the room she noticed that most of the group was already present and engaged in lively banter. Dr. Blair greeted her with a warm hug. His eyes held an unspoken question. "I'm good. I can do this," she answered.

He gently squeezed her arm and lightly bowed his head to her.

Amanda noticed that Jordan was already seated. When he saw her enter, he got up to meet her and take the guitar case from her hands. They had spoken about this and Jordan had offered his love and support. As they hugged, Amanda felt a rush of gratitude for this loving man. *He gets me. He gives me support but also my space.* She smiled at him.

"You okay?" Jordan whispered.

"Yup, I'm good. I can do this." The words anchored Amanda to the moment and the task at hand.

Jordan moved back, putting the guitar aside. "You look beautiful. Your eyes are absolutely brilliant."

Amanda smiled and offered a simple "thank you" but her heart soared. Those words always took her momentarily back to her childhood. She pushed back on the tug of sadness that threatened. *I can do this,* she silently affirmed.

Anioch noticed that Amanda's angelic presence was illuminated and pulsating with a new vibrancy and energy. Something had activated her and she was alive and mirrored Amanda's new radiance. He bowed to her. *You too look beautiful, my dear friend.*

The angelic being gently opened her wings. In that act, Anioch saw the true magnificence and the full range of her beauty. In the core of his angelic being Anioch sensed a connection to this guide and pondered the possibility.

Thank you, my beloved. Let me now offer you my name as it appears we are indeed connected on the angelic and human plane. I am Yrandia. With that she bowed. Anioch's heart soared.

Dr. Blair opened the session with a visualization and meditation. Once completed, he looked to Amanda, again asking without speaking. She nodded.

"Okay, tonight we are going to do something a little different," he announced. "We've talked a lot about our thoughts, our beliefs and some of our underlying fears. We've explored our limiting belief patterns and how we allow them to enter into our consciousness and become our reality. We've talked about our emotions and how each thought and response is really a choice. Now tonight, Amanda is going to share something. She listened to her heart and wanted to share its message. Please open your hearts and surround Amanda with that energy. This is an act of courage and love."

Amanda shifted in her seat and held her guitar close. She closed her eyes and took a deep breath.

Anioch noticed that her angelic guide shifted position to be directly behind her. The angel opened her wings and wrapped them around the young woman. Beautiful rays of light enveloped Amanda in a soft cocoon. A deep and calm energy filled the room.

Amanda spoke with a soft but strong voice, "For many years I lived my life like an abandoned child, without someone to speak for me or to love me. I withdrew and sank into a world that was cold and grey. But in order to quiet the voices that told me I wasn't worthy or deserving of happiness or love, I had to find my own voice—my true voice. I had to find a way to speak up for that wounded and abandoned little girl. This is the song I wrote for her. It's called Baby Blue."

Closing her eyes, she began to softly strum the guitar. In a voice both beautiful and clear, she sang:

"Give the child voice. Speak for her. Standup for her. Love her.
Let her step out of the shadows and stand in her righteous space.
Beautiful, radiant, new. Come sing, Baby Blue.

Speak for your child. Feel her stirring within.
Give her attention. Let her in. Come to know her.
Her innocence. Her vulnerability. Her grace.
Beautiful, radiant, new. Come dance, Baby Blue.

She stirs as the quiet unsettling
In the space between the beat and the breath.
She is real. A presence. Quiet yet real. Honor her.
Beautiful, radiant, new. Come breathe, Baby Blue.

Honor her for all the memories she holds.
Release her for the joy and laughter she wanted to share.
Comfort her for the tears she silently shed.
Embrace her from that space deep within your being.
Beautiful, radiant, new. Come fly, Baby Blue.

Make peace with her. Love her. Forgive her.
Shine the light of your love on her.
Let her enter into the radiance of the
Peaceful spot of the Whole and Holy you.
Beautiful, radiant, new. Come rest, Baby Blue.

Come rest, Baby Blue.
Beautiful, radiant new. Come rest, Baby Blue.
Make me Whole and Holy. Make me new.
Welcome home, sweet child, my sweet dear Baby Blue."

Amanda opened her eyes. She glanced at Jordan who sat motionless, his eyes filled with tears. In fact no one in the group, including Dr. Blair, was moving.

Suddenly, caught in a collective wave of emotion, there was one communal breath as if they had been awakened. The group broke out in applause and a rush of joy filled the room.

Warmth and a rush of energy passed through Amanda. She had never felt so present, so fully alive and awake. Amanda bowed, acknowledging the outpouring of love. But there was something more, almost an act of sublime reverence to some unknown Presence of Grace.

Yrandia, her angel retreated, but in passing, returned the gesture.

In that moment, Anioch was filled with awe. Healing grace was at work. He sang his own song of praise, and was joined in angelic song by the majestic Being known as Yrandia.

CHAPTER 27

And so the journey continued for Amanda and Jordan—deprivation, denial, and destruction were slowly replaced by a deepening love that in its purest form was limitless and unconditional. Days turned into weeks which quickly passed into months. An azure sky stretched out in every direction. Wisps of white feathered clouds danced along the horizon. The sun blazed. Jordan and Amanda drove along the back canyons that cut west just beyond the Pacific Ocean. The terrain was rugged and the underbrush dry from the relentless summer sun.

Jordan leaned into the winding road, shifting effortlessly with the rolling hills. He lost himself in the mix of wind, speed, sun on his face, and the distinct smell of salt and dry shrub in the air. He felt alive. He glanced at Amanda who was looking off into the distance with a slight smile. *Life is good.* He down-shifted and eased into a deep curve.

The sound of the engine connecting with the road was suddenly pierced by the high staccato of Amanda's insulin pump. Jordan looked over to check. He felt the small grip of fear that always accompanied the mechanical alert. It spoke to both the highs and lows of Amanda's blood sugar levels.

Jordan was learning all he could about Type One Diabetes... he was often reminded of the distinction between the types. "You okay?"

Amanda had pulled out her pump and was punching in information. "Yeah, just going a little low," she said without looking up.

He heard the distinct downward scale of cascading notes that alerted them to an impending glucose crash.

Amanda opened her purse and popped a large tablet in her mouth. Her hands shook slightly.

"Do we need to stop and get something to eat?" Jordan asked, checking the GPS to see how far they were from the next exit.

"No, I'm fine now," she responded, her voice distant and thin. "I'm not that low." She leaned her head back and closed her eyes.

"You didn't eat much for lunch." Jordan felt the knot in his chest. He knew from past experience this was a conversation that had the potential for going off track. *Don't push. She hates when I push her.* "I've got some trail mix in my backpack."

Amanda didn't open her eyes. "I'm fine," she replied flatly. "The glucose will kick in soon. Thanks, but I am not hungry."

"If we waited until you were hungry, you would only eat once a day." *Dammit! I pushed.*

Amanda sat up abruptly and turned toward him. Her eyes were cold. "I said I am not hungry. I know what I need to do." Her voice became sharp. "Give me a little credit. I've been dealing with this disease since I was eleven years old."

"I'm sorry. It's just that it scares me to know what could happen if you don't take care of yourself." Jordan stopped. *Lighten up, man!*

"I am trying to take care of myself. I am eating healthy. I know the carb counts and portion size of everything. I learned a long time ago I can't eat whatever I want. People have no idea how hard this stupid thing is."

Jordan kept driving. He wanted to understand. He really did. *Just keep your mouth shut.*

"I'm not implying anything. I know you are smart. I can't even imagine what it's like. It hurts me to see you dealing with this. I just want to support you."

Jordan moved the car to the right lane and took the southbound exit.

"Where are we going?" Amanda asked. "I said I was fine. Let's just go for our drive." Her voice filled with frustration.

She's annoyed now. "Let's just pull off. We can go talk somewhere. We can take our drive later."

"I really don't want to talk. At least not about this." Her words were short. The tension punched through.

Amanda pulled out her meter and loaded it. She adeptly pricked her finger and touched the strip. The meter flashed her blood sugar number. "See? I'm going up. I told you I'm fine."

"That's good. But I feel like we need to talk. I mean really talk. It's like whenever something comes up about your health we just talk past each other. I want to understand you, and I need to let you know what I'm feeling." Jordan saw a roadway diner advertising cold beer and sandwiches. It had outdoor tables. "We can grab an iced tea and just talk. Please."

Amanda sighed and nodded as she forced a smile.

They sat under a bright red umbrella sipping tea with a basket of vegetables, chili-seasoned jicama and a side of baked tortilla strips along with pico and guacamole. Jordan remained quiet, sensing the undercurrent of tension.

They stared at the food. Neither wanted to eat.

Jordan finally broke the silence. "Amanda love, please don't be angry with me. I know you've been hurt. I know others have let you down. But I'm not one of those people. I love you. I get nervous when I think about something happening to you. And so I try to step in... and in my own dumb way I'm trying to help. I know you think I'm being pushy or judging. I'm not. I guess somehow I just want to make it go away."

Amanda was staring down at the uneaten basket of tortilla strips.

He gently raised her chin. "Please don't shut me out. I want to be part of your life. *All of it.* I know I sound like some sort of pushy jerk telling you to eat. I don't mean to do that. It's just my worry talking." Jordan felt an anxious pull in his gut. He acknowledged it and moved the negative thoughts away.

Amanda looked into his eyes. She saw genuine worry and something else. *Love?* Her heart softened and the knot of frustration loosened. "I know that. I really do. But when we start talking about diabetes or my eating patterns, stuff about my body, I just get triggered. I mean, it's been a struggle for a long time. It's not just about highs and lows. There is so much more wrapped up in this. I've told you about the voices and all the people who shouted at me or ignored me... Well, even the damn diabetes has a voice. It's a horrifying choir and it all g-g-gets j-jumbled and m-makes me freeze." Her voice was breaking.

"I'm sorry 'Manda, I didn't mean to stir all of that up. Please don't think I'm shouting at you or controlling you. Please don't make me another voice in your head... Unless I can be the voice of love."

"Oh Jordan, my sweet. You aren't one of them. Deep down, I know that. I was dealt a kind of crappy hand, but I'm coping with it. Dr. Blair talks about acceptance. I'm kind of more resigned. I've been giving myself shots since I was a kid so I had to grow up really fast. I've counted carbs for as long as I can remember. I had to schedule and measure everything. Even when I was a kid I knew that eating ten potato chips meant a shot. So I chose not to eat potato chips."

Amanda moved away, sliding her chair to the side. She began to pick at the now cold chips, slowly crumbling one into little pieces on her napkin. She pushed the napkin aside and looked off into the distance. As she slowly turned back toward Jordan she let out a deep sigh. She dropped her voice while she shifted her gaze directly at him. "But it really did define me for a long time. I guess it still does, sort of. It led me down a destructive path, too. I can still hear my mom and aunt telling people, 'She's diabetic,' *like I was the disease*. At least that's what I heard."

❦

Jordan sat perfectly still, his hands clenched in small fists underneath the table. He breathed deeply, feeling the tension in his jaw. He willed his hands to unclench. He swallowed hard, recognizing the rise of emotion in his stomach. It was anger boiling to erupt in rage. Anger, not so much at the reality of the disease or for the moment but instead for the past responses by adults who could have protected the little girl. He leaned forward and held Amanda's gaze. Then he took a sip of the warm tea to wash away the frustration and helplessness.

He took another deep breath and willed his voice to be gentle. "I wish I could make all those bad memories fade away. There are so many wonderful things that define you." Jordan's heart felt heavy. He scolded himself for not listening to his own advice. *No, I was right. We need to talk about this. It's important and it isn't going to go away.* A quick thought of gratitude recognized they were now having the conversation and it was unfolding as it needed to.

"I know all of that in my head," Amanda said. "But I didn't know it then. I wanted to be like every other kid. But I was the one who had to leave class and go to the nurse's office when my blood sugars would crash. And I'd hear the other kids whisper and call me 'the sick girl'. I couldn't even eat birthday cake at a party." Amanda instinctively drew her arms close across her chest. Her right hand cupped and covered the small sensor taped to her forearm.

"But it was worse than that. My mom couldn't cope. She had her own troubles and I was one more reason for her to feel sorry for herself. Her moods would last for days or weeks. She was consumed by demons. I can see that now. But I didn't know any of that. I am trying to give myself some space now and see her as a person, not just my mom. She lived in her own self-created hell. She couldn't even see me, much less care for me. Kind of funny since I was the little girl trying to disappear."

Jordan shifted in his chair. He felt the sting of tears and looked away. He pushed his chair aside and took off his sunglasses as if checking for smudges. He grabbed a napkin and absently wiped them. Then he took another sip of pungent tea, pushing down the knot in his throat. *Be present, man.*

"But it wasn't always all bad," Amanda continued. "Sometimes she'd take me to the movies or to the park and we'd play. For that moment, I felt normal. But it never lasted. She'd sink back into her dark place. Sometimes she couldn't even get out of bed."

Jordan listened, knowing Amanda needed to tell her story. He knew the power in letting that story out. Anne Marie had offered him that gift of presence and he felt honored and grateful he could do the same for the woman he loved.

"You know," Amanda said, "I remember looking at my mom and thinking she was beautiful. She had been a dancer and still moved with such grace even when she was totally beaten down by life. I wanted to be like her. In my little girl's fantasy world, I thought we just needed a magical person to swoop in and see how beautiful and graceful she was and take us away. I'd wrap myself in her scarves and breathe in the smell of her perfume and lose myself in the music. That was the magic time when I could escape the nightmares." Amanda stared off, letting the words tumble out.

"I don't know what broke her. But she was drowning in booze and who knows what else. I'm trying to see her as a real person but it's hard. I get caught up in the hurt and the resentment. Sometimes I had to beg her to get my medical supplies. I felt guilty like I was making her life bad. I hated the disease, Jordan." Amanda struggled with her words. "But what I really hated was her... and myself."

Jordan moved close and wrapped his arms around Amanda.

Her shoulders shook. Her words came in short bursts as she tried to control the sobs. "Over time it got worse... I hated the shots and found that if I didn't give myself insulin and let my sugars go high... I could lose weight. Somehow I thought if I was thin, I'd be cool." There was a long pause as Amanda composed herself. "I thought I'd be beautiful." Silence again wrapped around the couple.

Jordan stroked Amanda's hair and softly whispered, "Oh baby, you are so beautiful. Inside and out. Everything about you is beautiful. Don't ever doubt that."

Amanda slowly pulled herself together and sat up. Her eyes burned bright and a look of resolve settled over her. "But I know now it wasn't about being thin. It wasn't about being beautiful or accepted. And it wasn't about food." She paused. "I think the food was a replacement for love. And I needed to show that I didn't need that either."

Jordan felt the words sink in. He flinched. "I don't ever want you to think I am trying to control any part of your life. I'm here to be your biggest supporter."

"And I love you for that," she said. "I just need to work through this. Things got really bad. Between the anorexia and high blood sugars I was on a dangerous path with lows and highs that threw me into ketoacidosis." She stopped again and her voice dropped to a near whisper. She looked down at her folded hands. "At some level I didn't care. I went into a diabetic coma." Amanda wiped the tears from her face. "I don't remember any of it," she whispered, "but every chance she gets, my mom lets me know how much I made her suffer." She looked directly at Jordan and held his eyes in an expression of raw honesty. She had spoken her truth.

Jordan's throat tightened. He fought the sorrow and rage. *What kind of mother would do that?* Instead of yelling, he chose silence, recognizing that his words would be dark and angry. *Amanda just needs to feel my love.*

The waitress came out to refill their tea, but then slipped away.

Anioch and Yrandia stayed near, sending love and healing light out onto the roadside patio.

Anioch whispered, "They were together during that time."

Yrandia smiled, "Yes, my beloved. I know that. It was written oh so long ago."

Anioch turned with a question on his lips.

"Hush, dear one," Yrandia replied. "All is as it should be."

The couple sat and listened to the distant traffic and the singing birds. A warm wave of peace washed over them.

Jordan asked, "So, shall we continue on our ride?"

Amanda smiled. "That sounds good. But I owe you an apology. I snapped at you."

"No, I need to be more sensitive," Jordan sighed. "Part of loving you is wanting the best for you. So I need to offer you the best of myself. I can't change your past."

Amanda pulled Jordan's hands and gently kissed them. She smiled at him. She pushed his hair back and gently brushed his cheek.

"I don't know for sure," Jordan said, "but I think our past can be a blessing and a curse. I probably sound like an asshole to even say that, right? But maybe it's about how we choose to both embrace and let go of the past. Maybe that's what really matters."

Amanda leaned in and kissed him. "Thank you for pushing me to have this conversation. My natural tendency is to avoid the tough stuff." She paused and looked deep into Jordan's eyes before adding, "I love you."

Jordan got up and pushed his chair aside and left space for Amanda. She slid out of her chair and into his open arms. They leaned into each other and lost themselves in a deep kiss.

Quietly, Amanda looked up. "Push me honey, please. But push me gently."

Jordan chuckled. "Sounds like a country song or something... *Push me gently, shove me slowly.*"

"Sounds naughty," Amanda giggled. "Maybe I need to write another song!"

CHAPTER 28

During quiet times, Jordan found himself reflecting on his life and the changes that were unfolding, as if led by some higher power. He had friends who knew him, understood him, and still loved him. He found satisfaction working with the surf team as he guided and listened to the kids. He felt a sense of purpose. He dug deeper into his studies.

A calm and ease came over his family, too. The old dramas disappeared. He thought of Anne Marie and Dr. Blair and felt a rush of gratitude for their wisdom and support. He felt the deepening presence of his angelic guide and knew that connection was a vital lifeline that grounded him in hope.

And there was Amanda. He loved her in a way he had never thought possible. A deep connection was there that he sometimes struggled to understand. He saw in her reflected back the wounded broken parts of his own once-scarred soul. But he also saw beyond that. Bathed in total radiant light, he saw her True Being and she was magnificent. He lovingly held that mirror for her, hoping she too would eventually see and fall deeply in love with her True Self.

Embracing. Letting go. Transformation. Grace. These words swirled in Jordan's mind as he ran along the beach. These words held their own energy and he knew their forces were pulling at his life. Thankful for their power, he accepted that part of the mystery of life was learning to trust in this Higher Power. Jordan knew one of his lessons was to let go of the need to know—to learn to be okay with the not knowing—and just accept that all was in order.

As a professional surfer who had played out in his head every move on the illusive perfect wave before every competition, he was now learning to let go and trust. *Let the current carry you.* He smiled when he remembered those words a young surfer had shouted after pulling out of a set. *Yeah little dude, you might be right.*

While he ran, he thought of Amanda. He replayed the conversation they had at the roadside diner over cold soggy chips. He recalled the deep sense of frustration as he struggled to make sense of things in the moment. He'd just wanted to make everything right... his idea of right. Now, with distance, he could see how the past held a tight grip on both of them. It was a process, a lesson. He needed to let go.

Jordan's mind paused and a word came again, *Grace*. He wasn't sure what it meant. But he knew he should explore it. *Let the current carry you.* Jordan broke into a sprint and breathed in the fresh morning air.

❦

Amanda slid into the chair next to Jordan. He gently held her hands. The rest of the group quieted down the light chatter as Dr. Blair opened a leather-bound book. This was the cue that the session was about to begin.

Jordan glanced around the room and saw friends. They had travelled far together. Everyone had their own story, broken hearts, crushed dreams, failure and loss. They were all very human. Their stories and the weight of life were deeply etched on their faces. During these sessions, Dr. Blair pointed to the possibility of who was really hidden behind their well-worn masks. Much of their time was spent gently removing the layers of old veneer, dark patina and rust of the hardened mask, revealing something new and more real and beautiful.

Jordan recognized that before joining the group, each person had found his or her own way to disengage. They were all proof that disconnection resulted in alienation, withdrawal, anger and angst. While the stories were different, the journeys each led to a personal breaking point. Each of them had been crushed, and out of the fragmented pieces new patterns were being shaped. The light refracted from these new shards and now as they were brought into the light they reflected more intensely and more beautifully. It seemed that somehow the punishing crucible of pressure had polished them and there was something left that, while worn, was rich and deep. Jordan's heart filled with love. He gently patted Amanda's hands.

Dr. Blair slowly began to read a passage, "Simone Weil writes, 'All the natural movements of the soul are controlled by laws analogous to those of physical gravity. Grace is the only exception. Grace fills empty spaces, but it can only enter where there is a void to receive it, and it is grace itself which makes this void'."

Jordan's heart leapt, *Grace! Here we go...*

The group was led into meditation. Jordan tried to quiet his mind and his body. But he felt excited as he always did when these moments

177

of synchronicity appeared. He centered himself for the lesson he knew was coming. He also knew the lesson might be shrouded, offering him the opportunity to dig deeper for the grain of truth his soul needed. He let go and slid into the silence. *Just let the current carry you.*

Dr. Blair ended the meditation with a question, "So, do you have any empty spaces to fill?"

The group sat in silence.

Finally a young woman spoke. Her voice was deep and had a gravely edge to it. "I think we all do. Well, at least, I know I do. That's been my struggle. What do I fill it with? I'm not sure I'd say I fill it with grace." She paused and leaned forward, grabbing her water bottle. She took a long drink and cleared her throat. "No, it's not grace. I mean I'm not even sure what that is. For me, it's more the quiet voice that whispers fear into my heart." She closed her eyes.

The rest of the room was still. They created space for her and filled it with love.

"That voice..." the woman continued. "When it fills the void, it makes me stop believing. It silences my real voice, and ultimately forces me to not so much let go but rather turn away from that True Self you keep talking about, Dr. Blair."

Some in the group nodded in agreement.

"It's not grace. Because when I listen to that voice and believe in it and feed it, it starts to become my reality. And there is nothing graceful in that," she said.

"Okay, Jess, what are you filling that empty space with?"

"Like I said, not grace." The woman smiled.

Dr. Blair returned the smile but did not speak.

The woman named Jess dropped her eyes. "Not getting off that easy, right?"

There were a few chuckles. Dr. Blair nodded to her, his sign to continue.

"So I have a question for you, Doc. Is there a shadow side of grace? I mean, I think we all would have different lives if we had filled up those empty spaces with grace."

"Well," said Dr. Blair. "We begin with the idea that we can't earn grace. I think that is what Weil meant here. There's no law of cause and effect. We can't do anything to make grace flow in or out. That's the beauty of it. It's just there for us. It's a gift because we are human and we need it. We just have to accept it and let it in to fill the void. The writer says, 'Grace itself which makes this void'."

And the session flowed on its own current at its own pace. They talked and under Dr. Blair's steady yet firm prodding, the shadows that filled the space were brought out into the light. In that light, they lost their strength. The light transformed each member who opened up and spoke of their hurts, fears, regrets and perceived inadequacies. Now fully exposed, the shadows seemed small and weak.

In the quiet and safe space of the circle, these souls were now connected in a restorative energy. Jordan watched as people lost their bravado and gained real confidence. Raised voices were lowered. Hesitant whispers took on strength. The connectivity created its own forcefield. Vulnerable yet authentic people emerged, resonating with their own truth. *We are filling this space with grace.*

As Jordan listened, an oceanic image came to mind. He felt the inner tapping. It was time to share. He waited for the pause and then began. "I get the sense we all learned to close ourselves off. We didn't acknowledge there was even a space inside. It's like we crawled into a protective shell, and over time, the shells were crusted with barnacles. Even though that hid and protected us, it also weighed us down. It hid our true identity and closed off our knowing of the space or the grace that was there."

"Go on, Jordan," Dr. Blair said. "Explain the metaphor."

"I don't know. The shell is a space, right? Whether it's an oyster, clam or just a sea snail that's bunking for a while, the shell protects what's inside. It's the container, but we confuse the container with what it houses."

"Okay, so what is that space? What happens when you chip away at that shell..." Dr. Blair prompted, "to remove the debris and barnacles? Does that change anything?"

"Hmm," Jordan pondered. "It bares the shell. But it is still the shell. It's the container. Yet when someone opens up that shell, they see the flesh, the real part of what's in—"

Emily, a cancer survivor who kicked the addiction to pain pills, interrupted, "But wait, Jordan. Once you open the shell, whatever is inside it dies."

Jordan shuddered and stared at Emily. She spoke truth. The sudden change to his metaphor was not exactly what he had in mind.

Dr. Blair leaned into the circle. "Well, that might be so. But somehow I think Jordan was going somewhere else. What's inside, Jordan?"

Emily slumped into her chair, "Sorry," she softly whispered.

"No worries. You're right. Well according to Emily, something now is dead. I guess that's true. The mollusk inside, the flesh dies. But I think there's something more." Jordan paused. *Grace.*

"I see a shell. It's hard and because of that it endures. Over time, I see the waves beating against it and pounding on it. The shell stays shut and gathers a lot of gunk. The exterior gets harder and takes on stuff that changes how it looks on the outside. It gets weathered and its texture gets rough and worn, but there's something else going on. There's a life in there and it's growing, doing whatever it is mollusks do. They open up a little bit because they have to breathe and eat in order to live. But mostly they stay shut."

There was a deep stillness in the room. The friends sat in their seats, some with eyes opened, others with eyes shut. They seemed to be breathing in and out in the same steady flow as if some invisible heart joined them and held them in synchronized rhythm.

Dr. Blair leaned in, folded onto his forearms, head bent down as if in contemplation. The room held the energy of a sacred space and light danced between the partially pulled blinds.

Anioch and Yrandia bowed, acknowledging the sacred circle and breathing in the energy of love.

"But sometimes in that brief moment of opening," Jordan continued, "there's a space where a tiny piece of sand or parasite seeps in. It gets inside and fills that space. In a void the oyster didn't even know it had, that speck starts to irritate the living breathing part of it. And the oyster responds. It tries to protect itself. But because it's hermetically sealed, those of us on the outside can't tell what's going on. But the insides are changing and transforming as it tries to heal itself. The irritant that creeped into that tiny space is what was necessary to change that simple mollusk to respond and transform the sand into something priceless. But it isn't until we chip away the hard shell and crack it open... only then can we see the treasured pearl. The oyster healed itself and became something more... grander, more precious."

Emily leaned back with a heartfelt sigh and smiled. Others mirrored her body language, and the group sat in silence for many moments. *Grace.*

Then Dr. Blair cleared his throat. "Wow. Lots of stuff for us to think about in that, Jordan. Thank you. I feel that grace touched and guided us tonight. For that I thank you all. So folks, I think we have some homework. I want you each to reflect on your outer shell and the grain of sand or grace... whatever way you want to think of it. What is it that's the irritant for you? How does it get under your skin? Can you give it gratitude or does it still piss you off? And what will it take for you to discover the pearl that's hidden in your deepest core? Where is the grace in your life? Where is your empty place and entry point?"

Jordan sat, quietly fumbling in his pants pocket, holding that small package Anne Marie had given to him so long ago. He sensed a strong connection with her at that moment. He smiled. He heard her voice, *"My treasure from the sea."*

CHAPTER 29

Amanda and Jordan went to say good night to their group leader. Dr. Blair flashed a broad smile. "Good stuff there, Jordan." Jordan nodded and they shared a quick handshake before heading outside.

Amanda wondered what their private discussions were like. Dr. Blair met with each one of them individually. He was a strong presence who challenged her to open up and go deeper. She marveled at his uncanny ability to gently guide her with nothing more than silence or a raised eyebrow.

As they walked into the cool night air, Amanda nuzzled close. "Jordan, that image was really beautiful. I am wondering, what do you think that pearl is for you?"

"Not really sure. I think I am more tripped up on Emily's statement that the oyster dies when you open it up. It makes it all sound a little less miraculous."

Amanda drew closer. "I kind of like it. It makes sense that somewhere inside of us we have to let go or die... so the real part of us— the special part of us—can let the sand in and begin to grow into something new and better. It isn't about dying but rather transforming. It's about opening up and cracking ourselves wide open to reveal our True Selves. I love it."

Amanda recalled what her life had been like. She knew she had stayed closed and small because she was afraid of everything. Fear wrote her narrative and her reality. She replayed now with less sorrow and more curiosity how her life had spun out of control after high school. Accepted into a fine arts college, she found refuge in a small campus tucked away in the rolling hills. A few faculty members had taken her under their wings. She had been told she had a good eye for color, lines and design. She dreamed of becoming a clothing designer but couldn't share her dreams with her mother. She knew that would be greeted with judgment and reproach, wrapped in a tightly packed sermon of ultimate defeat. So she'd held her dreams close, unwilling to give them any room or hope.

She softly shared her thoughts with Jordan while they drove back from the group session. He had heard bits and pieces of her story and was patient, knowing that Amanda would reveal herself in her own time.

"I'm beginning to understand that the little neglected girl inside of me created my life. Somehow I couldn't love myself because I never really felt love. So I guess it isn't really such a big surprise that I ended up in so many lousy and messed up relationships. That's what I was attracting into my life."

She told him about her days at college and how she always ended up with a guy who never stuck around. She'd demanded nothing because she believed she deserved nothing. She sought empty relationships, comfortable in their emptiness, notable for their lack of love. She wanted no more because she did not believe there could be more.

"I guess we all want something, right? I mean it's human to need love. But the shadow of love is control, and the outcome is destruction."

Jordan took his time responding. "It's sad in a way but it makes sense. You didn't know what love looked like or felt like. But I grew up knowing I was loved. Even so, I couldn't accept it. I turned away and turned into one of those jerks you are describing. You wouldn't have wanted me in your life." Jordan stopped and sucked in a breath.

Amanda felt the added weight of Jordan's words. While she still ached and hungered, she responded by retreating, by starving, by controlling the few areas she could. Now as she viewed her life through the lens of love and forgiveness, she realized the space that held her soul had become empty. Each rejection drove her further away from the Source of Love. She responded by isolating herself from friends, mentors, and family. If no one could get near, then they couldn't threaten or inflict pain. With each goodbye, whether spoken or not, her spirit was diminished, her light dimmed, and her soul slowly disappeared.

"I guess it has always been about choices. With each bad relationship I turned further and further away. I couldn't risk being hurt anymore. I had to stop feeling... because the only feeling I knew was pain." Amanda grew silent.

Jordan pulled the car into the small alley behind Amanda's home. He turned toward Amanda and drew her close, his face covered in her falling hair, and softly whispered, "Well however messed up we might have been, and whatever negative forces we were bringing into our lives, I'm grateful somebody decided we were worthy of each other."

Amanda lightly kissed Jordan and took a deep breath. She inhaled the warmth of their shared love and felt it deep inside her being. It filled her with gratitude and love.

Jordan too had isolated himself. He had turned away from love, not because he had not been given love, but because somewhere in his childhood the magical and mystical was taken away. He'd stopped believing in the miraculous, the majestic and ultimately in the Sacred: in Love.

Amanda was beginning to understand that he had embarked upon his path of self-destruction when he no longer believed in the beauty of life or the magic each moment offered. He had intentionally turned away from any form of love because some deep, still unspoken trauma had happened that wouldn't allow him to reach for the deeper connection he had once believed in.

∽৻৵ৎ৵

Jordan knew in his heart that it was time to share the most profound part of his past. He knew his Angelic Guide needed to be brought into the relationship and that his direct experiences needed to be spoken about openly. If he was going to love Amanda without fear, he needed to step into it fully and allow himself to be vulnerable.

He thanked his father for giving him that gift after admitting his own loss of angelic connection. Daniel and Jordan had grown closer after that afternoon on the beach. The act of forgiveness for father and son had begun a journey of reconciliation and reconnection on a human and spiritual level.

Jordan decided he would speak his Truth with humility and grace. He stepped into his old fear and opened his heart to share his deepest secret and most sacred truth.

"Amanda, I know that over time we've been sharing a lot about ourselves. We've been talking about some pretty deep stuff and ideas that are really getting more and more complex and going into a spiritual dimension. We've been super honest with each other and I feel I have to tell you something."

∽৻৵ৎ৵

Amanda's heart plummeted. The old voices started a low rumble in her head, pulling at her from a dark place. What was he going to say? The metallic taste of panic rose in her mouth. She sensed a goodbye buried within the loving words. She braced herself for the inevitable, but took a deep breath to steady herself just like Dr. Blair coached.

It's only a thought. The fear still gripped her. *It's only a thought,* she repeated and let her breath go.

"What is it, Jordan?" she managed to squeak out.

Jordan must have sensed a shift in her voice. He took her hand and softly caressed it.

Amanda moved away in an almost imperceptible shift. Jordan held her hand a little tighter.

"I have something I need to share with you. It's something I've really only shared with my dad. Anne Marie knows... in fact, she sort of knew it before I did."

Amanda's mind was racing. His words didn't make sense. She tried to quiet her mind and allow herself to listen with an open heart.

Jordan continued. His eyes were closed. "I guess I'm still not ready to be totally honest or open about this. It's something I can't risk ever losing again."

Amanda was confused. A swirl of crazy and irrational thoughts bombarded her at once. She tried to remain focused but her mind screamed, *What is he saying? Is he gay?* Maybe he's found someone new, or perhaps someone from his past? Amanda's stomach tightened and her throat constricted.

In response, Jordan caressed her more gently, not letting go of her hand and the connection it offered. "I know we kind of talk around it but... do you really believe in some kind of Higher Power?"

What? Where is this going? How could that be such a big deal? Amanda shouted at herself to relax. Jordan was asking her a question and it was clearly important to him.

"Yes, yes I do. I guess I do. I mean, I was raised Catholic but you know I have a hard time with the idea of religion and church. I don't really buy into the whole thing of God being up there removed from us and watching us... if that's what you're asking. But I do believe there's something bigger than us."

Jordan visibly relaxed. "Me too. And here's the crazy part. I know there's a whole other realm out there and also here with us. I know this, Manda, 'cuz I've seen it. I mean I actually saw it." He paused and stared straight into her eyes before adding, "I've seen my own angel."

185

Relief flooded through Amanda. She smiled, grabbed his hand and kissed it. "Wow, really? How wonderful and totally amazing," she whispered.

Jordan's relief was palpable. "I called him my secret friend when I was little. He was always with me. He is one of my earliest memories. We played together. He was magnificent. I mean really, he was beyond description. He made the whole world look magical. I felt safe. I knew he was always with me and always protected me. I mean, what an awesome way to go through life as a kid just feeling totally safe and loved. Every day was a gift of light and joy and fun."

Amanda noticed Jordan's face light up as he recalled the angel of his youth. What had she done to deserve this beautiful man?

CHAPTER 30

Amanda sat at her small kitchen table. The early morning light streamed in and filled the space with a soft glow as shadows danced across the pale green walls. Music streamed in from the living room. She lost herself in the moment and splashed bright colors on the canvas, humming while she traced small brush strokes, expertly filling in empty spaces with fine details of contrasting shades and hues.

Early morning was when Amanda felt the most alive and at peace. Her heart was open and the new day was like an invitation to breathe joy. This was a new feeling. A good feeling.

Even though Amanda had never felt the presence of the Divine in the dramatic way Jordan described, she believed him when he spoke of his angel and the profound transformation he'd experienced on that empty shore.

Her life was simpler, but somewhere deep inside she felt a subtle transformation taking place. *All in its right season.* An old Sunday school teacher had spoken those words. She never understood them at the time; they seemed like a rebuke to impatient children. But now they were beginning to make sense.

Just be okay with the moment and what is offered. That was the new lens she chose to look through. And with that frame of reference she noticed her inner child's cry for attention had quieted.

She continued to paint, a scene of bursting sunflowers emerging on the once blank canvas. *Girasol*, she liked the Spanish word for her favorite flowers. *Turning toward the light.* She dipped her brush in the mix of yellow and orange.

No dramatic epiphanies for me. I'm not dramatic so I am totally fine with moving on the slow track. I don't need an angel appearing out of nowhere.

Yrandia smiled and filled the room with radiant light.

A wave of happiness passed over Amanda. She quietly sang, "Come rest, Baby Blue. Beautiful, radiant new. Come rest, Baby Blue. Make me whole, Holy. Make me new. Welcome home, sweet child, my sweet dear Baby Blue."

With a smile she recalled how that night she had pushed back her fear to sing from her heart. In that moment of surrender, she'd felt something. Her mind wandered and swirled around the notion of the Divine. It was indeed *something*. A guide? A protection?

Perhaps some of the magic and grandeur Jordan spoke about was stirred in her when she saw and connected with a splash of color and felt the connection as light danced in the beauty of nature. At moments she knew she was connected to the earth and all its natural beauty. Jordan however, with his angel and visions, was connected to the ethereal heavenly realm. *Heaven and Earth. Heaven on earth.* She smiled.

Yrandia laughed.

Amanda was moved by poetry, art, music, dance and their creative energy—as she learned to quiet the voices, she noticed the space they once occupied was now filled with a sense of joy. She opened her eyes to the expression of nature through color, design, texture, shadow and rhythm. She honored this energy, but wondered if there was something more. Something bigger. When she listened to Jordan she could see him light up each time he spoke of that other realm. *His heaven.*

"Be patient and allow some space," a small voice whispered.

Amanda stood up and looked at the bright spring flowers that danced on her canvas. Her thoughts flowed untethered. *Where's my heaven?* She returned to the feeling of that Wednesday session when she'd found her voice and sung her truth. There was something transcendent—maybe her first real brush with a Higher Energy connection. Some part of her had awakened that night, and there was a yearning to feel that spark again. Amanda giggled. *Maybe there is magic out there waiting for me.*

"Indeed, my child. There is a whole magical world right here waiting for you." Yrandia danced and sang. "It is beginning, my daughter. For you can't hunger for something you don't really know. Now you are beginning to know."

Jordan began each day with a prayer of gratitude. He thanked the Universe for all the blessings of love and his new life. He recognized that he had been offered a second chance and felt humbled by the notion. This gift was a promise of time to redefine his eternity. Perhaps he had only been a fearless fool because at his lowest point he had so little to lose. In retrospect he could see that he hadn't been fearless but rather had embraced the false idea of separation and the absence of Love. In hopelessness, he'd created his reality and thus his personal hell on earth.

In his morning practice, Jordan contemplated life. In gratitude, he recognized that he was being allowed to discover the miracle of returning to Love and that by reconnecting with his angelic guide he was reconnecting to the Source of all life and creation. He expanded his morning contemplation to ask not only for Divine Guidance but to be in service to the Divine. He stayed open to opportunities to be a manifestation of Love. *There is a reason I am here. Let me be in service to that Reason.*

He set an intention to be present and to allow Spirit to work through and with him to create the intricate and majestic tapestry of life one beautiful strand at a time. With an open heart he stretched his mind well beyond earthly boundaries, reaching instead into the limitless possibilities offered by Divine Mind. Jordan affirmed Joy, Happiness, and Love. He sat in silence and let the small voice of wisdom whisper: *"What if Love, in its purest form, is the human manifestation of the Creator's Love? Am I that Love? Am I then the manifestation of the Divine?"*

Jordan's mind slowly began to shift and in that shift he began to understand that he was so much more than his body. The professional athlete who was adored for his physical strength began to see that a connection solely to the physical world, to his body, was limiting. As he moved past the idea of separation between the physical and the Divine, he began to fully connect to the idea that he was but a container of Divine Love. He was being moved from the conceptual understanding of life and purpose to a place of deeper knowing. Maybe his Purpose was to accept this Love. And so he sat and breathed in the question... *What is mine to know?*

He came to know in that quiet inner space that Love had been given to him not to hold, but rather to allow it to flow through and from him. Love's pure strength wasn't his to direct. Instead he was called to be in true service to this Divine Love. His true calling and place of power was manifested when he simply surrendered to Love. His purpose was to accept the gift, and once freely received, pass it on.

Jordan couldn't fully put into words what was being revealed. This energy of Love sang in his heart and fed his soul. Its raw, creative and expansive force resided everywhere. When he took the time to focus on the moment, the energy of Life beat with the very rhythm of all nature. It was in everything and everybody. When Jordan quieted his mind and closed his eyes to distractions, he could feel It. Buried there deep within his Being was a place where he could rest. And there he knew that all things were mysteriously connected by this life force and creative energy of Love.

In silence, Jordan knew It was a gift from the Heavenly Hosts that saved him on that deserted beach. That energy and life force now called him to pass on the powerful and restorative energy of Love. This energy—Love—was limitless and made present in every manifestation from the warmth and tenderness he found in Amanda's eyes, her breath, her kiss, to the love he shared with his friends and family, the care he took with his young students, and the protection he offered to his beloved ocean.

In each act of service imbued with Love, he found his refuge and glimpsed his destiny. The limitless gift of pure Grace and Love in action humbled Jordan. *What is mine to learn? What is mine to see? What is mine to do?* The silence held his words and blessed him as his angel stayed near and wrapped him in an arc of brilliant light.

"You know, Dr. Blair, I've been thinking lately that I am not being totally honest with myself."

"What do you mean, Jordan?" The doctor was sitting in his large brown chair. His face was nearly expressionless but his eyes danced. Even in a question, his voice was calm and reassuring.

"I mean, I know I've changed and my whole idea around life is changing. I am trying to make sense out of things and I think I'm a better person. At least I hope I am." Jordan paused. He could hear the hesitancy in his own voice.

"Okay. Help me understand what you are comparing yourself to. Sounds like there's a question in there." The doctor sat relaxed, his arms folded behind his head.

"Maybe. I don't know. Not a comparison really. I guess I am taking stock of who I am and what I'm doing. I'm trying to not be judgmental with myself or others. I hear you when you talk about the process and just relaxing into the questions. But man, there are so many questions and ideas that just pop up. And I'm really letting go of the pressures to be a certain way. But I'm still searching for that purpose thing. I kind of see myself as if I'm on this incredible journey of discovery, and I'm having amazing insights. But I'm still not really owning them. At least not all the time."

Jordan paused and got up from his chair. Something pulled at him. He stretched his back and rolled his neck. The doctor sat still and watched, waiting, knowing the questions were being asked in silence. Jordan sat down and leaned forward, elbows on his knees.

"The real me is more like a shadow skirting above the path. Not really connected. More an observer. The 'me' who's walking on the path isn't totally part of the journey. It's like I'm asleep, but now I think I'm being called to wake up."

"Okay, so if the real you wakes up, what would waking up look like to you, Jordan?"

There it was. The simple question that would force Jordan to dig deeper. *The question is... who is the real me?*

"I've been asking myself that, and I think it's where the honesty thing comes in. I have certain truths I only share with certain people. I'm not dishonest, but I'm not... well... I guess the word I'm looking for is... I'm not sure. Maybe the word is integrated. I am not fully integrated. Maybe waking up means being the real me all the time."

"Who is the real you that needs to show up every time?" The doctor's voice was quiet and calm.

Jordan smiled. He knew the deeper question would get asked. "I think it's the me who is present here with you, with Amanda, who comes out when I speak with Anne Marie and also now sometimes with my dad and even my mom. You guys have seen my true self, but I'm not ready to be that person with other people." Jordan stopped and crossed his legs. There was more. He wasn't sure what it was.

"What's holding you back?"

"I don't know. I mean I have all these ideas swirling in my head and it's hard to make sense of them. So when I'm with you guys, I feel like I can just sort through these ideas and I know you'll let me do that and not judge me. Somehow you guys get it. But I think other people don't. Yet when I hold back and kind of check myself, I feel like I'm not honoring the second chance I was given."

Dr. Blair shifted in his seat. He leaned forward, his head slightly cocked. "Help me understand what feels dishonest."

Jordan didn't answer right away but let the question sink in. When he did speak, his breath was ragged. "M-maybe it isn't dishonest. But it isn't real, either. I'm trying to live from a place of openness and compassion, I just don't know how to do that all the time. You know part of this waking up thing is realizing that I am not just this body. I heard this saying from some French priest or something and it really got my mind going. Something like, 'We are not human beings having a spiritual experience. We are spiritual beings having a human experience'."

"Yes, Pierre Teilhard de Chardin," Dr. Blair nodded. "He was a Jesuit priest. He was also a paleontologist which makes the quote so much more interesting."

Jordan sat forward and dropped his head. The words had sounded jumbled and confused. The well-ordered ideas he held in his mind lost their congruence when spoken. Both men sat in the silence.

Jordan took a drink from his water bottle then said, "I'm only now realizing that every thought I have has power because they are energy. It inspires me, sure... but it also scares me. It's like I have to be aware now of how and what I think and how I act. If I'm connected to something bigger—even protected by angels—shouldn't that demand something awesome from me?"

"I don't know, Jordan. That's a question you have to answer."

"No kidding, Doc. That's what we do here, right? I answer questions." Jordan smiled.

"Yes, that's why I am asking it." Dr. Blair sat up as if he sensed a flash of energy. "So what I am hearing you ask yourself is what are you supposed to do differently knowing now you are a Divine Being? You say you need to be awesome."

"Yeah, something like that. I mean a Divine Being by nature is awesome, right?"

"Okay, so then if you are stepping into and accepting that part of yourself, my question is, what part of what you're doing isn't awesome?"

Again the pause. Jordan sat. He didn't want to fill it with words. The silence felt good. *Your turn, Doc. I'm not asking the question this time.*

Dr. Blair sat and let the energy in the room settle. He closed his eyes. When he opened them he looked at Jordan and with a slight bow he began, "How are you showing up at school, with your friends and family, with Amanda, with the group? What part of that isn't awesome?"

"Come on, Dr. Blair. I don't do anything awesome. I just try to be a good person and listen. That's not anything special." Jordan could feel something brewing at a deeper level in his gut.

" 'Awesome' was your word, Jordan, not mine. Why do you think you need to be awesome?"

"Like I said, I think a Divine Being like that French priest calls us is just awesome by nature."

"May I offer a perspective?" The man's voice was low and calm.

Jordan smiled. What could he say? *No?* He nodded.

"Let's look at your impact on people. I see it. You are being yourself and in that you are touching people. How about Amanda? Or how about your dad? And let's talk about what your openness has done for the folks in our group. It may not be what you think of as 'awesome' but it is transformational."

Jordan closed his eyes. He knew Dr. Blair spoke the truth yet there was something still missing. He took several deep breaths to try to quiet his racing mind. He had learned that if he focused on his heart, strong intuition would come.

"Okay, I hear you. Maybe as I open up to others and am present, there's a restorative balance. As I am, what did you say... *stepping into this new way of being...* in some way it transforms me and others, too. But that's the honesty part I'm struggling with." Jordan sat still and stared into his hands. His breath was measured and slow.

"Go on. Where's the disconnect that makes it feel less than honest?"

"I don't know. I guess I need to just relax and trust that my authentic self is enough. Maybe I need to really work on the letting go and getting out of the way. If I am the instrument, then I need to trust the flow and that I will be used as Divine Power chooses. I have to stop being the maestro." Jordan tapped on his chest. "I guess wanting to be awesome is not a humble way to approach things. Okay, I see that awesome can be very simple. But simple isn't always easy. Maybe I think awesome needs to look way bigger and badder."

"I'd say that you are pretty damn awesome right now."

"A Divine Being having a human experience. That's cool."

"Maybe simple is awesome, Jordan. I want you to try something. Next meeting, just center yourself and let whatever moves you flow outward. Let's see what simple, awesome and transformative can look like. Can you do that?"

"Sure," Jordan replied. "I thought I did do that, but maybe not. Maybe the hotshot is still there, needing to be the best. I will try to let go and be that channel. Thanks, Dr. Blair."

"Thank you, Jordan. You know, your awesome self teaches me, too. That French priest, as you call him, also said, 'Someday after mastering the winds, the waves, the tides and gravity, we shall harness for God the energies of love, and then, for the second time in the history of the world, man will have discovered fire.' Reminds me of you, Mr. Surfer Pro."

CHAPTER 31

Jordan left the session feeling energized. Something was bubbling just under the surface. He could feel it but it could not be named. There was a deep pulse that pulled at him, creating a delicious sense of anticipation. The world was more alive.

Jordan eased into traffic and drove slowly. He reflected, with a grateful heart, how much his life had changed. Lost in the moment, his senses were fully engaged. Energy flowed through him. Beauty surrounded him. He smiled. The power of attention took only a small shift to be present, to notice and become one with the moment.

As he drove, Jordan slowed his racing mind. An awareness came in that open space of how much he had missed—how much of life had been lost in the rush and chaos of the small crowded world he'd created. The sweet fragrance of grass and sage filled his lungs. In the surrender, his senses burst. The life-giving air was transformed now with an added texture he could taste. He listened intently with an open heart. It was as if he was hearing the world for the first time. A cacophony of bird sounds called and answered and the air filled with a choir—insects buzzing, children laughing. The world blended in a note of rapture that sent his soul soaring.

As he eased onto the Coast Highway, Jordan felt cool breezes pass and touch him like a gentle caress. His whole being was alive. He felt the earth wrap around him, comforting and warm like an old sweater. The refreshing touch of evening dew soothed him and in the release he connected to something grander. Jordan surrendered and became part of the texture, web and weave of life's connective fabric.

He chuckled. He might not be awesome, but life sure was. *This is the space of magic and miracles.*

Anioch agreed and danced with the fading light and breeze singing a song of praise. *Thank you,* man and angel intoned.

Jordan turned his drive into a meditation. Once again he knew Spirit was teaching him, quietly asking him to be present and open... and in that act of opening, the gifts would come. *Life is good.*

The days passed as schedules ruled and life unfolded. Jordan had all but forgotten Dr. Blair's request: *Center yourself and let whatever moves you flow outward.* There had been a lot of good flowing inward and a slow awakening taking place. The request indeed seemed inconsequential.

It was Wednesday evening and as routine, Jordan pulled up to Amanda's home. She rushed into the car while pulling on a sweatshirt, then leaned over and kissed him though she seemed distracted. "Sorry I'm late. I just got off the phone with Emily."

Jordan backed out of the alley way. *Oh yes Emily, slayer of metaphors,* he mused.

"Well, she is pretty upset. Her fiancé, Brian, is in the hospital. Looks like a drug overdose."

Amanda was obviously worried. Jordan pushed aside his stray thoughts and listened. *This is serious.* "Oh wow. Is he okay?"

Amanda was texting into her phone while she spoke. "Not sure. Well I mean he's in the hospital so that's good. She found him and they have Narcan at home. She said she doesn't think she'll make it to the session tonight. I told her we would check in on her afterwards. Hope that's okay..."

"Sure, of course. That's fine. Man, that's got to be hard. I hope Brian's okay. How's Emily?" Jordan didn't know the man but Emily had been sober for many years. She seemed tough and in control of her life, but he sensed vulnerability underneath the layer of bravado. She had beat cancer only to find herself addicted to painkillers. The challenges she had battled and won left her with a sarcastic and somewhat fatalistic view of life. But as she opened up to the group, a softer side was emerging. Jordan tried to keep his mind centered on healing thoughts and avoid any judgment.

"She is upset. You know she's come by the shop a few times... and we've gone for tea. I think she is looking for friendship..." Amanda paused as she put the phone down. When she spoke again her voice was soft. "...like she just needed someone to listen. I wasn't sure what was going on but I could tell she was worried. I am trying to be that friend and be there for her. I can do that."

"You're a good person, Manda. You have such a kind and open heart. That's why I love you." Jordan reached over and gently caressed her arm. "I'm sure she appreciates you being there for her. We can be there for her. Whatever she needs."

Amanda softly kissed his hand. They drove in silence.

Jordan and Amanda were the last to arrive. Folks were sitting and standing in small loose clusters. The sound of soft chatter filled the air.

Emily was in her regular spot, talking with Carter. He was leaning forward with his arms wrapped around her shoulders.

Amanda leaned over to Jordan and whispered, "I'm going to go say hi to Emily. I'm really relieved she's here. It's a good sign and I'm hoping that means Brian is okay."

Jordan lightly kissed Amanda's cheek.

She moved across the room and slid into a chair next to her friend. Carter eased back and offered space. Emily looked up. Her eyes were red-rimmed and held a sadness that didn't match the smile. Amanda drew near and hugged the young woman.

Dr. Blair took his seat and people moved to take their places. He started the session as he always did with a centering exercise. Members were asked to close their eyes and begin a body scan, noticing areas of tension and releasing them. The collective breathing began to slow. Jordan felt himself easing into the quiet space, focusing on the inward breath. The gentle doctor talked them into the silence.

Anioch noticed the usual shift in energy and vibration when the circle became still, centered and focused. He mused at the power of stillness and wondered why humans were so loath to just breathe and become one with it. The angel contemplated and held his thought. *Power resides in the stillness. Be still and know your Power.*

Anioch joined the group and bowed to his beloved companion. Yrandia returned the bow with a radiant smile. *Indeed,* she silently answered. *Be still and know.*

The session progressed in its usual warm and gentle manner, but Jordan found his mind wandering, restless. As he forced himself to return again to the circle, he became aware that there had been a shift in the energy. *Pay attention!*

Emily was speaking. Her voice was full of deep emotion. "...They say my fiancé's going to be okay, but I'm worried." Emily stopped. She looked around the room and saw the kind faces and knew each had their own story of pain, struggle and redemption. She glanced at Amanda who softly nodded. Emily lowered her gaze and her voice, "He's been sober now for two years. I didn't see this coming. I don't know how I missed the signs. I mean for God's sake, I've been there. I just don't understand his resistance to getting help. He said he could kick this habit on his own, and I believed him. But I guess we were both wrong." Tears streamed down Emily's cheeks.

Amanda shifted in her seat and moved closer. She took Emily's hand and gently squeezed it.

With a wavering voice Emily continued, "I don't know... maybe he needs to start by being truthful. He keeps saying, 'I've got this'. Well I guess he doesn't. Maybe it's time for him to be more honest. Maybe he needs to call it what it is. He's an addict." Her voice broke and the sobs shook her shoulder. There wasn't reproach in the words, just a simple statement. The circle of friends waited and held the space with love and grace.

Jordan listened. His heart felt open. But there was something more. He felt something stir in him. Dr. Blair's words came back to him, *"Center yourself. Let whatever moves you flow outward."* Something was going on. Jordan shut his eyes and acknowledged the feeling. He silently asked, *What do I need to know? What is mine to do?* The silence drew itself around him. The moment was asking him to step in. He needed to be a part of it. *'Be present'* echoed in his mind. He waited. He opened his eyes and his heart and listened.

"He's such a good and loving person," Emily sobbed. "I've begged him to join a support group, but he says he can do this alone. He says as long as I'm with him, he's good. But I can't do it by myself. It just scares me... I don't want to lose him to this damn addiction." Emily buried her face in her hands.

The group was silent.

"We are here for you, Emily," Dr. Blair finally said. "I know I can only speak for myself, but I am fairly confident everyone here is willing to step in and help in any way we can to support you. You are not alone. You are loved." There were nods of affirmation around the room.

"Thank you, I know that," she sniffled. "And believe me, I don't know what I would have done these past months if I didn't have you guys. I think that's what is really making it hard for me. I know the strength and power that a circle of friends and the safe space you all can bring. But Brian refuses." She dabbed her eyes.

"He's stubborn and private. But I can't be his only support. I have my own shit to deal with. Sorry, but you all know what I mean." A slight smile filled Emily's face.

People shifted in their seats. Jordan stayed still and listened. His heart was beating.

"You know he says he's been to AA but it's not for him. He says that he can't get into all the Jesus and God speak. He is so anti religion. There is no getting past that point."

At that moment, Jordan felt a nudge somewhere deep inside and his gut tightened. *Let whatever moves you flow outward.* He heard the question he'd been asking in the form of a prayer: *What's mine to do?*

Anioch sensed the shift in the moment and recognized the opportunity that Dr. Blair had presaged. He remembered the angry young man who swore he controlled his own destiny and had turned his back on everything holy and sacred. The angel remembered his beautiful child lost in a haze of drugs and alcohol. Anioch wondered if Jordan felt the moment calling to him as well. *Be your authentic self, my child. That is the awesome you desire. Just be, my son. Just be and know that is enough.*

Jordan moved forward in his seat. He sat up straight and offered himself to the moment. He let the words flow, "Emily, if you don't mind, perhaps I can offer my perspective. I don't mean to imply that I know what you or Brian are going through. I know it is really hard and all I can offer you right now is Love and maybe some of my past to help." Jordan paused as if waiting for permission.

Emily smiled and softly answered, "Sure, Jordan. I'd like that. Thank you."

Jordan didn't know what would flow outward but he let go. "Well, I think I might know what Brian is going through. Maybe a little. For some of us, maybe all of us, it's a huge struggle to admit that you aren't in control. That seems to be a lesson I am learning over and over. I also know that the whole 'Let go, let God' thing can seem kind of preachy and fake. I know because I was there. I ran from that idea. I shut it out of every part of my life." Jordan stopped. *Let it flow.* He briefly shut his eyes and breathed.

Be the blessing, Anioch whispered.

Jordan felt a surge of energy and continued. "You guys probably have figured it out by now, but what I never admitted to you or really hardly anybody was that my surfing accident wasn't an accident."

The room was silent.

Time to be honest. "Yeah, well at that point in life I had lost faith and hope in pretty much everything. I was a slave to the drugs and believed in the fame and all the phony trappings of my glamorous life. I didn't believe in God. I didn't believe in much of anything. In fact, I sort of hated God and blamed my childish dreams on the hopelessness that defined my life. When the dream died, some part of me died... I was so bitter and empty I already felt dead. I wanted to die."

A heavy hush hung in the room. Dr. Blair sat quietly and held the gaze of those who looked to him to guide the group. He didn't speak.

He let the silence fill the room. He surrendered to the Grace he knew was present to guide the moment.

"I wanted to die because I felt like I was already dead. I mean I had lost all contact and connection with the Divine. I was an empty shell. A body. I numbed every sense that could betray me. I was angry. Angry and arrogant. Those were my default emotions. I was angry at the world, angry at my family, angry at myself. But I was really angry with this God who I said didn't exist. I had believed in God and angels when I was a kid. That dumb kid believed in all sorts of wonderful and delightful things. But that precious trusting kid got beat down. Everybody let me down. They stole my soul. And in that lonely place somehow I thought the only person or thing I could rely on in this world was me, the godless, joyless, angry grown-up me. And that person didn't offer too much hope."

Jordan sucked in a long slow breath. *Okay, I'm here. So am I really going to do this?* Jordan felt his heart pounding and his mouth was dry. Dr. Blair's words returned, *"Let it flow outward."* He leaned in.

"Okay, so what I'm about to tell you, I've only shared with a couple of people. When I was on that empty beach being sucked into the pounding surf, I discovered I wasn't alone. I mean something happened and in the instant I was sure I was going to die. I knew I was taking my last breath and it was over. I wasn't angry. I was terrified.

"As I was screaming for help, getting tossed in the wind and surf, I suddenly looked through the wall of water and I saw my own Guide... or angel... or whatever the right word is. There he was. The Being just like I had seen him as a child. It was him, that angel who had been my secret friend. He had always been with me, but when I trusted people and told them about him they said I was delusional. No one could accept it. All that magic and the miraculous and what gave me joy in life was medicated and talked out of me. I was literally disconnected from that part of the Divine. And that was the beginning of my descent into hell.

"But there I was tempting fate, I mean that ocean was pounding me and dragging me down. The champion surfer couldn't beat the sea. I was alone, afraid and knowing I was dying and my angel didn't try to save me. I could see him frozen on the shore. The phantom memory of my youth was there. He was real. But he wasn't there with me like when I was a kid. He wasn't flying and dancing and singing. He was quiet and looked sad. He wasn't guiding me. He was disconnected, remote and removed. In that moment, I was terrified. I think he was kind of... over me... and honestly? I can't say I blame him. I mean I had come to hate him, too. I didn't believe in him since everyone told me he was a childhood fantasy. I hated what his loss meant to me. So I really didn't blame him for just watching me drown." Jordan stopped as the memory drew him in.

Anioch winced at the words. It hurt him, at some angelic level, to hear the truth. He wondered what people in the room would think. How might it test their faith if they thought their angels could be *over them*? But he had to admit that the lessons learned that day on the beach were transformation for both angel and child. Anioch sent love to his courageous son and bowed to his beloved Yrandia who held the space in an arc of radiant light.

"But I didn't drown. I guess it wasn't my time," Jordan continued. "Whatever hold the drugs had on me that day were erased by the mass adrenaline dump and total fear I felt at that moment. So there I was asking for forgiveness, hoping my angel would do something... and the skies opened. I mean right before I got pulled under by this enormous angry wave, right there in those clouds there was a whole army of the most magnificent beautiful celestial beings. They filled the sky with light and their voices boomed like thunder. They spoke of time and things I didn't really understand. They exploded with an order and my Guardian Angel was pushed back into service. He swooped in like he had when I was little and I know he saved me."

Jordan closed his eyes. The fear of sharing his story was gone. He didn't need to hide it anymore. No one could steal his soul. He felt the tears brimming. But speaking his truth felt good. It felt honest. He opened his eyes and looked at Dr. Blair. The man sat motionless but his eyes were warm and filled with love.

"So here's the gift. I know that day I saw a Divine realm. I know now in the deepest part of my being, there is something spectacular beyond our grasp and sight. It's not the stuff of dreams or a childish make-believe world. It is real. I was transformed that day. I wanted to die. But I didn't die. I don't know why I was spared, but call it God, call it the Universe, Spirit, Source, Divine Consciousness, the All-Knowing. Call it what you want. It gave me another chance. And I am here trying to make sense of it and honor it.

"What I know in my core is that we are part of that Divine Presence. It is our birthright. We can ignore it and negate it but it is bigger than our human mind. We are connected to the Divine and are a part of it whether we know it or not. But what I am learning is that when we come to know and believe that we are all part of that Great Something, that Great Everything, only then can we begin to come into our own and grow past our addictions and other weaknesses. It's about Grace and it's in that Grace that we can become healed and whole. It's about connecting with our True Self and with each other. I think we each feel it here together, and that is powerful. So Brian doesn't need to call on God. He can surrender to whatever energy calls him, however softly that inner voice is. It only takes that first yes to step into the journey."

Jordan stopped. He had spoken his truth. In that moment, he felt a wave of peace pass over him.

Dr. Blair sat still, a faint flicker of a smile crossing his face.

Jordan felt relief. He didn't know what any of his friends thought, but it didn't really matter. He had taken his first step toward integrating the many sides of himself.

Anioch thanked the Divine Light for the grace that had been brought to the room.

Amanda looked at Jordan with eyes brimming with love and respect.

Emily quietly dabbed her eyes. "Thank you, Jordan. That was beautiful and inspiring. Maybe Brian will listen to you. I have to believe that someone can reach him."

Jordan felt a pulse of energy. *That,* he thought, *was awesome.*

CHAPTER 32

Jordan noticed Dr. Blair said very little as the meeting ended and the group dispersed. The energy in the room had shifted and the gathering of friends slowly moved out into the evening. Many were quiet and lost in thought. The doctor walked over and placed a warm and firm hand on Jordan's shoulder. In that simple gesture, there was appreciation and acknowledgment of what had transpired. Both men knew he had taken an important step.

Anioch sang to the Creator, knowing that all was as it should be. In that knowing, the Angel rejoiced and gave thanks, acknowledging that he too had taken an important step on his journey. The past blended perfectly with the present. There was healing and light.

Jordan and Amanda drove home in near silence. Jordan contemplated the immense changes in his heart and in his life. He glanced over at Amanda and his heart was full. In the space of gratitude, he realized he was sitting next to a woman who loved him fully. The light turned from amber to red. After slowing the car to a stop, he leaned over to gently kiss her.

She smiled. "Jordan, that was very courageous of you to bare your soul like that. I know it had to have been difficult, given your struggle with the past."

Jordan nodded. *She understands.* The light turned and Jordan moved into the dark night as a fog bank slowly edged onto the highway. His thoughts continued to dance around the edges of his new life and he rested in the sense of freedom the evening had brought. In all the challenges, he was beginning to see the blessings of pushing deeper to a place where he could fully embrace his self-worth.

He stole another glance at his beautiful partner. She offered him a place of refuge where he could share his deepest secrets and always be answered with love. He was better because of her. "I love you, Amanda," he admitted.

The words filled the space and hung in the air.

"Thank you, Jordan. I really know that deep inside my soul. I love you, too."

"You know, I think that is what all of this is about. This journey we are on and all the lessons we learn come back to love. You said I was courageous tonight. I didn't think I was. I was... just being honest. I was able to speak my truth because I finally wasn't afraid. I just pushed past it and found that place of strength."

Jordan paused to move onto the back roads. The fog was moving in and clinging closer to the pavement. The world took on a gauzy dreamlike quality. Jordan trusted the road.

As the car's engine purred in the lower gears, Jordan let his words flow. "You know, you gave me that strength to be honest. You love me for who I am and that gives me permission in a weird way to love myself. You make me a better person because you see me in a way that mirrors my better self. Does that make sense?"

Amanda gently replied, "Yeah, it does. I feel it too but you are better at putting it into words."

Jordan chuckled. "Well, I don't know about that. You're a pretty powerful poet."

Amanda gently patted Jordan's hand that was steady on the wheel, still maneuvering through the dense fog. "Honey, I think you touched people. You opened their hearts to a new possibility. None of us have seen angels but we know you and trust you. You gave us a gift, all of us. You allowed us to believe in what many of us doubt. You gave us the chance to embrace the possibility."

"It feels good, 'Manda. It's like I made peace with my past somehow... and with who I am."

Amanda moved in her seat to face Jordan. He kept his eyes on the road, maneuvering in the thickening fog. "I am so happy for you," she said, her voice soft and rich. "I think life takes us where we need to go one step at a time. We just have to have enough faith to take that next step. I'm so proud of you."

Jordan nodded as he down-shifted.

Amanda leaned in closer and dropped her voice to a near whisper, "But you know I feel like I also have a big step to take. Watching you tonight gives me hope that when it's my time I will have the courage and strength to do the same." Amanda paused, trying to find the words. "I can believe in that possibility and see a future where I am free... because you believe in me. Because you love me."

She sat back and looked out at the foreign-looking fog enshrouded landscape.

Jordan didn't answer. He knew she spoke the truth. Above the small car, two angels blazed and guided them on their path home.

CHAPTER 33

Amanda stepped into her apartment. She turned on the hallway light and headed to the kitchen to put on some tea. Tossing her jacket on the dining chair, she noticed that the sunflowers on the table needed fresh water. She lit a white lavender candle and breathed in the sweet aroma of her home.

Jordan had asked her to come to his house but she'd needed some time to herself. There was a lot to process and she felt both of them could use time to reflect. Learning to honor her inner voice meant she no longer needed to make excuses, apologize or do something she didn't want. She hummed to herself and appreciated that Jordan understood and made no judgments.

As she moved in the kitchen, she took her cell phone out of her purse. It was still on silent mode from the group meeting. There were several missed calls and a voicemail. She didn't recognize the number. She placed the phone on the counter and poured water and chose the loose tea. She took a deep breath. Her home was warm and cozy. It felt safe.

Yrandia stayed near. She surrounded Amanda in light and wrapped her in waves of love.

A light fragrance of the brewing tea filled the room. Amanda picked up her phone to listen to the message. A voice from long ago spoke into her ear and immediately stoked a dormant smoldering ember. Amanda closed her eyes and swallowed hard.

Yrandia opened her wings wider as the energy in the room shifted.

"Hello Amanda dear, this is Aunt Trish. I am sorry to call you out of the blue like this but it's about your mom."

Yes, Amanda thought, *somehow it is always about Mom.*

The voice on the phone continued in a near sing-song tone discordant with the message. "I don't want you to worry, honey, but your mom has taken sick. She didn't want me to call you, but I think you need to know. If you could call me back, I'll fill you in. I know it's been a long time since we've talked. But family is always family. I hope to hear from you soon, sweetie."

Amanda put down the phone and stared at it. She tried to take a deep breath then closed her eyes. "Slow down. Just slow down," she whispered, willing the voices to go away.

Physically frozen in place, that nearly forgotten ember started a slow burn as it morphed and glowed to life hidden deep inside that well-guarded space Amanda ignored and kept secret. She felt a dull ache in her stomach and tasted a bitter mix of adrenaline and bile. She breathed deeply to block that voice from the past, so similar to her mother's breezy breathless tone. With the precision of surgical steel, the haunting refrain struck into Amanda's heart. A dark cloud of dread seeped into the safety of her home. Outside, the heavy of blanket of fog hung ominously.

"Your mother has taken ill... family is family." The words were strangely incongruous.

Sometimes family isn't family, her mind shouted back. Her mother was sick. What did that mean? Amanda felt strangely detached as she observed her reaction. She willed herself to stay beyond the clutch of the hijack. "Be calm," she demanded as she continued to measure her breath.

She knew an emotional storm was brewing but at the moment she sat in the stillness and pushed the wave of rising voices aside. They did not speak for her. She wasn't even sure if they were speaking to her. As she let the reality sink in, old feelings of vulnerability and guilt mixed into a toxic brew that hung in the air.

The past months of practice and carefully constructed beliefs had been laid bare in one swift move.

Yrandia drew closer, softly whispering into her beloved's ear, "Turn to Love, Amanda. Turn to Love. There's always a choice. It is always a choice."

Amanda saw the candle flicker and gazed into its rising flame. Inhaling the sweet floral scent, she spoke a grounding affirmation: "I am safe. I am protected. I am wrapped in love and choose to find the blessing."

Yrandia bowed and smiled. "Yes, my dear. Choose each thought carefully." The room was draped in a soft glow.

Amanda picked up the phone and stared at the number. *Aunt Trish.* She hadn't thought of the woman in years. Her mind softly answered, *Why would I think of her?* Aunt Trish was her mother's younger sister. She had danced in and out of Amanda's young life leaving a trail of broken promises and a legacy of emotional scars where the smoldering ember now burned back to life. Sometimes she came disguised as a best friend or the caring aunt, only to disappear without notice, or worse in a blaze of shouting drama. She was the focus of countless childhood stories Amanda told herself that were wrapped in guilt, regret and unworthiness.

Memories flooded back, fueled by the dark smoke of that long ignored ember. Amanda felt the strangling pull of fear settle into her chest. She remembered the dark shadows of her childhood nights that blended into a heavy hazy mist with the morning sun. In her small room she recalled hearing but never seeing the phantom figures. Their hushed voices conveyed anger, hurt, reproach and painful imploring. Amanda recalled the muffled cries that always ended in slammed doors and squealing car tires. She knew who those phantoms were that filled the night. One of them—her mother—would appear in the morning drained and disheveled, waking her up with feigned sweetness, tossing off covers and opening the heavy drapes, willing the shadows of the night to retreat.

Amanda closed her eyes and saw the young girl who under the covers was filled with dread and guilt. *"Aunt Trish... please come back. I'll be good."* She smelled the smoke from her mother's long extinguished cigarette. These scenes ended with Amanda silently crying herself back into fitful sleep, waking up to her mother's call, *"Wake up, my sunshine."* But the small child was always left wondering if those phantom voices had been a dream. The half-filled glasses on the counter and stale smell of tobacco that welcomed her with her bowl of cereal served as silent confirmation.

As Amanda's mind flashed these childhood memories in rapid progression, she suddenly felt cold. She stared at the phone... that haunting voice of her childhood suddenly made present again.

"It's just a voice," Amanda told herself. But it was a real voice, not the one of her childhood nightmares. It was a real voice with a real message. Amanda felt herself being pulled into some strange vortex. The phantom memories long buried began to swirl at her feet. She curled up on her chair. She closed her eyes. "You have a choice. There is always a choice," she whispered over and over.

Her mind raced. She should call Jordan. She *needed* to call Jordan.

"Breathe," she demanded.

"And say what?" the small voice asked her.

"Be the grown-up," she told the empty room and uncurled herself. No, she needed to call Trish. She needed to own the moment and not become the scared child hiding under the covers. She pushed back against the chair and the invisible energy grabbing at her.

Yrandia whispered softly to Amanda. She knew that while her child couldn't hear, her heart was open enough to sense her presence at some deeper level. "Bend toward Love, Amanda. The answer is always Love. Be present. Be in the moment. The past is not a part of this moment. Fear is not here. Love is here. Right here, right now. You have a choice. And you choose Peace."

As Amanda stood up, she felt a warm flow of energy enter the room. The dark energy retreated. She smiled. She listened to the breeze in the palms outside her window. Moving over to the living room she settled into her cushioned chair.

Yrandia continued to lovingly whisper into the still apartment, "Find your balance. It is here in the stillness. It is in the breath. Breathe in peace. Breathe out love."

Amanda sat for a long time, candle slowly burning while the deeply buried ember lost its heat.

CHAPTER 34

On the other side of town, Anioch sensed a change in vibration. His connection to Yrandia was growing strong and he sensed her calling to him. He paused and held her in light, offering a blessing. He knew, as angels always know—the answer simply is love.

Jordan looked up from his book. He thought he heard a knock. He wasn't tired, still feeling a raw energy that had stayed with him since the meeting. He put down the book he'd been flipping through and stretched after he got up from the sofa.

He looked outside to see the heavy fog beginning to lift. A strong northerly wind pushed the slender palm trees and rocked the towering pines, creating the banging noises as branches collided. The surf was loud and the crash of the sea pounding on the shore carried in the howling wind. Jordan wondered if perhaps a big storm was coming. He poked his head out the open door and felt the change in pressure.

The charged night called to him. The approaching storm matched his restless energy. He slipped on his running shoes and jacket before stepping outside. The wind was cold as it rushed against his skin. The ocean beckoned. It always beckoned when the energy of a storm was near.

He headed to the deserted shore. As he walked, the swirling sand whipped at his feet, creating small spirals. The wind pulled the sand from the shore and stung his face as it sailed along. Sensing something more than a change in weather, Jordan breathed in the salt air and surrendered to the unbridled pulse that tugged at him.

"What's going on?" he quietly asked himself.

The meeting had been cathartic and rich with emotion so this pulling unease seemed strange. He reached the open beach and began his run, willing himself to release any anxiety, knowing that worry was wasted energy. Under the dark night sky, he spoke a prayer of gratitude ending in a near whisper, "...All is well, and so it is."

⌘⌘

Amanda dialed the number. After two rings, Aunt Trish picked up, her voice groggy and sleep-filled.

"Hi, it's Amanda. I got your message." She tried to keep her voice calm and light.

"Oh honey, thank you for calling me back. I know it's been a long time. But you know how things can get busy."

Amanda could hear the hesitancy. She let it go and willed herself to stay present. "No worries. Life does seem to get hectic." Her heart pounded and she felt the urge to fill the space with idle talk. "I hope you are okay. So what's going on?" Amanda forced her mind to stay focused and not run in a thousand crazy directions.

"Yes, yes. I'm sorry sweetie, not the type of message I like to leave. But like I said, your mom is sick and in the hospital. They're running tests. She didn't want to get people all spun up. You know how she can be." Her aunt paused as if trying to choose her words.

Amanda listened and breathed in an effort to stay in the moment. Amanda heard Dr. Blair's calm voice telling her to acknowledge the feelings that pulled at her, but not to lose herself to them. *"Don't get triggered."* Always the advice of her mentor.

Fear. Dread. Those were the most immediate feelings. There was bitterness, too. Amanda nodded silently and bid them farewell. *You don't serve me now*, she noted. *Stay present.*

"What are they testing for?" Amanda heard her own voice, grateful it didn't belie the fear that bubbled just below the surface. Her adult voice was in control, leaving no space for the cries of the young child.

"We thought maybe she had the flu or some kind of virus. She just didn't seem herself. But she wouldn't go to the doctor. I mean, I don't have to tell you how stubborn your mom can be." Trish let out a choked laugh.

Amanda could picture her aunt with a burning cigarette and a half-empty beer bottle nearby.

"Okay, but you said she's in the hospital. If they're just running tests, why is she in the hospital?" Amanda's voice rose with her frustration. *Just talk to me like I'm an adult*, she wanted to shout. But instead she closed her eyes and silently recited her mantra: *I am peace. I breathe in Peace. I am love. I breathe out Love.*

"I just think it would be good if you came to see her. You know, before the next results come. She'd like that, Amanda. She misses you." Trish began to softly sob. "She wouldn't go to the doctors for a long time, sweetie. I tried to get her to go."

Amanda knew there was more than what her aunt was sharing. She stayed in control. "I can drive up. But I'd like to have some sense of what's going on. Is it serious? I mean, you must have some idea what they are testing for." A wave of calm washed over Amanda. She sat completely still and noticed her own matter of fact tone. It was as if someone else had taken control while she watched.

Aunt Trish choked back the sobs and continued, her voice weak. "Well, we're hopeful it's only a bad bronchitis infection. I don't know, honey. I just think it would be good for you to be here." Trish was getting quieter.

Amanda knew words were being chosen to avoid the truth. But it was getting late and clearly Trish was not in a state of mind to offer more. "Okay. I need to get some things in order here if I'm going to drive out. What hospital is she in? Tri-Valley?"

"Well... no, Amanda honey. She moved. You knew that, right?"

Amanda couldn't help but smile at the absurdity of the question. *No, actually I didn't.*

"Let it go," she said under her breath then responded softly, "I guess I forgot that. What town is she in and what hospital?" Her mind shouted out, *Just give me the facts so I can get off the phone.* She remained quiet.

Amanda let out a low sigh. As she waited for her aunt to respond, the dark feeling of dread re-entered the room. It found its way back into her private refuge, slipping in between any space she left unobserved and unprotected. Its tentacles grabbed at her feet and hands, slowly wrapping around her heart.

She closed her eyes and willed the negative energy to leave. She visualized a radiant ball of light covering her and her home in pure light. Adult monsters couldn't be allowed to take over. Not now.

Her aunt's gravelly voiced pierced the silence, bringing Amanda back to the moment. "She lives in Holyfield now. She's at Community General. I'm staying in her apartment. I'll text you the address."

"Okay," Amanda said, thinking quickly. "I'm guessing I can drive there in about six hours. But it's late and I have to get some stuff together. I'll let you know when I hit the road. You get some rest. You sound tired. I'm sure this will all be fine." Amanda knew the words rang hollow but she didn't want to talk anymore. She'd heard enough.

"Yes, you too, sweetie. I am sure the tests will come back fine. Your mom will feel so much better when she sees you. She loves you. She... always has..." Trish's voice trailed off.

"Good night. I will see you tomorrow." Amanda hung up.

Her mind was racing, a swirl of raw emotions. Recrimination and judgment fought for control. *You should have been with her. You never call. You are selfish.*

"*Stop!*" she yelled to the empty apartment.

Yrandia bowed, glad to hear her child speak out. There was power in that command. She knew Amanda was stepping into her own strength instead of shrinking to the fear. Yes, her child was learning to return to Love.

Amanda stared at her tea cup. Her quiet evening was shattered but in the stillness her inner voice came to her, breaking through the dim churn of nameless voices that blended into the now howling winds. The voice called her to pay attention. They were the questions she grappled with as her homework from Dr. Blair. In their simplicity they called her to shift into the moment and escape the insidious creep of fear. *What is mine to do? How else can I look at this situation? If it is a call for help, or a call to serve, I can choose how to respond. It is always my choice. Always.*

As Amanda's mind pulled in a dizzying mix of practical concerns for trip planning, there suddenly came a fleeting thought of Jordan's angel. She heard Jordan's voice clearly telling her that angels need to be asked to help. She recalled their conversation and how he explained the concept of free will and how angels waited for humans to ask for intercession. "It's a night for angels, I guess," she softly whispered.

She smiled, amused by the random thought, so she got up. It didn't feel silly or childish but rather totally right. She spoke in a clear voice, "My dear angel, I believe you are with me. Please guide me. Let me be strong and do what is mine to do."

She paused and looked at her warm apartment. She felt safe and secure. She bowed her head and closed her eyes. She softly placed her right hand over her heart. She sensed a presence with her and was filled with gratitude.

Her voice remained calm as she lowered it into a whispered prayer, "Please be with me in my thoughts and actions that I stay aligned with Love, always with Love. Open my eyes so that I may see with the eyes of my True Self. Keep me safe and protect me from my own small voice. Let me be a channel of peace and love. Thank you. And so it is." Amanda felt moved to end with a slight bow.

Yrandia blazed with Angelic joy. Her heart opened wider and blessed every corner of the room. She channeled Divine grace into her child's beautiful heart.

A flash of light lit the space and thunder rattled the windows. Amanda opened her eyes. The candle blazed and Amanda's pulse quickened.

In a surge of energy, Amanda softly spoke into the night, "I choose Love."

CHAPTER 35

Anioch and Jordan were alone on the empty beach. Anioch flew just above the fast moving man. The angel loved running alongside his beautiful child. He delighted in the mad dance of nature as the ocean roared, the wind howled and the rain pounded. Jordan fell into a steady pace, taking in the sights and sounds of life that surrounded him. Jordan needed motion and speed in his life. Running next to the thrashing surf was therapeutic for both angel and man. The ocean still called to Jordan but he hadn't overcome the last vestige of fear. The block remained.

As Anioch surrendered to the wind, he sensed a shift—the atmosphere was changing. His thoughts drifted once again to the angelic call he had heard earlier from his Beloved. He couldn't name what was shifting but he knew that all things conspired toward good and that all was in order. An undercurrent of peacefulness pulled him along even amid the power of the rising storm. Anioch remembered Yrandia's wise words, *"All is well and as it should be, dear brother, and must be..."* and sensed her presence among the crest of the waves and the explosive flashes from the distant lightning. He leaned into the storm and felt the raw magnetic pull of the earth. The power of nature was in full display. His thoughts again moved to Yrandia. She too was a magnificent force of nature.

Jordan quickened his pace. The thunder immediately followed the jagged bolts and panoramic displays of electricity that lit up the sky. The storm was closer now. Pulsing electricity was in the atmosphere. Jordan thought of Amanda. The winds picked up as the waves pounded the shore, inching closer as the tide rolled in. A flickering memory of another storm-battered shore came to Jordan. But he was not frightened nor haunted by the memory. Rather drenched by the rain and pushed by wind, he remembered the ancient prayer: *"May you trust God that you are exactly where you are meant to be."* He spoke to the screeching wind, "I am where I am supposed to be and for that I am grateful." In his heart he knew that stormy day on the same shore was a gift and he felt comfort in the thought.

Amanda's call to Jordan went straight to voicemail. *Where is he?* She left a quick message, not wanting to provide details. She heard the loud claps of thunder and the driving rain against the window. *Where on earth could he be with this storm?*

She knew she had to go to Holyfield. It wasn't a choice. It occurred to her that the old patterns were falling back into place. Once again she would need to be the adult in the situation and carry her mother and aunt. But she also knew that this time it felt different. There was something deeper and grounded. Amanda could feel it but it didn't paralyze her like it had when she was a child. Some part of her surrendered to it and understood the field had changed. She wasn't lending her mother support or a shoulder to cry on after one of her countless breakups. It wasn't listening to the laments of a bad decision after another job lost or a bad business deal. It wasn't one of the countless other meaningless slights or misunderstandings that had always set her mom into a spiral of doubt, grief and depression. No, this time it was stated as a simple fact. Her aunt said that her mom was sick.

Amanda pondered the reality that Aunt Trish bothered to call, which led her to believe her mom must be really sick. Amanda knew she had to be there and be present in a way she hadn't been before. She sensed there was a big lesson in all of this; for all of them. She steadied herself and silently asked for strength.

Amanda began to plan what she needed to do to get ready for this unexpected trip. As she moved about the apartment, the scared and wounded child screamed for attention. Amanda willed herself to focus and pushed the young child's voice aside. "Guide me, please. I am strong. I am protected."

Yrandia stayed near and wrapped her child in rays of interlacing light.

She sent a text to her boss saying she'd call in the morning. She threw a load of clothes in the washer and pulled out her old suitcases. She looked at the weather in Holyfield. "Holyfield? Who knew I'd be going there?" she mused. She planned to be gone for a week or two... together again with her mother and Aunt Trish... fully mindful of all the landmines buried in their collective past.

❦

Jordan returned energized from his run. He saw that he had a voicemail. He listened to it and immediately sensed an underlying urgency in Amanda's perfunctory message. He wondered what had happened in this short period of time. His mind tried to whisper that he had somehow let her down. Something happened and he should have been there.

He pushed the sabotaging thought aside. It didn't serve him to think like that. He called her back and she picked up after the first ring.

"Hey, I just got back in. You okay?" Jordan's voice was still breathless and held a telltale intensity he had not intended. He slowed his breathing. *Let go of the worry!*

"Yeah, I'm okay," Amanda answered, then added, "Actually, I'm not totally sure. I got a call from my aunt. Seems my mom is sick and Aunt Trish says I should come."

Jordan could hear her hesitancy. "Wow, I'm sorry. I can come over. The storm's passed so I can be there in a few minutes. Let me just change clothes."

"No, no that's okay. I'm getting my things together. It's late and I gotta figure out stuff to get in line. I feel like I need to go and it sounded kind of urgent. I know my Aunt and I'm thinking things must be pretty serious... or beyond her coping abilities if she had to call." Amanda paused and with a touch of sarcasm added, "Not to say she really has any coping skills. So in truth, I don't know how bad it is."

It took a moment for Jordan to process what she was saying. "I understand but I can be there to help you. Whatever you need, Manda. I won't bug you but I can be there to support you in any way. I don't want you to feel alone."

Amanda paused. "Thank you, sweetheart. I appreciate that, but right now I feel like I need to do this and just focus." Her voice was kind yet firm.

"Okay. I understand," Jordan lied. "You know I am here. You know that, right? No matter what." A tight knot began to wrap around him and gripped his chest. What was he resisting? He offered love but there was something else... something pulled at him. He pushed it aside.

"And that's why I love you. You are my rock. I just need a little space right now to get organized. I feel like I have to be a grown-up." Her voice was now stronger and steady.

Jordan exhaled. He understood. This was hers to do. *Let it be.* "Okay, I get that. But being a grown-up doesn't mean you have to do this alone." Jordan didn't want to push, but he also didn't want her pushing him away. It crossed his mind that the haunting figures of her past might be pulling her back into the dark places she'd fought so hard to illuminate. He didn't want to see that happen and fought against the negative story he had created about Amanda's family.

It was as if Amanda read his mind. Her words cut through his jumbled thoughts. "Jordan, I'm okay. I can't really explain it but I have this weird inner calm like a warm blanket is wrapped around me. I always knew this day would come. In some way, I think the past months have been preparing me for this. I need to really step into this, whatever *this* is. My inner voice keeps telling me to answer with love."

Anioch recognized the strength of the words and saw Jordan physically respond by relaxing.

"Okay, I hear you and of course trust you. But I just have to say it again, I am with you. You know that, right?" Jordan's voice was softer now.

"I know that," she replied with a smile in her voice. "I know that with every fiber of my being. I love you so much." Amanda got quiet. "You know what, I did something tonight I've never done before..."

Her voice had a dreamy quality to it. More silence. Jordan waited. His silence begged her to continue.

"I was struggling with all of this and felt momentarily vulnerable like every childhood monster was clawing at the door to come in. I had to find a way to stay strong. And in that moment I thought of you. There was this moment of clarity and I knew what I had to do. I asked my angel to be with me and to guide me." He could hear a spark of joy as she spoke the words. "You taught me that. And when I did that, everything just sort of melted and got a whole lot less scary. I have you to thank for that."

"Wow, that is awesome, my love. Really awesome. That makes me feel so much better. It makes this feel somehow directed and okay. I am really happy for you." Jordan felt his voice catch and a wave of deep emotion wash over him.

Anioch blazed as the words echoed. He danced above his child and laughed with wild abandon. A ray of light spread from his core that radiated out into the room and beyond. He channeled pure joy. He immediately thought of Yrandia and imagined how she must have filled with angelic bliss. After all this time on earth, she finally was being brought into the sacred space opened by the act of petition. Anioch sent his light and love to Jordan and gently exhaled a silent command. *"Be still, Jordan."* Then he followed with an angelic burst of pure Source energy to his beloved Yrandia.

Jordan hung up, trying not to give attention to his worry and focusing instead on the happiness he felt for Amanda and her Guardian. He prayed for wisdom and faith. He didn't know what this next phase of their journey would be but in that moment chose to turn and surrender to Divine Order.

A faint echo of unsettledness—like a hollow reverberation that followed his heartbeat—was still there, but he didn't dwell on it. There was the small whisper beckoning to him to take charge, to be in control. But he resisted. This wasn't his. His inner voice reassured him that Amanda needed to step into her own life. This wasn't about him.

"Send love. Just send love."

Jordan turned around. He'd heard a voice. It was clear and commanding. He knew he was alone in his apartment but felt compelled to answer aloud, "Yes."

That was the answer. Just send love and know that all will be as it should be.

Again the voice spoke, *"All is well."* Jordan looked up and smiled, "Yes, Ani. All is well."

"Yes," Jordan affirmed a second time.

He smiled and Anioch danced.

CHAPTER 36

Amanda stopped by Jordan's house early the next morning, bringing coffee and fresh baked muffins. Jordan kept the conversation light, trying to read her emotions. He sensed resolve more than worry. Peace more than fear. Stillness more than chaos. She looked beautiful, her eyes were bright and radiated a calm presence that Jordan felt when he held her in his arms. Something about her had changed. It was as if some deep reservoir of strength had opened and was finding its way up to the surface. When they hugged, a strange image of a warrior princess passed before his mind's eye.

Anioch saw the image too and recognized the archetype. He knew Amanda was preparing for a big lesson—a battle, if you will.

Yrandia was brilliant and fully prepared to guide her child on this important journey.

Anioch and Yrandia shared the strength of their magnificent auras. The angels knew that their lives were intertwined and they vowed strength and love to the other.

Jordan felt some new energy in the room and wondered if the Warrior Princess was Amanda's soul assignment. The thought humbled him. He wasn't there to protect her. Whatever this trip brought was hers to do and not his to take away. He was there to love her and trust.

He pulled her close and whispered into her ear. His words flowed from an opening deep inside his heart. "You are strong and beautiful," he said, his voice soft and calm. "You always have been and always will be. You are loved and worthy of love. You always have been and always will be that, too. I love you with my whole heart and my whole soul and I am with you every step of your journey. The voices from your past can't quiet the voice of your heart."

Amanda's eyes filled with tears. She softly replied a simple, "Thank you." She lifted her head from Jordan's shoulders. "I feel like the Universe has conspired for some time now to prepare me for this. Meeting you has changed me in profound ways. I don't know what is coming my way but I know I am better and stronger and more capable to find the right answer because you love me." The room was filled with the elevated vibration of gratitude and love.

The angels touched wings and held their children in a circle of love. Yrandia knew that the road ahead was filled with steps and passages into love, forgiveness and letting go.

Amanda folded herself back into Jordan's deep embrace. "Thank you, Jordan. My aunt didn't say it, but somehow I know what I am going to. I am going to begin that last part of the journey that will end by my saying goodbye." Amanda softly began to weep.

Gently Jordan stroked her long hair. He let her cry. It was a good release. He held her close and felt the gentle beating of her heart next to his. *All is well*, he prayed. He then gently spoke, "I know, my love. I feel that and I want to protect you from pain and hurt. But I can't. I can only hold you in light. And I will do that every minute of every day. I am here and I will be by your side at a moment's notice. Just call... please... just call."

The two held on to each other while their angels enveloped them in a radiant arc of light and love.

Amanda pulled up to Community General Hospital. A stark building built in the brutalist style, its mass of concrete was surrounded by an expansive parking lot dotted by late-blooming mimosa trees. Their delicate pink blossoms contrasted with the dark outlines of the hospital.

She looked past the sea of asphalt and focused instead on the perfect blue sky. It was a sunny day with just a few wispy clouds gathering along the horizon. She rolled down the window. Sounds and smells of the vibrant energy of life greeted her. *Sometimes you just have to pause and listen*, she mused. The trees rustled in the breeze and distant birds chirped.

As she breathed in the fresh air, she felt a sense of dread that rested deep in the pit of her stomach. She named it. It was fear. All the centering exercises she had done on the long drive, all the affirmations for healing, peace and wholeness began to slip away and the calm she'd clung to slowly unraveled as she walked the pathway to the unwelcoming building.

At the hospital entrance, the same old dark energy crawled up to her when the door slid shut. The sounds of life were quieted. The place of healing felt like a sealed tomb, cavernous, sinister and sterile. Amanda stopped and squared her shoulders. She silently willed herself to be present and to become the channel of healing light she needed.

The dark energy offered to guide her. She clutched her hands together. *One step at a time.*

She could hear her own small footsteps echo in the long hallway. The gravity of the moment clawed at her, grabbing her by the throat. A muffled sob caught in her chest. *Somewhere,* she thought, *within these dimly lit corridors my mother is lying surrounded by these thick walls that are keeping out the light and the sounds of life. But I am the healing light. I am the sound of life.* She continued to silently speak, trying to push aside the dark thoughts.

Amanda had a room number and wove her way along the various wings. She walked past strangers carrying flowers and balloons, coming to celebrate the miracle of birth or the miracle of healing. Others seemed lost in thought, processing their own world of worry.

Amanda hated hospitals, only knowing the worry, pain and loss they represented. What would she say to her mother? *Let it go,* she willed her mind. *Just walk.* One step at a time. *When it is time to speak, you will speak.*

But she worried about the wounded child. What if the child was the one who wanted to speak and demanded the stage? How could decades of hurt be erased literally overnight, or by one diagnosis?

She walked and wondered what type of foolish path she had embarked on, thinking that if she just changed her perspective she could simply wipe the slate clean of the past trauma and pain. The child began to shout at her and she felt stupid and alone. "Just walk," she firmly demanded.

Yrandia matched every step. She sensed the negative energy swirling around her child. The angel created an invisible arc of light to protect her from the pulsing dark waves. The guardian knew that these insidious questions and thoughts could open up the invisible door leading into a swirling, murky vortex that would grab Amanda and drag her deeper into that empty space she'd recently escaped. Her beautiful child had come too far, trading the dark world of shadows, choosing instead to step into the light. She would not let her lose her footing now.

The angel whispered to her beloved, "You are a child of the Divine. You are light and love." She would not let those heavy chains of past illusions grip her beautiful girl.

Amanda saw a small patio and turned toward it. She needed air. Walking back into the sunlight, she sat on the iron bench and felt the warmth enter her body. She closed her eyes. She hadn't expected to feel this disoriented. She wished she had accepted Jordan's invitation.

After a deep breath she whispered, "Dear angel, please hear me. I know you are here with me. Give me strength, be my strength. I know I am not alone but I am scared, really scared. Please walk with me. I can't do this alone. Wrap me in light and love." Tears rolled down her face.

The wind picked up and Amanda heard a voice speak to her. *"You are not alone. You are a child of the Divine. You are light and love. You are all goodness."*

Amanda opened her eyes. She blinked to let the world come back in focus. The once small voice she'd worked so hard to find and needed to practice to tune into was no longer small.

A burst of energy passed through her. She remembered Jordan's inspired words: *"You are strong and beautiful. You always have been and always will be. You are loved and worthy of love. You always have been and always will be that, too. I love you with my whole heart and soul and I am with you every step of your journey. No voice from your past can quiet the voice of your heart."*

She stood up, "Okay Amanda, you can do this."

Amanda opened the door and walked back into the brooding edifice. She felt small but not alone. The gift shop was right around the corner so she stopped in and bought a bouquet of wildflowers and lilies. The saleslady rang her up. Without a word their eyes met. A warm smile made the building suddenly seem less dark, less ominous.

Amanda made her way up to the sixth floor. The door to her mother's room was closed. She waited, listening for some sound of life. But all she heard was a low buzz and muted voices off in the distance.

Life seemed suspended. Amanda took a deep breath and entered the room. Heavy plastic curtains darkened the space. A faint trace of antibacterial scents mixed in with the cool air.

Her mother was turned on her side, asleep under the covers. She looked small, barely filling up a corner of the bed. Amanda saw the tiny ripple of the rise of the thin blanket.

Amanda's eyes adjusted to the light. Could this be the right room? She barely recognized the small, frail woman as the one who had danced and sung with a breezy boozy sway. The red hair was matted down and shocked with gleaming white roots. Once radiant rouged cheeks were sallow and sunken. She looked like a waxed version of Amanda's mother. Time had robbed her not only of any trace of beauty but of any visage of life.

Amanda turned away. Her worst fears were realized at the sound of her mother's raspy, rhythmic breathing.

The covers moved as the figure beneath them shifted, perhaps sensing Amanda's presence. The pale woman's eyelids fluttered. As she moved, the IV bottle began to gently sway. Claire shifted her head and her eyes turned toward Amanda. They stared back, blankly, not recognizing her daughter. Those pupils shined like tiny black pinpricks on a canvas of hazy pink.

Amanda blinked and looked away. Her own eyes welled with tears. She did not want to greet her mother like this so she walked to the window to slightly open the drawn curtains. "Here, let's get some sunshine into this room." Amanda willed her voice to be light.

Her mother pushed herself into a seated position and instinctively brushed the stray hairs aside, licking her parched lips.

Amanda knew her mother didn't recognize her and wondered what medications were pumping through the IV. She carried the large bundle of flowers to the bedside, an offering of life and joy. "Hi, Mom. It's me, Amanda." Her voice was a sing-song. She bent in to give her mother a peck on the cheek.

Claire leaned in. "Amanda. Oh my goodness, Amanda. What a wonderful surprise. Let me look at you."

Amanda felt her mother's cold hand reach out and push her slightly back so she could look at her and take her in.

"Oh Mandy, why look at you. Oh my. And I look like a total wreck!"

Amanda smiled. There she was... the mother she remembered, unchanged by the ravages of disease, still worried about how she looked. "Oh, Mom." The half-statement hung in the air.

Claire's voice dropped to a whisper, "Oh Mandy, you came. You *came*." She coughed slightly and turned her head. "If you could give me some water, please, that would be sweet."

Amanda poured from the pink plastic pitcher and handed the cup to her mother. She noticed that those hands were bruised and yellowed. "Yes, of course I came. As soon as Aunt Trish called."

Amanda busied herself setting the flowers on a nearby nightstand and moving the guest chair closer to the bed.

She reached again for Claire's hand. Lowering her gaze she studied that hand, so different from the ones that had bathed her, brushed her hair, held her own small hands as they crossed the street. The same hands that turned angry and harsh. Hands that slapped her, marking the indelible welts that never really went away.

Amanda patted the clammy hand, now letting the fleeting thoughts pass away. *Let it* go. These hands belonged to a woman she barely recognized.

Her mom drank deeply from the cup. She struggled with a slight cough.

"I'm here now, Mom. You don't need to talk. We have time. Just rest."

Her mother took smaller sips from the straw that hung from the pink plastic cup. She smiled slightly and closed her eyes. She squeezed Amanda's hand. A small gravelly voice slowly spoke, "I hoped you would come. But I would have understood if you didn't."

Amanda noticed a small tear forming on the corner of her mother's closed eyelid. "You rest. We'll catch up slowly. I have nowhere else to be but here."

Yrandia watched as her child spoke. She saw beautiful luminous light sparkle around Amanda, extending out to her mother and touching the outer edges of the older woman's pale aura. Yrandia sent love to them both. She knew, as angelic guides do, that this was a special time for mother and child. She glanced above Claire's head to reconnect with her ancient sister and Claire's angelic guide, Xandra.

Xandra bowed a deep and welcoming bow. The years had separated them but there was much that still connected them to each other. "Welcome, my sister. I've missed you."

"And I you, my beloved," Yrandia replied. They touched wings and formed a protective arch over mother and child. "It is as it should be," Yrandia whispered. "Indeed it is. I've waited for this day. We knew it would come."

Xandra was a radiant Being with deep amber-colored eyes that glowed with a rich light. Her face was framed by long curls of gold. Yrandia had missed this beautiful Being who had been her early Guide. She mused how different this magnificent Being of Light was to the earthly daughter who lay almost lifeless, pale and drained of all radiance of the true Life Force.

Amanda got up. She felt a wave of brooding energy pulling at her so she moved closer to the sunlight. She wished she could open the window and let in the fresh air. She looked back at her mother whose eyes silently followed. There was something in those eyes. Beyond pain or even sadness. There was an intensity as if something was burning deeply inside or behind.

Claire held Amanda's gaze. Amanda took a small instinctual step back. She looked away. Claire blinked and the moment passed.

"I'm here and you just rest. You don't need to worry or feel rushed." Amanda moved back to the bed, gently caressing her mother's hand.

Claire smiled, this time a broader smile. As she took in a deep breath she closed her eyes.

Amanda noticed how her mother's chest rose under the blanket and heard a dry rattle as she released that breath.

Claire kept her eyes closed as she softly spoke, "Oh sweetie, I am really so very happy to see you. We need to get ourselves right. I need to do this right. This time I've gotta get it right." Then Claire opened her eyes. Amanda could see they were brimming with tears.

Yrandia and Xandra bowed and filled the room with waves of love. They knew that time stood still, waiting for the release of the past, the opening of hearts and the flow of pure energy that forgiveness provides. They joined in a low and beautiful chant knowing that their Purpose was to join with these two women on their journey of healing.

"Shhh, Mom." Amanda's voice was a gentle hum blending beautifully with the angelic song. "Just rest. We are good. Right here. Right now. We are good. I'm here. I'll be here right beside you. Just rest." Amanda gently slid onto the bed and squeezed next to her mother.

Claire stroked her daughter's hair. "You deserve better. You always deserved better. I tried, baby. I really did."

"I know that. It doesn't matter, really. That's all in the past. Right now let's try and find a place of peace, okay?" Amanda felt the words in her heart as she spoke them.

Xandra bowed, recognizing the words of Wisdom and Truth. The angel lifted her head and smiled at Yrandia. "You've guided our daughter well. Her heart is open. Her words are inspired."

Yrandia bowed and felt a swell of angelic pride. Yes, their daughter was special. "Her journey has been a difficult one, but every step has led us to this moment. Sister, we always knew it. Divine will has no whys." The two angels embraced as arches of light draped the drab hospital room.

Claire shifted and faced her daughter. "A place of peace? That sounds perfect. I think we deserve that. You were always special. So kind and smart and so beautiful. I hope you know I always thought you were beautiful."

Amanda felt the sting. Her breath caught. "*I hope you know I always thought you were beautiful.*" Old wounds, long buried, opened. The ancient invisible scars from the past were laid bare by these words. Amanda recognized the pain and willed herself not to let it grab her heart.

Yrandia drew close. "You are a child of the Divine. Perfect in every way. Complete and whole." Amanda shifted in the bed and nodded, then closed her eyes. Yrandia sent love to the small child who had ached and longed to hear those words. "You are beautiful."

She had waited for years but those words were never spoken. In their absence, Amanda wrote a life story negating the need to be beautiful. Being beautiful didn't matter. But the small child still waited. And here in this space of stale air and gray nothingness, the salve of healing was offered. The words seeped into the vacuous places of denial. "*You were always special. I hope you know I always thought you were beautiful.*" Amanda felt the tears coming and swallowed hard.

"Thank you, Mom. Thank you."

Claire looked at her daughter, puzzled by the deep emotion. "You've always been strong and beautiful. I've always been proud of you for being such a good person, and I told people what a beautiful daughter you are. I hope you know that. I hope you always knew and know how much I love you."

There in the space between mother and daughter, Jordan's words silently hung. Amanda felt something move and in her heart she knew that a plank in their shared bridge had appeared. It was now waiting for her to take the next step. Healing was going to happen one step at a time.

Amanda found her voice. "Well, it's always good to hear that. I always thought you were the most beautiful woman in the world. I wanted to grow up and be as beautiful as you." Amanda smiled. It wasn't so hard. She accepted the gift she was being given and was grateful for it... even after all these years of waiting.

CHAPTER 37

Amanda jerked in the chair. She must have fallen asleep. She was momentarily confused but as her eyes adjusted to the dim light, she saw her mother resting comfortably in bed. It was early afternoon. The day seemed endless as if time had stood still.

Stomach growling, she got up and stretched. *No word from the doctor.* The nurse had said he had a full schedule and would be by as soon as the test results arrived. *And of course Aunt Trish is a no-show.* Amanda sighed as she bent at the waist to stretch and shake out the kinks that had settled into her back and neck after the drive and hours of sitting.

Perhaps sensing movement in the room, Claire opened her eyes and smiled.

Amanda moved toward the bed. She gently stroked the stray strands of hair that fell over her mother's face. "I'm going to get a quick bite of lunch," Amanda called to her. "I'm feeling hungry. Can I get you something?"

"Oh of course, sweetie. You must be *starving.*"

Amanda ignored the dig. "I'll be right back. I don't want to miss the doctor."

Claire nodded. "Sure, Mandy. I'm fine. Trish said she would be here. I wonder what happened. She should be here soon. You know Aunt Trish. She runs on her own time."

Amanda let a slight smile escape. *That's an understatement.*

She found signs pointing to the cafeteria. As she turned the corner, she noticed the small courtyard she'd seen earlier that morning. It was bathed in sunlight. *What a pretty little spot,* an oasis within the center of the brutal structure. Amanda noticed miniature roses clustered on vines that lined the walkway. A small bench was tucked under an ivy-draped trellis. "I'll eat my lunch there," Amanda whispered to herself. With just the simple view of the small sanctuary, she felt her energy shift. *Funny.* The concrete walls so quickly obscured the world and the calm that waited just beyond.

Amanda arranged her lunch on the bench. The afternoon sun and warmth enveloped her. She breathed in the fresh air as she nibbled on the sandwich. She checked in with Jordan by phone and a deep calm slowly entered, releasing the strain of the past hours. She closed her eyes and listened to the birds. Their chatter brought her into the present moment. She could smell the mix of flowers and grass and felt transported into a state of peace.

Amanda was lost in a place of shifting thoughts when she felt a tap on her shoulder. "Aunt Trish!" She stood to embrace the woman and caught the scent of stale cigarettes. Then she felt her aunt lean into her. Amanda suppressed the urge to push away and instead chose to lean in to the hug, releasing the rush of old half-formed memories brought on by the smell of her aunt's hair.

"Amanda, sweetie, thank you for coming." Trish's voice was heavy, draped in weariness. Amanda detected a hint of beer on her breath.

Aware of her own body tensing and back tightening, Amanda again resisted the pull of the shadow and chose to let go. *Be still and choose love*, she silently prayed. "Of course I came. I'm glad to see you, Aunt Trish." Amanda's voice remained calm. She moved her half-eaten sandwich aside and motioned for her aunt to sit down. "I've been with Mom. She's resting right now. I know you told me she was sick but she looks worse than I expected." *Strong and direct.*

She noticed her aunt take a small step back. The old roles were shifting. Power was transferred in that moment.

"I know, honey. She does look tired but I didn't want to worry you over the phone. I thought it would be better to have you here." Trish tugged on her purse and fumbled with the zipper.

"I understand." Amanda held her aunt's gaze and reached for her hand. "So tell me what's going on. What are they saying?" Amanda planted her feet firmly on the terra cotta brick and sat up straight.

Her aunt's voice was small and the woman looked down while she spoke. "She isn't well, honey." Silence hung in the space between them. "They say it's cancer. I think it's pretty bad."

Amanda let out a long breath and sat with the word: *Cancer*. She wasn't really surprised. But hearing the word still hit hard. That word had power.

The silence seemed to vibrate. Amanda's thoughts raced. She had always known this day would come. She had always known... but had been unsure if it would be a car accident, a fall, some dramatic self-inflicted wound or an illness. "Cancer," she replied, letting the word sink in. Calm enveloped Amanda. It seemed as if someone else had taken control over her body and she was just an observer. "Okay, so not that it really matters, but what kind of cancer?"

"It's showing up in the lungs," Trish replied. "The tests are to s-see if... to see if it's s-spread." Trish's voice caught. There was more silence.

Amanda sat and waited. She could hear her aunt exhale.

Still fidgeting, Trish continued, "They took more tests, like I told you. So we should know more very soon. That's why I called you. I thought you would want to be here to get the results." Her aunt fumbled in her purse, pulling out a pack of cigarettes.

Amanda pointed to the No Smoking sign stuck between two rose bushes. Trish pushed the pack back into her purse and pulled out some chewing gum, offering a piece.

"No, thank you," Amanda quietly replied.

Amanda weeded through her thoughts. Aunt Trish, and probably her mother too, had known about the cancer but didn't call. Rather, they waited to tell her about it until it was possibly too late... *To see if it spread...* Anger bubbled to the surface.

Yrandia drew closer and softly whispered. "Be calm, my child." The breeze picked up and the small delicate roses danced on the supple stocks. "Anger won't serve you. Be present. You know the answer is always rooted in love."

The light breeze caressed Amanda. Her eyelids fluttered shut. *I'm here for a reason. Let me stay open to this moment.* The words percolated up and she was thankful for them. She opened her eyes and looked at Trish. At that moment she saw the woman not as her aunt but as a vulnerable scared child. In that moment she decided she would not respond to the woman the way her aunt had responded to her all those years before.

Something touched her and she knew this was a journey of forgiveness. It was time to begin the process of letting go. The wounds were old and needed to fully heal. That would happen only with deep forgiveness. She looked once again at her aunt and offered her love.

Trish looked up and caught her gaze. A small smile crossed the woman's face. Her eyes were brimming with tears. *She is a wounded child*, Amanda thought. She offered more love.

As they sat together on the patio, birds continued to sing. No words were spoken. Amanda had a thousand unanswered questions but knew there was time to ask them later. Now it was right to sit in the breeze and just let the moment be.

Trish covered her eyes and bent forward, her head dropping into her hands. When she looked up her eyes glistened. Amanda watched and waited. She studied the woman and for the first time, the vision was not clouded by memories. Trish looked tired and spent. Her skin was flushed and rough in spots. Her lips were surrounded by a patchwork of fine lines.

A pang of sadness brushed Amanda's heart. She had only ever seen this woman defined by years of longing, hurt and disappointment. Through the eyes of a child. Now in the slanted sunlight, in the shadows of this quiet garden sanctuary tucked away in the corner of Community General Hospital, she saw a vulnerable, scared, tired woman.

Suddenly in that moment, deep in Amanda's heart, she realized that she was looking at a reflection of herself before love had saved her.

Yrandia smiled. "Yes my child, learn this lesson. Look with the eyes of love. See that we are all reflections of each other. Know that beneath the surface you share the same bond of Divinity."

Amanda stared at her mother's sister and was overcome with emotion. "Oh, Aunt Trish." She bent over and wrapped her arms around the woman. She smoothed her hair and softly whispered, "It's okay. It will be okay." She felt Trish's small frame begin to shake as low sobs rose from the woman's chest.

"Oh Mandy, your mom is so sick. I just couldn't tell you on the phone. I didn't want it to be true. I didn't want to say it. I couldn't say it. I somehow thought that if I said it out loud, it would become real. And I don't want this to be real." Trish sank deeper into Amanda's arms and cried.

Nothing more needed to be said. Amanda closed her eyes and let herself disappear into the moment. This was real. All she ever wanted as a child was to be held and told it would be okay. Everything would be okay. She knew now that she could offer that to her aunt.

Yrandia stayed near. She saw her child's beautiful light emanating out into the courtyard, filling the space with the healing energy of love and forgiveness, mixing with the life force emitted by the birds, flowers and all of nature that danced and swirled mystically joined on the earth plane.

The older woman's angelic guide hovered close by and closed her eyes, opening her wings to encircle the now sacred space hidden deep within the hospital's walls.

Yrandia joined in, closing the sacred circle and pondering how many years she and her companion guides, ancient Beings of light, had waited for the journey of these connected human souls to move to this destined point of joining. All the years of fear, anger, resentment, pain and hurt had served as stepping stones along this path to meet at this moment.

And now that outpouring of comfort and love flowed in an act of forgiveness. It was not as once hoped... but it was as it should be.

Yrandia and Trish's guides joined and sang a song of praise to Divine Source. Grace descended and ascended, gently wrapping aunt and niece in warmth and hope.

CHAPTER 38

The afternoon sun was dipping into the western sky as slanted rays filtered into Claire's hospital room. A small knock on the door punctured the quiet. Amanda and Trish sat up and pushed aside the books and magazines they had turned to as they waited.

A man dressed in neat khakis and a polo shirt entered the room. He greeted Claire who was sitting in the bed, then moved toward Amanda with an outstretched hand. His neatly trimmed hair was flecked with a mix of grey and sandy brown. His eyes warm. *A kind spirit.* She took the proffered hand and warmly shook it.

Yrandia sent waves of light as the sun dipped.

"Good afternoon. I'm Doctor Gagnon," he said.

"Nice to meet you. I'm Amanda Martin, Claire's daughter."

Claire sat up and began to speak as a deep rattle rose in her chest. The doctor turned toward her but waited, alert as she lost herself in a spasm of coughing and gasping. He gently patted her and whispered, "Breathe through your nose, Claire. Slow it down."

Amanda's mother looked into his eyes and labored to slow her breath until the spasm subsided.

Amanda poured her mother fresh water. Claire waved it off and leaned back into the bed clearly exhausted. Small pearls of sweat glistened on her forehead. Trish wet a small cloth and gently dabbed her sister. Amanda watched.

The doctor quietly checked electronic records and moved systematically through a physical examination. Once finished, he circled the bed and asked a few questions to assess her discomfort and pain. His voice was gentle and calm. His attention was directed and he leaned in when Claire responded.

Afterward, he turned toward Amanda and Trish. "I think it would be good to let Claire rest for a bit. We can talk in my office," he said and then turned back to his patient, "if that's okay with you, Claire."

Amanda glanced at her mother who nodded in agreement.

"I'm fine, sweetie. I told the doctor earlier that you and Trish will be a part of any discussions. So go ahead. You can fill me in later."

While weakened by the coughing spasm, Amanda took note that her mother still had an air of quiet resolve. Bending over to kiss Claire's damp forehead, she softly whispered, "Remember we are making a place of peace, right here, right now."

Claire smiled and whispered back, "I love you."

Xandra bowed deeply and with one strong stroke of her wing set the room into a slow moving vortex of love that glimmered like falling snow in the darkening room.

Trish watched and sensed some sort of strange movement. The air felt different. She wondered what had changed. The sadness that had consumed her every waking moment was lifting. Something deep inside of her was moving. She stayed still.

Her angelic guide sang a song of thanks. The miracle of a shift was beginning. That guide looked toward Yrandia and Xandra and the three angels embraced and danced. Human time had brought them to this moment of unity. But in the realm of the Divine it was always this way: love and light, peace and joy. "Awaken our beautiful daughters, awaken. Now is the time!" the angelic trio sang and rejoiced.

Sister and daughter followed the doctor to the door. "I'll be in my office in about an hour," he said, handing them a business card that had the office number on it. "We can talk then."

"Thank you, doctor." Amanda extended her hand to offer a handshake.

Instead, he took that hand and held it in both of his own. He looked into her eyes and smiled.

Amanda felt her heart skip a beat. She knew then what she had dared not acknowledge during that call last night. *It was only last night,* she mused. It felt like years since she'd heard her aunt's greeting on the phone. She let out a sigh and gently nodded back.

He patted her hand once again. It felt warm and reassuring. She looked down. *We are putting ourselves in your hands.*

Amanda walked the corridors alone, going past dinner carts and the fluid movement of the evening routines. The peace and calm that had surrounded her in the garden now gave way to a dull ache deep in her chest. Aunt Trish had spoken the diagnosis; Dr. Gagnon's gesture of comfort foreshadowed the prognosis.

She turned to find the door to the small garden. Daylight had all but faded. Small lights flickered in the patio. A full moon was rising low on the eastern horizon. The cool night air rushed toward her and she could smell the evening dew settling onto the small mounds of grass. She missed Jordan. She missed her home. But here she was.

She turned to one of her new mantras: "I am exactly where I am supposed to be."

Amanda sat on the small bench draped in shadows. In an hour the unspoken would be spoken. Doubt would be erased and she would have to step deeper into a new reality. For now she had this small gap where the full truth didn't have a complete name.

She turned to the darkening night sky and said a simple prayer, "Let me be strong. I am strong. Let me be at peace. I am peace. Let me be wise. I am wise. I trust that all is as it should be in Divine Order, conspiring always for good."

Amanda quietly drank in the stillness. The birds had returned to their resting spots. It was still too early in the season for night sounds. Time had turned everything upside down. Yet she knew deep in her core, this moment mattered. Everything that had come before this moment no longer held sway. The false narrative of a long gone childhood had been crushed under the stark clarity of this moment. Every practice Amanda had been cultivating was now called upon to support her. How she framed this challenge and the gifts it offered was important, consequential and held deep meaning.

Yrandia surrounded her earthly daughter with large unfolded wings. She read her child's heart and knew it was pure.

Amanda felt strangely calm as she sat in the stillness. There was a lesson here. She could see the lesson as harsh and crushing. Or she could see it as infinitely good. She would choose to find the good. She slowed her breath and tried to drop into the silence but she felt that someone was nearby. Opening her eyes, she saw a man kneeling near one of the small rose beds though she hadn't seen anyone on the patio when she'd entered.

He was cutting a rose. The man looked up and smiled at her. His face was shrouded in shadows but she could see his smile. He stood and moved closer. In the diffused light, his eyes reflected joy. Amanda thought they shined with pure kindness. She returned his smile.

As the stranger walked toward her, she decided he was older than she had originally thought. Tall and built like a runner, even in the half-light she could now see that his face was framed in well-worn lines that burst around his eyes. His was a face of a life well lived.

He reached out and offered a red rose to Amanda, bowing slightly.

Amanda stood and smiled. It was a beautiful long-stemmed rose.

When he lifted his head he spoke in a deep but gentle voice. Its cadence was soothing and filled the small space with a resonant tone like an ancient hymn. "There's always beauty around us. We just have to open our eyes to see the possibilities. Gifts, like blessings, often come disguised or discovered in the most unexpected places. Curious how I find the most exquisite roses here in this most unlikely spot. They grow in the shadow of this building. You just have to open your eyes to see them."

Amanda took the flower and drew it close, taking in the rich fragrance. It was indeed perfect. She wanted to speak but before she could find the words, the stranger was gone. He left as quickly and quietly as he had appeared.

She looked around bewildered. She knew it wasn't a dream because she held the red rose in her hand. The man was gone but in his place she felt a surge of energy. The first stars peeked out in the night sky. A hushed silence hung in the air and a feeling of reverence wrapped around her. Amanda breathed in the rose's scent one more time. It was real.

Funny. No, *curious,* she thought, I only saw pink and white miniature roses clustered on small bushes. How had she missed such long and beautiful roses earlier?

Yrandia bowed in adoration for the beauty and perfection in the Divine Plan. The mystery touched the Being of Light who marveled at how all things indeed conspired for good. "All in its right time. All in its right season," she sang.

CHAPTER 39

The three women sat together in the social worker's office getting information to support them after Claire's discharge. Claire was smartly dressed, a touch of makeup on her face and her hair neatly arranged. She wanted the visit to be as normal as possible. "It's just another medical visit," she insisted.

Amanda looked out the large picture window and noticed the sun breaking through the passing clouds. *Funny*, her thoughts wandered, *life goes on*. The sun shines. It rises and it will set. The stars will come out. The clouds are passing by effortlessly in the breeze. Life is normal. But nothing is normal. She pushed those thoughts aside and turned toward Claire. "You okay, Mom?"

Claire smiled. Her eyes looked tired but something burned behind them. There was softness in them, peacefulness. "Believe it or not, sweetie, I am fine. I really am fine..." her voice trailed off. She reached for the small glass of water that the social worker had poured for her.

Silence surrounded them but it wasn't uncomfortable. The words still filled the space within the confined office that held the three women who had survived years of shared battles, some small victories, many retreats and countless draws.

The reality spoken into being tightened invisible threads around the well-appointed office, further weaving the web that had joined the three of them. The threads were ancient but made new. Life's tapestry for each was a different texture, one woven and accented in brilliant hues and the other two in muted colors serving more as the background to the still unfinished piece of art.

Hospice, Amanda let the word twist in her mind. Somehow it translated to *hopeless*.

Yrandia knew her child's heart and again softly sang, "Choose hope."

Trish walked to the door. "I'm going to get a cup of coffee. Do you want anything?" Her voice was flat. Amanda and Claire both knew she needed a cigarette.

"I'm good, thanks," Amanda answered. "Mom, how about you?"

"Thanks, I am good with the water." Claire took another sip from the glass.

Trish hurried out of the office.

Amanda moved toward her mother. In the slanted afternoon light, softened by the shadows that framed the room, for a brief moment Amanda saw the young mother of her childhood.

Claire turned to her daughter. Her eyes were soft and a hint of a smile danced across her face. The dim lights hid the passage of time and the ravages of the disease growing inside. Claire's hair was pulled back in a loose ponytail and it bobbed as she moved. "Come here, Mandy. I think we both could use a hug right now."

Amanda moved into her mother's arms. She buried her face in the bend of Claire's neck. Each woman let go and sank deeply into the warmth of the embrace.

Xandra and Yrandia blazed with joy and gratitude. Every hurt and grievance melted away in that moment of release. The accumulated years of pain and disappointment, self-loathing and recrimination evaporated in the power of human touch. The unkind words and long festering wounds they had created vanished. In that moment there was only love. The seeds of forgiveness were taking root and growing strong.

Xandra and Yrandia sang a song of deep gratitude.

"Oh my sweet sister, truly the greatest blessings and gifts come disguised and hidden awaiting discovery."

Xandra touched her angelic partner's wing and they danced.

Yrandia heard again the words of the kind stranger. They were deep and wise. She wondered if perhaps he was some sort of higher consciousness being similar to an angelic guide.

Xandra knew her companion's thoughts. "Humans can also be great gifts and sage prophets." Both angels laughed and filled the office with radiant light. They moved together to surround mother and daughter in a circle of protective energy drenched in beams of dancing light that reflected the colors of the rainbow.

The miracle of healing had begun. Here in this sacred space, thoughts of death, and conversations to prepare for the end had been breathed into a holy and sanctified spot of forgiveness, healing and transformation. Two lives were ready to put down their swords and armor and surrender to peace. As they dropped the armaments of past battles, they moved gracefully in the weightlessness of release, free to blend their hearts on the final passage of their conjoined journey.

Yrandia began a chant of ancient song. Xandra answered the ethereal call for healing.

"Let there be light."

—"I am the light."

"Let there be peace."

—"I am the peace."

"Let there be hope."

—"I am the hope."

"Let there be love."

—"I am the love."

"As I let go…"

—"I am restored."

"As I let go…"

—"I am made whole."

"As I let go…"

—"I am that, I am."

"And so it is."

—"Amen."

The magnificent angels swirled and sang and danced and filled the room with Divine Light.

The social worker, who had retreated to her inner office, looked up from her work. She sensed something in the air and smiled. She was well versed in the mysteries steeped in the moment of reckoning between the human mind, heart and soul. It was a mystery she chose to embrace as a miracle… or as Dr. Gagnon, ever the physician and man of science, called "a shift in perspective." Either way, it was real and profound. The social worker added to the ancient chant, offering her own silent prayer of gratitude.

Amanda and Claire stayed close and held each other. Neither felt the need to speak but instead drifted into a beautiful wave of calm.

Claire closed her eyes. Her breath became lighter and less labored. It felt good.

Amanda opened her heart and contemplated the profound peace she felt. "It's a miracle," she softly whispered.

"Indeed, my Beloved, it is," Yrandia replied.

As the angel spoke, the social worker stepped into the private space, reserved for grieving families, standing in the doorway. She paused and noticed a warmth and visible glow in the room. As she moved to close that adjoining door and allow them a bit more time, her eyes met Amanda's and she bowed. "Yes, miracles often come disguised." With that the social worker stepped back and closed the door.

Amanda's heart raced and she smiled.

CHAPTER 40

Jordan felt his heart sink with the news. "I'm so sorry, 'Manda. I don't know what to say. I can get there in a few hours and at least be there to hold you." His small inner voice spoke to him, *"You should be there. This isn't something Amanda should face alone."* But he didn't speak these words. He knew Amanda and Claire's history. So he listened. That was what he needed to offer for now.

"I'm okay. I mean it's hard, for sure, and I feel like I am just winging it. But somehow I am okay." Amanda's voice was calm and strong. "We're moving Mom back home tomorrow. For now, we are going to take it one day at a time. She is strong enough at the moment to be at home and that's where she wants to be. She is really taking this well. It's all so strange."

Amanda paused.

"I spoke with Kayla earlier today," Amanda continued, "and I will be able to do a lot of the purchasing and accounting remotely. She was super understanding. We really don't know what we are looking at... as far as time... but we will make this work."

Jordan listened. He sensed that right now she needed to speak through the logistics. He would listen with an open heart. He could remain present.

"You know I am seeing a side of my mother I never knew existed," Amanda said. "She is calm and taking all of this with a lot of grace. It's like I am seeing her for the first time as a real person and not just my mom..." Amanda's voice trailed off.

In the pause, Jordan spoke, "Well that's good, right? I mean this is all really big stuff for you both to work through. I don't think it gets a whole lot bigger than this." Jordan was carefully choosing his words, not fully knowing how mother and daughter were maneuvering through this new reality.

"Yeah, it's big. But now that it's happening, it isn't as scary as I always thought it would be. I don't know, maybe getting her home will be good for both of us. Aunt Trish is kind of a mess but I am trying really hard not to get sucked into her drama."

Aunt Trish, Jordan thought. He hadn't met her. Actually he had never met Amanda's mother either. He had seen pictures of both of them. They were both quite beautiful, each having their own unique quality of beauty. It was clear to Jordan that Amanda had taken after her mother's side of the family as far as looks, although the few pictures he had seen of her father showed a handsome man with dancing eyes and a captivating smile. Jordan however saw them all in his mind's eye as troubled souls who'd lived life on a turbulent surface, caught somehow in a current they never learned how to navigate. *Currents,* he pondered, *maybe more like riptides.* But somehow, he thought, Amanda had her own beautiful soul that survived despite the drama these women had created in her young life.

Amanda's voice brought Jordan back to the conversation. *So much for being present,* he silently scolded himself.

"I'm going to be coming home to get a little more organized. Right now I'm not going to make any long-term plans but I left in such a rush. I need to get things in some sort of order."

Jordan's heart leapt. *Yes!* "Oh yes, my love, that makes total sense. Selfishly I am thrilled, but I know you will have things to do. Just let me know what you need from me. I promise to stay out of the way. But just say the word." Jordan didn't want to add to her burden but secretly hoped Amanda would stay with him even if their only time was to rest in each other's arms.

"Thank you, honey. I will let you know as soon as I firm up my plans. I really miss you."

There was a hint of sadness in her voice and Jordan could hear the exhaustion. "Oh 'Manda, I miss you something crazy. I wish I could hold you and make this all go away." Jordan closed his eyes. He didn't tell her that she was always present in his thoughts during his days.

He heard Amanda sigh. Her voice sounded far off. "There have been moments when I feel like I will wake up and this will all have been a dream. But right in the middle of that, something inside tugs me back and I know I can't wish this away. I met this interesting stranger when I was having lunch by myself in a tiny garden right in the middle of the hospital. It was the weirdest thing."

Jordan wondered where the story was going but willed himself to just be there and to listen.

Amanda continued, "I was sort of meditating. I've been taking these pauses a lot. Well anyway, this man just appeared out of nowhere. One moment I'm alone. The next he is there and I can feel his presence. He was in the shadows picking a flower from the rose bed. The strange thing was I had noticed all these beautiful miniature roses earlier. They were clustered together in shades of pink and peach. But there was this man with these kind eyes. He's an older gentleman but there was something about him, a presence that initially made him appear younger. I don't know how to describe it, he just brought this beautiful calm to the garden. And then he handed me a beautiful long-stem red rose. It's gorgeous. And he said, 'Gifts and blessing often come disguised.' Then he was gone. I was left with this rose, this sense of inner peace and a good story. Except that the words keep coming back to me. Later the social worker used almost the identical phrase, as if she knew what happened in that garden. I think I need to pay attention to them."

Anioch was near Jordan and shifted when he heard Amanda's story. He raised his energy, recognizing the profound wisdom in the simple words. He didn't know who the stranger was but in his heart he believed the man was a messenger. The angel unfolded his wings and drew a circle of light around his child and extended his vibration of love across the illusory distance to his dear friend Yrandia. Strangely he missed her, too.

Jordan felt his pulse momentarily quicken. He smiled. He was learning to read his body and was coming to understand that these bursts of energy were a sign of his angel's presence. "Wow, that's pretty deep. I got goosebumps. I'd say you've got some pretty amazing Divine light around you." Jordan felt a warm wave of peace wash over him. At that moment he knew deep inside his being that Amanda and her mom were being guided. *All is well and as it should be.* In that simple knowledge, he felt a deep sense of calm.

"I feel that, too. I feel it right now. Like I said, my mom is so calm but I am really surprised that I'm not freaking out. In a crazy way this is the most at peace I think I've ever felt. It's like I am here doing what I need to do. I guess there is a real sense of purpose for me and it isn't about me."

Amanda's voice had taken on a richer deeper sound. Jordan imagined her slowly twisting her blonde hair as she gazed off. He wanted to hold her close but pushed the thought away. *Listen man, just listen.*

"You know in those moments of pause I was telling you about, I practiced the freeze frame a few times like Dr. Blair taught us. I had some really interesting imagery pop up when I asked, 'What do I need to know about this situation'."

Jordan nodded, fully understanding the reference to a technique to gain heart and mind coherence. It was a powerful practice that Jordan and Amanda were both beginning to explore. He was intrigued to hear more.

"So I asked that question and went into my space of ease. What I saw was a little girl dragging this giant chest around. It looked like one of those pirate treasure chests. It was covered in all sorts of heavy chains with big locks. As the little girl pulled it, she started walking toward this beautiful illuminated path. As she turned onto the path, the heavy locks opened and the chains began to drop off. The treasure chest was released and opened up. She was now free from the weight of that old chest. She started running and dancing into the light and the path was filled with flowers and butterflies flowing out of that old chest that had been transformed into a beautiful gilded case. It was such a powerful image for me. I mean right there I knew that all this old stuff I've hung on to and kept locked up just doesn't serve me. I don't need to drag the old chest and chains along with me anymore. That's what my heart wants me to know. I can't explain it, Jordan, but I believe it with my whole heart. This is the hardest thing to know that my mom won't be here forever, but somehow the Universe is sending all these signs that it's okay. It's going to be okay." Amanda paused and lowered her voice, "Actually I feel almost guilty saying it, but there is great good. Does that sound wrong?"

Yrandia smiled as she listened to her child. "Oh my beautiful girl, it is not wrong. It is as it should be. All is as it should be. Listen to your heart. All your answers rest there." Yrandia spread her wings across the small divide in the large hospital where mother and daughter and their two angelic guides rested. Yrandia touched Xandra who was close to Claire's side but aware of the transformation. Both angels bowed and illuminated the space they shared.

"The miracle of forgiveness," Yrandia whispered.

"Yes, it is. Letting the illusions drop away to reveal that the truth has been there, always. Therein lies true peace," Xandra sang out, rejoicing in the revelation of the unlocked treasure chest and the unfolding of the bright path.

Jordan smiled. "No, there is nothing wrong with thinking like that. I think it's totally amazing and wonderful, my love. Really, it is. Your stranger friend was right. What a gift you are being given. You can free yourself from all these chains. This is your time for you and your mom. Your heart is speaking to you. But I don't have to tell you that, right?"

Anioch listened and was touched by the perfect alignment of all these human souls. He was awed by the connection of humans and angels and in that moment joined with his angelic sisters as they combined in a hymn of gratitude and joy. The circle of love continued to expand.

CHAPTER 41

"There is a profound mystery that I am trying to wrap my head around." Amanda leaned on her elbows in front of the warm glow of the bonfire Jordan had built on the beach. She rearranged herself, folding into his arms. "It's like I am seeing my mom for the first time as a fellow human being. My head knows in some cold clinical way that she is dying. Saying it just seems unholy. But because of that knowing, really in spite of it, I feel like I am closer to her than I've ever been. It's like I've finally found a way to love her. And as I lean into that love, it seems that somehow she has transformed. She is more real. I don't get it. Why do we have to wait for something like this to change how we see things?"

Jordan listened. These were deep questions and he didn't have any answers. He had learned from his own past that each person has to come first to their own questions... and if you stay with them long enough, the answers come in their own time.

He stroked Amanda's hair and gently kissed her. He let the silence sit as the fire crackled.

"Why did it take this disease to disrupt our stupid story? How stubborn are we? Or scared? We're only making the time count now that it's precious. That seems tragically silly. All the energy we expended fighting... and now I don't even know what we were fighting for or against. We were just locked in the fight. And for what? To be right or to prove some point? It simply doesn't make any sense."

Jordan listened. The angels listened. Anioch was simply happy to be near Yrandia. He had missed her in a way he didn't know was possible in the angelic realm. She had grown more luminous as her child slowly awakened. Anioch was grateful for the lessons being offered. He continued to learn. This entire journey of guardian on the human plane was one vast lesson for the now not-so-novice angel. The human world was truly a mystery shrouded in illusion.

"If only humans could see from a new lens and recognize their True Identity," Anioch thought in his angelic telepathic way. "Then they could love freely. Then they could be love made manifest every moment. Then they would understand eternity and so much pain and conflict would simply melt away."

Yrandia bowed and said softly, "My dear companion, you are growing so wise. Soon you will be considered a sage guide." Both angels laughed. It was good to be home. They gently caressed each other with their beautiful outstretched wings. The fire glowed. The ocean roared.

Jordan sat up and pulled Amanda by his side. He noticed how the fire had begun to dance in the night wind. He heard the waves crashing on the shore. Their small space on the beach was transformed into a sacred circle. Jordan felt it and honored it. He had listened and now it was time to speak.

"I know and understand what you are saying. Somehow we don't appreciate people or blessings until we lose them... or very close to it. And if we are lucky we wake up as if something has been lifted from our eyes. In that moment, we see life from a different place. It's like we are on a higher plane, or the blinders have been removed. For the very first time we see the whole of life. I know that in that one brief moment on the beach I woke up. The trick now is finding a way to stay awake."

Jordan softly kissed Amanda. The fire crackled. The waves broke on the shore. The heavens rejoiced.

Life took on its own routine and pace as the weeks passed. Amanda settled into her new role as caregiver. She worked out an arrangement with her employer, her Aunt Trish, and the hospice provider who allowed her to split time between Holyfield and Seaside. While she was away, Jordan busied himself with school and work and Amanda arranged video calls with Dr. Blair who remained a strong supportive anchor.

The cancer continued its ferocious assault on Claire's body. But her mind remained alert. She seemed to be filled with an unquenchable curiosity and trying to fit the past into the present. Her spirit grew stronger with each passing day.

Amanda tended to her mother with a tenderness and compassion she didn't know she possessed, grateful for the support she received from the hospice caregiver and the marvelous network it offered.

Trish stopped by with no discernable pattern. Amanda noticed that her visits were becoming more sporadic but she was grateful her aunt at least provided support when Amanda went home for short trips.

Amanda and Claire spent their days reminiscing and telling stories from their respective frames of reference. Claire tired easily but looked forward to spending time outdoors. She advised Amanda on how to tend to the small garden she had planted in the back before she got sick, and took great pleasure as Amanda harvested the fresh vegetables. Together they would prepare the meals using herbs from Claire's potted herb gardens.

Mother and child sorted through old photos using the pictures as prompts and entry points for reminiscing and old stories retold from a new vantage point. Amanda was amazed to hear her mother recount stories from her own childhood and she was grateful to have the opportunity to see life through her mother's eyes. Amanda's heart softened as she began to understand that loneliness was an underlying and constant theme in her mother's life. She came to understand that in her own way, her mother had tried to protect her as best she could.

Yrandia and Xandra were as inseparable as mother and daughter. But the angelic realm was free of the petty interferences that seemed to so often cloud and block earthly relationships. Indeed their bonds were ancient and predestined. Each angel knew her purpose and filled it with an outpouring of unconditional love.

Xandra knew, as angels do, that her beautiful child had a primary purpose on this earthly plane. As Claire's earth time drew down, Xandra wrapped her in warm layers of radiant light. "Be the lesson you were meant to be," she whispered to her child. "You are here to love. Love yourself first, dear one. Forgive yourself first, dear one. Then all else will flow."

In those moments, Claire felt waves of peace and calm. She had vivid dreams. She felt herself running through dew-soaked grass, laughing with the joy of a young child. She could smell the grass and feel the summer sun on her skin. She dreamed of her own mother and felt safe as they gazed at passing clouds, describing the large castles and animals that filled the blue sky. Claire knew something was changing in her and she stopped fighting the small voice. Instead she listened and asked for the dreams to come and wash away all of the old hurts. "I had a dream about your grandma last night," she said.

Amanda looked up from her computer. "Yeah, was it good?"

"I was a little girl. We were playing and laughing. It was wonderful. I woke up with a smile. You didn't know your grandma, but she would have loved you. She had the most beautiful voice. You remind me of her. I miss her a lot."

Amanda got up and moved near her mother.

Claire was looking out into the garden. Her eyes were misty. "I wish I could have been a better mom to you. She was a good mom. But she left me when I was so young and I had your Aunt Trish who needed me. I think about how I just sort of shut down and didn't know how to be light like my mom." Claire's voice was filled with emotion.

"Mom, you were the perfect mom for me." Amanda heard the words and smiled. She didn't know where the words had come from but in that moment they were true.

Claire looked up at her daughter and smiled. "Really? All I wanted to do for you was keep you safe and let you have a dream. I know I made mistakes and I know that when it really mattered I gave up. But I didn't really give up on you, honey. I just didn't want you to hurt anymore. I always loved you." Claire dropped her head into her hands.

Amanda listened and tried to make sense of what she was hearing. There was deep regret in the words. Her heart told her it was time for her mother to release those chains as well. "Mom, I know you loved me. I know that deep inside. I am who I am because you never gave up on me. Everything that happened was for some good. I believe that now. You need to know that. I love you." Amanda pulled her mother close to her chest and kissed her gently on the top of her head.

"Thank you. I hope you can truly forgive me. I need to know that. I think your grandma coming to me is a sign that I need to let go of things. I was angry at her for dying and leaving me alone and I felt frightened. But I don't want to be scared now. I'm not angry at this cancer and I'm not scared of what's coming. I just need to know that you and I are at peace. That's all that matters." Claire shut her eyes.

"We are at peace, Mom. And I love that grandma is here, too. It makes it right. For now let's just share our dreams and our memories. I love hearing your stories and really seeing you not as my mom but as the beautiful woman you've always been."

And in the sunlit kitchen mother and daughter took one more step on their journey of reconciliation and healing.

Amanda watched and kept track of the subtle changes and held them close to her heart. She gave her mother space to share her thoughts and prayed for the wisdom to keep the judgment at bay. This was a time to listen and to love. This was a time to forgive and rewrite their history. And so Amanda let Claire lead them on whatever path Claire needed to pass.

CHAPTER 42

It was a bright and clear morning and Amanda had an idea that perhaps an outing would be good for her mom. The new medication provided much-needed pain control and Claire's spirits and energy seemed high.

"Hey Mom, I was thinking maybe we could go out to Sunset Beach for the day. The weather is gorgeous and I'm guessing the summer fruit would be at its final peak. What do you think?"

Claire's eyes lit up. "Oh honey, that would be lovely."

Amanda's heart felt light. "We can drive down the coast and stop by the beach along the way. It should be pretty empty now that school is back in session."

"Maybe we can grab a bite at the old diner at the end of the pier," Claire suggested. She moved to the bedroom to change her clothes.

"You mean Long Board?" Amanda asked. "Gosh, I haven't been there for years. They had the best shakes."

"And the best greasy fries," Claire added, laughing.

Holyfield was about an hour from the coast, nestled between the low foothills. Amanda and Claire had spent many summer days on the beach. Those days were some of Amanda's fondest childhood memories. She was happy at her mother's exuberant response.

Daughter and mother drove along the windy road through the still green hills that cast shadows along the blacktop. The sunroof was open and a warm breeze danced through their hair. Amanda saw her mother close her eyes and tilt her head up into the welcoming sun. *Girasol*, she thought. Both women smiled.

The air smelled clean with a hint of drying grass. Amanda reached over and softly patted her mother's hand.

Claire looked up and gently touched her daughter's face. "This is heaven, Mandy. You next to me, the wind in my hair and sun in my face. I feel like I am flying. It is perfect."

Amanda felt her throat catch but her heart soared. She turned the car onto the Coast Highway and headed west toward Sunset Beach. The drive through the canyon hadn't changed since her childhood but as they got closer to the small beach community Amanda noticed more strip malls and hotels clustered along the once vacant marsh lands. Time had changed the small seaside town of her youth. Amanda pushed the thought away. *Stay in this moment*, she willed herself.

"Look, Mandy," her mother pointed. "It's the old pottery shack. I didn't think it was still here."

Amanda remembered the hours they had spent combing through displays of local pottery and handicrafts from local artists. There was a small community studio behind the patio where Claire and Amanda had painted their own pottery pieces. Amanda remembered watching her mother mix beautiful colors to create bursts and swirls that rivaled any sunset. Amanda still cherished the few pieces she had kept.

"Hey honey, do you remember the vases and plates we made?" Claire asked. "I mixed those crazy colors but you were so serious. I just wanted you to have fun."

Amanda had an idea and pulled into the old pottery yard. "Let's see if they still have that studio, Mom. I would love to paint something with you."

Claire's eyes lit up. "Oh how fun! But only if you play and spice things up. You have such a good eye for color. "

Amanda put her arm around her mom as they pushed through the small wooden gate. "Well, you know I learned from the best. I wanted the most perfect flowers and strawberries and suns on those darn plates and vases. But man, you just painted with abandon and I thought your pieces were the most beautiful works of art. The reds and golds, purples and blues were pulled right out of nature. Funny, I never thought about it before, but I think I fell in love with color right here watching you."

Amanda felt her eyes begin to well. She rested her head on her mother's small shoulder. Claire smiled.

Xandra and Yrandia hovered as their beloved daughters sat side by side. Claire picked out a large angled box with a knobbed lid. Amanda chose a plate. That had been her favorite pottery piece as a child. Mother and daughter giggled and reminisced while they painted.

Amanda mixed greens and blues, capturing the subtle beauty of a summer sea. She let go of form and lost herself in the act of joyful creation. She noticed how the texture and mixture of the paint took on the swirling energy of a wave. She smiled and thought of Jordan. *He would like this.*

Claire slowly painted delicate vines and small budding flowers, turning the plain ceramic box into a burst of springtime beauty. Tiny green leaves and pink-tipped white petals draped along the climbing vines. Amanda watched as her mother transformed the box into a magical garden.

The conversation slowed as Claire lost herself, dipping the tiny brush into an array of soft spring pastels. Amanda watched as she added beautiful butterflies taking flight from the boxed lid. *Oh my, it looks like the treasure chest in my dream.* Amanda felt a wave of love wash over her.

The angels sent radiant beams, feeling the higher vibrations emanate from the shared love and release of creative energy.

"Your child is growing more beautiful each day," Yrandia whispered.

Xandra nodded. She looked at the woman who in fact wore the ravages of cancer in her small stooped frame and drawn face. But she too saw the light emanating and stretching out from her. "Yes, she is. And your child has served as a wise guide. Funny how earth time transforms things."

Yrandia smiled and responded, "Indeed, that is true." The angels watched as Amanda mixed colors and captured the raw beauty of nature while Claire painstakingly paid attention to the minute details, creating a masterpiece of emerging spring.

"It is as it should be, dear sister."

"Indeed that also is true," Yrandia replied.

Mother and daughter left their pieces. "We'll call you when they are ready," the young shop owner said as she moved the plate and box. "These are going to be absolutely breathtaking once they are finished. Both of them are gorgeous."

Claire smiled. "We used to come here when she was a child. I still have her plates. They are my most treasured possessions."

Amanda looked at her mom. She didn't recall ever seeing them or hearing her mom praise her artwork. "You still have them, Mom?"

"Of course I do. I've moved them a million times... even when I got rid of other stuff. But not those, honey. They remind me of the good times. You would smile, so proud every time we'd pick them up, all shiny and transformed from the kiln."

"No. I don't remember that. I wasn't sure you kept them." Amanda didn't add, *I didn't think you even liked them,* though she had believed it.

"When we get home, remind me to show them to you. Like I was saying, when I look at them I remember the little girl who wanted to turn something plain into something beautiful. That's you. You have a special touch."

"Your box from today is unbelievable. I think we changed roles a bit."

"Maybe you are right. Your plate is a vast wide ocean. Endless possibilities. And mine is a garden. Planted seeds of pure potential emerging into full bloom. I wanted to paint hope."

Xandra knew her daughter's thoughts and sent her love. Yes, she was transforming into luminous beauty.

Amanda and Claire turned back onto the highway toward the old wooden pier. They shared a lunch like they had shared so many times over the years. They spoke of long forgotten yesterdays, each drawing from a separate well of remembrance. Amanda's heart began to open wider, listening to her mother's memories. She realized their shared past, while the same, was in fact so different when viewed through the lens of another person's view of life. Those childhood stories she'd guarded were being challenged, and in the heat of the challenge something deeper and more real was emerging.

Again, today she saw her mother as something more than just her mom. Today she saw her in the light of an intentional guide trying to model the excitement of pure creativity. She hadn't ever seen her mother as a gifted artist but instead as some wild alchemist who splashed colors into life. But today she chose to let the artist emerge. She knew her daughter had learned enough and now she was free to express her heart. Today she chose to paint hope. And in that moment, Amanda felt deep love for this woman.

"You tired?" Amanda was watching her mom, amazed by Claire's energy that day. The sun was slowly shifting on its westward trajectory. The breeze had picked up a bit. "We can head back home if you want."

"What I want is for this day to never end." Claire looked at her daughter who held her gaze.

"Yeah, me too. It's a good day."

As they slowly traversed the empty beach, Claire stopped and pulled her daughter close. "I know I messed a lot of things up. I could have done more for you. But I hope you know that every second of every day I have loved you more than life itself."

Amanda turned toward Claire and in that moment she knew this was a truth. In that moment every grievance she had hung on to slipped away. Amanda stepped into a place of acceptance, and as she did so the miracle of grace washed over them. "I know that, Mom. I know it wasn't easy. And I am grateful for that. I can honestly say I really do know that now."

Yrandia and Xandra rejoiced. Xandra dipped low onto the earthly plane. Her angelic heart swelled. In this moment the healing energy of forgiveness radiated outward and bound these two humans who were united before time. This was their special moment of release and surrender.

Claire stepped wholly into her Purpose to serve as the instrument of healing. At that moment of true forgiveness the illusion vanished. The angels knew there was nothing left that needed to be forgiven as the love had always been there. Divine Order was restored.

Mother and daughter embraced. As the waves gently lapped the shore, the angels sang. The sun bathed them with a warm glow of light and love.

"All is as it should be, dear sister," Xandra softly sang.

"As it always has been, my beloved," Yrandia responded.

Amanda and Claire began the drive home. Their hearts were full and each was lost in thought. "Today was magical," Claire sighed.

"Yes, it was," Amanda responded. "You up for one more moment of magic?"

"Oh, what the heck," Claire smiled. "I sure am."

Amanda turned off the canyon road and headed east.

"So I am guessing we're going to Willow Lake?"

Amanda nodded. "Best place for a late summer sunset."

"That's what they say." Both women laughed.

Amanda helped her mother out of the car. They were parked along the high ledge of the small lake that was surrounded by scrub pines. She looked at the gravel path that led down to the shore. "You able to do this, Mom?"

"Oh come on, you, I'm not that decrepit yet."

Amanda looked again at her mom but saw the smiling and dancing eyes. She opened the trunk and grabbed her guitar and an old quilt.

Snaking their way down the rocky path, they stopped along the way as Amanda paced herself to her mother's breathing. The sun was slowly shifting and would soon begin its descent. Amanda spied a perfect spot near the lake under a pine. She spread out the blanket and they sat. They could feel the warmth of the ground. The air was still filled with the sounds of life as the summer cicadas hummed and birds began their late day chorus.

Amanda pulled out her guitar and began to softly strum as her mother leaned against her back. Amanda breathed deeply. She wanted every moment of this day to enter deep into her bones. This was a day worth remembering, every sound, every smell, and every beat of her heart.

"Thank you for this. I couldn't have planned a more perfect day. This is the day I always dreamed of spending with you." Claire's voice was soft and her eyes filled with tears. "Play a song for us."

Amanda stopped and thought. She smiled as she slowly started to strum and play the chords of a song from her childhood. It was the tune her mother had sung to her when she was sick or they just needed time to heal from some wasted battle. The sunlight danced between the branches of the trees and sparkled on the glassy lake.

Claire listened and said one word: "Perfect."

"Sunshine on my shoulders..." Their voices blended in perfect harmony as the angels listened to that John Denver tune, silent in the miracle of the moment.

Xandra was filled with a love so deep she rose higher off the earthly plane. She knew that she and her earthly daughter would be leaving this space sometime soon. But she knew the beauty and grace of this moment would live on in Amanda's heart. Grace was present and a miracle made manifest.

In this tiny place along the lake surrounded by birds and trees, earth was transformed and heaven revealed. Yrandia was filled with awe. She watched and listened. Her daughter sang and she knew the Divine Plan of forgiveness and redemption was being made complete. She stayed silent and bowed to Source, the Divine Director.

When Amanda and Claire finished the last refrain, they embraced. Each knew that all wounds were healed. Their hearts were full. Whatever the next days would bring, they were united and ready.

Amanda smiled and softly said, "Thank you."

Claire understood and added, "Yes, thank you." The sun dipped below the now purple foothills and the soft hoot of an owl filled the air. "Perfect," Claire sighed.

"Indeed, perfect," Amanda replied.

CHAPTER 43

Amanda knew she had to take a quick trip home. She spoke with the hospice services and Susan, the nurse who came to check on her mother. Her visits were becoming frequent. Claire spent more time napping. She was visibly slowing down, and the medications had been increased to help manage the pain. Amanda even had to coax her mother to eat.

"Everybody is different and there is no set pattern how this goes," Susan said as they sipped tea in the small living room. "There's no saying how much longer your mom has. But it is fine for you to go home for a few days. Claire is in a good spot and I know you don't totally believe it but your Aunt Trish is actually very good with her. You have to take care of yourself and your life, too."

Amanda nodded. She was grateful how she had been able to continue with her life and job during these past months. She needed to meet with some buyers and vendors for the upcoming holiday season and the Christmas markets she had lined up for the boutique. She looked at Susan who had become like a surrogate mother during these past months.

Susan's brown eyes were warm and her voice always calm. "You are a wonderful daughter, Amanda. I hope you know that."

Amanda nodded. She was thankful for the kind words. "Thank you. I actually feel more like a daughter these days. We've always had a different kind of relationship. You sure it's okay to go?"

"Honey, listen to your heart. It's the one telling you to go home."

Amanda looked away. She felt the tug and needed a few days. "Okay, it will be short. Jordan is going to come back with me. It's so great how he and Mom seem to have a special connection. She really likes him. But you have to promise to call me if there is any kind of change. I don't care what time it is. I can get here in a few hours."

"You know I will. But don't worry, we will have time." The nurse patted Amanda's hand. It was warm and the touch was soothing.

The two women sat in silence. The room was bathed in the soft autumn sunlight. Amanda swirled her tea as she breathed in the rich aroma of cinnamon and other spices. She nibbled at a cookie and looked at the ceramic plate adorned in orange and yellow flowers. She smiled. She could see now how uninspired her childhood art was. They had pulled out the old plates and used them every day. Her mother had stored them in the hutch, ceremoniously putting them in small stands. *"No need to keep them wrapped up. Seems to defeat the purpose to put our treasures away. Right?"* Claire's face had lit up when she added, *"If I don't use them now, not sure when I will."*

"I'm going to miss her," Amanda said. "Six months ago I would never have said that."

Susan lightly brushed her arm. "You guys are lucky. Lots of people don't get the time—or don't use the time they have. It's remarkable how much you two have grown. I tell people about it. It is really special."

Amanda knew in her heart the groundwork had been laid long before the diagnosis. There were forces at work and for that she was grateful. "Yeah, I can't imagine if we hadn't had this time to heal. It has changed me in so many ways."

Susan smiled. "It's all about forgiveness. The magic happens in that space."

Amanda prepared for her return home. She had her calendar meticulously planned to make every moment count. She knew this would be her last trip home while still in caregiver mode. Next trip she would return to settle back into her life without the responsibility... without her mom.

CHAPTER 44

Anioch was excited to be back within Yrandia's energy field even if only for a brief human moment. As he dutifully served his child during Amanda's absence, he noticed that a part of him yearned for the warmth of Yrandia's grace.

During this time of separation, Anioch spent time reflecting on his early studies as a novice angel. He had sat through lectures on the capacity for humans to love. He heard of Spirit's intentional creation of a void and hunger in the human soul... to be used as an entry point for the desire to receive and impart love. And he now vividly recalled the lesson on humanity's current state of slumber.

The lesson taught that connection and unity were needed to drive humanity toward awakening. The eternal lesson of course was that awakening was simply the process of noticing that the connection and unity already existed. *All is One.*

Anioch had waited for the return of his Beloved. His angelic heart leapt when he felt Yrandia's radiant energy. He watched as she drew near in a blaze of pure light. Her aura was now magnificent. Anioch bowed deeply as a rush of love enveloped him.

"Dear sister, I have longed to rest in your presence again. I offer you blessings and love. It is a gift to have you near."

Yrandia bowed and smiled at her partner. "Oh my Beloved, my heart is full. There is much for us to share. This passage is truly one of grace for my daughter. The lessons have been profound."

The angels flew together and joined in a swirl of energy that exploded into the heavens while Jordan and Amanda walked arm in arm along the sun-drenched boardwalk. The ocean rolled in and out as gulls screeched and laughter filtered from the shoreline below.

Flying above their children as they had done from the beginning of their earthly days, Anioch watched Jordan lean in and gently kiss Amanda. The angel no longer recoiled at the show of tenderness and love.

As he flew effortlessly, he asked Yrandia why the Universe allowed so few people to experience love. "Teach me, please. Why would Source allow these beloved creations to live in a state of disconnection and disunity?"

Yrandia smiled a truly magnificent smile, all glory and light.

Anioch had been taken aback the first time she had radiated all of her beauty. Now he basked in it. He gave thanks for her brilliance as it reminded him again and again that Divine creations were truly wondrous, magical and wholly marvelous.

"Dear Anioch, as you know, this world here is not True Reality. The material world is only a reflection of a slumbering mind. It is all an illusion."

"A slumbering mind? But why do they stay asleep when there is so much beauty surrounding them?"

"Ahh, you must remember they see with their human eyes, not the eyes of the Indwelling Divine. With that narrow vision, they believe the world is limited in time and space. They choose to replace love with fear and believe in scarcity over abundance." Yrandia's radiance glowed.

Anioch listened and let the unspoken words resonate deep within. "Love," he repeated. To the young angel the earthly idea of love seemed no more than an empty word. He had seen humans turn love into an expression of lust, greed, power and control. But he knew this was not what Yrandia spoke of. "If Source is Love and an angelic Guide's Purpose is to impart true Love, why then is the human condition so pitiful, empty, and devoid of Divine Love?"

"I hear your ponderings. Yes, their condition appears pitiful. But we don't pity them, do we? We love them. We hold them in that light and healing vibration of real Love. That is what is ours to do."

Anioch lifted his wing and gracefully twisted in the wind, peering at his companion. She smiled. Her face was a canvas of angelic love, serene and supremely beautiful.

She bowed and bent her wing. "It's fine and good and holy. You know that. Love born of Source cannot be extinguished. It is the strongest force in the Universe. It is the mysterious energy that holds All together. These humans just choose to disconnect and enter into that place of darkness. But we always return to Light and Love. That is our joined journey Home."

"Indeed, but knowing this to be true, why do human's get so disconnected? How does that happen? And why?"

"Dear one, know that while the Divine Spirit is eternal, humans can lose touch with the Indwelling Divine. Look at my beloved daughter, Amanda, and your dear son, Jordan. It was that crushing of their faith—not their Spirit—that disconnected them from our pure essence... and in that loss of faith, it diminished our power to intercede."

"Loss of *faith*?" the novice echoed.

"Yes, Anioch," she comforted. "We are born of faith... and we, like human beings, are dependent on Faith's gift of Grace. Miracles happen in a shift, in a short humble prayer, through the outpouring of a stranger's love, and in the possibility it invokes. That alone is enough to draw us closer to our charges. It is through that first act of faith followed by the response of Grace that our interconnectivity allows us to guide and guard them in the Creator's Plan."

Anioch began to better understand and appreciate the true interweaving of all that coexisted in the Universe. The thread of Love connected everything. An invisible web of mutual dependency held everything together. It was indeed the Divine energy that pulsed through all Creation that maintained order and balance.

"My dear Anioch, our purpose is to serve. We are Messengers of Love. You ultimately answered Jordan's plea and in that instance you returned to the flow of service. The heavens opened to pull you back, just like your gentle touch reached me. We are connected, all of us, always."

Anioch was moved. He gently bowed and spread his wings. They had served each other. What a splendid Universe he rested in and shared.

Yrandia opened her wings and reached out to Anioch. They touched in a spark of light and energy. The majestic Being, who was now a part of the young angel's swirl of energy, knew there was balance in this flow of giving and receiving. As Yrandia imparted the wisdom and truth, she felt her energy sizzle and her aura blazed. All was well. She breathed, deeply content in the moment.

The lessons continued. The young angel was filled with questions. "If man is beloved, why does he suffer? When I traveled with Jordan, I saw poverty, hunger, sadness and fear. I saw hopelessness and hate. Why are babies left to suffer? It makes no sense."

Yrandia spoke silently but the energy passed over the earth like a soft breeze that brushed over the ocean and danced in the hovering palms. "Source imparts Love to all Beings. They are all Beloved. The key to understanding the earthly plane is to understand the responsibility placed upon each soul and spirit. I know the disparity may appear unjust. But Source, in infinite wisdom, does not judge based upon wealth, education, status or achievement. Rather eternal grace, while ever-present, is experienced in the human incarnation of the Divine Spark. It is eternal yet joins in the journey and is learned by degrees. Man chooses his reality by the energy of his thoughts."

"Humans choose these experiences?" Anioch puzzled. "If I could have peace and abundance, why would I choose war and scarcity?"

"Because, my dear, the soul searches for growth. The answers are often shrouded in darkness and silence. But suffering is a choice. The lesson can be learned without the accompanying pain and suffering. It is a choice to see the lesson as a blessing instead. Growth is inevitable along the path. How one learns is the choice." Yrandia pulsed in a deep and radiant shield of light.

"Suffering is a choice? I suffered that day. Me—an angel—I felt that pain and it was unbearable. Why would they choose that?"

"Why did you choose it, Anioch? Why did I choose it, for I too suffered? We know our True Identity and yet we descended."

Anioch felt the weight return to him of that moment of disconnect and despair. "My God, what pain they must endure."

"Suffering is born from impatience, in the forgetting that only Love is real. The rest is illusion. We have to find the good. It is there. It is the fertile ground and resting place of the soul. But sometimes we have to dig and clear the space where Love abides." The Ancient Sage breathed deeply and the air moved. "The Universe does not judge nor deny grace. Rather each man chooses to either open his Spiritual Eye to the ever present Grace and abundance or to keep his Eye closed and wander in darkness and live from a place of scarcity and fear."

"I see that and it makes me weep. This world is beautiful and magnificent. It is paradise. But man pollutes and destroys. Out of fear humans fight for more. More what? When will they wake up and realize they have enough?" Anioch still did not fully understand.

"Indeed," Yrandia nodded. "Whole segments of the world live in blindness. It is out of this twisted perspective of fear, loss and separation that humans suffer: not because of lack but because of their inability to see and accept the rich blessings. They believe that they must grow big and strong to be powerful. But instead they must shrink and reduce to become Authentic and Powerful."

The fronds of nearby elegant palm trees swayed gently in the breeze of Yrandia's breath. "The hope of mankind rests with a shift in

262

perception. It requires letting go and stepping into a higher consciousness at both the individual and collective level."

"Why don't they let go?" Anioch pleaded. "I see what they hold on to and I do not understand. The illusion is not worth the effort of holding all this pain so close to their hearts. If letting go means stepping into Divine Reality, why do they cling so tightly to their self-created hell?"

Yrandia acknowledged that few men understand the power of their own thoughts. "It is Spirit's intention to honor all creation and offer the richest blessing to those who would come to recognize their True Selves. Indeed, few recognize they have the potential to create a reality of Wholeness and Oneness."

There was a hint of sadness in the angel's voice. The skies darkened.

"Understand, my dear one, the human soul has different evolutions which are neither right nor wrong, neither more nor less. Ultimately, it all is measured against the blossoming of love and the connection between the human heart and the Spirit of the Soul. The human soul has all of eternity to evolve."

Anioch felt Truth in this simple but powerful transmission.

Jordan and Amanda fell silent as they stepped onto the shore. They stood barefoot in the wet sand. Their angelic Guides hovered above. Each was lost in the moment, the rolling tide, and the inaudible call pulling them into their inner awakening.

Yrandia traced a circle of light around the couple below. She continued, "Some humans are born with a higher level of understanding and therefore a greater responsibility. What they do or do not do with their gifts is their choice. If the focus of each day is on mere survival—a physical hunger, repeating in an endless cycling caught in the hunt and fight—then that is their truth. Fear is their truth and it welcomes a range of accompanying heavy emotions. Each person progresses accordingly and is aligned to the vibrations their choices bring. Every thought from each of Source's creations is answered as if it were a prayer. That is why, my Beloved, we must guard our thoughts and the vibrational levels they reach."

Anioch received Yrandia's thoughts and was filled with tremendous gratitude for the ancient wisdom that was being passed to him. He hungered to better understand the human condition and with that understanding become a better servant and Messenger of Love.

Yrandia's voice took on the slow and steady cadence of the rolling waves. It provided comfort and calm as the words of hope resonated deeply in Anioch's angelic core.

The material plane was drawn in to match her rhythm and blend with the angelic wavelength. The sea swelled, spraying Jordan and Amanda. They stood on the shore lost in an embrace and without fully knowing the miracle of Transformation, they were showered with healing light. They let Love pierce their open hearts like the saltwater that lapped at their feet. They treasured the few hours they had together.

"It feels so good to be here with you. I've missed you so much. But right here, right now, the world seems right. I can just get lost in the immensity of the ocean," Jordan marveled. "Something about its timelessness and expansiveness speaks to me. Back when I surfed I used to get that feeling all the time... but I suppose I can get that same energy just being nearby." There was time to talk about what they both knew was coming. For now they enjoyed the respite the sacred shore offered.

Amanda smiled. She understood and felt the same strong pull deep within her. There was an almost primal connection as if the whole of heaven seamlessly intersected with earth at the shore. "This feels like home. Thank you, my love, for 'pushing me gently' to take this moment to pause and reconnect." Amanda stood still snuggled close to Jordan. She closed her eyes and melted into the moment. *Right here, right now, all is well.*

Moments later, she opened her eyes and looked up at the man she loved. She could see the longing in his eyes as he gazed off into the endless horizon. "You love the ocean, Jordan. I am wondering when you will get back in and do what you love. The surfer needs to be the surfer."

"Someday, sweetheart. I will know when I am ready. If I'm really truthful about it, at some level I actually doubt my surfing ability. I wonder now how much of that was talent and how much was my angel protecting me from my own stupid arrogance."

"Well, I'm not pushing you. It's just when you speak about surfing you light up. It seems to feed your soul and connect you to something bigger than yourself."

"I can't fully grasp the immensity of the ocean. Rivers flow into it. Rain comes from and returns to it. In a way I feel like I was born from it. You can take out one drop but the ocean remains undivided. The missing drop doesn't diminish the grandness, but that drop is of no less substance than its source. It is the ocean. I guess I see that as our relationship with Spirit. We are that drop of the Source. The Source isn't diminished. It is Whole in whatever manifestation it presents. We return to Source and are pulled into its vastness when we step back into it."

Amanda smiled. She appreciated their intimate soul connection. She gently kissed him, knowing he was connected to another dimension.

"You know, we can float on the waves," he mused. "Some are gentle and rock us; others are big and move us. We can't harness them. But we can surrender and be carried. I find real peace and power in thinking of myself connected to the waves. I'll get back in one day and when I do I will let my angel ride with me all the way."

Yrandia opened her wings and raised her angelic voice, "Humans are much beloved by our Creator. They have within themselves all that they need to manifest a life here on earth that is blessed and whole. Yet they do not see that what they seek... dream of... and even fight for... is already present in each moment. The gift rests in their undiscovered Self. It is not in the giving that the miracle of enlightenment occurs but rather in the conscious and simple act of receiving through deep surrender. They journey to far-away lands believing in ancient tales of salvation. Yet the simple Truth is that the unspeakable 'I AM That I AM' dwells within each human being. With that knowledge and the faith it breeds, there is no room for fear. Fear cannot abide in the space of Love. Most humans cannot let go of their small self to awaken to this ancient, eternal Reality. Heaven is here as close to them as their own breath and their beating heart." Yrandia inhaled sharply and in a rush of wind commanded: "Be Here Now."

A burst of energy surged through Anioch as he pondered those words and the earth below shook. The young couple on the shore lost themselves in a deep kiss.

Amanda spent the next few days focused on getting all the remaining details of her life in order. She knew that she would need to be fully present when she returned to Holyfield and felt that these hours of preparation would provide her the space to be at peace and immersed in the final steps of this journey. She spent the nights with

Jordan and in those hours they shared their day. It was in the small and simple that the magical and mystical resided. Each small pull added to the texture of the invisible web that time was weaving.

"I think I've got everything lined up for the markets. Funny how so many small things keep falling in line. The local artisans will get a good boost out of the exposure and the boutique is setting itself apart. I even talked to one vendor who is interested in my mom's artwork. She wants to transfer the patterns onto fabric. The colors are really gorgeous. Who knew all that crazy painting my mom did would be transformed one day?"

⚬⚭⚬

In the evening, Jordan listened. He marveled at Amanda's calm presence, noting a depth and aura of assurance he hadn't seen before. As he studied her face, Amanda stopped and held his gaze.

"What are you doing?" Her voice was soft with a hint of a giggle.

"Me? I am listening to you and thinking that I love you more than I thought possible." He pulled her softly toward him and gently kissed her lips. "You are amazing."

Amanda chuckled. "I don't know about all that. It's so good to be here with you. This is so big and deep it is going to take me a long time to sort out. But there are times, mostly at night, when I miss you so much."

Anioch listened as Jordan and Amanda wove their conversation in an intricate interlace of subjects like life and death, fear and surrender, hurt and forgiveness yet always returned to love. Anioch turned to Yrandia and bowed. "I too am so happy to be back within your presence. It gives me joy to be with you."

Yrandia stretched her magnificent wings. "Oh my dear brother, it is a true miracle to watch how our children have grown. They are luminous."

Anioch saw that the small room was filled with a deep glow that pulsated at the outer edges. "This is a place of love," he whispered.

"Indeed it is," Yrandia softly replied.

Both angels wrapped themselves in an angelic embrace and sang a song of praise. Their song turned to laughter as they surrendered to the shared bliss between heaven and earth.

Amanda and Jordan shifted on the couch and leaned in closer. "I love you, Jordan. I know that to be truer than anything else in my life."

The vibration of love filled the entire space and radiated out into the world.

❧❧

Jordan and Amanda took turns during the drive north to Holyfield. They had gotten a late start. A light rain fell and a heavy mist blurred the landscape. A large full moon danced alongside the car and mixed with the mist, creating a soft amber glow.

Amanda turned the radio up to let music fill the space. In her heart she knew the next few days or possibly a week would be important and impactful. She felt at peace and strangely calm. "When my mom and I went out to the lake a couple weeks ago, I took my guitar. It was a magical moment for me. I played a song that she used to sing to me when I was a little girl. I always liked it, but there at the lake, it was the first time I really heard the words." Amanda paused. "Funny how I've gone through so much of life never really paying attention. This experience has really taught me that. I need to be more present."

Jordan waited.

"I am hearing things now that I heard before but never thought about. Like being present. Dr. Blair says that a lot. Or getting centered. I never understood what he meant until now. Now I am here with you. I hear the music. It is lovely. I hear the windshield wipers. They are a backdrop. But I *hear* them. I can *feel* you. I *sense* you. I hear your breathing and I can smell that special smell that is you. I feel the motion of the car and can hear the mist as it sprays, and the passing of the wheels on the road. When I look outside I can see the mist and haze blend with the light of the moon. I can really see how it changes the fields and the colors of the landscape. I never noticed before. I would just have driven right by. But now it's like I am awake."

Jordan understood. He could feel his body, aware of his breath and the rise and fall of his chest. He understood. He waited.

"I wonder if knowing how precious time is has made me wake up. I don't just sing words with a pretty melody anymore. Now when I sing I hear a prayer. I connect with it. '*Sunshine on my shoulders...*' It means something to me now. That memory will stay with me forever."

Jordan smiled. "I know what you mean. Listen to the radio. What's playing right now?" He turned the volume up and softly began to sing the refrain. Amanda immediately recognized Ben E. King. She looked at the dark night and luminous moon and laughed. "This is perfect!"

As she joined in with the lyrics she softly whispered, "I'm not afraid, I'm really not."

Jordan turned the volume and joined in the chorus laughing as they chased the light of the moon.

The angels in the backseat rocked to the rhythm and added their voices, *"Oh darling, stand... by me, stand by me... stand by me."*

CHAPTER 45

The car pulled into the long curved driveway. Amanda noticed a black SUV parked next to her aunt's old Civic. A light was burning in the kitchen. Amanda's pulse quickened. *Calm down,* she softly told herself.

Jordan pulled their bags from the trunk.

"I wonder who is over this late?" she asked.

As the couple entered the small home, they were welcomed by the soft purr of Chloe the cat, whose long tail twisted around Amanda's leg. The comforting smell of baking bread filled the house.

Trish came into the hallway carrying a book, then moved closer to embrace Amanda. "Hey, glad you made it. I was a little worried with the fog." The scent of bread and cinnamon hung in her hair. *No cigarette smell*, Amanda noticed.

Jordan put down their bags and received a hug as well.

"How's Mom?" Amanda quickly asked as she scooped up the still purring cat.

"She's pretty tired these days. But she's in good spirits. Dwayne is with her right now. Amazing, those two. They seem to have really hit it off. It's like they've been friends forever."

Dwayne, Amanda mused. She hadn't heard about him before. *Curious.* She let her questions hang unasked.

"I'm baking bread right now," Trish said. "For some reason Claire has been having these cravings. Mostly she isn't hungry, but you know I'm happy to do what I can."

Amanda smiled. "Thanks for being here. It means a lot to Mom. The bread smells wonderful. Reminds me of childhood."

"I know, right? Might be one of the best smells in the world." Trish grabbed one of the bags. "Here, let me help you with this."

Jordan tugged it back. "I got this. 'Manda, you two go on and see your mom. I'll get everything put away."

Amanda kissed him on the cheek. "Thanks, honey." She was anxious to reconnect.

Amanda and her aunt turned toward the small hallway leading to her mother's room. "So who is this Dwayne guy?" she asked. As they passed the small dining area, she noticed a bud vase with a beautiful long-stemmed rose. *Late in the season for roses.*

"Oh, he's here to cover for Susan. She had some family thing come up and had to go to Arizona for a few days. But she's been calling to check in. So sweet. Anyway, the hospice center sent Dwayne over to make sure your mom gets seen and we get taken care of. They wanted to move her to a facility, but she didn't want that. Dwayne promised to be here so we wouldn't have to make that choice. And he's been great. He comes every day. I mean... look how late it is and he's still here. They just sit in there and talk for hours. Sometimes he reads to her. It's like they're old friends."

"Oh, that's good. But I hope everything is okay with Susan." Amanda felt a small wave of unease. She relied on Susan's advice. "Will she be gone for long?" She tried to keep her voice soft and the question neutral to not belie her concern.

Her aunt didn't seem to notice. "I think everything is okay. She didn't really say. She should be back soon, but your mom seems to be really comfortable with this new guy."

Amanda and Trish stood in the doorway. Claire lay in bed propped up by pillows with a large white down comforter covering her. Her hair was pulled back. In the soft glow of the bedside lamp, she almost looked like a child.

In the floral-clothed side chair, a tall man in jeans and a black turtleneck sat bent over a book. He was reading to Claire in a soft calm voice. "If you want to become whole, let yourself be partial. If you want to become straight, let yourself be crooked. If you want to become full, let yourself be empty. If you want to be reborn, let yourself die. If you want to be given everything, give everything up." Amanda noticed that he had his shoes off. She glanced at her aunt's feet and noticed she too was wearing nothing on her feet but socks. *Curious.*

When Claire shifted, he stopped and put the book in his lap. A warm smile crossed over his face, causing a splash of lines to curve out from his eyes. "Lao Tzu."

Amanda's mind flashed recognition. She stood still staring at the man. *How do I know him?* "Oh..." Amanda didn't understand but she smiled.

Claire's voice was weak but carried a brightness, "Oh Mandy honey, I am so happy to see you. Come here. Let me hug you!"

Amanda stepped into the room. She bent down to kiss her mother. She was surprised by how much smaller and frailer Claire had gotten in the past few days. The skin of her mother's cheek was dry and cold. Her breath had a strange smell that made Amanda want to pull back. *Decay,* was her first silent thought.

As Amanda's eyes adjusted to the light, she looked more closely at the stranger in the wing-backed chair. He was watching mother and daughter, eyes twinkling as if illuminated from some magical interior light source.

He began to stand as Amanda moved to greet him. "Hi, I'm Amanda, Claire's daughter." She offered her hand and the stranger warmly took it.

"I'm Dwayne. Your mother has told me a lot about you. It is a real pleasure to meet you."

She noticed the beautiful spring box was on the nightstand and colorful pictures hung on the wall. The room had been transformed. Color and beauty surrounded them.

As if reading her mind the stranger said, "Your mom's artwork is too beautiful to keep hidden. They are treasures and must be shared."

Amanda nodded. There were small and large canvases placed on every open space. Claire's face was filled with a radiant smile as she watched her daughter eye each piece of art.

Amanda stood still and listened to the voice. She recognized it but couldn't place the man. "Oh yes. It is magnificent." As she drew her hand back she added as if an afterthought, "I am happy to meet you, too."

She paused to look deeper at this man, Dwayne, who held her gaze. His eyes were filled with pure kindness.

Amanda continued, "I know this might sound weird, but I am pretty sure we've met before. You just seem so familiar."

Claire moved in her bed, patting the covers in a gesture Amanda recognized from her youth. She moved over to her mother's bed and softly sat down.

"Well, I don't know," he said. "Could be, I suppose. But last week was the first time I met your mom and aunt."

And when was the first time you met me?

Trish moved into the room near the man.

Amanda smiled. She liked him, too. "Who knows? Maybe our paths crossed here in Holyfield?"

Dwayne smiled back. "Maybe." His voice dropped and was gentle as he added, "Well Claire, it's getting late and I am sure you want to catch up with your daughter. Plus you need to rest." He placed the book near the box of hope.

"Thank you, Dwayne," Claire said brightly. "It is always such a joy to be with you. I do hope you can come by while Amanda is here. I think you two would hit it off. She's my gentle guardian soul."

Amanda noticed that Dwayne softly bowed in her direction. There was something calming about his presence. In fact she noticed an overall sense of peace in the room. Even Aunt Trish sat happily in the floral chair with a soft smile framing her face. *This is an oasis. A sanctuary.*

As Dwayne leaned over to wish Claire a good night, Trish jumped up. "Oh my, wait, I need to cut you some bread to take home."

Dwayne stretched his arms. "You didn't think I would forget, did you? I mean the deal was I'd bring you flowers in exchange for your baked goodies."

Trish left the room with a giggle.

The rose! Amanda's mind flashed on the bud vase in the dining room. Her mind focused and it was as if the fog had lifted. She was briefly transported back to the small garden bathed in an earlier full moon. *That's it. He is the stranger with the rose.* Her heart raced. Her mind shot into a thousand different directions.

Dwayne turned and looked at Amanda again as if reading her thoughts. His eyes twinkled.

Curious. She remembered the words he had offered that day in the small hospital garden: *"Gifts and blessing often come disguised."* And here he was filling their house with calm and peace. *So strange yet so perfect.* Her heart filled with a deep warmth as if some inner stream had flooded her with a sense of pure love. Again she looked at this serene stranger. He winked at her and grabbed for his wool cap and slipped on his shoes.

Amanda followed him to the door. As he stopped in the kitchen to wait on Trish's offering, she quietly asked, "How is she? I mean, she looks even frailer than when I left."

The mysterious man reached for Amanda's hand. His touch was warm and comforting. "Physically she is nearing the end. But you know that. Susan told me you've had those conversations. I sense you are all prepared for that. Your mother is making her final acts of peace. She is getting ready. I don't think it will be long. She is very open and is really making sense out of things. She is in a good place. She is truly a beautiful soul."

Amanda's breath caught. It sounded strange for him to refer to her mother as "a beautiful soul." *That is what she is,* her mind responded. *That is what she will always be,* her heart answered.

Amanda's thoughts stood still and her heart swelled. She looked at this man, Dwayne. "This is the first time I've thought of her like that. A soul."

He smiled. "It is probably a good time to begin to embrace the idea. It will be very helpful." His voice was soft and low but it resonated and Amanda could feel it deep in her chest as the words entered her heart. "It's late, Amanda. You've had a long drive. If you don't mind, I am happy to come by tomorrow. I am here as much for you as your mother."

Amanda stopped and looked at this kind man. *Who are you?* "Yes, that would be very nice. There's a warm and peaceful vibe in here and I'm thinking that has a lot to do with you."

She walked him to the front door but at the last second he turned to her. "I think it has far more to do with your mother and her guide. You too are a part of this. I am just here to bear witness. The miracles are all yours."

He opened the door and the cool night air pushed in. Amanda noticed the pool of soft light cast by the full moon on the gravel path. *A lighted path.* The thought brought comfort. Then she recalled the words this man had shared on the first day of their journey... *he* was a gift.

"Wait, please. I need to talk to you." Amanda stepped out in the night air.

Dwayne paused.

"You remember that evening on the hospital patio, don't you? You handed me a rose just like the one in the kitchen. You said something to me and it has stayed with me. This is no coincidence is it?" Amanda's heart was racing.

"There are no accidents and no coincidences in life," Dwayne answered, "if we stay alert. I do remember. In fact, when I am called to the hospital and find a rose, I always stay alert. There you were, alone and clearly troubled and sad. I didn't know what the Universe wanted from me, but I learned a long time ago, if we offer to be of service, the heavens will find a way to place us in service. So I am here for you and your mother."

Amanda listened. *Who are you?* she wondered again. "Well, thank you for being here. I sense you've touched my mother and aunt. There is a real calm in the house."

"It is all working as it is meant to. Susan's family matter opened up this opportunity and here I am. I recognized you when I saw your picture in the living room. I know there is a purpose behind this... and I dare say a gift for me as well. So thank you, Amanda, for the gift you bring to me." Dwayne's voice had an almost hypnotic cadence to it. It flowed effortlessly.

Amanda didn't understand what he was saying but decided the strange man would reveal himself in time. "I don't have any idea what I could offer you but I do thank you. I can't help but think you are supposed to be here for us. And for that I am grateful." Amanda smiled as she remembered the evening they first met. "It was a full moon when I met you, right?"

"I believe it was. The most beautiful roses bloom in the light of the moon." He softly laughed. "Amanda, I think you will be called to do wonderful things. Stay open. You had a mystical experience that will reveal itself to you in time. I know that to be true as someone who walked the same path. So just be open and follow your heart."

With that he stepped closer and gently embraced her. Amanda felt an electric warm energy enter her body. For a brief second she had a thought, *He's an angel!* She felt his body move and a laugh filled the night air.

"You are a blessing, Amanda. A true blessing."

She watched as he walked down the path lit by twinkle lights, the moon casting long shadows. He didn't look back but she could hear him softly hum.

Amanda stayed outside as his car pulled away. She turned to the house and saw Jordan waiting for her in the doorway. *"Be open and follow your heart,"* Dwayne's words echoed. She walked toward Jordan and melted into his arms.

CHAPTER 46

The days passed. Time felt suspended. An almost hushed reverence hung in the air. Trish stopped by every morning and evening. Amanda noticed a new calm in her aunt and something she couldn't quite name. *Surrender,* she mused. It was good.

"Expansive," Dwayne repeated. He was seated at the kitchen table with an open book near him. He held his glasses in his hand.

He must have been a teacher, Amanda thought.

Dwayne continued in his deep soft tone, "There's a point in our lives where we choose to either shrink and contract and shut off life or instead to grow and become expansive."

Amanda listened as Dwayne and her mother quietly discussed an idea from the book.

Claire had moved into the warm kitchen and sat in the overstuffed chair they had brought in from the living room so she could be near the large garden window.

Amanda continued chopping the last of the fall vegetables from the garden, preparing soup for the evening meal.

"Expansive," Claire repeated. She started to laugh. It came out as dry snorts. "I don't know why, but it just seems funny to me." She stopped.

Amanda put down her knife and looked at her mother. She had noticed Claire spent most of her waking hours asking questions, listening intently to Dwayne as he read select passages from an endless source of books. She also seemed to enjoy thinking out loud as if trying to reconcile and make sense out of thoughts and events.

Jordan had noticed too and asked Amanda to pay attention. "I think Dwayne's first words to you carry a lot of power. I feel like this is all unfolding as it should and there is a great gift here for you and your mom."

Amanda had agreed, so she stopped and listened.

"Look at me," Claire chuckled roughly. "I am just a tiny shell of myself. About as unexpanded as I've ever been. But I get it. I feel more open than before. More alive than before. I am sitting here right now so full of life. It hurts like hell to breathe, but with each breath I know

I am alive. I feel the sunlight. I smell these flowers. I hear sounds of life and I feel such love. Damn, if it didn't take my having to shrivel to the point of almost nothing to feel so expansive."

Amanda felt tears run down her cheeks.

Dwayne got up and hugged Claire.

Jordan listened and understood.

"You are a wise soul, my dear Claire," Dwayne said softly. "A very wise and expansive soul." His large frame wrapped around Amanda's mother.

Yrandia and Xandra encircled the room with their angelic presence. Right there the angels knew the small sunlit kitchen was as close to heaven as the world could know.

"Oh my wonderful sister, this is such a perfect gift," Yrandia spoke.

"Indeed it is. After so many years of fear and fighting, here we are finally bringing our earthly sister to her true place of greatness. She chose this as her purpose and is stepping into it with such grace." Xandra was magnificent. As her earthly daughter had shrunk, consumed by disease, the angel had grown deeper and richer in beauty and light.

Anioch watched and absorbed the lessons. The novice angel understood.

Xandra was filled with angelic pride. She knew her role and had always stayed true to it. She and Claire had made a pact in the space before time. Xandra was to always guide her child toward this place of balance. Claire had chosen to be teacher and student, to serve both mother and daughter. Claire's purpose was to impart this important lesson on forgiveness.

Xandra knew that ultimately all things needed to be stripped away on the earthly plane to reveal the illusion of separation and the gift of expansion, of healing, and finally of forgiveness. Claire's act of love to serve as master teacher was a gift. On the earthly plane, she required forgiveness and in that act gave the gift of freedom to her daughter. And through that gift, both mother and daughter were healed. *Such was the mystery*, Xandra pondered and praised.

Dwayne's voice was rich and deep. He gave human voice to the angel's thoughts, "Claire, you are a beautiful gift to all of us. Your beauty transcends this body. Your soul is so alive and will always be alive. You are a pure channel of the Divine. An instrument of Divine Love." Dwayne paused.

Claire's eyes glowed. "I am. I am. I always was but I didn't know it. I was distracted by other stuff I thought mattered. But now that it's all disappearing, I can see that none of it was real. *This* is what is real. Right here, right now. This expansive feeling of love and joy and peace is all that ever mattered."

Claire stopped. She moved her body to face Amanda.

"Amanda honey, my heart is so full right now," she continued. "Anything I could have ever wanted in life seems small and silly compared to this. It's like I am totally alive and awake for the first time. It really all comes down to this. All that matters in life is love. And when I think of that love, I see it is you. I messed up a lot. We both know that and in my heart I know we've healed. But in the end, what remains is love."

As she spoke, the angels began to sing. Dwayne stood and bowed. Amanda stood still. Tears streamed down her face. Something had forever changed.

Claire closed her eyes. Her voice became soft, "My beautiful daughter, you showed me love and mercy. I didn't deserve that love and grace from you, but you gave it to me anyway and now that I am so weak and counting the days, I know you gave me the greatest gift ever. You gave me the chance to put aside my own self-doubt and self-hatred and you let me see myself through your eyes. You forgave me and let me forgive myself. Now I understand it. Expansive. I have become expansive. It's all about love. That's what's limitless. That's who we are. Once I was able to love myself—because you loved me—it all just made sense. We are love." Claire began to cry.

"And so it is," Xandra sang. "The separation is healed as all things join in the infinite expanse of love."

Anioch bowed as the lesson of Truth washed over the small kitchen in Holyfield. The heavens rejoiced as one human soul fully awakened.

Amanda and Dwayne helped Claire to the bedroom. Claire removed her shoes before she entered her mother's bedroom. Dwayne had explained that in many ancient spiritual traditions shoes were not worn in sacred spaces. Amanda entered the room and felt the peace. *This is a holy place,* she thought. The long journey of forgiveness and healing drew closer to its end. The two angels took their positions knowing that all was well in heaven and on earth.

Claire slept. Amanda waited. Jordan held vigil. Dwayne held the sacred space. Trish came in and out and in her own way made peace.

There were candles and music, poems and prayers. The room was filled with love. And when the time came, Dwayne stopped reading the ancient poems and opened the window. "They say it lets the soul transcend."

Xandra closed her eyes and began a solemn chant. She turned and slowly began a dance of movement and light. As she opened her wings, the heavens began to stir.

Yrandia watched and sent love to her sister. A swirl of twinkling light gathered speed and a small energy field blended into a vortex of twirling energy.

Xandra continued to chant. She touched Yrandia and kissed her on her face. "I love you, my Beloved. It has been an honor to inhabit this space with you. Earth time for me is ending, but our souls are joined in eternity. I will be with you as I've always been with you. I bid you love and light."

Yrandia opened her wings and joined in a blaze of colors.

Anioch watched in awe at the grandeur of the moment.

Yrandia joined the chant and sang a hymn to her angelic companion. "You have done well, my dear. Your child is blessed and whole. I thank you for the gift you've bequeathed to my daughter. All is in order and as it was destined. Blessings, my sister. Blessings."

Xandra bent down and the energy in the small bedroom changed.

Dwayne touched Amanda's shoulder. "Be near her."

Amanda moved and sat at her mother's side and stroked her hair. Claire's breathing was shallow and raspy. "I love you, Mom. You taught me how to forgive and love. I know you are at peace. It's okay to let go now. We are all okay here and will hold you forever in our hearts."

And in that moment, a soft breeze passed through the room. The candles flickered. A morning bird began its song to the rising sun. Claire quietly surrendered as Xandra welcomed her into her arms on the angelic plane while Amanda cradled her below.

"All is well and as it should be," the angelic sisters rejoiced and bowed in honor. Anioch watched and marveled. The lessons were rich and deep and he was humbled.

❈

The small group gathered at Willow Lake. Amanda carried her guitar down the gravel path she had walked a few months before. She felt a deep connection to the place. Memories of her mother rushed at

278

her and for a moment she believed that if she turned around she would see her mom. *I miss you*, she silently whispered. *But I know you are happy and safe and free of pain and worry.*

Amanda heard the low warble of a distant bird. She pointed out a spot to the rest of the group. "Down there."

Trish carried the beautiful painted box with springtime blooms and dancing butterflies. The box carried Claire's ashes. Claire had named it the Hope Box. Amanda now understood why her mother had been so meticulous that day. She'd had a purpose for it. The memory of the day made Amanda smile. She breathed deep. The forest held her mother's spirit.

Jordan walked beside Amanda. His heart was full of love and gratitude. He too breathed in the deep smells that the pine forest shared. It smelled of life. The damp soil was soft and the sun had lost its warmth, but he knew this was a sacred place where Amanda and Claire had touched each other's soul. He knew the woman he loved had been deeply transformed over the past months. The grace she displayed only deepened the love he felt for her. He watched her as she looked out across the tranquil blue lake. The dancing rays of sunlight framed her face and she looked like an angelic being. His heart burst with love.

Dwayne and Susan unfurled the quilts and created a circle with the wildflowers they had picked up at a local stand.

Amanda placed a single sunflower in the center. "Bend toward the light," she softly prayed.

Dwayne opened his backpack and took out a book of poetry. The small party settled in for a celebration of Claire's life. In that forest glen surrounded by towering pines, graceful willows and the shimmering blue lake they sang songs, shared stories and honored the woman they each had come to know and love.

The afternoon ended with Amanda playing what she now called "Claire's Song." The whole group blended their voices in the final chorus.

The forest was still. On the other side of the lake a soft whooshing sound pierced the silence. A shadow passed, a slender snowy egret landed in a cluster of amber colored grass. Amanda pointed. The group smiled.

Dwayne looked at Amanda and bowed.

Yrandia knew that he understood. Yrandia bowed as well. There hovering above the pristine bird she saw the brilliant amber eyes of her Beloved who blended in with the beauty of the forest. They had returned to the circle of love.

"All is as it should be," both angels silently praised. "And so it is."

CHAPTER 47

Amanda returned home. It felt good. So much was the same and yet in many ways everything was different. Reflecting back on that foggy night, the cryptic voicemail and the conversation with Aunt Trish, Amanda could see that her life had been forever changed. As she unpacked, she thought about the journey and the deep life lessons she had been offered. Now with distance and the ability to step into the role of observer, she saw that unexpected turns in her path were a true blessing leading her back to her own heart. She heard Dwayne's deep voice echo the ancient words in her quiet mind, *"Each separate being in the universe returns to the common source. Returning to the source is serenity."*

As she sorted through her belongings and tried to bring order to her home, she recognized she had returned to a different life. All the stuff was the same but she had changed. Transformed. She was seeing with new eyes. "It's nice to be back," she whispered to her empty house.

She saw the familiar vase that had held sunflowers on that stormy night. The old hand-painted container had transformed into a priceless treasure. It held deeper meaning and connection for her. She thought of her mom and smiled.

As the first few days passed, Amanda found herself settling back into a routine. But the energy had changed, too. She felt connected to her actions. She paused to appreciate simple moments. She thought of the potential in each seed as she planted a small garden. She savored the smell that filled her home when she baked bread from her mother's recipe book. She breathed in the smell of the ocean and stopped to listen closely to the waves as they broke on the shore. She allowed herself to sink deeply and feel the love that filled her as she rested in Jordan's arms. She savored each special and tender moment, knowing now the preciousness of each hour and minute.

Amanda woke each day and set an intention: "I will be a blessing today." Feelings of joy, wonder, peace and bliss entered her world and opened her heart to the new energy they brought. As she lived from a place of connection and intention, she became surrounded by higher vibrations of love and joy that seeped into her soul. Where she once saw obstacles and difficulties, she now saw possibility and blessings. Her perception of reality had radically changed. And she liked it.

A new passion evolved for writing poetry. The words flowed, speaking in their own language of lessons learned and the power of grace and love. *Let my lessons serve a purpose*, she prayed. During moments of silence she reflected how these past months had offered her the gift of letting go. The act of forgiveness had been a spiritual release, not for or from her mom, but rather for and from her True Self. Through the process of forgiving, she had ultimately freed herself. She felt brave and no longer needed to disappear.

In a protected seaside cove Amanda set up her easel and lost herself in the colors of her new radiant world. "Life is good," she whispered. Her world felt like a new blank canvas and she was free to paint her own masterpiece unencumbered by the past or fear.

She took time to reflect on her new life, recognizing that her mother was a gift and had been one of her master teachers. Her past no longer dictated her present as she had not only made peace with it but thanked it. As she released herself from the grip of the ancient and invisible shackles, she was able to love herself and reconcile and reconnect with her True Self. The once withdrawn and shy woman was now able to step into her own power as the individualized expression of the Divine. That transformation was the miracle.

Food became a newfound pleasure as it nourished her, no longer a thing of inner and outward control. She marveled at the miracle of her body and even found a space to offer gratitude for diabetes. It taught her about balance and made her aware of how interconnected everything was to life and wholeness. She honored herself as a complete being and felt connected to all of Life.

And of course there was her relationship with Jordan. She marveled at how much they had grown as individuals. She never imagined that her life would be this rich and blessed. All of her growth and awakening was supported by his generous act of being present and serving as a channel of love. He was a constant for her during every twist and turn. She also knew that her mother's passing and the healing it offered was an essential step for her to be able to receive the gift of love. And for that she was deeply grateful. *May I also be a channel of love*, she prayed, knowing the power of reciprocity.

❧ ❧

And so the days passed, slowly, gently, without expectation or hurry. Man and woman discovered their inner joys, shared their truths and as their hearts continued to expand, their love grew. They journeyed deeper, moved closer to their inner Light, and their souls formed a union of sacred Love.

"Hey sweetheart, now that you've had time to get somewhat settled in, I was thinking maybe we could visit my friend Anne Marie. I have been wanting to do this for some time but things got a little complicated with your mom's illness and all."

Anne Marie was the first person that Jordan had connected with in a spiritual way and had been a constant source of strength, understanding and deep friendship. "I've told her a lot about you and she has wanted to meet you. I think you two will really connect."

He had shared so much with Anne Marie and felt that the timing was now perfect. He saw Anne Marie as a sort of surrogate mother figure. He knew she held a special place in his life and he wanted to finally bring together these two women he loved.

Amanda smiled. "I know how much you love her and I am all for having a big circle of people to surround us in love. Sounds perfect."

Jordan picked Amanda up and set out on the freeway heading northeast into the still rising sun. It was a glorious spring day. Nature was in full bloom and bursting in sheer delight. A soft breeze danced along the blossoming trees. Tiny petals of pink and white cascaded down from the lush tops. The sweet fragrance of blossoms and grass mingled in the air. Jordan was happy to be alive. Amanda sat beside him, her hair blowing in the wind. She flashed a radiant smile and wrapped her arms around him.

Jordan stole another sideways glance and smiled. *God, she's beautiful.* She had put on a little weight and it added to her beauty. She was radiant. Her hair and skin were bright and full of color.

"I know you'll like Anne Marie. She is one of the most real people I've ever met. She has this way about her that is serene, but not in a weird way. I don't know, she just seems grounded and in touch with everything and everybody she meets. I guess maybe I'd say she is grace-filled." Jordan stopped and looked at Amanda.

She smiled. "She sounds lovely."

"Yes, and she has a presence about her that just makes you feel at peace. She's also really intuitive. She sensed my angel before I even knew that I believed in him. I know her love and prayers played a big part in my recovery."

Amanda sighed a deep sign of contentment and smiled. Jordan went on talking as the radio played and the morning awoke in all of its glory. As she heard his stories about Anne Marie, she thought of the special people who came to her when she needed their presence. "I think maybe she's your Dwayne. That perfect stranger who appeared just when you needed her and touched your life." She silently thought of her garden stranger and the idea filled her with joy. *There's always beauty around. We just have to open our eyes to the possibilities...* She gently touched the bouquet of red roses she held on her lap.

Jordan maneuvered his car along the canyon roads. Anne Marie had moved further inland to the open spaces of the backlands. The geography changed as they drove east. The jagged ocean cliffs gave way to gentle slopes and wide stretches of rolling green hills. Wildflowers grew in verdant meadows, dotting the horizon in splashes of yellow and blue. Amanda pointed with joy at a cluster of tall sunflowers swaying in the gentle breeze. A solitary hawk circled and danced in the wind. The world was alive and nature fully awakened and radiating her glory.

Anne Marie and her husband had bought a small horse ranch where they tended to their garden and animals. She dreamed of opening a healing center. Jordan slowed down trying to follow the navigation system.

Off in the distance he noticed a small white house surrounded by elegant tall willows. "That must be Anne Marie's home," he exclaimed. He recalled how she had lovingly described it and this was the picture he had painted in his mind. It was perfect. He could feel the peace and sense the love as they approached, as if a soft energy field enveloped it and pulsed with generative joy. *This already is a healing place.*

He drove to the fenced yard, and Anne Marie stepped out onto the wide veranda and waved. "Hello, my treasure from the sea," she hollered.

"Well hello there, Florence," Jordan chuckled.

Quickly Jordan and Anne Marie were embracing. Amanda stood back and allowed the friends their space and time.

Jordan brought Amanda forward and with a reassuring embrace and love in his eyes introduced her. Anne Marie stretched out her arms and warmly welcomed Amanda. They instinctively hugged heart to heart.

When Amanda pulled away she looked down at the ruffled roses then up at Jordan and whispered, "Leave it to Dwayne to be part of this hug."

The day at Anne Marie's ranch was a joyous reunion. Jordan felt the strong connection he had always shared with this kind woman. He had missed their visits. They had such a strong bond and he felt himself fully relax and allow his heart to open. It occurred to Jordan that it was like coming home... even though he had never been to this beautiful spot of land.

A tremendous sense of harmony surrounded the ranch. The vistas were beautiful, its hills filled with color and light. It was a true refuge, holding the energy of healing. *Love abides here*. Jordan felt like he had found a small piece of heaven.

Amanda watched and listened while Jordan and Anne Marie talked. She sensed the deep love and respect they shared. She settled into the surroundings and let the feeling of peace wash over her. She breathed in the sweet air and felt connected to the earth and felt renewed.

Anne Marie talked about her new life as a rancher. She was so happy to be close to nature and Spirit.

Amanda listened and relaxed in the warmth that emanated from the land, the sun, the air and company.

Anne Marie slowly started bringing Amanda into the conversation. She spoke to Amanda openly, as if she knew her from some long forgotten past. She told her that she looked remarkable, as if comparing against some other image.

Then she must have noticed Amanda's puzzled look because she took Amanda's hand in hers and said, "I know you don't know me, but I met you once. You were very ill and I just happened to be drawn to your room. You weren't on my floor, but something beckoned me to your side. You were a patient at South Bay, at the same time as Jordan, in fact."

Jordan jumped. *What?* His heart pounded. That sense of recognition that registered when he'd first met Amanda at Dr. Blair's stirred in him. *What is Anne Marie saying? Did I meet Amanda there? I don't remember.* He listened intently. There was something more. He saw confusion on Amanda's face.

"I'm sorry but I'm not sure I understand," Amanda babbled. "I wasn't ever at South Bay. How could that be?" Her eyes looked nervous and unsure.

"I'm sure you don't remember," Anne Marie consoled. "You were transported from Creekside Clinic. You had gone into cardiac distress and early organ failure which required more intense medical attention than the Clinic could give. By the time you arrived at South Bay you were comatose. When I visited, there was very little hope you would survive. You had gone into sepsis. Truth be told, you stunned most of us when you pulled through. Even non-believers begrudgingly conceded that your recovery was 'miraculous'—not unlike yours, Jordan." Anne Marie smiled toward Jordan.

He recognized those dancing eyes. It meant there was a story to be told.

Amanda sat confused, trying to process this new information. "But I don't remember ever being there," Amanda said, brow wrinkled in concentration. "No one ever mentioned it to me before. I was released from Creekside. I remember that but I don't remember anyone talking of sepsis or organ failure. You'd think I would remember something like that."

"Wait, do you mean Amanda was only at South Bay while she was comatose?" Jordan asked, trying to figure out the pieces of the puzzle.

"Not exactly," Anne Marie answered. "Amanda, your prognosis was so bad your mother decided not to request extraordinary intervention if you went into cardiac arrest again. Doctors had explained to her that the anorexia was severe. And the diabetes complicated your already fragile state. You were so weak and frail. Your little body couldn't battle anymore. They said your organs had been irreparably damaged. So they sent you back to Creekside to be placed into hospice care." Anne Marie's voice was calm and the words simple. Amanda struggled to make sense of this new narrative. *What is she saying?* It was as if the words made no sense.

"So I was supposed to die?"

Amanda's question hung in the air. The small group was wrapped in silence as if nature had momentarily caught its collective breath.

In that moment of pause, reality hit. Jordan's mind raced. He bolted upright and looked at Amanda after an image flashed in his mind. The near wasted remains of that young woman... his prayer inside her door.

Jordan grabbed Amanda's hands, wanting to feel her warmth. He remembered. Yes, he had met her before, as he took his final walk through the darkened hospital corridor before his release. He had entered that door and seen her. *"Thy will be done,"* he had asked.

"My God," Jordan spluttered. He closed his eyes as the immensity of the moment washed over him. "My God," he whispered again.

"What? I'm missing something here." Amanda's voice was high and filled with questions. Her mind was racing. She felt dizzy and her breath was short. *What am I supposed to know!* She tried to quiet her screaming mind and move toward center.

"I saw you there, Amanda." Jordan's hand squeezed her tightly. "I saw a broken, frail woman. You looked almost dead. Something led me to this little room. A woman—I guess it was your mom—had run out crying. I snuck in as if I felt your need. My heart cried out. I couldn't just leave you. But I didn't know what to do... so I prayed. I didn't pray for you to get better, since I didn't know if that was right for you. All I could think of was to offer you love. *'Thy will be done,'* I prayed."

Jordan stopped and caught his breath. It all seemed surreal.

He looked at Anne Marie and then Amanda. "And now here you are, the most real and beautiful p-part of my l-life." Jordan's voice caught and his eyes filled with tears.

Anne Marie watched. She was part of this tableau. She had prayed for both of them. She had sensed their Spirits when they needed mercy and grace and felt the presence of their Angelic Guides. And here they were sitting on her front porch unraveling the mysteries of the Universe's perfect plan.

Jordan's voice was thick with emotion. "Amanda, I f-felt called and r-responded." His mind was racing and he tried to find the words to make sense of all of this "My God, you are a miracle. I prayed for you, not for me, not out of some selfish need or want but because you, this total stranger who seemed so alone, so desperately needed it. Some part of me knew that. I didn't touch you, but I know now that the small prayer did." Jordan spoke with his eyes closed.

Amanda listened transfixed. She slowed her breathing and moved her thoughts to her heart space. *What does this mean?*

"You lived. I lived. And here we are." Jordan's voice was a near whisper. "Anne Marie saw both of us as we lay near death and yet we are here together, the three of us, sharing life and love. This is a miracle."

The three humans sat together on the large veranda contemplating the miraculous while three angels hovered above and rejoiced in the revelation. No one spoke. The breeze carried bird songs and the soft nay of nearby horses.

"I learned so long ago," Anne Marie broke the silence, "that the hand of the Divine works as it wills. We can fight it or allow it to flow through us and create miracles. I prayed for each of you to find your truth and purpose. Now here we are connected on this path. Take this for what it is. For me it is a confirmation of this Divine plan for each of you..." Anne Marie's voice trailed off as she turned and gazed out to the vast expanse of her yard. *All is well.*

She turned back and looked at the young couple. Her heart swelled with love. "Divine Will truly has no why. The good or bad in our eyes is always a blessing that we might not see or appreciate at the time. But time is relative. Amanda, your illness brought you close to death, but to the Divine it was really a beginning. From that place of pain and suffering, you were allowed to grow and become the beautiful woman and spirit you are today. And the growth will continue."

Amanda held the wise woman's gaze and bowed.

Anne Marie then turned toward Jordan and met his tear-filled eyes. "Jordan, you are a living breathing miracle. And the love that you have found in your life only serves as proof that Spirit knew you had a reason and a purpose. Seeing you both sitting here right now filled with so much love is a miracle."

Jordan and Amanda moved in closer, feeling the powerful words of affirmation.

Anne Marie's voice blended with the whisper of the wind in the tall grass, "Amanda, no one held much hope for you. It was hard to pray for you, but I sensed that if you passed, there would have been a void in this world. You had a gift that had not been shared. I prayed that Divine Will be done with you."

Amanda was silent. It did not escape her that Jordan had echoed Anne Marie's simple prayer in that dark hospital room.

"Despite that bleak prognosis, it was Spirit's will that you live. As I look at you, my heart is filled with such joy. Here you are, beautiful and strong, nowhere near that empty shell of a woman. It is not because of me or because of Jordan, but because even then you were open to Spirit. I can't believe the physical change. It's dramatic. But I think the true miracle has been the rebirth of your Spirit. I can sense the power and energy of your Guide and it is vibrant and strong."

Amanda stirred. Could Anne Marie really sense something like that? "What do you mean? What do you see?"

"Amanda, it's not what I see. But I can sense their presence. I can sense their weakness or strength. And yours is vibrating at a level that is pure power right now." She turned to Jordan and added, "In fact yours is, too. They are connected—not unlike the two of you."

"Spirits and angels connect?" Jordan barely asked the question.

"Sometimes," Anne Marie responded. "Where there is true love, the energy extends beyond the human plane, transcending the boundaries of our dense earthly plane. You two have a very special bond, a love that isn't of this earth." Her voice was light and curious.

Amanda sat back. Her mind was filled with a swirl of questions. But she knew these mysteries weren't for her mind to understand. *See with your heart.* She closed her eyes to let the words and new reality sink in. Had her mother been willing to let her go? *"I never gave up on you,"* she'd said. *It doesn't matter. It all conspired toward good. Grace had been offered then as it was offered now.*

Amanda opened her eyes and took in the beauty of the world that surrounded them. Here she was alive, in love, fully transformed. Her organs were not ravaged, her heart had not failed and in fact her soul was filled to the breaking point with love and joy. Jordan, a complete stranger, had prayed for her... and even then he had been able to touch and connect with her deepest Self. Their pasts had touched. What did that mean for their future?

Jordan stood up. He touched Anne Marie gently on the shoulder but said nothing. Then he touched the small package he always carried with him, that tiny gift that she had given. *"Someday you will connect with this and its purpose will be clear to you."* He could sense she knew. She smiled at him and gently nodded.

He headed down the steps toward the open meadow.

Amanda watched him, not sure what was going on. She looked at Anne Marie who again nodded slightly. Amanda understood. She got up and followed Jordan.

Amanda reached Jordan and wrapped her arms around his waist. He brought her close. They walked in silence.

Anioch and Yrandia stayed near to their children. They flew together nearly intersecting. Their children had found their past and in it they were defining their future.

Jordan headed toward a small cluster of willows. They swayed in the spring breeze. The grass was green and slightly moist. He took off his sandals and watched while Amanda took off hers. *This is a sacred space.*

The grass was moist and the earth warm under Jordan's feet. The air was filled with the smells and sounds of life. The sun shone brightly through the canopy of long slender leaves.

Jordan took Amanda in his arms. He looked into her eyes, the same eyes that had given him hope and love. He looked into his one true reason and hope and saw in them the mirror of his own soul. Spirit had allowed her to be a part of his life. His prayers for everything good in this world were answered through her.

The angels whispered in unison, *"Thy will be done."* And so it was. And so it is.

Jordan saw in that instance his Purpose: to Love without reservation. He held his destiny in his own hands. The Universe had conspired to create this one moment and it was his choice how to live within it. He bowed and breathed in deeply.

"Amanda, I've always asked for signs. I used to do it as a kid. I'd dare my angel. It was a game. But I guess I never completely outgrew it. I still look for little signs; you know those pats on the back. But this is more than a pat on the back, more like a kick in the pants. I *knew* you. I *felt* you. I *prayed* for you, for your future. And here you are with me. I know with my whole heart that you are my future, my destiny, my life, my eternity. Amanda," he said, dropping to one knee. "I want to spend the rest of my living days with you. I guess what I'm trying to say is, will you marry me?"

Amanda's breath caught. She hadn't expected it, not yet. Marriage. Commitment. Forever. These were big words, awesome life-altering decisions. This one answer would change her whole life for today, tomorrow and forever. She had always run, but she knew that the running had brought her right here to this moment. It was right. It was real. Jordan was everything she had dared to hope for and believe in. He was what she had stopped believing in. The fairy tale. And yet here she was filled with love, hope, faith, and miraculously totally alive, looking at the face of her forever.

Jordan brought out a small packet from his pants pocket. He handed it to Amanda. "Anne Marie gave this to me the day I left the hospital. But now I know the gift wasn't just for me. I don't have a ring yet, but I know this is a perfect symbol for us."

Amanda opened up the pouch and found a small yet perfect pearl. She smiled. A gift from the sea. A hidden treasure formed slowly over time, buried beneath a shell that was strong enough to weather the ocean's storms and the tidal churn.

She remembered that night when Jordan spoke of the oyster and the pearl. She smiled. It was the perfect reminder that out of the challenges comes transformation. From the moment of introduction of that tiny grain of sand, resides the potential for transcendence from the ordinary to the infinitely extraordinary and priceless. It was indeed perfect.

"You, my love, are my gift from the sea," she said, her voice so low it was barely audible. She looked up and in a stronger voice, answered, "Yes. Yes, Jordan. A thousand times yes!" Amanda melted into the arms of the only person she had ever loved and lost herself in his touch and kiss.

Anioch and Yrandia flew into each other's comforting aura and praised the Universe. *"Thy will be done,"* rang from their lips and love radiated out in a joyous hymn to the far stretches of heaven and earth.

Anne Marie smiled and laughed as she saw the sun shine and momentarily blink. She heard the mountains ring and the birds join in a chorus of praise. She saw the couple lost in an embrace under the weeping trees. *Life is a wonderfully unpredictable trip*, she thought. And then she thanked Source for the gift of life and the power of love.

CHAPTER 48

Amanda waited above the secluded cove. She watched as friends and family gathered on the shore below, pausing to gaze at the glistening ocean. The water sparkled like a smooth blue jewel. The sky was clear and distant islands were visible in the far off horizon. It was a beautiful day. *Perfect.*

"You are stunning, my dear."

The warm and kind voice brought Amanda back to the jagged overlook. She turned and smiled at Dwayne who handed her a small red rosebud. "Well, you look quite handsome, too," she replied, gently kissing his cheek.

He opened his arms and wrapped her in a hug. "You are beautiful, Amanda. Absolutely radiant. I love your dress." He softly touched the draping fabric.

Amanda smiled. "Thank you. Does it look familiar?"

Dwayne examined it in the reflecting sun. He saw tiny white flowers, tips dipped in pink, climbing on a slender vine. "It is a work of art," he whispered.

"Yes," Amanda laughed.

Dwayne hugged her again. "You brought a bit of your mom here, didn't you?"

"Of course. She's with me all the time. I borrowed this imagery from one of the pictures you hung in her room. I see potential and hope in these tiny buds... they are still connected to the vine... the source that holds them but they are blooming and becoming their own beautiful self. I've named the whole fabric line Clarity."

"Perfect." Dwayne smiled and bowed. "Okay my dear, pin me with the rose and let's get ready. You have a circle of love waiting for a wedding."

Amanda smiled and gently fastened the boutonniere on her garden stranger. "You ready?"

Dwayne handed her a bouquet of wildflowers tied in a loose ribbon.

Amanda paused one more time, scanning the horizon, then softly giggled, "Wait, one more thing. We are entering a sacred place so...

shoes off." They both laughed and tossed their flip flops near the low growing shrubs.

Jordan made his way toward the small altar under a flower-draped arch. He stopped in front of his parents and hugged each one of them.

Charlene held her son tight and softly caressed his cheek. "My beautiful radiant son. I love you."

"Thanks Mom, for everything, but mostly for believing in me and loving me."

Daniel stood up and held his son. He tapped him on the shoulder and smiled. "You know, you are always protected... and always loved."

Jordan smiled and tapped his father's shoulder. "So are you, Dad, so are you."

Jake and Jenna both hugged their brother and smiled.

Amanda came down the footpath surrounded by blooming succulents. She smiled at the family and friends who lined the shore. Jordan was waiting near the arch with Anne Marie by his side. Dwayne led Amanda to the small table that held a watercolor portrait of Claire. Amanda removed the solitary sunflower from her bouquet and set it beside the picture. *I know you are part of the light now. I bend toward you.*

Then, Dwayne stopped and kissed Amanda softly on the cheek. "Beauty surrounds us, and you, my dear, are a gift and a blessing to all. I love you."

Amanda gently hugged him. "I love you too, my beloved garden friend."

Jordan took Amanda's hand and brought her under the arch of light their angels had formed.

Anioch and Yrandia hovered and held this small refuge in rays of love. They both vibrated with boundless love and pride, feeling an angelic connection that mirrored the miraculous joining of man and woman. The earth below and heavens above fairly echoed as hearts and souls joined to offer a blessing upon the young couple. *"This day we too are joined, my beloved,"* the angels sang.

Anne Marie opened the ceremony with a prayer. Dr. Blair came forward and turned to the gathering. His face was bright and his smile matched the lightness of his voice. "Today we celebrate love. Today we celebrate hope. Today we celebrate Amanda and Jordan. We come together to create a space of worship and blessing to hold this young couple in the light and power of love. I have a special poem to share from a beautiful and gifted poet."

He paused to pull out a small sheet of paper. Briefly looking up to the sky, he offered a slight bow. All the angels present returned the bow.

I loved you before my heart took flight,
Before my feet touched the earth, or my eyes gained sight.
I loved you in my ancient soul for you are part of my ancient soul.
And we waited, we waited to answer Love's call.

We were joined in that sacred place where light meets the
*   darkness,*
And ancient stardust dances
We were joined before time and space
Our souls one... waiting for Love's call.

And here in the dark place of slumber,
You spoke silent words of hope and offered love
We were not strangers for our souls knew
And my ancient soul awakened.

You called me like the whispering wind
Timeless words stirred the sleeping Spirit within
And we listened, we heard. Believe. Know
We are called to Love.

You pulled me in like the eternal tide
Beckoning the lost seafarer back to the safety of the shore.
"Return to Love" was whispered in the wind
And I answered, "Yes." Let me begin again.

We were joined before our first breath
We will be joined long after our last
For we are ancient starlight
Radiant stardust, released to dance, to soar, to love.

And so Jordan and Amanda were married in the secluded cove on the now crowded beach among friends, family and angels. Their vows were a simple confirmation of love, commitment, hope and faith. Jordan slid the beautiful pearl ring on Amanda's finger. Her smile was as bright as the sun. "My gift from the sea," she softly whispered.

Charlene and Daniel quietly wept, each deeply touched by the love they felt for their son and their new daughter, pondering the transformation in Jordan and in their own lives. Charlene wiped a tear while Daniel gently bowed to his angel who he knew was nearby.

Murial and Roshan rejoiced in the perfection of the day. Murial sent love to Anioch, "You have done well, my dear. Indeed you've done well."

The souls gathered on this stretch of beach held the sacred space. They watched Amanda and Jordan state their truths and unite their lives. Each had been touched in some way by the healing power of grace, forgiveness and love. Friends and family remembered their own journeys and how they each had intersected with Jordan and Amanda. Those private stories—valleys of sorrow and peaks of joy—all culminated in this moment where they stood in witness to the sacred ritual.

Anne Marie offered a prayer of thanksgiving, "We are all witness to this miracle of love. Love brought Amanda and Jordan together. We are all united in love and are part of this great mystery of Life. May we all live from the sacred place where love and peace abide. May we honor the Divine that dwells within each of us. May we find strength in the quiet moments when heaven and earth join and our angels whisper to our hearts. For all that is good, we give thanks. We are the blessings we deserve."

The host of angels who had gathered on the shore raised a chorus of song.

The service concluded with every soul present offering a joined blessing to the young couple. Amanda and Jordan were introduced, and lost themselves in their first kiss as husband and wife.

All the guests joined the heavenly choir and cheered. A small group of friends who had shared Wednesday night meetings, surf club practices, games of chess, broke out in song, *"Oh darling, darling... stand by me..."*

Anioch blazed as never before. Yrandia sang a prayer of praise to the Creator of All. The sun shone, the sea sparkled brightly as the waves rose and crashed with the ocean's full force and strength. A rainbow arose and framed the couple in a tapestry of light and mist, creating a veil of translucent shimmering drops.

This was a celebration of new and everlasting love. For God's will had been done as had been ordained from the beginning and now written into eternity. The energy of Love lifted the Spirit of each person on that shore, raising the vibration of the planet, and the Universe hummed. For here on this journey, a man and a woman dared to walk the path in faith allowing Divine grace and the Will and Wisdom and power of Love to gather them all in. And so the angels sang with joy and praise as Love flowed like the rising tide and rippled out in a wave of pure energy.

Close to the shore a distant bird drew close, wings fully outstretched, gliding in the breeze. It landed gracefully in the white mist of the shoreline. The slender white egret stood still as a silent sentry in the blazing sun.

Dwayne nudged Trish who bowed in reverence. *All is well.*

And so the story ends just as it began with a heavenly choir singing its unending hymn of joy and praise. A new life borne of love was ushered into a dimly lit room at South Bay Medical Center. Hope Anne Collingsworth filled the room with a loud, full-throttled cry as her parents wept with joy.

Anioch and Yrandia smiled as only angels can and enveloped the room in angelic warmth and love. Nurses and doctors who passed by saw a row of shoes lined up outside the room. Those who entered felt a certain strange energy amidst the gathered family. Charlene and Daniel wept tears of joy. Anne Marie took pictures as she bowed ever so slightly to all those present—seen and unseen.

A full moon rose and the room was bathed in moonlight. Dwayne offered a simple prayer, "Namaste." Laughter filled the space and the tall kind man set a vase of beautiful red roses in front of Amanda. "Beauty surrounds us." In a soft voice he whispered to the young mother, "The most beautiful bloom under the full moon."

Amanda nodded and smiled. "Indeed they do."

And so the circle of love and life continued to expand. From the highest reaches of the heavens to the depths of the sea, the miracle of birth touched and renewed each soul. A new angel, Ephie, hovered near the baby, shining with deep angelic pride and singing an endless hymn of praise.

EPILOGUE

As the day drew to a close, the small seaside cottage was bathed in light. Amanda cradled their tiny daughter close to her heart. Jordan sat in the small wicker rocker and held the image in his mind's eye as his heart swelled with unspeakable love. His mind wandered to all the blessings in his life. *All is well*, he silently affirmed.

Anioch bowed and responded softly, "Indeed."

Jordan stood and stretched, leaving the rocker slowly gliding.

Amanda's eyes danced. "You okay?" she softly mouthed.

Jordan nodded and answered with a broad smile.

He went out to the small yard. Anioch followed close by, sensing the energy that surrounded his child. The angel felt a wave of excitement. *Yes!*

Yrandia moved close to the bay window and watched. She laughed as man and angel trudged along the back path toward the ocean. *Indeed, my love! All is well and as it should be.*

Jordan followed the sandy footpath. The time had come for him to conquer the one last remnant of fear held in his heart. He turned down a dimly lit stretch of beach that was drenched in dusk's purples and golds.

He heard the voice of his beloved ocean, felt the warm sand under his feet and the breeze as it danced across his face. He stopped and looked at the broad expanse of the coast. This was the beach of his youth and a place of great joy and pain. He closed his eyes and willed himself to be fully present and feel the deep connection of his past and present... and to his eternal future.

He opened his eyes and gazed at the endless horizon. *I am ready to let go of my fear. I am a child of the Divine. I am unlimited and unstoppable.*

He pulled his old board across the deserted sand. As he neared the churning water he felt the sting of the cold Pacific. He smiled and let out a soft chuckle.

Anioch stayed near. "This is good, my child."

Jordan laughed as he went deeper into the waves. The water was cold but familiar and welcoming. His skin reacted while his heart jumped. He closed his eyes and let go. He dove in and felt his body relax. He came to the surface and let out a shout of joy. "I'm back!"

The surfer swam effortlessly, calm, big, strong strokes. Waves rolled over him. He felt the power and strength of the tide pulling him. He breathed in the salt air. *I'm home.*

Jordan opened his eyes and got on his board and paddled. Once again, he was one with the ocean, the current and the waves. The rhythm and energy propelled him. His focus narrowed to the push and pull as he swayed, waiting. Waiting for the perfect wave. He knew it would come. He felt it before he saw it and readied himself, every muscle leaning into the building momentum. He was grace in motion.

He rose on the wave and looked at the setting sun. The beach was covered in light. As he shifted into the ride, he heard a voice that sang out to the heavens, *"Today the long wait is over. Let go, my child, and be free. All is in order."*

A familiar but long forgotten surge of energy ran through Jordan. Every part of his Being was alive. As he let go and let the wave ride him, he saw his childhood angel, shining and bright, drawing rainbows.

"Ani!" Jordan's face burst into a broad smile.

Anioch turned to witness the smile of his beloved child returned to pure Love. "Come, let's play and rejoice!"

Jordan let out a howl, "This is *awesome!*"

Once again angel and child rode the waves and shared in the joy that was theirs, total and complete as the sun set in a blaze of glory and light. Together man and angel joined and sailed on a sublime and perfect Angelic Wavelength.

AFTERWORD

In October 1994, I was anxiously awaiting the passage of the Crime Act Bill by Congress. I had recently been hired by the Department of Justice to join the Immigration and Naturalization Service. The offer of employment was dependent on Congressional funding. In anticipation, I closed my law practice and found myself waiting. For the first time in a long time, I was not working. My youngest daughter, Shelly, had just started kindergarten and there wasn't even a child in the house. It was a strange and somewhat disorienting place. What was I going to do with this free time? Well I did what everybody does... I wrote a book!

Over a three-day period, I wrote what would be the basic foundational structure for *Angelic Wavelength*. For about three hours a day, I completely lost myself in the act of writing. The words just flew onto the page. It was one of the most exhilarating creative moments of my life. I can still recall the energy I felt as if some sort of strange portal opened and the story just tumbled out.

The three nights following my morning writing sessions, something strange and magical happened. The first night I didn't give it much thought but when it repeated itself twice more, I knew I needed to pay attention. Each night I found a single white feather in my top dresser drawer. When this happened for the third and final time, I brought in my two youngest daughters, Jackie and Shelly, and showed them the white feathers.

Jackie was nine years old and has always been my artist and dreamer. She immediately attributed the feathers to the angels who were watching me as I wrote "the angel story." I still remember her radiant smile as she danced around thrilled with the notion that angels were near us.

Shelly, the kindergartner who has always been grounded and pragmatic, let out a sigh and rolled her eyes. "Mommy," she said seriously. "You know those feathers are from your pillow."

Twenty-four years later, I have to laugh recognizing now how those two different responses perfectly signaled each of their beautiful and unique approaches to life. I have to admit, I was more in the "angels are here watching over me camp." There was something deliciously creative and almost sacred that surrounded me those three October mornings.

On the third and final day of my grand writing adventure, I saved my manuscript and printed it before I walked over to the school. This was the first hardcopy I made. I was frugal and mindful of the page count and didn't want to waste paper and ink. The first draft of the story was almost finished. The next morning, the kids all off to school, I went to the computer ready to finish the story. I searched and searched but could not find the file. Bordering on the edge of frustration, I stopped and decided I would let the children's father search for it. I had a healthy respect and growing fear of technology.

Search as we may, we discovered that early draft of *Angelic Wavelength* was the only victim of a virus that was running through the greater San Diego area. It seems that the *Natas* virus had found my "masterpiece." I was intrigued to discover that *Natas* is Satan spelled backwards. There was something strangely curious that only my angel story had been destroyed. I had competing emotions of sadness, anger, and frustration. The early seeds of a dislike for technology took root.

I looked at the ninety-five-page document and was sure it would be a long time before I would have the sweet luxury of time again to retype those pages. I moved to a place of acceptance and put the manuscript aside vowing I'd return to it.

Life had different plans for me. I started a new job with the Feds and had little time for creative endeavors. The Universe then conspired to further complicate my life as I was involved in a serious car accident in June of 1995 which led to a series of major life changes. In all of these moves and changes, the only hard copy of *Angelic Wavelength* disappeared. I let go of the notion of writing a book and accepted instead that the act of writing was in itself a gift.

Fast forward to 2013, and I experienced my personal "long night of the soul" and I was begging the Universe for help and calling out, *"I need something to feed my soul."* The Universe answered my call and I found myself returning to a long forgotten spiritual path. Kind and generous people were placed on my path and almost effortlessly I literally stumbled upon a Unity church at the same time I was accepted into Georgetown University's Executive Coaching Program.

It was only after my Learning Circle Advisor at Georgetown urged me to reconnect and share my poetry that I dug up the now wrinkled manuscript my husband had found in a box a few years earlier. A dear friend typed it up and handed the clean copy to me stating, "Barbara, you know there is no ending." It seemed that I was now ready to finish it.

As I read it for the first time in many years, the words and storyline struck me. The spiritual depth and wisdom on those pages were remarkable—not so much for what they said but rather because those ideas and beliefs had not been a part of my worldview in 1994. But reading them later in 2014, they mirrored the teachings I was only then learning. Somehow these deep truths had found voice through me.

What was perhaps more remarkable was the strange feeling of foreshadowing. It was as if I had been transported in some sort of time warp when I wrote Jordan and Amanda's story. The trajectory of two of my children, Shelly and Michael, were there woven into the story in prescient detail many years before their life-altering events.

When I noticed the connection to my family's life and the spiritual teachings that were beyond me, I felt a responsibility to finish the book. There is something magical and miraculous in the backstory. The basic structure of this story was written through me in three days; white feathers delivered; destroyed by a curiously named virus; disappeared and reappeared twenty years later as if on cue. Time stood still and seemed to wait for my soul to catch up. Only when I was sufficiently humbled and ready to accept the responsibility to care for the message, something spoke to me and urged me to move beyond my fears and return to the story.

So, dear reader, I offer to you this labor of love. Wonderful people came into my life to support the release of this story. I know it was never mine to keep or claim. I hope it touched you and drew you closer to your inner voice. I am profoundly touched and transformed to have played a part in bringing this story to life. I wish you peace, joy, light and love. May your angels continue to guide you on your journey.

Namaste,
Barbara

ACKNOWLEDGMENTS

The long journey to completing this book would not have happened without the love, support, and dedication of my family and many dear friends. At its core, this is a love story and this story exists today because I am blessed by a circle of love. I want to thank my husband, Michael, who gave me the gifts of love, time and space to finish this decades-long project. Thank you for believing in me and always pointing to my better nature. Thank you to my children—Nicole, Michael, Jackie and Shelly—who served as my inspiration, allowing me to see through the eyes of love. You fill me with love and pride and it is a source of profound joy to watch you on your life journeys. Being your mother is a true blessing. To my extended family members who make up this raucous tribe, thank you for the gifts you have each brought into my life.

The path to completion was filled with lots of small miracles. At every important inflection point, the Universe brought the right person into my life to either whisper a word of encouragement or to take on a heavy lift. To each of you, and you know who you are, my deepest and most sincere thanks for being present, believing, loving and always laughing.

There are a few special earth angels I have to acknowledge by name. Maxine Thomas, thank you for picking up those old marked up pages and transcribing them. I know that was an act of love and this book would not have happened without you. Eric de Nijs, you pushed me outside of my comfort zone and coaxed me to share my writing. Thank you for that. Lisa Colburn, I thank you for seeing the potential in the story and serving as that bridge to the next phase. Finally, Demi Stevens, you were the book whisperer. Thank you for your gentle yet firm touch. You encouraged me to dig deeper and find that active voice. You are more than an editor. You are a friend. You lovingly tilled the garden and brought out the beauty that was waiting to be discovered. You are a wise guide and I am grateful you were brought into my life. Thank you for believing in me and moving me from being a writer to an author.

To all of you, my deepest appreciation. As you have been a gift to me, I give back to you the love in prose and hope you enjoy the ride.

ABOUT THE AUTHOR

BARBARA QUIJANO lives in the Washington, D.C. metropolitan area with her husband, Michael. She has four children and a large extended family including eight grandchildren. She served in a variety of senior leadership positions during her twenty-four years in Federal service.

She is a certified Executive coach, licensed attorney, and native of California. Barbara's philosophy of life is to embrace each day as a gift and an opportunity to be in service. She is guided by her daily affirmation, "I am an expression of Divine Love... I stand as an agent of HOPE: Helping Others' Purpose Emerge."

www.ingramcontent.com/pod-product-compliance
Lightning Source LLC
Chambersburg PA
CBHW031549240626
47153CB00002B/435